Wicar's Legacy

Don Stratton

To Pauline

The infectiousness of crime is like that of the plague

Napoleon Bonaparte

Wicar's Legacy

1

HUNTER MCCOY BARELY HEARD GENEVIEVE SWIFT'S frantic whisper from nine hundred miles away in Sarasota, Florida—but her terror came through loud and clear.

"Hunter," she said in a voice shaking with palpable fear, "someone's in the house."

"What? Listen. Get out of there now, fast. Go to the neighbors. Call 911. Go."

He heard a muffled crash in the background.

"Hunter!" she shrieked. "It's a man. I—" She cried out, then a thud.

"Genevieve," he shouted into the phone then watched in horror as—*call ended—call ended—call ended* scrolled across the screen.

What the hell just happened?

While too self-disciplined to panic, it still took all his self-control to steady himself and call 911.

He told the emergency operator he'd been talking to a woman at her home in Sarasota when an intruder attacked her. After identifying himself, he gave the dispatcher Genevieve's name and address. To the operator's credit, she took him seriously and made the necessary connections to a dispatcher in Sarasota who told Hunter the police were on their way.

Desperate for news, he repeatedly tried calling Genevieve's phone but got no answer. Between calls, he contacted the airport and managed to get the last seat on an American Airlines flight leaving Charlottesville, Virginia at 6:55 pm that would get him to Sarasota around 10:30.

With little more than an hour to make the flight, he rushed back to the loft apartment he maintained not far from his office and lab at the University of Virginia School of Medicine, packed a bag, drove to the airport, got through security in record time, and boarded just before the gate closed.

THE CROWD ROARED, WANTING MORE BLOOD. Despite the exhaustion clouding his consciousness, Hunter managed to duck, but still the blow that bounced off his head rattled him to the core. He stumbled backward, trying to regain his balance as the man with no face closed in for the kill. Stunned, he had to think fast. The faceless man was a monster, even bigger than Hunter's own solid six foot-two inch frame. An approving partisan cheer went up from the man's colleagues who were guarding the mouth of the cave and its lone prisoner, Hunter's brother, Marine Sergeant Gary McCoy.

Knowing his only chance was to lure the man into a mistake, Hunter feigned another stumble and let his hands drop as if he was wiped out. Seeing his chance, the monster launched a flying kick directly at Hunter's chest that would have finished him had it landed. Hunter timed it perfectly and leaned to the side just as the man's horizontal body flew past, hitting nothing but air.

When the monster landed, and before he could recover, Hunter was all over him. He twisted the man's arm behind his back then snapped it off, ripping it free from his body. Blood spurted from the torso, covering Hunter in gore. As he backed off, horrified, he watched the creature slowly rise and with his one good arm rip off one of his own legs. Then he began beating Hunter with it.

His brother Gary reached out from the cave, beseeching him for help.

Struggling again, Hunter lashed out and heard a sharp female cry. He continued to flail until pinned down by several strong arms.

"Mr. McCoy. Look at me. Open your eyes. Do it now."

Confused but unable to move or escape, he fought to open his eyes. Bright light assailed his retinas. Reflexively he closed his eyes again.

"It's all right. Try to relax. You're okay. We're here to help."

Help? What the—?

"Sir. You've been hurt. But you're safe now. Just relax."

Relax?

"That's it. Good. That's good. You were having a nightmare. Breathe. Take a deep breath. Let it out slowly. That's good. Now do it again."

Slowly he began to reopen his eyes, squinting at first, getting used to the brightness. Two young men in blue scrubs were holding him down. He was lying in a bed. A woman in a white jacket was wiping his forehead with a damp cloth.

"I'm Dr. Virginia Olesin," she said. "You're in Sarasota Memorial Hospital."

"What? Why am I here? What happened?"

"You were hit by a car. You're lucky to be alive."

Hit by a car?

"I put eight stitches in your scalp. They'll dissolve on their own. Your left shoulder was dislocated. I reset it. It'll be sore for a while but there'll be no permanent damage. You have no internal injuries that we could find. Other than that, you've got lots of bruises and scrapes. Like I said, you were lucky. How are you feeling?"

"I've been better," he said, only now becoming aware of the ache in his shoulder.

Then it came back to him in a jolt of anxious recollection—*Genevieve*. He was in Sarasota to find Genevieve. The phone call, a man had attacked her, he'd called 911. He'd gotten a flight from Charlottesville to Sarasota. He'd been unable to reach her and hadn't heard from the authorities. He remembered trying to rent a car at the airport. Then—then, he couldn't remember anything after that.

"Where was the accident?" he asked, trying to make sense of things.

"The police report said it was a hit-and-run, just outside a car rental agency at the airport."

Hit and run?

He tried to sit up, but dizzy from the sudden movement, lay back on the pillow. "I've got to make a phone call."

"Of course, but you should try to relax." She walked out of the room, leaving him alone.

He realized he didn't have his cellphone, or his wallet for that matter. Where were they? Had they taken them? He clutched at the bed's handset and punched the call button. When the nurse arrived he practically shouted at her.

"My cellphone. Where is it? I've got to make a call right now."

"It's probably in the emergency room. Take it easy. I'll go check."

"Hurry."

Ten minutes later she was back with his phone and wallet, but then placing her hand on his forearm asked, "Mr. McCoy, do you know someone named Genevieve Swift?"

"What? Yes. Why?" he frowned, picking up on the tension in her voice and demeanor. *Something's wrong.*

"Um, well, she's here in the hospital."

"Here? Is she okay?"

"She's been hurt."

"How badly?"

"She's in a room downstairs. They brought her into our emergency room last night—"

"I've got to—" He moved to get out of bed until the nurse pushed him back.

"And she's going to be okay. You can see her later."

Nuts to that.

Throwing back the covers, he swung out of bed and stood wobbling on the cold tile floor. Then the room began to turn. The last thing he remembered was the nurse wrapping him in a bear hug that dragged both of them to the floor.

DR. VIRGINIA OLESIN HAD JUST SHAKEN him awake and was examining his pupils. Satisfied, she said, "I understand you tried to storm our emergency room to find your friend."

Hunter found the handset with the bed control buttons and brought himself to a semi-sitting position, fully alert now.

"Is she okay?"

"She's doing much better. She suffered a blow to the head at her house last night. Apparently, there'd been a break-in. A neighbor found her when his dog wouldn't stop barking. He called 911. When she came around in our emergency room she was a little delirious and kept asking for someone named Hunter. Your nurse wondered if that might be you and came up to ask you. When you leapt out of bed both of you crashed to the floor."

Relieved that Genevieve was all right he asked, "When can I see her?"

Dr. Olesin smiled, backed up to the door, looked out into the hall, and nodded. "How about right now?"

Genevieve, in all her tall, slim athletic beauty, wearing a robe over a hospital gown, and with a bandage similar to his own covering the back of her head, appeared in the doorway and rushed across the room to his bedside.

"Mon chéri."

"Don't wear him out," Dr. Olesin admonished her. "He's had a concussion, and you need some rest, too."

Genevieve kissed him and their hands found each other while the doctor and nurse left them alone. For a moment neither of them spoke. He gently cupped the bandage accenting her shiny black, shoulder-length hair. "Are you okay? What happened?"

Glancing around to make sure they were still alone, she hiked up her hospital gown, stood on one leg, and raised her lovely bare thigh.

Completely ignoring the small bandage just above her knee, Hunter chose instead to carefully examine her wonderfully naked thigh.

"I was asking about the bandage on your head," he said, "but I have to tell you, this view is definitely making *me* feel better."

Back on two legs she smoothed her gown and flashed him that familiar superior smile. "Good." Then, turning serious, she touched the bandage on *his* head. "They said you were in a car accident. Where was it? Were you driving?"

"I'll tell you what I know in a minute; it's not much. Tell me about you first. We were on the phone and—"

Genevieve put her fingers to his lips to shush him, sat down, and spoke in a low voice.

"I'd just gotten to my place after work last night, around five. I parked in the carport and headed for the side door, but before I could insert the key I noticed the door was open a few inches. I knew I'd locked it before I left in the morning.

"I stepped into the kitchen, trying not to make a sound. It was awful. Every cabinet door was open, every drawer was open, even the refrigerator door. I remember walking into the living room. Everything was a mess there too. That's when I called you. Then I heard a noise and knew someone was still in the house. I turned and saw a man. He must have hit me, because I don't recall anything after that. I woke up in the emergency room with a major headache and a cut on my leg. I must have been a little delirious because apparently I told everyone I had to find you."

"That sounds delirious all right. You didn't recognize the man?"

"No, but I had a plan."

"You had a plan?"

"Right."

"Was it a good plan?"

"I thought so at the time."

"So what was your plan?"

"I was going to put *you* in charge of finding out who did this and why. That is, until they told me you were here, too."

He smiled and nodded. Neither of them spoke for a while.

Genevieve pressed her hand to his cheek. "I know we didn't plan on you coming down for another two weeks, but in spite of what happened to you, I'm glad you're here now."

He chuckled and lay back against the pillow. "Now that I think about it, spending time with you *is* dangerous. I mean, look at our history. When I'm at the medical school, doing my job, nothing even remotely alarming happens. Then we get together, and people come out of the woodwork trying to kill us. They tried in Spain and Portugal two years ago. They tried in Belgium and Italy last summer. I mean I should get combat pay. Spending time with you is downright life-threatening."

She brought her face close to him and sweetly asked, "Hunter?"

"Yeah?"

"Which shoulder was dislocated?"

"The left one, why?"

She punched him hard in the right arm. Then, bringing her face even closer, she kissed him—a long slow kiss that he returned in full. Finally coming up for air, they gazed at each other silently for a moment before she said, "But we do have fun, don't we?"

He sighed, lay back, and thought about that. It was true. The only thing keeping them apart was the Atlantic Ocean. She worked in Paris as a curator of pre-twentieth-century western art at the Louvre, and he was an assistant professor of physiology at the University of Virginia Medical School.

Now, for the first time ever, they were both on the American side of the pond, even though they were working in different states. Best of all she was here for a whole year. But it was late spring, his classes were over for the semester, and his schedule allowed him some free time. He'd be able to stay in Sarasota with her for a while.

He pressed the call button. The nurse returned almost instantly.

"Ms. Swift is going to spend the night here—in this room. Could you ask someone to roll in another bed?"

Both the nurse and Genevieve gaped at him.

"Hey," he said, putting his hands up in supplication, "someone seems to think you're a punching bag and maybe that same someone tried to turn me into road-kill. I'm not letting you out of my sight until we find who did it and why."

The familiar recurring nightmare he'd had, fighting the monstrous man in front of the cave, was a constant reminder to Hunter that he was never far from the guilt he'd experienced at not being able to save his brother's life.

He'd been in charge of a Marine unit sent to capture a terrorist leader in the mountains of Pakistan. His brother Gary had been part of the squad. He'd made a personal vow after losing Gary that he'd never let anyone in his care be harmed again. Right now, Genevieve was at the top of that list.

Whoever you are, I'm coming for you.

2

McCoy brushed dirt off his torn pants and tucked in his soiled shirt as he and Genevieve exited the hospital. Wet from an early morning rain, the bright Southwest Florida sun reflected diamond-like glitter off the surface of the parking lot puddles. Once Dr. Olesin had signed the papers that cleared them both for release, Hunter had called the parking attendant at the entrance and asked him to get them a cab, since they'd both arrived by ambulance.

Still uncertain about the extent of the threat to Genevieve, Hunter nervously scanned the area. Had the incident been just a one-off burglary attempt gone bad, or was she a deliberate target for some reason? He was damn well going to find out, but in the meantime he planned to stay as close to her as possible.

Genevieve had told him her leased BMW convertible was at the house. Now that he thought about it, he didn't even know if he'd actually picked up his rental car. Had he been in the car at the time of the hit-and-run, or was he walking? He made a mental note to call the rental car company and find out. The receipt in his wallet showed he'd rented from Budget.

The cabby drove them through a quiet neighborhood just south of the Ringling Museum. She was renting an old one-story home nestled among the mega-mansions on Sarasota Bay. "I love it here," Genevieve said wistfully. "Or at least I did. Look at that great view across the water. You can see it from almost every room in the house."

Hunter had to agree. The view was spectacular. A cool breeze swept inshore off the bay and gave pleasant relief to the otherwise warm late spring afternoon.

"It's hard to believe," she continued, "this place is considered a teardown. The land is worth more than the house. Eventually someone will buy it, demolish the house, and build a mansion like the others you see around here."

Hunter was about to escort Genevieve inside when a Sarasota police cruiser pulled up, crunching the gravel on the driveway. The uniformed driver got out and approached them. "Ms. Swift? I'm Sergeant Karen Ball with the Sarasota Police Department."

"Hello, Sergeant. This is my friend, Hunter McCoy."

Sergeant Ball, a diminutive woman with a blond ponytail who looked as if she could handle herself, acknowledged him with a small nod. "Ms. Swift, I responded the day before yesterday when we got the 911 call—actually two 911 calls. When my partner and I got here you were unconscious on the floor. We sent you off to the hospital. I also interviewed your neighbor, the one who found you."

"It's not my house, Sergeant Ball, I'm just staying here for a year as part of a curator exchange program. The owner is Phyllis Durham. She's staying at my place in Paris. I'm with the Louvre, and she's with the Ringling Museum of Art."

Sergeant Ball thought about this for a moment. "So she's doing your job while you're doing hers?"

"That's right."

She smiled and nodded. "Must be nice."

"It has been until—this." She waved her hand at the house.

"And you, Mr. McCoy? Do you live here as well?"

"No. Two weeks ago Genevieve invited me to come and stay here with her for a while. I'm a professor at the medical school in Charlottesville, and my schedule allowed me to do it. I heard her being attacked while we were on the phone and came down right away, ending up in the hospital myself. I was one of those two 911 callers."

"Do you have some identification?"

Hunter showed her his faculty ID. Then, because he figured he was going to need her cooperation, and probably that of other local cops as well, he showed her his Virginia State Police ID with his detective shield.

"You're a medical school professor and a state police detective?"

"It's complicated, but yes."

"I see, sort of. I guess."

Sergeant Ball addressed Genevieve. "Here's what I'd like you to do. I want you to go through the house and see if anything is missing. Given what's happened in there, it appears that whoever did this was looking for something. If you had anything of value hidden away for safety in a special place, check to see if it's still there. While you're doing that you might also consider whether you know anyone who might have done this. I have some paperwork to do in the cruiser. You and Mr. McCoy—Dr. McCoy, sorry— go ahead. Take your time."

As they entered the house through the same door that Genevieve had found open two nights ago, Hunter sensed her trepidation. She took his arm and held it tight.

"It's okay," he said, steadying her, "I'm right here this time."

"Look at this place," she said, gesturing broadly. "He was even more thorough than I remembered. Every drawer in every room, dumped out."

Hunter agreed. All the closets were in disarray, as if the intruder—like the policewoman had said—was looking for something specific. The sheets were off the bed, the mattress off the boxspring, furniture overturned.

Twenty minutes later Sergeant Ball came in. "Any luck?" she asked Genevieve. "Can you tell if anything is missing?"

"No, not that I can see. "If he was looking for something, I don't know what it was."

Sergeant Ball took her notebook. "Do you know anyone who might do this—someone who doesn't like you, someone who'd want to mess with you this way?"

Genevieve didn't even have to stop and think about it. "No. No one. I've only been here a month. I haven't made any enemies that I know of. I can't even give you any kind of description of the man who hit me. I only know it was a man."

"How about height, build, color, clothing he was wearing?"

"Really nothing. He was maybe taller than me. It just happened too fast."

"All right, how about this? Has anything else unusual happened, maybe something at work?"

"No. Nothing."

Sergeant Ball watched as Genevieve squinted and furrowed her brows.

"Ms. Swift? Did you think of something?"

"There was something a few days ago," Genevieve said reflectively. "Not at work though, it was here at home. But it was probably nothing."

"What was it?"

"That desk over there." Genevieve pointed to the corner of the living room, where a wicker desk was now overturned with its drawers pulled out. "I know this will sound weird, but when I got home after work, my planner—she reached down and picked up a notebook from the floor—this one, was *open* on that desk."

The sergeant and Hunter looked at each other, not comprehending.

"I know it sounds crazy, but I always close it when I leave, always. It's just a thing I do. Anyway, that's the only strange thing I can think of."

Sergeant Ball wrote this down and closed her notebook. "I'm afraid that's all I can do for now. I'll complete my report, and you can pick up a copy at the station after ten o'clock tomorrow morning. You'll need it if you plan to submit an insurance claim. Here's my card. If you think of anything else, give me a call."

As Hunter walked Sergeant Ball outside he noticed a car he hadn't seen earlier pulling away from the house.

3

"IT AIN'T LEGAL, AND I AIN'T DOIN' IT." JAMES KNOX dug in his heels and crossed his arms over his scrawny chest.

The well-dressed woman stood on the splintered front step of the run-down old house that matched the other decrepit homes in the area and fixed him with a kindly but exasperated stare. Ever since she'd recruited him to help with her plan, he had gotten more and more uncomfortable with it. She was growing tired of his whining but knew she couldn't do it without him.

"Of course it's legal. Think about it. How could it be *illegal*? You're not stealing anything."

"Well why dontcha just give it to 'em then?"

"Look, James, you don't need to know that. I have my reasons. You can do this. It's not illegal. Just do it, collect your money, and get on with your life. You're going to be fine."

In the end, James had to agree. He needed the five hundred dollars she was paying him. Now, as he approached the three, huge, arched glass doorways at the entrance to the John and Mable Ringling Museum of Art, he felt the full weight of his seventy-five years and nervously patted the package through his light jacket. Of course he knew the jacket wasn't necessary. He was in southwest Florida, for crying out loud. It was eighty-five degrees and the sun was shining. Still, he knew the museum was air-conditioned and the jacket wouldn't look out of place. He hated that his financial situation left him no other choice. Feeling the familiar chest pain that constantly reminded him of his mortality, he popped a nitroglycerine pill under his tongue.

Earlier, he'd checked his profile in the mirror at home and knew the small, framed painting didn't show. Part of it was stuffed down the front of his pants, securing it in place, and the rest of it lay flat against his belly as he climbed the front steps to the museum. For once he was glad he was a skinny old man. Maybe no one would give him a second look.

Wearing a baseball cap with the visor tugged low over his brow, he hoped he looked like any other Florida retiree spending a day at the museum. He pulled open one of the large glass doors at the entrance, walked in, and was immediately greeted by the female attendant on duty. The badge hanging on a strap around her neck identified her as a Ringling Ambassador.

"Welcome to The Ringling, sir," she said, handing him a map. "Is this your first visit?"

Sucking in his belly even more to obscure the treasure hidden under his jacket, he swallowed hard and lowered his head in deference to her official status. "Yeah, just gonna wander around, you know. Look at the pictures, kinda."

Two days before when he'd made his first and only other visit to the museum, a different ambassador had been on duty. He hadn't wanted to risk it, but he wanted to see for himself precisely where he was supposed to place the thing. Now, confident of the location but still afraid of being caught, he turned left through two more large glass doors into what he'd learned was Gallery 21. According to the wall plaque it was dedicated to Art in Europe and North America between 1850 and 1940.

He tried to act casual while he shuffled through it, but was unnerved by the feeling that the human figures in the large paintings were eyeing him accusingly, as if to say, "We know what you're going to do."

At the far side of the room, he turned right through the open doorway into Galleries 20 and 19. The descriptive plaque on the wall said the two galleries contained the actual walls and furnishings of the library and salon of Jacob Astor, the wealthy nineteenth-century New York businessman. John Ringling had bought them in 1926 at a sale prior to the demolition of Astor's New York mansion. Both rooms felt cold to James as he scuttled through to Gallery 18 and then on to his ultimate objective—Gallery 17.

She'd told him specifically that the painting had to be placed in Gallery 17 in the museum's south wing. When he arrived, a young couple and an elderly woman were moving slowly through the room. One of the guards, who he'd learned strolled regularly through the galleries, was watching them. As soon as they all moved on he'd get to it. He dried his clammy hands on his pants and forced himself to look interested in the art on the walls. Finally, everyone left the small gallery.

Do it now, right now.

He quickly pulled on a pair of thin gloves as he'd been instructed, removed the painting from under his jacket, and set it on top of the large glass display case filled with silverware from the eighteenth century. Then he placed the folded note carefully on top of the painting—just as he'd been told to do.

His mission complete, James wanted to get out of there as fast as he could. He exited through a door in Gallery 17 that led him out onto the promenade encircling the vast central courtyard of the museum. He turned left and forced himself not to run as he strode stiffly to the walking bridge connecting the south wing he'd just exited, past an enormous replica of Michelangelo's *David*, to the north wing.

Rather than enter the north wing, he turned left to the Searing wing of the museum, and walked through the

Joseph's Coat Skyspace, empty during the day. Exiting the other side, he left the building. Once outside, he descended the steps and waited for the tram.

Please, Lord, let me get outta here. I didn't do nothin wrong, I didn't take nothin. Just let me get outta here so I can go home.

In spite of the nitro, James felt another pain in his chest. After a three-minute wait that seemed much longer, the tram rolled up to the museum entrance and stopped. The driver stepped out and chatted amiably with the passengers. Five riders got off and James and three others got on for the return ride to the Visitors Pavilion, where he'd first entered the Ringling complex. James sat on the backward-facing seat at the rear of the tram, too anxious to talk with anyone. He gripped the metal vertical strut holding up the tram's roof as it slowly pulled away, Almost immediately the tightness in his chest increased. He loosened his collar and began to breathe deeply. The tightness continued and became a pain in his left shoulder.

I can't breathe.

Clutching his chest he turned around in his seat to get help from the other passengers. A lady noticed and yelled at the driver to stop. James gasped twice and collapsed sideways on the seat. During his last moments of consciousness, he remembered the strange words of the woman who'd hired him.

You're important, James. You're the first salvo in stopping the Legacy.

TEN-YEAR OLD CHLOE SLINDE stood next to her mother staring in silent wonder at the dramatic oil painting set up on the easel in Gallery 3 of the museum's north wing.

The brightly colored sixteenth-century painting by Lucas Cranach depicted a pious Saint Jerome, dressed in brilliant red, doing scholarly work on the Bible. Strangely, though, he wore the face of Cardinal Albrecht of

Brandenburg, as if the cardinal himself were Saint Jerome. It was, as the placard explained, a self-serving attempt by the cardinal to clean up his somewhat tarnished reputation for luxurious living and unseemly relationships with women. Saint Jerome was, after all, a devout scholar whose fourth-century translation of the Hebrew and Greek scriptures into Latin became the official version of the Bible as recognized by the church. Cardinal Albrecht, who'd commissioned the painting, had no such scholarly abilities himself.

Chloe glanced at her mother, who seemed focused on the cardinal's beefy face in his guise as St. Jerome. Chloe found herself entranced by the huge lion on the floor, looking menacingly at some birds. Tilting her head in concentration, she thought something was odd about the lion's face. It looked wet. On an impulse, she reached out and touched it. She was right. It was wet.

"No, Chloe," her mother scolded her. "You don't touch things in a museum."

Startled, the girl put her hand to her mouth. When she licked her fingers she discovered that the wet face of the lion tasted a little soapy.

Much later, on the drive back home from the museum, Chloe said, "Mommy, I don't feel good. My tummy hurts."

4

THE MAN WHO'D DRIVEN AWAY EARLIER HAD RETURNED and was observing from his parked car waiting patiently for the couple to leave. In truth, he had little patience and hated it when he was forced to exercise any. Still, he had to get them both together. It had to be set up properly. So he lit another cigarette and continued to wait.

HUNTER AND GENEVIEVE SPENT MOST OF THE AFTERNOON trying to put the house back in order.

"I just don't get it, Hunter. I don't have anything anyone would want."

"Someone apparently thinks you do. That's what we have to focus on. What *could* you have that would be so important someone would do this? Do you have access to anything at work that might be valuable? I mean you do work in an art museum."

"Yes, but it's not as is if I have the keys to the kingdom. I can get into the Education Center, where my office is, but I don't have a key to anything else in there, like the library or the conservation lab."

"What's that?"

"That's where art gets cleaned or repaired if it's damaged by age, weather, water, things like that. They also do other things to preserve the art holdings. Then there's an above-the-flood-plain storage area where the excess art is kept. I don't have keys to that either."

"Excess art?"

"Sure. Most people don't realize it, but all museums have more art than they have space to display. A sort of industry standard is that close to 80% of a museum's holdings are in storage at any one time. In the past few years much of the Ringling's excess art has been transferred to secured vaults at the Tampa Airport's Freeport Naff, a relatively new state-of-the-art facility for housing valuable paintings and other works of art for both individuals and organizations."

"Wow."

"Yeah."

"What about paperwork, historic documents, things like that?"

"Again, I have no more access than anyone else. The art library is in our building, and it does have a huge collection of volumes from the sixteenth to the twentieth centuries. I'm sure they're quite valuable. The research collection is open to the public and they can browse through it, even though they can't check things out."

Hunter thought about that. It occurred to him, not for the first time, how little he knew about art. He believed he had an open mind and had always enjoyed art, but the more he listened to Genevieve the more he realized his knowledge meter was pinned on empty. He'd been that way about antique furniture, too, when he'd first started teaching at the med school in Charlottesville. Because he didn't know much, his appreciation was equally meager. But then he started seeing Annie, who owned a local antique shop, and he slowly learned about antiques. Now, he owned several pieces and was always eager to learn more. That was the way it worked. First comes a little knowledge, then later, the appreciation. He grinned to think he was going through the same cycle with Genevieve, slowly learning about art.

Not getting anywhere speculating, they drove downtown to a place called Mattison's City Grille off Main Street and ordered burgers and sweet potato fries at their sidewalk patio grill under a large covered roof. They ate in silence, each still trying to come up with answers, anything that might explain what happened to them.

Genevieve broke the gloom. "What about you?"

"What do you mean?"

"Well, we're not having much luck trying to imagine what *I* might have that's so important. How about we look at you? Why would someone try to run you down with a car?"

He'd actually been thinking about this a lot. He didn't have any active investigations going on. Nobody from his past with the Department of Defense was after him. At least he didn't think so. Anyone who might conceivably want to go after him was either dead or in prison somewhere. Besides, no one knew he'd be in Florida.

Wait a minute. Maybe that's it.

"Maybe someone *was* after me and decided to lure me to Sarasota and figured threatening you would be a good way to do it," he said. "Maybe that's what the hit and run was about. Someone planned for me to be at the airport."

He thought about that for a minute and then dismissed it. "If someone was after me they wouldn't have to lure me here. It's no secret that I'm in Virginia at the med school. They could get to me just as well there. Also, no one knew I was going to be here. I didn't tell anyone. I didn't even tell my two postdocs where I was going, just that I was taking a few weeks off and putting them in charge of the lab. So no one in Virginia knew I was coming here. I didn't even tell my dad in Michigan. What about you? Did you tell anyone I was coming?"

"Let me think." She closed her eyes for a moment.

He watched as she searched her memory.

"Yes, I did tell someone—my friend Monica. She's the only one. I told her you'd be here in about two weeks."

"Who's Monica?"

Genevieve smiled. "That's right, I haven't had a chance to tell you about her. This is really interesting. About a week ago I got a call from Monica Arseneau. She was an art student at the Sorbonne the same time I was there getting my Ph.D. in Renaissance history. We got to be pretty good friends and spent a lot of time together, but then lost track after we finished our schooling. Anyway, she saw my name in a Ringling newsletter explaining how I was going to be here for a year on an exchange program. It turns out she works as a graphic illustrator for a company in Sarasota. She actually grew up right here, on Lido Key. Of course I didn't know that when we were in school, or if I did, it didn't mean anything to me at the time, never having been to Florida.

"Anyway, we met for lunch and had a great time catching up. It was fun to see her again and relive some of those days. I *did* tell her about you and that you were coming, but that's it." Genevieve paused. "No, wait a minute, that's not true. I also told Gretchen, Gretchen Ceisel. She's the museum's conservator. She runs the art conservation lab I told you about. We had lunch together several times."

"That's it, nobody else?"

She shook her head, thinking. "No. Nobody else. And I can't imagine why either of those women would want to threaten you or me."

"So," he said, "we're back where we started."

Back at Genevieve's place they decided to put the mystery out of their minds for the time being and enjoy the rest of the evening. Genevieve found a Diana Krall album on her laptop and synched it to a portable Bluetooth speaker that she brought out to the lanai overlooking Sarasota Bay. The sun had already set, and the stars were just beginning to appear. Hunter opened a bottle of pinot noir he'd found in her under-counter wine cooler, poured two glasses, and joined her. They sat watching the lazy nighttime running lights on boats moving slowly across the water. The Ringling Bridge and the lights of downtown

Sarasota and Lido Key were the perfect background to a tranquil scene.

They reminisced about how they'd met two summers before when they both became involved in the adventure of looking for a lost manuscript that ended with their saving the Large Hadron Collider from destruction by a crazed scientist. Then the previous summer they had tackled a criminal at the Caravaggio Neurological Institute in Sorrento. By the end of that case they knew they had to work out the differences in their circumstances. In spite of living on either side of the Atlantic Ocean, they vowed they were going to be together, somehow.

Later, as they strolled to the bedroom, Hunter slipped his hands under Genevieve's tee top from behind, and she sighed as he cupped her breasts and gently stroked her nipples. Clothes were shed. The trauma of the past few days slipped away, slowly replaced by a timeless rhythm as old as humankind and yet somehow as new as now, until spent, they collapsed in a dream of pleasure, aware only of each other.

HE HEARD IT BEFORE HE SMELLED IT. Never a sound sleeper, Hunter had gotten up to use the bathroom and heard a quiet hissing noise coming from the back of the house. As he walked through the small home the smell became unmistakable.

Gas!

He roused Genevieve and told her they had to get out of the house. They quickly dressed and went to the kitchen door that led out to the carport. It wouldn't open. *That's strange*, Hunter thought, and tried it again. It didn't appear to be locked, but it was jammed somehow. The front door wouldn't open either. Next he tried the slider to the lanai. It too was blocked. Through the glass he could see a piece of two-by-four lying in the track, preventing it from sliding open.

What the hell's going on?

He remembered seeing an iron on the kitchen counter and raced back to get it. He ran to Genevieve, who was trying to force open the slider, and yelled, "Get back and cover your eyes." He hurled the iron shattering the glass. But as he was preparing to kick out enough remaining shards for them to escape, a figure appeared on the lanai. It was a man dressed completely in black.

What the hell?

The man smiled beneath his black ski mask, and with the flick of his thumb ignited a lighter and tossed it through the broken glass into the gas-filled house.

5

CARRIE SLINDE TRIED TO REMAIN CALM as Dr. Joyce Durocher examined her daughter at the Pediatric Clinic for the second time in two days. She'd brought Chloe in earlier to see Dr. Joyce because she'd been running a fever and had felt queasy ever since their trip to the Ringling Museum. Nothing Carrie had tried seemed to help. Chloe's fever wasn't too bad initially but when it got to 103 Carrie had called the clinic and they said to bring her right in. During that visit Dr. Joyce had told Carrie to give her children's formula acetaminophen—Tylenol—and keep her home until her temperature returned to normal. She should see that Chloe got plenty of fluids. If she was no better, bring her back in and she'd run some tests.

Carrie had followed those instructions, but Chloe didn't get any better and her temperature refused to drop, so they were back seeing Dr. Joyce.

"Hi, honey," said Dr. Joyce. "Can you tell me if it hurts anywhere?"

"My tummy." Chloe said, frowning.

"She's had diarrhea, doctor, for the last two days. And she has no pep. She's very tired."

Dr. Joyce carefully probed Chloe's abdomen and listened to her heart and respiration. "I'm going to do some blood work," she said, putting her stethoscope away. "That should tell us what's going on."

"Is there a needle?" Chloe asked tentatively.

"Yes, Chloe, but we're really good at that here. You'll barely feel it," said Dr. Joyce.

Carrie could almost feel her daughter's dread. "Chloe, remember when Dr. Joyce took blood once before? Afterward, you said you hardly felt a thing."

"Uh huh."

"You were very brave, Honey."

"Uh huh."

Dr. Joyce drew the blood, and as bad as she felt, Chloe was brave again. Then Dr. Joyce took Carrie aside. "I want you to take her home now and make her comfortable. Stay with the Tylenol and fluids. As soon as I get the test results and examine them, I'll call you, okay?"

Two hours later Carrie got a call from Dr. Joyce. "Mrs. Slinde, I want you to bring Chloe to the emergency room at the hospital right away. I've already called them and they know you're coming. I'll meet you there and explain."

At the emergency room they admitted Chloe and immediately started an IV line and began giving her antibiotics. By now Chloe was very listless and her blood pressure was extremely low. When Dr. Joyce got there she took Carrie aside, out of Chloe's hearing.

"She has septicemia with a bacterial infection that we're trying to get under control. That's why she's getting IV antibiotics right now. I'm afraid this is a serious situation."

"Oh, my God. Will she be all right, doctor?" Carrie asked, taking her hands.

"She should be, if we can stop the infection. But you have to be prepared. This could get worse."

Carrie put her hands to her mouth and choked back a cry.

Little Chloe Slinde didn't respond to the antibiotic treatment Dr. Joyce had prescribed. She and her staff were doing all they could, but now Chloe had developed blisters tinged with blood on her swelling arms and legs. Equally threatening was her drop in blood pressure. The hospital staff was concerned about her going into septic shock.

Carrie wasn't doing well either. Chloe was all she had, her husband having left almost immediately after Chloe's birth. She'd still been in school at New College in Sarasota, and Chloe had been the stabilizing factor in her life, giving it meaning and purpose during the dark days after Kevin left. Mother and daughter were as close as child and parent could be. Any time Chloe was sick, Carrie had nursed her back to health. The few times Carrie was ill, Chloe, even at her very young age, did all she could to make life better for her mom. They were a pair, a loving singularity, unstoppable together—until now.

As Carrie gazed down on Chloe in her bed in the hospital pediatric wing, she thought how small her daughter was, how vulnerable. Dr. Joyce had been in an hour earlier and told her it didn't look good. Chloe's systems were beginning to shut down in a condition called Multiple Organ Dysfunction Syndrome. She explained that once that started, the prognosis was very bad. She'd told Carrie that she should prepare herself for the worst.

Carrie bent over her and kissed Chloe's cheek, wiping away a tear. "Come on, baby, fight," she murmured. "You can beat this," she begged, even though in her heart she knew the battle was over and the fight was lost.

6

TIME IS ALMOST INFINITE ON A GEOLOGIC or cosmic scale, but can also be incredibly short. Events can happen over eons or in fractions of a second. There's the split second between turning the key in your car and ignition. There's the split second between the arrival of a nerve impulse and the subsequent contraction of a muscle. A batter has a split second between the release of a pitcher's ninety-mile-per-hour fastball and his decision to swing the bat.

As Hunter stomped on the flame in the gas-filled house he reacted in a split second but it seemed like an eternity as he waited for an explosion or a fire or whatever was might happen. He waited. He waited some more. Nothing. Nothing happened.

Thank God. "Get out, he yelled to Genevieve."

He raced back into the bedroom and grabbed his Beretta 9 mm from the nightstand, checked the magazine, and ran back to the slider where Genevieve had just exited. Furious at this second threat to Genevieve, he darted out to the lanai, where he scanned the yard for the man in black with the sickening smile. He saw nothing. The man was gone.

Hearing a car start he raced toward the sound, around the side of the house to the street. A sedan with no headlights squealed its tires and thundered straight at him. With no time to bring his Beretta up, he was forced to dive to the side, hitting the pavement and rolling onto his good shoulder. Jumping immediately to his feet, he took a stance and fired five shots into the back of the fleeing car. It continued on, disappearing around a corner. Catching his breath and cursing, he pocketed the Beretta and headed back to the house.

Genevieve waved her cellphone from the front yard. "Who should I call?"

"911," Hunter said, gasping.

The police arrived within eight minutes along with the fire department, followed by the gas company. Once the two officers did a thorough search and verified that the man Hunter had seen was no longer around, they allowed the guy from the gas company to go inside. A few minutes later the gas man showed them where the gas lines had been disconnected from the gas water heater in the closet off the kitchen, as well as to the kitchen stove and a small fireplace in the living room.

Someone had gone to a lot of trouble to kill them. Hunter figured the would-be killer had gotten into the house while they were away having dinner downtown. He had disconnected the lines, shut off the gas flow with the outside valve, and waited until they were asleep. Then he simply opened the line again, filling the house with gas.

They each gave statements to the police. The cops confirmed what Hunter already knew. The doors and sliders had been deliberately blocked from the outside to prevent anyone inside from escaping. The two of them gave what little description they could of the man who'd thrown the flame into the house. Hunter described the vehicle as a late model SUV of some kind. He didn't get the make. It was black or brown. He couldn't offer any explanation of who the man was or why he might have done this. Was it the same man who'd attacked Genevieve and ransacked her house? Was he the hit-and-run guy?

To be on the safe side, they spent the night in a nearby motel, sleeping fitfully and finally getting up at 8:30 A.M. With all the police and the gas company activity, Hunter knew they hadn't had enough sleep, but he had a lot to do. They ate the motel's surprisingly adequate continental breakfast and drove back to the house. Unfortunately he had no choice but to put on the same grubby clothes he'd been wearing when the car hit him at the airport. His pants had a large tear on the left front thigh area and featured several scuffmarks from where he'd hit the pavement. He still had a bandage on the back of his head covering the stitches, and his shoulder hurt where Dr. Olesin had reset it. The black and blue original color was starting to turn a sickly yellow-green. Coupled with the bruises and scrapes on his face from the hit and run, he was a pretty frightful sight.

He drove Genevieve to work and then took the Beemer to the Budget rental agency at the airport. He was reluctant to leave her alone, but figured she'd be safe at work, and he had to recover his luggage. Earlier, the police had told him that the rental car company was holding it. It turned out he'd never actually taken possession of a car. The hit-and-run driver got him as he was walking out to their lot.

The next item on his list was to pick up the police report on the B & E at Genevieve's house. He drove south to the police station downtown indicated on Sergeant Ball's business card. Fifteen minutes later he was given the report, then headed back to Genevieve's house, where he found a place in the closet to hang his clothes and an empty drawer for his things. He showered, shaved, and changed into clean khaki chinos and a green polo shirt, finally beginning to feel human again for the first time in three days.

He decided to call his dad and tell him where he was. He hadn't planned to leave Charlottesville for another two weeks and would have called him before he left, but after the call from Genevieve, he hadn't had time. It was important to Hunter that his dad always knew where he could reach him. Ed McCoy lived alone in a cabin on the shore of Lake Superior in the Upper Peninsula of Michigan, just north of Marquette. Hunter actually owned the cabin, but his dad lived there year around and took care of the place.

The last time he'd been up at the cabin, just a month before for a weekend, they'd talked about Genevieve for hours. Ed McCoy had been delighted and hoped it meant that Hunter would settle down now and get married.

"Dad, how are you?"

"I'm fine, son. Been doing a lot of trout fishing with Henry over on the Yellow Dog. Sometimes I think that man is tryin' to mother me. He's always asking how I'm doing, if I need any help around the place. You know, just like a mother hen."

Hunter smiled and thought to himself, great, that's just what he'd asked Henry to do. Good to know the man was true to his word, not that he was surprised. Henry and his dad had known each other since high school and they'd been best friends ever since, including their stints in Viet Nam with the Marines.

"Well, good for Henry, Dad. I just wanted to let you know I'll be staying with Genevieve in Sarasota for a while. You've got my cell number, so call anytime you need anything, okay?"

"All right, son. Thanks for calling. Bye."

"Wait, Dad?"

"What?"

He knew he had to be careful here. "Have you had any more, you know, incidents like the last time?"

"I'm all right, Hunter. I know you're worried. I'm being careful. I got Henry."

"All right, Dad. I'll call you soon. Bye."

Hunter sighed. His dad had been starting to show signs of dementia. But when he was examined last month at Marquette General Hospital, they had identified a small benign tumor on his brain that explained the symptoms. The good news was that it was operable, and they were setting up a date at the Mayo Clinic in Rochester,

Minnesota to have it removed. He could continue to live alone, but Hunter *still* worried about him living in such a remote area of Marquette County. Nevertheless, Ed McCoy wouldn't hear any talk about moving into town. He'd always lived in the woods and that was that. Consequently, Hunter tried to spend as much time with him as he could, although his work in Virginia kept him away most of the year.

He stashed his suitcase under the bed, and returning his mind to Genevieve, decided he'd do a reconnaissance of her house and grounds. He figured that her attacker must have been waiting in the living room next to a large bookcase, partially hidden by an artificial potted palm tree when she'd entered. When he saw her on her cellphone, he hit her.

The police had already questioned the neighbor who'd found her, but Hunter thought he'd give it a shot as well. He determined that his Irish luck was still working when he saw the man was having coffee on the covered lanai of his large beachfront home next door, a house that was definitely not a teardown.

He walked over to where he assumed the lot-line was and waved at the man, who appeared to be in his eighties. The neighbor lifted his coffee cup in salute and signaled for Hunter to come on over.

"Hi, I'm staying with the lady next door. The one you rescued a few nights ago with your 911 call." Hunter reached out to shake his hand. "The name's McCoy, Hunter McCoy."

"Curly Winston," the completely bald man said, petting the small dog sitting next to him.

"What was going on there last night? Sounded like gunshots, then the police and the gas guys. What happened?"

Hunter explained and then thanked the man for calling 911 when he'd found Genevieve on the floor.

"Boy, I'll tell you, that was something. Thanks to my dog, Spot here, we found her."

"Well, both she and I are glad you did."

Hunter looked at the dog, an all white bichon.

"Your dog's name is Spot?"

"Yeah."

"But he doesn't have spots."

"I know. It drives him nuts."

"I see." *Hmmm.*

"Say, would you like a cup of coffee?" Curly rose and headed toward the Keurig machine on the counter of his beautiful outdoor kitchen with granite countertops and the biggest outdoor grill Hunter had ever seen.

"Sure. That'd be great." While he made it, Hunter thought, not for the first time, that he'd have to get one of those things. He knew he wasted way too much coffee, throwing away half the pot when he'd had only a cup.

Curly Winston handed him the mug and they sat down. "You're staying with her, you say? Is she all right?"

"She's okay. In fact she's back at work."

"You know," he said, "I feel bad that we haven't gone over to meet her. I know she hasn't been there long, but that's no excuse on our part, my wife Sophie and I. We should have gone and introduced ourselves."

Hunter reached over and patted the old man's shoulder. "Believe me, you're a good neighbor. Who knows what would have happened if you and your dog hadn't been there? His barking probably scared the guy off."

Hunter wondered whose 911 call had reached the authorities first, his or Curly's.

"I know you talked to the police and they probably asked you this already, but did you see anything unusual going on over there, anyone prowling around, anything like that?"

"No, the place is totally quiet. Your friend is like a mouse when she's home. I never saw other cars there, nothing. The groundskeeper who comes once a month is the only other person ever there. We all use him. He's great. But that's it, and he's not due for another week."

Hunter finished his coffee and got up. "Well, thanks again. I'll be staying with her at her place for a while."

"Good to know, and Hunter?"

"Yes?"

"We'll have both of you over for dinner and a drink real soon."

7

THE PREVIOUS EVENING ON LIDO KEY

THE STORM OFF THE GULF OF MEXICO rapidly moved inshore after sunset. Flashes of lightning followed eight to ten seconds later by concussive explosions of thunder, amplified the gravity of the evening. The angry sky had turned black. Six tall royal palm trees separating the enormous pool from the grassy area that ran to the shore bent toward the mansion under the strong westerly wind.

The five men from the five families who represented the current members of the Legacy assembled at the leader's lavish seaside home on Lido Key, just west of downtown Sarasota. The others had arrived from Europe in the last twenty-four hours and were staying in guest quarters in the mansion. They had just completed a sumptuous dinner and retired to the seaside mansion's library to begin their meeting. They sat around a large table with the leader, Tintoretto, at the head.

By Legacy convention, during the meetings each of the members was referred to by the name of one of the Old Master artists whose paintings they owned. Tintoretto had been the Legacy's leader for the past ten years. All five men were wealthy and powerful entrepreneurs in their own right. Besides Tintoretto, the group included Rembrandt, a banker from Zurich; van Dyck a shipping line owner from Paris; Correggio from Lille, France, who operated granite mines in Italy; and finally Botticelli from Prague in the Czech Republic, who owned automobile manufacturing plants. Tintoretto, the host for tonight's meeting, owned a biochemical manufacturing company in Sarasota and oil leases in the Gulf of Mexico.

Tonight, in accordance with the tradition of the Legacy, they were gathered to select Tintoretto's replacement and approve the next five-year plan for their joint enterprise.

Rain pounded on the roof and the floor-to-ceiling windows at the far end of the library. Lightning flashes and thunderclaps were coming closer together.

The operating rules of the Legacy had been in place for over two hundred years. Membership turned over, either by death or mutual agreement, from one generation to the next. Occasionally one of the family's lines ended when a member produced no children. In that event one of the other families nominated a candidate for membership who, if approved, would carry on. Never had there been more than seven or fewer than three members. All plans were put to a vote and the majority ruled. And, since no abstentions were allowed and the membership was always an odd number, every vote resulted in a decision. The individual members didn't always like it, but the system was efficient.

Recently Tintoretto had acquired a piece of information that troubled him considerably. The others weren't aware of it yet but soon would be. Before turning to the main purpose of the meeting he knew he had to tell them. He had to convince them that what he'd discovered was a serious enough threat to the Legacy's plans that it required their immediate attention.

Tintoretto called them to order. "Gentlemen, I must bring you up to date on two issues of critical importance. Issues that if not corrected, have the potential to interfere with our agenda."

The members of Legacy sat stone-faced, waiting.

A flash of lightning and an almost simultaneous clap of thunder literally shook the room. The men looked outward nervously. The lights dimmed for a moment and then returned, as if Tintoretto had called on the rising storm to accentuate the gravity of the news they were about to hear.

"First—and I suspect not one of you is aware of this—our family's history is being carefully scrutinized by a professor at Cambridge University in England. The man's name is Addison Swift. I became aware of this through an article in our local newspaper after the *Cambridge Evening News* carried a story on his research, a story that was syndicated worldwide. The story referred to two scholarly papers he'd written. I read both of them, and they leave no doubt as to his ultimate intent."

"And what's that?" asked Rembrandt, the banker from Zurich.

"Nothing less than locating and repatriating our family's historic art."

"Good luck with that," scoffed van Dyck, the shipping magnate. "None of us even carries the name anymore, and it's been over two hundred years. And remember, the five of us are the only descendants who still have any of the paintings."

"Unfortunately I'm afraid that's no longer true," Tintoretto said. "An outsider has one of them. My Jacob van Ruisdael was recently stolen from my home."

"What? How?" demanded Correggio from Lille, standing up from his chair with both fists on the table. "How did that happen?"

"How did they get past your security?" Rembrandt asked.

"I don't know." Tintoretto tossed back his thick mane of white hair. "But it's gone. They must have gone over my gate at the entrance, crossed the open grassy area to the house, smashed the window—somehow they knew which one—grabbed the painting and left. For some reason the alarm didn't sound. I checked with the alarm company. They reported absolutely no interruption of service. Their records show the house's alarm system was up and running at all times."

"Do you have any idea who did it?" asked Correggio.

Tintoretto stared hard at the other four men and paused before answering. "Yes, as a matter of fact, I do."

He had their attention now. They all gazed at him, eager for an explanation.

"Professor Addison Swift has a daughter. Her name is Genevieve Swift."

He met each one's eyes individually. He wanted them to see the threat the way he did. When he knew they were ready, he continued.

"A month ago Genevieve Swift began a one-year appointment as a visiting curator at the Ringling Museum of Art here in Sarasota. I don't believe for a moment that it's merely a coincidence that the daughter of the man investigating the history of our family's art just happens to show up here at the Ringling, and my painting goes missing shortly after."

"But if you're right and she, or they, are behind it, how were they able to identify you as a descendent, and moreover how would they know about your painting?" Correggio jabbed a finger at Tintoretto, looking for an answer. "How could they—"

"They couldn't," Rembrandt interrupted. "The steps Tintoretto has taken—the steps we've all taken—to shroud our family history are unbreachable."

Botticelli, the automaker from Prague, spoke up. "Gentlemen, I agree with Tintoretto that it's likely Ms. Swift is working with her father, and I'm afraid it's possible they've learned more about the family lineage than we'd like to think. I also agree it's likely she's behind the theft of his painting and plans to use it to further her father's work."

Tintoretto could read the palpable concern in the faces of the others. He nodded gravely. "The inescapable conclusion," he said, "has to be that if they've identified me as a descendent, it won't be long before they know about the rest of you as well."

"We've got to stop them," Rembrandt said, with Correggio, and van Dyck agreeing. Botticelli sat stone-faced and said nothing. Tintoretto knew this was the moment he'd been waiting for.

"As you all know, the terms of the Legacy require that we hold a vote to elect the chairman for the next five years," he said. "This new potential threat to our larger aims has to be dealt with swiftly and decisively. It's my contention that our response needs to be carried out under the direction of whoever we elect as chairman. Therefore, I propose that we conduct the election now, before proceeding any further."

Tintoretto stepped over to the bar adjacent to the huge fireplace in his book-lined library, where he poured two fingers of his favorite twenty-five-year-old single-malt scotch while the others huddled. He couldn't make out their conversation, but could easily imagine it. Except for Botticelli who was somewhat of an enigma, generally keeping his thoughts to himself, he knew them all very well.

Ten years before, in his first term as chairman of the Legacy, he'd told them about an investment opportunity he believed could potentially make them vast amounts of money while simultaneously solving the collective problem of what to do with their inherited art pieces. The investment opportunity became the enormously successful and lucrative art storehouse enterprise known as the Freeport Naff at the Zurich Airport.

Over the next four years the Freeport Naff grew into a huge financial success. Then—at the urging of Botticelli, the automobile manufacturer from Prague—the Legacy decided to sell their shares in Freeport Naff and take what promised to be a sizeable profit—and it was. Each of them enjoyed an almost five hundred percent return on their original investment. That left Quentin Naff as the sole owner of his own enterprise. He'd come up with the idea for the freeport, but had needed the Legacy's funding to realize it. Naff had also opened freeports in Asia and in the United States.

Everything had gone well until Naff swindled them out of the historic paintings they'd been storing in his freeport. For this egregious act they decided to seek revenge. At their next meeting a year later, the group adopted a five-year plan called *Payback*. Firstly, *Payback* would grant them the satisfaction of revenge for the heinous crime that Naff had perpetrated against them. But—at least in the minds of three of the four European members of Legacy—they were also doing it for another, more noble and lofty reason. They were righting what they saw as an untenable injustice to society that the freeport concept was fostering by hiding art away in vaults and keeping it from the public. Tintoretto didn't personally share this particular goal with them, but he understood it.

The group had relied on Tintoretto to mastermind the plan and elected him chair again. And their plan had been working. Successes had been achieved in Europe, America, and Asia.

But there was still much work to be done, and the Legacy was convinced they were the means to achieve it. Further, Tintoretto had been the right choice to implement the program, and now with this new threat they knew he'd be the right choice to continue as chair for a third five-year term.

Tintoretto returned to the head of the table and said, "Are there any nominations for chair?"

Rembrandt, the banker from Zurich stood. "I believe I speak for all of us when I say that we need you in charge now, more than ever. Therefore I nominate you, Tintoretto, as chair for a third five-year term."

Correggio seconded.

"Are there any other nominations?" Tintoretto asked, knowing there'd be none. When none were forthcoming, they proceeded and he was elected to a third five-year term. They congratulated him, poured themselves drinks from the bar, and returned to the table.

Tintoretto lifted his glass. "A toast." The others lifted theirs. "To the Legacy," he said, "and to a quick and decisive solution to the current problem and then on to the next five-year plan. Tonight I'm going to tell you about a new and amazing tool that my company has developed that will be a huge help to further our *Payback* goals."

An enormous clap of thunder rattled the windows.

8

REFRESHED AFTER THE COFFEE WITH CURLY WINSTON, Hunter put on his sunglasses and headed back up Bay Shore Road to the Ringling. One thing he'd discovered about Florida is you need sunglasses. The sun was much brighter than in Virginia and certainly brighter than Michigan. He entered through the Visitors Pavilion, bought a ticket, then strolled past the gift shop and stepped outside onto the grounds.

The guide sheet he'd been given said the entire place covered sixty-six acres and included the palatial home of the circus king, John Ringling, and his wife, Mable, along with an expansive art museum, a circus museum with the world's largest miniature circus, a rose garden, and beautiful grounds that featured exotic, spreading banyan trees and bayfront views.

Rather than take the tram that many visitors seemed to favor to cover the sprawling grounds, he checked his map and decided to walk the relatively short distance to the Education Center and Genevieve's office. He called her on his cell, and she met him at the front door. After checking in at the security desk and getting a visitor badge, he followed her to her office on the second floor, where she sat at her desk and he took an empty chair.

"You look a lot better than you did this morning or yesterday," she said with a smile.

"What? You don't like the mud-stained hit-and-run look?"

Her smile vanished immediately. "I'm glad you're okay, Hunter, and I'm glad you're here."

"Same here."

They studied each other until smiles slowly came back, each remembering the previous night.

"I've missed you," he said.

She leaned over and kissed him. "And I you."

"I stopped at the police station and picked up Sergeant Ball's report. I also met your neighbor, Curly Winston. Nice man."

"Thanks for seeing him. I'll really have to thank him when we get home."

"You'll get your chance. He and his wife are going to invite us to dinner." Then, turning serious, he said, "That guy who tried to torch us last night meant business. He knew exactly what he was doing and whom he was doing it to. It's obviously related to the break-in at your house and the hit-and-run attempt, but who's doing it and why? That's the question. We've got to figure that out, and I haven't a clue."

"Maybe I do."

"What?"

"I've been sitting here this morning trying to come up with a reason someone would tear up my house. I was thinking about my planner. Remember I said I found it open on my desk at home? Something else was odd about it. I'd forgotten it at the time."

"What was that?"

"It was the page it was opened to, April sixteenth. I remembered because that was the day I called my father. We don't call each other that often, so I remembered it."

Hunter frowned. "I don't get it."

"When I recalled our conversion, I remembered what I wrote on the planner. Look. I brought it with me."

Genevieve opened the planner and pushed it over to him.

Citizen Wicar

"Citizen Wicar? What's that, a piece of deck furniture?" he asked, confused by the meaning.

"It's not a what, it's a who."

"What's he a citizen of?"

"No, that's his name."

"His name is Citizen?"

"No," she said, laughing. "During Napoleonic times, the use of the term 'Citizen' was the emperor's attempt to establish a gender-neutral pronoun. The man's actual name is Jean Baptiste Wicar."

Questions still painfully obvious on Hunter's face, she continued. "Okay, okay, I'll admit, I didn't know that either until I looked it up."

"Ah ha."

Ignoring the "gotcha" she continued. "Anyway, it seems that Wicar was one of Napoleon's chief officers in charge of plundering art. You have to understand that art looting had become a standard practice for Napoleon's victorious armies as they marched across the continent, and there was a practical side to it. Wars cost money. Napoleon used pilfered art from the conquered territories to raise funds to support his armies. The looting had another purpose as well. Napoleon hoped that by showcasing and displaying the great artistic treasures of the conquered in the newly converted Louvre museum, he could raise the sinking French morale back home."

Hunter thought about this and couldn't resist pointing out the obvious. "So—you work at a place full of stolen art. The Louvre, I mean?"

She grinned. "I suppose I do."

"So why is Wicar important today? I mean, what's your father's interest?"

"He's doing research concerning some of the stolen pieces."

"Hi, Genevieve, who's your friend?"

They both looked up to see a cheery-faced woman of about thirty with very short, spiky red hair, wearing a white smock blotched with multicolored paint, carrying a cup of coffee.

"Oh, hi, Gretchen, this is Hunter McCoy. I told you about him. He's staying with me for a while."

Gretchen lifted an eyebrow and gave him an approving smile, putting out her hand. "Gretchen Ceisel. Very happy to meet you, Hunter."

Hunter smiled and shook her hand. "Same here, Gretchen."

"What's up?" Genevieve asked.

"I'm still trying to figure out what caused the paint loss in the Lucas Cranach."

"Paint loss?" Hunter asked. "What do you mean?"

"A week ago, a portion of one of the sixteenth-century paintings in our permanent collection developed—I don't know what—a loss of pigment, enough to disfigure it. I'm restoring it now, but I'd like to know what caused it. Anyway, I've got to get back to it. Nice to meet you, Hunter, see you at lunch, Genevieve. Bye."

Genevieve paused until Gretchen was gone. "She's one of the many nice people I work with here," she told Hunter. "Like I said, I love this job. It's been absolutely wonderful, until—"

"—The bad stuff started happening."

They locked eyes. Neither of them spoke. He knew what was coming. A superior smile slowly spread across Genevieve's face.

"Hunter?"

"Yeah?"

She just stared at him for a moment. He rolled his eyes, waiting for it.

"You did it, you know."

"I know, but in my defense, maybe it's contagious."

"You just finished a sentence for me."

The superior smile persisted. When they'd first met three years before at the Bibliotheque Nationale in Paris where she was working at the time, Hunter had thought—and still did—that Genevieve was the most beautiful woman he'd ever seen. In fact, he soon learned that she excelled at everything and only had one fault as far as he could tell. She used to finish his sentences for him. To be fair, she had worked hard to correct it and only did it occasionally anymore.

"You got me. Oops," he said.

"Well, don't let it happen again, Buster. I'm watching you." She did the thing where she pointed two fingers at her eyes and then pointed them at him.

He noticed that she'd been picking up American phrases and mannerisms at a rapid rate. He loved the way they sounded with her French accent.

"I'm having lunch with Gretchen," she told him. "Want to join us?"

"Another time," Hunter said. "Right now I'm going to see what I can find out about the break-in at your house."

9

"HEY, GENEVIEVE. READY FOR LUNCH?"

Genevieve reluctantly lifted her eyes away from the Lucas Cranach canvas being lovingly restored by Gretchen Ceisel. "This is amazing, Gretchen. The lion's face is almost back to normal."

Glancing briefly at the painting, Gretchen shrugged and said, "Come on, I'm hungry."

Just then Hilda Swanson, the director's receptionist, swept into the conservation lab and with her usual high energy level spotted Genevieve and headed in her direction. "Genevieve, you'd better get yourself over to the director's office on the double. He's looking for you."

"The director is looking for me?"

"Yes, and he's not happy about something. He's had me trying to find you from the minute I got in this morning."

Genevieve had been at the museum all morning, but only briefly in her office with Hunter earlier. Before that, she'd spent most of her time in the library seeing what she could learn about Jean Baptiste Wicar.

A wave of anxiety washed over her normal jubilant self. *What's this all about?* She thought. *Have I done something wrong?*

"Why does he want to see me?"

"I don't know for sure, but I think it might have something to do with the old guy who died yesterday on the tram."

Someone died on a tram? "What does that have to do with me?"

"I don't know but you'd better get over there right away. He's upset about something."

With an apologetic glance at Gretchen, Genevieve followed Hilda out of the Conservation Lab on the first floor of the Education Building and went up one flight to the director's office. Hilda went in first and announced that she'd found Genevieve. Genevieve heard the director's sharp voice through the open door. "Send her in." He didn't sound happy.

Dr. Elias Bertram, the newly appointed director of the Ringling Museum of Art, was standing behind his desk in his bookshelf-lined office. A large window behind him overlooked the central courtyard of the Ringling, dominated by the sixteen-foot-tall copy of the statue of Michelangelo's "David." Original paintings lined the walls, and every book on the shelves had been placed so that regardless of its depth, the spines presented a perfectly even line. His ornate desk was free of clutter, with only a small framed painting lying on it. Sharon Grandholm, the assistant curator for pre-twentieth-century Western art, Genevieve's immediate superior, was also there, and Genevieve felt somewhat less anxious when Sharon smiled a greeting to her.

A tall, thin man, Elias Bertram was wearing a black suit, white shirt, and red bowtie, his dark hair neatly combed to the side. At fifty-four he looked every bit the chief executive he was—and he wasn't smiling.

"Come in, Dr. Swift." He indicated a chair in front of his desk. Remaining standing, he pushed the small, ornately framed painting across his broad desk toward Genevieve. "Can you tell me what that is?"

Startled by the man's abruptness and having no idea what he was talking about, she picked it up and examined it. The painting was a misty seascape showing a river and town in the background with a wash of white puffy clouds against a gray-blue sky. It looked to be Flemish, about seventeenth century. She pointed to the lower right hand corner. "According to the signature, it's a van Ruisdael. I didn't know we had this in our collection."

"You haven't seen it before?"

"No. Why?"

Beginning to feel she was being put on the spot for something—she didn't know what—she frowned and said, "Dr. Bertram, what's this all about? What's going on here?"

Without softening his tone he just stared at her. "What can you tell me about this painting?"

This was getting annoying. On top of the horrific experiences she and Hunter had just been through—facts she'd deliberately chosen *not* to share with her colleagues—she didn't need this third degree from the director.

"What is this, some kind of exam? You're not sure of my abilities?" This was the rudest anyone had been to her since she'd arrived from Paris.

"No, Dr. Swift, on the contrary, I have every confidence in your ability. Now what can you tell me about this painting?"

Unwilling to take this anymore, Genevieve started to rise. "Look, am I being accused of something here? Please tell me what's going on."

Dr. Bertram, clearly not used to being addressed in this manner, adjusted his bowtie, took two deep breaths, apparently as much for effect as physiology. "You're not being accused of anything, but if you do know anything about what's going on here and don't tell us, you may be."

Really irritated now, Genevieve was on the verge of storming out when the director picked up the painting. "A docent found this lying on top of the glass display case of German silverware in Gallery 17 yesterday afternoon. She was alarmed because it was just lying there out in the open. I'm sure you realize we don't leave valuable paintings on top of display cases, even if it isn't one of ours."

"It's not one of ours?" Genevieve asked, confused. She looked to Sharon Grandholm, who nodded in confirmation.

"No, but we know where it came from—sort of."

"Sort of? Why would someone give a painting to us that way? Why not just donate it?"

"Exactly."

"I mean if they wanted to do it anonymously, all they'd have to do is ask, right?"

"That's the normal way," agreed the director who looked at her and added, "unless . . .?"

"Unless they don't own it," she said.

"Exactly."

Genevieve furrowed her brows. "But if that's true why would someone leave a possibly stolen painting here? Why not keep it or try to sell it?"

"There's more," said Bertram. "Security examined CCTV footage of the gallery, and we can clearly see the painting being placed on the display case yesterday by an elderly man."

"Can you identify him? Do you know who he is?"

"We haven't identified him yet, but we will."

"How can you be so sure?"

"Because the police have his body. After he dropped off the painting he casually got on a tram. On the ride back to the Visitors Pavilion, he had a heart attack, or something, and died."

Oh—the dead guy on the tram.

"Mon Dieu!"

"Exactly. But that's not all, Dr. Swift, there's more, and that's really why you're here. It most definitely involves you."

Here it comes, the reason he called me in.

"Lying on top of the painting was this note."

He handed the note to Genevieve, who unfolded it and saw immediately it was handwritten in a smooth cursive style

The van Ruisdael is just the first step in the dance
Have Genevieve Swift trace its history
Her father's life hangs in the balance
If she's unable to solve its mystery

Genevieve blinked in astonishment. "My father's life?" she said out loud.

A chill washed over her. *What is going on here?*

The Swifts were a close family, everybody involved in their own scholarship. Family get-togethers were like tiny academic seminars, with each Swift equally fascinated by the other's work. Genevieve remembered how happy her parents were when she—their only child—was admitted to a doctoral program in Renaissance History at the Sorbonne. They'd always stayed in close touch, through her first position as a curator at the National Library in Paris, and later when she switched to the Louvre and became an assistant curator of pre-twentieth-century Western art, the position from which she was currently on a yearlong exchange program with the Ringling.

Director Bertram studied the confusion on her face. "You're saying you have no idea what this is about?"

Still stunned by the threatening nature of the note, even more than the accusatory tone of the director, Genevieve shook her head. "No, I don't. I have no idea what this is about or what my father has to do with any of this." Then, reflecting on its implication, she added, "or why someone would threaten him. And I've never seen this painting before just now."

But I'm damn well going to find out what it means.

10

THE GRAVEL CRACKLED UNDER HUNTER'S FEET as he walked slowly from the Beemer to the Education Building to meet Genevieve. People were beginning to leave after their day's work, and the long narrow parking lot required more vigilance than he was giving it. He almost walked into a parked car.

He was sure the break-in at Genevieve's house, the hit-and-run attempt on his life, and the man who had tried to torch her house with both of them inside were related. Most people went through life without a single event as serious as any one of those happening to them, but three life-threatening events in three days? No way was that a coincidence.

Hoping Genevieve was having better luck than he was, he took the elevator to the second floor and found her at her desk.

"You don't look happy," he said, stating the obvious.

Genevieve gently pounded both fists on her desktop. "I'm not, I'm not happy at all." Then she went on to tell him about her encounter with the director. He listened, saying nothing.

"But even more than the director's attitude, I'm upset because I don't know what to make of the painting or the note with the reference to my father that was left in the gallery." She showed him the copy she had made of the note.

Hunter examined it. "It refers to a mystery. What mystery? Is there something mysterious about the painting?" he asked.

"Not that I'm aware of. Jacob van Ruisdael was a seventeenth-century Dutch artist, one of the great masters, credited with giving landscape painting a soul. His paintings were more than just an accurate depiction of nature. He gave them a feeling of human psychology and emotion. A major influence on his work was his uncle, Solomon Ruisdael, his father's brother, also a landscape painter."

"So which do you have here, Jacob or Solomon?"

"Oh, it's a Jacob van Ruisdael for sure. The signature is clear."

"What do you suppose 'trace its history' means?"

"I've been working on that all afternoon. The head of library services has been looking into it, too. She's very knowledgeable and offered to help. Also Sharon Grandholm, my boss, is doing all she can."

"Maybe the link to your father will help. Have you called him?"

"I was just about to. I wanted to see what I could come up with on my own first. I'm afraid the answer is not much, so it's time to call him."

He checked his watch. 5:15 P.M. "It's ten-fifteen in Cambridge."

Genevieve took out her cellphone. Hunter sat back and listened to one side of the conversation as Genevieve first told her father about the events that had led to their simultaneous hospitalizations and the attempt on their lives at her house last night. She repeatedly had to assure him they were both all right now. When she related the story of the open planner page with Citizen Wicar written on it and the van Ruisdael painting and strange cryptic note left in the museum, he must have had a lot to say. Genevieve mostly listened, and Hunter watched her take notes on a pad. After fifteen minutes or so, she thanked her father, promised they'd be careful, and hung up.

"Well?" he asked, stretching his long legs and crossing them at the ankle. "What did you learn?"

She sat back in her chair and paused for a moment, apparently trying to assimilate everything she'd heard.

"It's highly probable that the painting—the van Ruisdael—was part of the loot taken by Wicar during Napoleon's campaign in Italy. According to my father's research, on May 17, 1796, the Duke of Modena—having just been defeated by Napoleon's army—signed an armistice that stated, among other things, that he was to hand over twenty paintings to the Emperor's representative at the scene."

"Would that be the good Citizen Wicar?" asked Hunter.

"Correct. Except that Wicar took fifty and not twenty paintings. True to the signed armistice he dutifully gave twenty to Napoleon, but kept the remaining thirty unreported paintings for himself."

"Aha," said Hunter. "So if the good Citizen Wicar followed the army around to every defeated dukedom, repeating this practice, he'd eventually—"

"Collect quite a treasure trove," Genevieve finished. "And that's exactly what he did. According to my father, when Wicar died in 1834, he bequeathed almost fifteen hundred works of art to his home town of Lille, France."

"Genevieve?"

She rolled her eyes. "I know. I just—"

"Forgot for a moment?"

"There, we're even now," she said smugly, the sentence finishing temporarily completed.

"So, was this painting stolen from Lille, then?" asked Hunter.

"Apparently not. The museums there have no record of this particular painting."

"Then how does your father know it was part of the Modena loot?"

"Ah, now here's where it gets interesting." Genevieve got up and retrieved a can of fruit juice from her small refrigerator, and offered one to him. He turned it down in favor of bottled water.

"Modena is an ancient town on the south side of the Po River in Italy. It features a university that dates back to the twelfth century. Their library holdings are incredible, and my father was able to track down, in their archives, a list of the fifty paintings that Wicar took in the Modena theft. Wicar apparently assembled this list for his own use. Remember, he only reported twenty to Napoleon. This list, along with the fifteen hundred works of art all went to Lille after his death. My father found it in the records. By cross-referencing this list with other documents, my father was able to determine the twenty paintings that went to Napoleon."

"And our Jacob van Ruisdael wasn't among them?"

"Correct. And," continued Genevieve, "the remaining thirty paintings were not listed among those bequeathed to Lille upon his death."

"So what does that tell us?"

"Now we get to my father's interest in the whole thing. He's now assembled a list of the thirty paintings that came from the Duke of Modena that were not turned over to Napoleon, and not bequeathed to Lille. So where did they go?"

"Well, it's been over two hundred years," said Hunter. "They could be anywhere,"

"Or?"

"Or they could still be in the Wicar family—the descendants of the family."

"That's my father's point. He's trying to identify the family lines from Jean-Baptiste Wicar to the present."

"Why? Surely these descendants haven't broken any laws or even have any responsibility to give the paintings back if they do have them. Isn't there some kind of statute of limitations on that kind of thing?"

"It's a gray area. There are still an estimated one hundred thousand works of art looted by the Nazis that still haven't been repatriated to the owners or families of the owners. In the United States alone there are paintings, sculptures, and other works of art with provenance gaps from the time of the Nazis that imply a continuing need for research on rightful ownership."

"So this case," Hunter said, "with the actual lists of paintings and the proof that they were looted, it would seem to be quite easy to make the case that any descendants of Mr. Wicar would be holding the works illegally and therefore have to turn them over."

They both sat for a moment and considered all of this. Hunter took a long drink from his water bottle. "The note implies a threat to your father. Where does that come from? If it's from some heir of Wicar, how would he, or they, know your father was even looking into it? Has he published any of this?"

"Yes, two papers in historical journals."

"Well, there you go. Unless the heirs read academic journals, I can't imagine how they'd ever learn about it."

"I'm afraid there *is* a way, and I think I know what it is."

"What?"

"The *Cambridge Evening News*—the local newspaper—interviewed him. The story was picked up two months ago by news affiliates all over the world. The Wicar heirs could have seen it anywhere."

11

HUNTER CLOSED HIS EYES, CLASPED HIS HANDS behind his head, and turned his face to the ceiling in Genevieve's office. His duties at the med school involved teaching physiology to first year students, but he was also a scientist and director of the Vascular Smooth Muscle Research Laboratory. He knew how the system worked. Published scholarly research was almost exclusively read by other academics doing research in the same or a similar area. The necessary scientific terminology in a typical published paper would make it almost unintelligible to a nonspecialist in the area. There was so much technical language a layperson would need a translator for almost every sentence.

Genevieve's dad, Professor Addison Swift, authored publications in scholarly research journals that Hunter assumed were also primarily written for professionals and might be somewhat difficult for outsiders. Occasionally though, a reporter would hear about some research he thought might appeal to the public at large. After interviewing the scholar, if the reporter was good at his job, he'd write a story in common language that could be understood by the general public, and it would run in a magazine or newspaper. Hunter had had this happen to him twice—and apparently it had happened to Professor Addison Swift two months ago.

He turned to Genevieve. "Who, and why here?" he asked, almost rhetorically. "If this painting—the van Ruisdael—is one of Wicar's stolen paintings and was in the hands of a descendant, who was he, and equally important, why did it turn up here at the Ringling Museum of Art in Sarasota?"

Genevieve turned to her computer. "Let me try something." Genevieve checked the Sarasota White Pages online for anyone named Wicar. No hits.

Looking over her shoulder, he said, "Try a larger area."

"Okay, I'll try the entire state of Florida. There have to be some people named Wicar."

He watched while she searched. Apparently there was no one named Wicar in the entire state.

"It's been over two hundred years," Hunter said. "The name could be spelled differently. Also, the descendants might have different names today through marriage."

"My father said he's been trying to trace the descendants using genealogy software. He said it's much harder to trace from a historical figure to current individuals than in the reverse direction."

Hunter stared at the ceiling again. "Why was the painting left here at the Ringling? What did that note say again?"

Genevieve read it aloud.

The van Ruisdael is just the first step in the dance
Have Genevieve Swift trace its history
Her father's life hangs in the balance
If she's unable to solve its mystery

"What does that sound like to you?" he said. "I'm not sure it's a threat as much as a warning. Maybe someone is trying to tell you about a potential danger to your father. Someone is telling you that you have to solve a mystery related to this painting or he could be in trouble. Maybe this came from a friend, someone who wants to help but doesn't want to be identified."

Genevieve knit her brow. "I can't imagine who that might be. Also, what mystery? Is it just that this painting was stolen by Wicar? That didn't take long to find out. There has to be more to it than that. There has to be something else."

"Agreed," Hunter said. "There has to be something else."

This was getting them nowhere. Still, he couldn't get rid of the nagging feeling that something obvious was eluding them. "Why Ringling?" he considered out loud. "Let's review what we know; maybe that will help."

He and Genevieve had played this game before.

"Okay," Genevieve said. "You go first."

"All right. One. Your father is digging into the background of the Wicar descendants who may be holding pilfered art. After reading the news article about what he's up to, they get nervous. Will the bad publicity mean they have to give it back? So far they haven't been individually identified, but if he keeps it up, maybe they will be."

"Two. Me," she pointed at herself, "my father's daughter—a Renaissance scholar. I show up at the Ringling about the same time. Is that just a coincidence?"

Hunter shrugged. "Three. A likely stolen Wicar painting is mysteriously left at the very same Ringling."

"Four," Genevieve countered, "a note relating to the painting and linked to me and my father is left with the painting."

Hunter nodded. "And don't forget what happened to us. That's got to be linked too."

"Agreed," she said. "Five. My house is burglarized and I'm mugged."

"Six. Someone tried to kill me with a car."

Genevieve nodded. "Seven. We're locked in my house and nearly firebombed."

"So," Hunter said. "Was the painting left at the Ringling specifically because *you're* here? And what is the significance, if any, to your planner being opened to the page you'd written Citizen Wicar on? Was the guy going through your house a few days before he attacked you?"

Three hours later, after a quiet dinner and back at Genevieve's house they retired to the deck to watch the afterglow of the earlier sunset. Suddenly the tranquility was shattered by what sounded like a high-powered rifle shot smashing the glass of the newly replaced lanai sliders to smithereens. Hunter grabbed Genevieve and threw her down to cover her body as glass shards rained on the deck. Looking out at the water he saw a boat just offshore with its outboard motor idling while the driver lined up for another shot. Hunter grabbed the round metal patio table and used it as a shield as he backed Genevieve inside. He pulled out his Beretta, ran toward the dock, hid behind a tall palm, and fired at the gunman. The man ducked, gunned his engine, and took off.

Hunter leaped onto the dock and pulled the lines free from the Boston Whaler, with its 200 horsepower Mercury outboard, that Genevieve's landlady had told them they could use. The key was in the ignition; Hunter fired it up and within seconds was roaring after the shooter. He headed out toward the center of the bay at top speed with Hunter in pursuit. He apparently couldn't manage the rifle and the boat at the same time, so he focused on getting away. Hunter didn't know the rules for boating after sunset but assumed speeding wasn't allowed, even in the center of the bay. With any luck the authorities might intervene. Meanwhile he kept after the man at full throttle.

They raced across the bay and then under the Ringling Bridge that connected downtown Sarasota to Lido Key. Hunter was gratified to see that he was slowly gaining on the boat ahead, which was beginning to turn to the right past huge homes on what he'd learned earlier was Bird Key. And then the boat was out of sight. Where had it gone?

Hunter slowed to listen for the shooter's motor just as a bullet tore through the windshield inches from his face. He jerked the wheel and pulled the boat around in time to see the man had turned into a small cove and was now behind him, lining up for another shot. Hunter ducked and swerved, aimed his boat directly at the shooter, and pushed the throttle to full. Steering with one hand, he raised his gun and fired two shots at the gunman, who was now speeding away back out into the bay and back under the Ringling Bridge, this time in the opposite direction. If the man had a night-scope on that rifle, Hunter was seriously outgunned.

He zoomed past nighttime sailors, who raised their fists and swore at them to slow down. Where was the water patrol? The man headed under the bridge to Longboat Key and into the pass that Hunter knew opened out into the Gulf of Mexico itself. For the first time Hunter checked his fuel and saw he was almost empty. Reluctantly, he pulled back on the throttle and watched the boat roar ahead and disappear into the night. Breathing heavily, he slumped back into the seat and waited to see if the man would come back. Ten minutes later it was clear he had made a run for it.

Hunter turned on the running lights and slowly returned to Genevieve's house where he docked the boat. She rushed out to meet him, and he took her in his arms.

"He got away."

She saw the shattered windshield on the boat. "Are you all right?"

"Yeah, but I'm really beginning to dislike this guy."

12

THE SARASOTA POLICE DETECTIVE who answered the call Hunter made after the boat chase was the same one who responded after the earlier attempt on their lives following the gas episode. Again, they weren't able to supply any information about who the man was or even if it was the same guy. And, if it was the same guy, why he was after them at all? They finally got to bed, exhausted, about two in the morning.

At ten thirty the morning after the boat chase, responding to an email she had received from the director, Hunter accompanied Genevieve to Elias Bertram's office. Genevieve had previously told him that the administrative assistant's name was Hilda Swanson, and he assumed it was she who met them in the outer office when they arrived. She stared at Hunter, no doubt wondering who the big guy with Genevieve was. When she ushered them in, two men were already present.

"Who's this?" demanded the tall fussily dressed man behind the desk, whom Hunter assumed was Bertram.

"This is my friend, Hunter McCoy," Genevieve said. "He's going to help me find the answers."

"Absolutely not," the director said. "This is an in-house issue. I'll be directing it, and we'll deal with it that way. There's no need to have any amateurs from the outside involved." Looking directly at Hunter, he added, "You're excused, sir, please leave."

Genevieve gasped. "Dr. Bertram, if you—"

"No, no, Genevieve, it's all right," said Hunter, open palms toward her as if holding her back. "The director is correct. This *is* no time for amateurs. I'm sure he and the local staff have had considerable experience dealing with criminals and cracking enigmatic codes. And I'm sure he can personally call on the help of the right people at Interpol in an instant if the investigation calls for it."

The other man in the room perked up at this last statement and cocked his head, studying Hunter with renewed interest.

The director stared. "Just who *are* you, sir?"

"Me? Why I believe you just called me an amateur."

Sensing he was anything but, the other man in the room moved forward. "Mr. McCoy, I'm Kyle Klinger, Head of Security. I suggest that you and I have a private chat in the outer office. If you'll excuse us, Dr. Bertram."

Klinger stepped outside, and Hunter followed. A clearly irritated director was left behind with Genevieve.

Klinger closed the door to the director's office. "Hilda, could you give us some privacy for a bit?"

Hilda Swanson, eyeing Hunter dubiously, gathered up her purse and rose from her chair. "No problem. I'll go have a cup of coffee."

Klinger took Hilda's chair and motioned for Hunter to take the guest chair. "Now, Mr. McCoy, perhaps you'd be so kind as to tell me who you are?"

Hunter was pretty sure he'd need Klinger's cooperation, so he told him that after his stint as a Marine captain in Afghanistan, he had worked for several years as an investigator for the Intelligence Agency of the United States Department of Defense. He showed Klinger his credentials indicating that he was still active. He explained that he was also a detective with the Virginia State Police and showed him his current credentials to prove that as well. Finally, he explained that throughout his years of work for the DOD and the Virginia State Police he had often worked with Interpol, tracking and capturing international criminals whose activities were of interest to the security of the United States. Further, he still maintained all of those contacts.

He explained that seven years ago he'd retired from full-time service with each organization so he could earn a Ph.D. in physiology and was currently an assistant professor of physiology at the University of Virginia School of Medicine. He still maintained a quasi-active status with all three law-enforcement organizations, however, and had agreements with each that they could call on him whenever their investigations involved higher education or at any time they thought his input could be useful.

Finally, he told Klinger that it was his other—more personal—line of work that he thought could be most useful to Ringling in the current instance. He explained that whenever his duties at the medical school allowed, he often undertook what he called "find-and-correct" work. He'd agree to find something or find out something that a client had lost or didn't understand, something that caused considerable anxiety and loss, either personal or financial. He'd investigate, find the answer, and then correct the negative consequences produced. For these services, he had no set fee. He only asked that when he'd accomplished his task, the client would pay whatever he thought it was worth.

Klinger sat and stared at him. Then he said, "Anything else?"

"Nope, that's pretty much it."

"And Dr. Swift? Is there more to her than we know as well?"

Hunter told him about Genevieve's considerable help two summers before, in tracking down and stopping the madman physicist, Arnaud Laurendeau, who was responsible for killing young scientists assigned to the Large Hadron Collider at CERN, the European Nuclear Research Organization. She'd helped him prevent a terrorist attack on the facility during their search to find a lost copy of a Renaissance manuscript.

He also explained how she'd been instrumental in tracking down Willem Hofmann, who'd been responsible for fostering illegal and unethical human brain research as a means for personal revenge. He explained that Genevieve's amazing ability to decipher coded messages and their hidden meaning was unequaled and had been essential in each case.

Again Kyle Klinger sat and stared. He unwrapped a stick of gum and popped it into his mouth. Then he raised his eyebrows and extended the pack to Hunter. "Would you like one?"

"No thanks."

"Of course, I'll have to verify all of this," Klinger said, chewing thoughtfully.

They reentered the director's office. "Dr. Bertram," Klinger said, "I'm going to check on some information Mr. McCoy gave me, and if it checks out, I strongly believe it would be to the Ringling's advantage to have him assist in this matter."

Genevieve and Hunter were asked to step out into the outer hall while the security head and the director had a chat. Hunter smiled, imagining the conversation inside. He was sure the director was a good guy and only doing what he thought was best for the institution; but still worried about Hunter's motives.

Finally the door opened, and Klinger came out and handed Hunter his card. "Give me a few hours and then come over to the security office, say three o'clock? It's directly across the driveway from this building. You'll see the sign. I'll have you checked out by then."

Hunter left Genevieve to work at her desk and used the intervening time before his meeting with Klinger to grab lunch and learn what he could about the hit-and-run attempt on his life. He drove to police headquarters and showed his detective shield with the Virginia State Police to the sergeant at the front desk. That got him a productive sit-down with Division Commander Rand Conrad.

Conrad informed him that sharing a police report with a victim wasn't standard procedure, but given Hunter's state police connection he'd stretch the point. Hunter learned that there were two witnesses to the hit-and-run. They didn't agree on the make or even color of the car. Neither could come up with any part of a license plate number, much less a state registration. However, they did both agree on two things: the vehicle had suddenly accelerated just before hitting him, and the driver, a man, was the only one in the car. The driver was definitely aiming at him. It was no accident. CCTV wasn't much help either. It did show the incident, but only from the front and Florida cars only have a rear license plate. The car was a dark blue Ford Taurus. The driver had a baseball cap pulled down low over his face. Hunter knew they'd never catch who did it without a lot more information.

After thanking Commander Conrad for the information, Hunter headed back for his appointment with Klinger. The security entrance was in the west end of the south gallery of the museum on the ground floor. Access was off the same parking lot he used to get to the Education Center and Genevieve's office.

Klinger's office was the complete opposite of the director's; furnished with a plain metal desk and several file cabinets in institutional green. Klinger's chair was identical to the three placed around the desk. The floor was made of standard-issue, off-white ceramic tiles. A metal coat rack stood in the corner by the door.

"McCoy, your creds with the Virginia State Police checked out. I'm a former Florida State Police detective, and my colleagues were happy to cooperate in looking you up. I also checked with the University of Virginia, and—to my complete surprise, I have to admit—you actually *are* a professor. Things were a little tougher with the feds. Eventually, though, I did manage to get through to Director Deacon Wogen of the Defense Intelligence Agency, who said you're a good man and I'd be lucky to have you help us."

"As I said earlier, Mr. Klinger, I'm at your service."

"Kyle, please. And what do I call you?"

"McCoy or Hunter, either will do just fine."

"Fine. Now here's something for you to know, McCoy. Dr. Bertram, for obvious reasons, would like to keep a lid on the painting and note affair. That was his reason for not wanting an outsider—namely you—involved.

"Also, as you can imagine, he didn't much like your sarcasm in his office earlier. I tell you this, because while I agree you might have something to offer in this case, you'd better tread lightly when dealing with him directly. It won't take much on your part to cause him to throw you out. Are we clear on that?"

"I got it."

Hunter chuckled quietly to himself. *That would be an amusing picture, the director trying to throw me out.*

"All right. I've got something for you." He handed Hunter a clip-on security badge with his name on it that gave him authoritative access to everything. "I don't know where this investigation is going to take us, but you might find that handy."

Klinger stood up and they shook hands. Hunter left, sure that the pass would undoubtedly help him move about the Ringling property. The problem was he had no idea where to begin.

13

TINTORETTO SAT ON THE UPPER LANAI off the large office of his home on Lido Key, staring west out over the calm waters of the Gulf of Mexico. It was ten in the morning on Saturday and he was in the shade, with a large fan slowly and silently turning overhead. The other members of the Legacy had already left and were returning to their homes in Europe, having completed their business meeting. Five years from now the next meeting would be at Botticelli's home in Prague, unless there was a need for them to meet sooner.

Tintoretto turned his attention to their newly approved strategy for implementing the next phase of the Legacy's agenda. But first he had to deal with the Swift woman and her father, the Cambridge professor. He hadn't told the group specifically what he was going to do about the situation, just that he would take care of it. In addition to the Swifts he knew he also had to eliminate the threat posed by Hunter McCoy. What he'd been able to learn about this man had led him to commission the failed hit-and-run. He'd determined that if McCoy were working with the Swift woman, he'd be a dangerous adversary. The agenda would have to wait until they were all neutralized.

Three of the other four members of the Legacy, cousins of one kind or another, always felt the revenge component against Quentin Naff was less important than the other outcome of *Payback*—their plan to close freeports everywhere. As for Botticelli, he was still an enigma, and Tintoretto never quite knew where the man stood in regard to Naff. And he'd been surprised by the man's support at the meeting given their history over the unfortunate circumstances of the death of Botticelli's son.

For Tintoretto, revenge and payback was the number one motive. It was all about the theft of the Wicar paintings by that ungrateful bastard Quentin Naff. That's how he thought of them—the Wicars, the thirty paintings that were in the family. Each of the five Legacy members had six paintings. The members knew of course that they'd been passed down from Jean-Baptiste Wicar, their distant relative. And they, like their ancestors before them, knew they'd never be able to sell them nor even safely display them in their own homes for fear they'd be identified, although some had, including Tintoretto.

No, he and his cousins knew they had to find a safe place to keep them. And yet, like all people who own fine art, they wanted to have access to it as well. They wanted to see it, to enjoy it. Otherwise, what was the point? When Quentin Naff told him about his plan for a freeport, it sounded almost too good to be true. They would have a permanently safe place for the art, in a setting that would give them access to it in beautiful surroundings commensurate with the value of the paintings. The five of them funded Naff's endeavor, and against all odds, it had grown far beyond any of their expectations.

They all agreed they'd been premature in selling their interests back to Naff after the first four years. True, they'd made a huge profit on their investment, but had they stayed in they'd have made even more. Naff had since expanded internationally so that now he owned freeports in Europe, Asia, and most recently, Tampa, Florida.

When it came right down to it, Tintoretto wasn't personally a great lover of art, not nearly as much as his four cousins. Maybe it was because they were more European in their outlook than he was, he wasn't sure. Of course his wife, Marie, loved art. So much so she was even on the Board at the Ringling Museum of Art.

It had been Botticelli who'd wanted to sell the art in the first place, all thirty paintings. He saw the cover of the freeport as the perfect opportunity. Transactions carried out under its roof were free from the prying eyes of the authorities and the taxman. They knew they could never sell the pieces openly, just as their ancestors couldn't, because it was looted art in the first place and the provenance would be suspect. But now, under cover of the freeport, they could carry out any transactions they wanted.

Six years earlier, Botticelli had finally talked his cousins in the Legacy into selling. They'd agreed that each of them would keep one painting at home as a sort of paean to the family tradition but would place the other twenty-five—five from each cousin—in the new Freeport Naff-Zurich while they looked for a buyer. The theory was that once the operation grew large enough, when other wealthy art owners began storing their art there, one of them could be approached and asked if they'd be interested in buying the paintings. The Legacy theorized that even if the purchaser knew, or even suspected, it was looted art, they wouldn't be dissuaded from buying because the art would stay there for them to enjoy and no one would know.

In return for their having funded his capital investment in the freeport, Quentin Naff had agreed to help find a buyer for them from among his clients. After all, they'd reasoned, he knew all of them and the cousins didn't.

One of Quentin Naff's new renters, a German industrialist named Horst Mueller who hadn't yet transferred any of his own paintings to his vault at the freeport, agreed to purchase all twenty-five paintings for four hundred thirty-two million dollars, a price that was at least twice what they'd expected to get. They readily agreed to go ahead with the sale and authorized Naff to expedite it. What happened after that was a disaster.

Once the paintings had been transferred from the Legacy's vault to the vault of the German industrialist, Naff

informed the Legacy that the buyer had fled, along with the
paintings. Further, the money transfer—the cash to be paid
to the Legacy under the roof of the freeport—had not
occurred. The Legacy, smelling a rat, accused Naff of
swindling them. Of course they had no proof and could
hardly go to the authorities and claim the theft of their
paintings. They only had two options: suck it up or seek
redress in any way they could.

And so it was that five years ago at the last meeting of
the Legacy at Rembrandt's house in Zurich, they launched
the agenda they called *Payback*, to right this wrong. As far
as Tintoretto was concerned, the purpose was simple—
revenge, and if possible, recouping their financial loss as
well, with interest. Oh yes, there'd be interest.

What he hadn't counted on were his cousins. While
they too hated Naff and wanted to get back at him for what
he'd done to them, they'd developed another reason to shut
Naff down. It had always bothered them that they couldn't
openly enjoy the Wicar paintings. They felt that people
should see beautiful art. Certainly the painters of the great
masterpieces must have felt that way. Surely they wanted
their work seen.

What had been happening in the art world though, in
recent years, was that great art—the life's work of the great
masters—had become capital. The super-wealthy were
buying it, not for its artistic or historic worth, but purely as
a financial investment. Naff's great freeports were
becoming bank vaults rather than safe houses for the
temporary storage of art the owners didn't have room for on
their walls. For all Naff's insistence that he was supplying a
safe place for the art so that owners could periodically
switch out the pieces they had at home with their art in his
storage facilities, he was actually supplying a shelter for
their money without government oversight.

Tintoretto's cousins in the Legacy found this practice
ludicrous. They had hated that they were never able to

freely display the Wicar paintings when they still had them, and came to the conclusion that Naff and his freeports were continuing that practice by allowing clients to treat art works as investments and not display them so they could be enjoyed and studied. And worst of all, because the art could be held indefinitely, it was essentially being locked away forever.

So while Tintoretto's ultimate goal was to ruin Naff and extract revenge, the other cousins' main goal was more altruistic—the closing of the freeports in order to literally "free" the art held therein.

The emails Tintoretto had received earlier that morning confirmed what he already knew. *Payback* was beginning to work. The Legacy's *Payback* agenda included spreading rumors among clients at the freeports that the facilities weren't as safe as the art owners thought, and that local governments were preparing to shut them down for tax fraud. *Payback* also included rumors that Naff was taking illegal commissions on transactions between art owners under the freeports. All of this had been having an effect. Three more owners with large inventories in Freeport Naff-Zurich had pulled their holdings, bringing the number to twelve at that facility alone. Worldwide, Naff had suffered the loss of twenty-seven clients with holdings worth an estimated 1.4 billion dollars. And best of all, Naff had no idea the cousins were behind it. Yes indeed, revenge was sweet. He smiled for the first time that day.

In the last month, Tintoretto had—without telling the other four members of Legacy about it—prepared yet another campaign to discourage owners from keeping their art in Naff's freeports. He had told them about it for the first time at their recent meeting at his seaside home in Lido Key. Much to his dismay, Correggio, van Dyck, and Rembrandt were horrified by his plan and voted it down. Botticelli voted with them, but was strangely silent during the discussion. But then, Tintoretto had always found the man to be an enigma, especially so after the tragedy involving his son.

Still, the Legacy couldn't have the authorities looking too closely at their affairs. That meant that Professor Swift, his daughter, and McCoy had to be stopped immediately. So far, the man he had surreptitiously hired to do this had failed badly. He had to correct that and do it now.

Back at the desk in his study, Tintoretto opened his computer and checked his email. Then he activated his wife's email account. He'd never had any interest in her stuff before, but thought he'd see what she was up to. It didn't take him long to get bored; it was all bridge dates, mahjongg, luncheons, and emails to and from Ringling addresses. He didn't know any of the museum people, refusing to have anything to do with the place. He'd gone once with her to a reception but couldn't stand the stupid small talk.

Then he spotted an email heading from JW with the subject line showing "He'll know." Intrigued, he clicked it open.

After reading the email, he sat back in his chair and stared straight out at the Gulf of Mexico, unblinking. He didn't move for a long time. Finally, having decided on a course of action, he closed his eyes and slowly, slowly smirked.

He hadn't noticed it until he got up.

"Where's my paperweight?" he said out loud.

14

DIRECTOR BERTRAM SAT AT HIS DESK, still a little nervous about having the outsider, Hunter McCoy, working with them, even though he had to admit the man's credentials were impressive. He supposed it would be all right, since Klinger would be dealing with him most of the time anyway.

He reached for the day's mail and sifted through it to see if anything was important. It looked like the usual junk assortment he got every day. One letter stood out though: a standard white business envelope with a wide black stripe down the left edge about an inch wide. It reminded him of what he'd heard as a boy about the way a Catholic priest was informed that the bishop was transferring him to another parish. The black stripe signified bad news even before the envelope was opened. The letter was addressed to him, and there was no return address. The postmark was local. Inside was an unsigned note in a large printer font.

The clock starts ticking on May third.
Exactly twenty-one days later the Ringling
Museum will be ruined.
This is not a blackmail situation.
Nothing is demanded from you to prevent this.
There is nothing you can do to prevent it.
It will happen.

He put the note down on his desk and just stared at it. *What is this?* he thought. He read it again. Coming on the heels of the painting left in Gallery 17 and the note associated with it, he was afraid this wasn't just a crank letter—someone trying a little vandalism through the mail. *No,* he thought, *this is not good.*

"Hilda!" he called.

The door opened and Hilda appeared. "Yes sir?"

"Call Klinger and get him over here on the double."

Five minutes later the security chief was reading the note the director handed him.

"What do you think, Kyle?" Bertram asked when Klinger set it down.

"I don't know. Do you get crank letters like this often?"

"Never. I've never gotten a letter like this one."

They talked about its implications for several minutes before Klinger said, "Let's call McCoy in. See what he thinks."

After a little grumbling at the thought, the director agreed, knowing that they needed all the help they could get if this threat turned out to be legitimate.

HUNTER READ THE LETTER AND LOOKED UP. "What about the envelope?"

Klinger handed it to him. "It doesn't help much other than a local postmark."

Hunter examined it. "What about this black line? It looks like it was done by hand with a felt-tip marker. Does that mean anything?"

Feeling a little sheepish, Bertram told them his recollection of the Catholic practice.

"This certainly qualifies as bad news if the writer is serious," Hunter agreed. "What about the date, May third? That's today. Does that mean something?"

"Not to me," Klinger said. "What about you, Director?"

"I can't think of anything. May Day is May first, and Cinco de Mayo is May fifth. I don't know of any significance to May third."

"How about a significant event in the history of the museum? Anything particularly good or bad happen on that date?" Hunter asked.

He watched as Bertram and Klinger thought that over. Neither could come up with anything off the top of their heads.

"Let's try something else," Hunter said. "If you're going to set a deadline for something to happen, why twenty-one? It would seem more likely you'd come up with twenty, or twenty-five, or thirty, not twenty-one. I have a feeling that both of the numbers have some significance to the letter writer. May third is an important date to him. So is the number twenty-one. I think we need to focus on that."

"I think there's something else we need to focus on," Bertram said. "Is this note somehow related to the van Ruisdael painting and the note that was left with it? These are two pretty strange events to happen within a few days of each other."

Hunter frowned and shook his head. "It seems unlikely to me. On the one hand, with the painting, the donor is actually giving something of value to the museum, along with a strange note somehow warning Addison Swift of a danger to him personally. Nothing there suggests a threat to the museum. Also, while the note is anonymous, Professor Swift is named specifically. Plus that note is handwritten in a poetic way.

"This note, on the other hand, is typed in straightforward prose and is a definite warning of an impending catastrophic event to the Ringling Museum itself. It doesn't name anyone. It clearly isn't a warning. It isn't even a threat, since it has no caveat to it. There's no 'do such and such or I'll ruin the museum.' Instead it goes out of its way to say this isn't a threat. It's a fact. In twenty-one days from May third the museum will be ruined."

"I don't know, McCoy," Klinger said. "I agree with what you said, but the two notes coming so close together does suggest they're related somehow."

"I don't like this," said Bertram. "What does ruined mean? He doesn't say destroyed, set fire to, blown up, or anything like that. He says ruined. How do you ruin a museum?"

Hunter said, "I think it would be useful to examine the museum's history to see if the date, May third, and the number twenty-one can be tied to anything significant that might give us a clue to what they mean."

"All right," Bertram said. "I don't want to bring any more people in on this than we already have, so I'll go to the computer and see what I can find myself."

"I'll do the same," Klinger said.

Hunter headed to Genevieve's office to meet her after work. Neither felt like cooking so they went to Mattison's Forty-One, where they dined on a variety of delicious appetizers. Genevieve had a glass of un-oaked chardonnay, while Hunter ordered his favorite, a perfect Manhattan on the rocks. He told her about the new note and the meeting in Bertram's office.

"I'm not happy with the way the director's been behaving, but he's sure got a lot on his plate lately," Genevieve observed.

"A lot on his plate? You're picking up American idioms pretty fast."

"Did I use that one correctly?" she asked.

"Yup. You sure did. And you're right. He's pretty shaken up about this threat to the museum."

"Shaken? Is that another one?"

"It means this has him very upset and confused. Or as Elvis would sing, 'He's all shook up.'"

"Shook up. I'll have to remember that."

"Ruin is a strange word here," Hunter added. "I don't think ruin would be the correct term if the writer plans some kind of physical destruction to the facility. You'd use the word destroy or something like that. Ruin suggests something softer but equally devastating, like maybe bringing the museum down financially somehow."

They continued speculating through dinner, and on the drive home. Later, in bed, their attention turned to other more enjoyable matters.

15

"ADDISON. THERE'S SOMEONE DOWNSTAIRS," Belle Swift whispered to her husband, shaking him in the upstairs bedroom of their home in Cambridge, England. "I think he's in the study."

"What?" The large bearded professor threw back the covers, awakening quickly. "In the study?"

"Yes. Maybe we should call the police."

Professor Addison Swift got out of bed, stepped into his slippers, and quietly moved to the bedroom door. It was open, the way they always left it. He listened. Someone was definitely in the study. He checked the bedside clock: 2:40 A.M.

Addison Swift was a big man, but no longer young. In the old days he would have stormed in on the intruder with righteous indignation and throttled the bastard to within an inch of his life. But time and a series of heath issues suggested he should follow Belle's advice and call the authorities. He looked back at her and pointed to their nightstand phone. He punched his left palm with his right index finger, mimicking what she should do. She nodded and picked up the phone.

For maybe five minutes the professor maintained his position at the door and just listened. Then, unable to just stand there and wait any longer, he slipped out of the bedroom and began to descend the stairs. Straight ahead was the front door of the old two-story house. The study was to the right. As he made his way down he heard shuffling noises; there was no question about it, someone was in there. At the bottom of the stairs he slowly peered around the corner. A man with his back to the professor was going through his file cabinet.

Who is he and what the hell is he looking for? he thought, outraged at the intrusion.

Just then he heard a crash and broken glass from upstairs. The intruder spun around and saw Swift. He jerked his head left and right, and then quickly climbed out the open window he'd apparently used to enter the study. Swift ran to the window just in time to see the intruder stop, pivot toward him, point a gun, and fire a shot. The glass above his head shattered as the open panes were hit.

At about the same time a Cambridge police car roared up and almost hit the man, who appeared to panic, firing at the police car. Taken by surprise by the violence of the intruder, they didn't react immediately, so the man approached the car and shot the driver at point blank range, killing him instantly. The policeman's partner drew his weapon, and as the intruder's eyes shifted toward him as his next victim, the officer shot first. The man staggered backward and fell. Professor Swift, speechless, still stunned from the earlier gunshot, watched the surreal scene unfold.

A half hour later, deeply shaken by the events, Addison and Belle Swift sat quietly holding hands in the study while Detective Chief Inspector Ian McCormick of the Cambridge Police Department tried to piece together what had happened. The detective had asked the professor to look at the dead man before they'd taken the body away to see if he knew him. Swift had never seen him before, and the man apparently carried no identification.

"Professor Swift, can you tell if anything is missing or what the man might have been looking for?" McCormick asked.

"Both of us are 'Professor Swift,' Inspector, but I assume you're addressing me," Addison said.

"Sorry, of course," said the DCI. "Do you both share this study?"

"Yes, we do," Belle Swift said. "We each have a desk here, as you can see, and we share the rest."

"So, is anything missing?"

Addison looked at Belle, who shrugged.

"When I reached the bottom of the stairs and looked in the study," Addison Swift said, "the man had my file cabinet open and was going through it. When he heard the crash from upstairs, he turned and saw me."

"That was me, Addison. I knocked over the bedside lamp and the bulb popped," his wife said.

Addison nodded. "I thought as much. Anyway, the man left the file drawer open. And he had one of my files out and was apparently going through it."

"Can I ask what the file contained?" Inspector McCormick asked.

"Of course. That file and all the others in that top drawer contain papers and materials on my current research topic. I've been looking into the history of the art looting orchestrated by Napoleon in Italy at the close of the eighteenth century. I'm a historian, you see. The looting was quite extensive, and many museums throughout the world ultimately turned out to have one or more of the stolen works of art. Many have been returned to their rightful owners, but some are currently in litigation, and others are still in limbo. No one has claimed them, and the museums aren't pushing it, as you can imagine."

"Professor, the dead man took one of your files when he ran. We found it on his body. We'll keep it as evidence for the time being, but I'd like to show it to you and ask if you can think of any reason someone would specifically want it."

McCormick's young sergeant handed the folder to the inspector, who handed it to Addison Swift. He glanced at the label on the folder and then looked up at the inspector without opening it. "I was afraid of this. I thought this might happen."

"Sir?"

"Part of my research is trying to trace the current location of what I believe to be thirty paintings looted from the Duke of Modena in 1796 and kept by Napoleon's chief art thief, Jean-Baptiste Wicar. Wicar didn't turn them over to Napoleon as he should have, and they weren't part of a large art collection he left on his death to his home city of Lille. My hypothesis is that the pieces have stayed in the Wicar family, probably handed down to his descendants. This folder contains my efforts to identify them."

"I see," said Inspector McCormick. "I would imagine they might not be happy with what you're trying to do. How successful have you been?"

"Not successful enough for anyone to be worried, I can tell you that."

"Even so, if they know you're looking, they have to be concerned. What would happen if you do identify them and you find they have the paintings? That's what, two hundred years ago?"

"It's complicated. Let's say someone has the paintings today. They didn't steal them, their ancestor did. Even if they wanted to give them back out of a sense of trying to right a wrong, so to speak, to whom do they give them? The Duke of Modena is long dead. Do *his* heirs have a right to them? How do we identify them? If you ask for my best guess, I'd say they're going to stay right wherever they are today.

"As a historian, I'm interested in following their path to the present. They might not even exist anymore. Often such thefts are destroyed, either accidentally or because the current owner doesn't have any innate appreciation for their artistic value and is worried that they might be held liable somehow. It happens a lot, I'm afraid."

"Can you think of anything else, professor? Anything else unusual going on?"

Yes, there damned sure is something else going on, he thought.

He explained about the recent attack on his daughter in Sarasota.

16

"HUNTER, WAKE UP."

He rubbed his eyes and yawned. For a change he awoke without the bad aftertaste of a nightmare. "What is it?" he asked, rubbing his eyes as Genevieve thrust her cellphone at him. He swung up to a sitting position on the bed and looked out over the bay. It was still dark, but the faint light of dawn was slowly creeping over the water.

"It's Kyle Klinger. He wants to see us."

He checked his watch: 6:15

"What's up, Kyle?"

"We've got a situation. You and Genevieve need to get over here now. I'm at the Ca' d'Zan."

"The what?"

"The Ca' d'Zan. Genevieve knows where it is. Get over here now. I'll meet you in the reception entrance." Then he hung up.

They got dressed and Genevieve drove the five minutes it took to get to the Ringling. They took the road in front of the Education Center. As it curved to the right, Sarasota Bay began to appear on the left. She pulled into the gravel parking lot just as Hunter began to see an enormous, exotic-looking palazzo on the Bay.

As they got out and headed for the visitor's entrance, Genevieve said, "This is the Ca' d'Zan. It means House of John."

"For John Ringling?"

"Right. It was John and Mable's winter residence, built in 1926. I read somewhere that it cost over a million dollars at the time. The style is Venetian Gothic, said to reflect their taste and love for Italy, one of their favorite vacation destinations."

"Pretty impressive."

"It is. Wait till you see the inside."

They walked around to the back of the mansion, where they saw Klinger standing outside on the top of a ramp leading to what Hunter assumed was the visitors' entrance.

He signaled for them to follow him as he entered a glass-enclosed solarium. They passed through ornate gilded double doors into what Genevieve said was the east ballroom. Immediately he could see the opulence of the place, and not for the first time was grateful for the understanding of fine historic antique furniture he'd gained from Annie. The room's signature feature was a beautiful French *bureau-plat,* or writing table, on a Turkish silk carpet, and a suite of chairs with antique tapestry upholstery illustrating Aesop's fables.

"In here," Klinger called. He was already through the next room—the west ballroom—and had turned left out of sight. They followed him through the doorway into an enormous room, two stories high with a banistered balcony on three sides. Several antique furniture groupings created individual seating areas for conversation. Ornate tables were set up for cards and other games. The ceiling, at least thirty feet overhead, had stained glass skylights and was framed by pecky cypress wood beams. An antique piano stood in one corner and a writing desk in the other. Klinger was waiting at the writing desk.

"Over here," Kyle said.

Reluctant to pull his eyes away from the spectacular sights everywhere in the great room, Hunter finally moved to the writing desk.

"Look at this," the head of security said. "It doesn't belong here. It's not ours."

He pointed to a glass paperweight on the desk. "I already checked. There are no prints on it."

Hunter picked it up and examined it. It was about the size of a tennis ball that was slightly flattened on the bottom giving it the shape of most paperweights. The reddish orange glass had what looked like an orange colored fly etched into it on the surface.

"How did you find it?" he asked.

"The early crew that gets the house ready for visitors spotted it. They dust this desk every morning, and this piece was never here before. None of them recognized it as belonging in any other part of the mansion. It wasn't here yesterday morning, or they claim they would have seen it for sure."

"Do you have CCTV video for yesterday? Someone must have dropped it off during the day."

"We do, and that's why I wanted both of you to view it with me. See if you recognize anyone."

Klinger led them to a small closet in the back of the house, where he retrieved the video from several security cameras. "We'll go back to my office. We can view it there."

Hunter and Genevieve drove back to the parking lot at the Education Center and within five minutes were seated in the security chief's office in front of a monitor. He fiddled with the controls until he found the camera angle that focused on the desk and paused the video.

"Okay. No paperweight there. Let's see now. This is 9:30 yesterday morning. I'm going to speed it up, so keep watching until it shows up." They watched as groups of people moved quickly through the room, gawking at everything just as Hunter had earlier. Finally, at 3:44 P.M the paperweight showed up. Klinger hit the pause button.

"All right. I'm going to back it up slowly. Let's see what happens."

A group of eleven people moved by the desk, with a docent apparently telling them what they were seeing. There was no clear picture of any one of them actually placing the paperweight. The camera showed the backs of their heads. Kyle played it backwards and forwards several times to no avail. It was clear that someone in the group had put it there, because it wasn't on the desk before they passed but was visible afterward. Hunter counted five men and five women, and a little girl with one of the men.

"Do you recognize anyone?" Klinger asked.

"No, I've never seen any of them before," Genevieve said.

"Same here," said Hunter, "but then I hardly know anyone in Sarasota."

"All right. I'll try to trace these people back to where they checked in at the Visitors Pavilion and see if any of them used a credit card," Klinger said. "Maybe I can get some names that way. That's going to take a while."

"Let me see that paperweight again." Hunter took several pictures of it with his phone's camera.

"Do people often leave things here at the Ringling, Kyle?" Genevieve asked.

"Sure. But it's usually stuff they accidently left behind. Purses, sunglasses, umbrellas, stuff like that. This is definitely different. Given the drop-off of the painting the other day, I thought we'd better check into this."

"How about if Hunter and I go back to my computer and see if we can find anything about this paperweight? We'll use the photos he just took."

"Okay. You do that while I see what I can find out about these people."

Back at her desk Genevieve opened her laptop and got on the Internet, while Hunter brought up the photo of the paperweight on his cell.

"Any ideas?" he asked.

Genevieve slapped the desktop. "Of course. I should have recognized it immediately. That's not a fly, Hunter. It's a bee. It's a Napoleonic bee. Here, I'll show you."

In a minute the screen was filled with symbols. She scrolled down and there it was. The bee, exactly as it was on the paperweight. She clicked on the image and it enlarged along with some text.

"Look at this, Hunter."

> *Golden bees (in fact, cicadas) were discovered in 1653 in Tournai in the tomb of Childeric I, founder in 457 of the Merovingian dynasty. They were considered as the oldest emblem of the sovereigns of France.*
>
> *It is interesting to note how the bee was one of the main symbols for Ancient Egyptian Pharaohs, The Merovingian dynasty, and Napoleon's Coat of Arms. No other symbol (not even the Reed or the Eagle) has survived consistently as a regal symbol for such a long time!*
>
> *Used as a symbol of immortality and resurrection, the bee was chosen so as to link Napoleon's new dynasty to the very origins of France.*

"Okay it's a bee."

"Right," Genevieve said, "And it's definitely a link to Napoleon. Here, look at this." She pointed to an image of his coat of arms. "You can see them on the imperial mantle draped over the crest."

They sat and stared for a moment, trying to take it all in.

"So what's going on here?" she asked. "Is this supposed to be some kind of message? It must be connected to the van Ruisdael and the note warning my father. But what does it mean?"

Hunter tapped the image on the screen. "Yeah. Is the paperweight itself valuable in some way, or is it just meant to keep us looking? But then, what are we looking for?"

17

HUNTER PHONED KLINGER AND TOLD HIM they'd learned that the image on the paperweight was a bee and the exact replica of the symbolic bees on Napoleon's official coat of arms.

"Napoleon?" he asked. "Does that have some significance we should be aware of?"

It suddenly occurred to Hunter that neither Klinger nor the director knew anything about the connection of the van Ruisdael painting to Napoleon or to Wicar. There just hadn't been time for Genevieve to share any of this with them, as she'd only recently learned it herself from her father.

"Yeah, it does. We'll catch you after lunch and explain."

He was in Genevieve's outer office and on his way in to tell her this when he saw she was already on her phone. He came in and listened to her side of the conversation.

"Oh, mon dieu. Are you all right?"

She covered the mouthpiece with her hand and mouthed, *"My father."*

"I can't believe it," Genevieve said. "Is mother all right? Yes, okay. I'll stop asking questions and just listen. Go ahead."

Hunter could tell that whatever her father was saying, it wasn't good. He went on for a full ten minutes. Again Genevieve took out a notepad and wrote copious notes. When her father finished, she said, "Thank God you're both all right. Yes, I'll tell him right now. He's here. Goodbye."

She met Hunter's worried gaze. "We've now got a fifth incident to add to the four that happened to us."

"What?"

"A man broke into my parents' house during the night." She summarized the story, her voice shaking, "He'd stolen a file from my father's cabinet and had it on him when he was killed. It contained his research notes on his efforts to trace the Wicar descendants."

"Thank God the shot missed your dad. Even if somebody's nervous about what he might learn, that's pretty extreme. You say he really hasn't uncovered much yet?"

"That's right. Of course they don't know that."

"Yeah," Hunter said, "and since they didn't get the file they were ready to kill for, they still don't know it."

"Oh."

"Right. They may try again. Do the police know who the dead guy is?"

"Not yet. But if his fingerprints are on file somewhere, they should know soon."

Hunter knew this could take a while. It was never quite as fast as they showed in the movies or on television. But it was their only lead.

"The police told my father they'd tell him as soon as they identify the man. He said he'd call us when he knows."

"What else did you learn?" From all the note taking she'd done he guessed there had to be more.

"He believes he's traced the paintings to a specific branch of the Wicar family, down to the early nineteen hundreds in France. The surname he has is Drouet. He believes all thirty paintings were in the hands of this branch of the family at one time. The line's gone cold after that, but he's got some genealogy experts at Cambridge hard at work trying to pick it up again. He says these people are the best at what they do, and if anyone can do it, they can."

"Did you tell him about the attacks on us at your house?"

"Yes. They're very worried about me. I told them that as long as I had you here, I'd be okay. He told me to tell you not to let me out of your sight."

Hunter smiled. "Good. That's my plan. Unfortunately, it's my only plan."

Genevieve pushed back her chair and ran both hands through her hair and around her neck leaning back with a big stretch. "You know, it's one thing to be worried about our safety. It's altogether another thing to be worried about theirs."

"Did the police say they'd keep an eye on the place?"

"They said they would."

"We've got to meet with Klinger and the director," said Hunter. "They need to know about the Napoleonic connection and Wicar. They also need to know that whoever's behind this isn't afraid to use deadly force and that they have a long reach if they can attack us here and your parents in England at almost the same time."

"You're right. It's time. Let's do it after lunch."

TWO HOURS LATER, AFTER A LUNCH during which neither of them turned out to be very hungry, they sat down with Klinger in Bertram's office. Genevieve began by describing her father's research and the link between Napoleon and Jean-Baptiste Wicar. She said her father believed thirty of the fifty paintings Wicar took from the Modena heist were still in the hands of Wicar's descendants.

"He's been trying to trace the line and believes that he'll eventually be able to do it. He also says that the van Ruisdael painting the dead man left here at the Ringling is one of the thirty. He has no idea why it would have shown up here. Even if he can identify who currently has the paintings, it's an open question as to whether they can be repatriated back to the owners after two hundred years."

She went on to explain about the Napoleonic bees and that the image on the paperweight that was left in the Ca' d'Zan was an exact duplicate of those on the Napoleonic coat of arms. Again, the question was who had left it and why.

Hunter took over at this point. He described how the police report indicated that he'd been the deliberate target of a hit-and-run driver at the airport, and that earlier that day someone had broken into Genevieve's house and ransacked it, clearly looking for something, then attacked her when she came home.

"Once out of the hospital we returned to her house, where someone blocked all the exits and tried to kill us with a gas explosion. Then a man in a speedboat fired on us with a high-powered rifle as we sat outside. We reported all this to the police. At almost the same time, someone broke into Professor Addison Swift's residence in Cambridge, England. He's Genevieve's father. The man tried to steal the professor's file relating to his efforts to trace the Wicar family descendants. He fired a shot at the professor and was killed by the police. We're waiting for him to be identified."

Klinger and Director Bertram sat silent and aghast at the recitation.

Hunter turned to the director. "You were right to keep this quiet. Until we've learned what's going on and who's behind it, the fewer people who know about any of this, the better."

Bertram nodded, obviously shaken. "I wish I'd known what you two had been through when I called you into the office. I wouldn't have been so hard on you both."

Hunter accepted that. "We don't know what we're up against. One man might be behind all four incidents aimed at Genevieve and me, but with the almost simultaneous action against her father in England, it's a good bet that more than one person is involved."

Klinger spoke up. "I just got word that the man who left the painting at the museum has been identified. He was a retired construction worker named James Knox. He lived alone, and according to his neighbors was in poor health and probably depressed. As far as I can determine he had no connection to the museum at all. Where he would get a painting like this and why he would leave it here, along with the note, is a mystery."

"He had to be doing it for someone else. That's who we have to find," Hunter said.

Klinger nodded. "Agreed."

"What about the second note threatening to ruin the museum?" Hunter asked. "Were either of you able to make any sense out of it?"

"Sorry, no," Klinger said.

"What about you, director?" Hunter asked.

"The museum has lots of events that occur during the spring and summer that sometimes happen around May third. But without knowing what year we're talking about, it's impossible to pin it down to a particular event. Over the past ten years we've had three exhibits open on that date. There was nothing particularly unusual about them."

"Well, we'd better keep looking. If the note means what it says, we only have twenty days left," said Hunter.

18

THE CONSERVATION LAB AT THE RINGLING reminded Hunter of most labs he'd seen and worked in over the years: concrete floors, lab benches filled with equipment, storage cabinets with chemicals and supplies, a refrigerator, empty lab tabletops for quick setup and takedown. Really, the only things not found in an ordinary laboratory were the several works of art in various stages of restoration throughout the room.

Gretchen Ceisel was waiting for them. At the meeting with Klinger and Bertram earlier, Hunter had told them he believed the next step called for a thorough examination of the van Ruisdael painting. This meant expanding the circle of people who knew about the painting to include the conservator. The director called her in and explained the situation, including the contents of the note with its admonishment to "solve the mystery of the painting." If there were a mystery to the physical painting itself, it would be Gretchen's job to find it.

Since its arrival, the painting had been stored in the director's safe. Now it was sitting on a small easel on one of her workbenches.

"Lovely," Gretchen said to Genevieve and Hunter. "Too bad it's not one of ours."

"So what will you do to it?" Hunter asked.

"First of all, I won't do anything *to* it. It doesn't need cleaning or restoration. It's been well taken care of and is in excellent shape. But I'll give it a thorough examination. If it's got a secret physically contained within it, I've got the equipment, and believe me, I'll find it. Give me a couple of hours and check back. If I find anything before then I'll call you."

They left Gretchen to do her thing and headed for an appointment with Sharon Grandholm, the resident curator of pre-twentieth-century Western art, and Genevieve's immediate supervisor. She, of course, knew about the painting, as she'd been in the director's office when Genevieve was first summoned there.

"Please come in," she said, beckoning to Genevieve. Then she raised an eyebrow at Hunter.

"Sharon, this is Hunter McCoy. Hunter, Sharon Grandholm, my boss, so to speak."

Sharon laughed at this. "A boss? Wow, I don't think I've ever been called that before. Anyway, I'm hardly her boss. We're more colleagues than anything."

Genevieve brought her up to speed on Hunter's part in the investigation and that both the director and Klinger had vetted him. She told her, without going into too much detail, about the three attempts on their lives and the event with her father in England. Sharon was stunned, to say the least.

"I had no idea. My God, what's going on here?"

"Indeed," Genevieve said. "That's what we're trying to find out."

"Maybe the person who broke into your house was looking for the painting that showed up here—the van Ruisdael," Sharon offered.

Hunter looked at Genevieve. "Makes sense. It'd be valuable enough to warrant the effort and small enough for your attacker to tear your house apart."

"If that's the case," Genevieve said, "then whoever arranged to have the painting dropped off at the Ringling is clearly not the same person who broke into my house."

"Right," he said. "So if that's true, that brings up another question. Is the person, or more likely persons, who are possibly looking for your painting the same ones who want to stop your father from tracing the lineage to the other Wicar paintings?"

"And," Genevieve said, "since I'm his daughter and you're helping me, is that why we were targets in the first place?"

"And," Sharon added, "would the painting have been left here at the Ringling if *you* weren't here? As I recall, it's a message to you *personally*. If so, it would seem that someone is trying to warn you. The note writer might actually be on your side somehow in this thing."

Hunter nodded, impressed. "We've been considering that possibility," he said.

Genevieve shook her head. "What I don't get is this. If someone is trying to help, why not just *do* it? Why not just tell me what's happening? Why the obscure note? What are they afraid of?"

"Maybe that's it," Hunter said. "Maybe someone is on the inside in this thing and can't surface visibly for fear of being discovered. The painting and the note could be the only way they have of letting you know."

"And the bee. Don't forget the bee," said Genevieve.

"The bee? What's that?" Sharon asked.

"Oh yes. We didn't tell you about the bee," said Genevieve, who then explained about the paperweight. "We examined CCTV video and saw exactly when it was left on the desk but we couldn't determine who did it. Kyle's working on that now. It must be related somehow— maybe another prod for us to keep looking."

Hunter's phone rang. It was Klinger. "We just got some information on James Knox, the dead guy on the tram who dropped off the painting. The police interviewed his neighbors, and one of them saw a woman in her late sixties visit him twice before he died. She stayed about an hour the first time and a little less the second time. Interestingly, that second time was the morning Knox died. He gave a description of her to the police."

Hunter got the neighbor's name and address and thanked Klinger, then told Sharon and Genevieve what he'd learned. "If Knox was hired to place the painting, this woman might have some of the answers. I'll go see the neighbor, Genevieve. Why don't you see if you can get the paperweight from Kyle and have Gretchen examine it too? Who knows, there might be a clue in there."

"Good idea. I'll do that."

HUNTER DROVE TO THE ADDRESS Klinger had given him. It turned out to be a little old home on the north side of Sarasota not far from the airport, meaning it was not far from the museum either. The small lawn hadn't been mowed in weeks, so it was way overdue, given how rapidly vegetation grew in Florida's wet, humid summers. Palms and other trees that looked as if they'd never been trimmed appeared to be engulfing the house. It was badly in need of paint and would have stood out as an eyesore except that those around it didn't look much better.

He parked on the unpaved street with an open storm sewer running across the front yard, walked up to the front door, and knocked. A few minutes later a little girl, no more than five, opened the door. "Hi, mister."

"Well hi, are your parents home?"

She disappeared, and soon a man in his seventies took her place. In sharp contrast to the house, he was clean-shaven and neatly dressed. "Hi," he said, managing to make it sound like a question.

"Mr. Gallagher, my name's Hunter McCoy. I'm working with the Ringling authorities trying to find out what happened to your neighbor, Mr. Knox." He showed him the badge Klinger had given him.

"He's not my neighbor, he's my son's neighbor. This is his house, and the little girl, Candy, is my granddaughter. I'm here temporarily, trying to help him over a rough patch."

That explains the contradiction in the man's appearance and the house.

"I'd invite you in, but . . ." He waved his hand and rolled his eyes as if to say, I don't want to be in there myself. "Maybe we can talk out here on the step."

"That's fine. I understand you saw a woman visit Knox on the morning of the day he died at the Ringling."

"Yes. She stayed about forty-five minutes. I only saw her when she came up to the door and then when she left. They were in his house during that time. She was very well dressed. Not what you'd expect in this neighborhood. She was in her late sixties, I'd guess."

"Could you tell if he was happy to see her or not? Did they appear to be on good terms?"

"Hard to say. I guess so. At least nothing stood out. They shook hands at the front door when she left. Funny though, now that I think on it, it was almost like they had sealed a deal of some kind. It was that kind of handshake. Do you know what I mean?"

"Yes, I do. That's a good observation, Mr. Gallagher. Did anything else stand out that you remember?"

"No, not that comes to mind."

"And you say she didn't have a car? Where did she go?"

"Well, that was a little weird too. She walked to the corner, that one over there, and turned right behind the high hedges, and then faster than I would have thought possible, she was in a car driving past the house and out of sight."

"What do you mean? Was she driving or was she a passenger? Was somebody waiting for her?"

"That's the weird part. She was driving, and I didn't see anyone else in the car, but it happened too fast. It takes time for a person to open a car door, start the engine, and drive away, you know? It was almost like the door had been open and the car was running. It was that fast. I don't know. It just seemed weird to me."

Hunter thought that over. "Can you describe the car?"

"Sure, It was a big black Lexus sedan, again, not what you expect in this neighborhood. And before you ask, I didn't get the license plate or even the state. I wasn't looking."

"That's all right, Mr. Gallagher, what you've told me is a big help. Thank you."

"Good for you," he said. "Now if I could only find a way to help my son. Drugs and alcohol, you know." He shook his head in despair. "But we're working on it."

Hunter could only imagine the heartache of the man.

As he drove away, he refocused his mind.

I've got to find this woman.

19

THE SUN, LOW IN THE SKY TO THE WEST, cast dark shadows that contrasted with the purples and oranges slowly replacing the uniform light of the day. It was the time before sunset that photographers crave and lovingly refer to as the "golden light," the time when colors are most vivid and images jump from the frame. It was also Quentin Naff's favorite time of day.

Naff, seventy-nine years old, five-foot-six, and slim as a boy, sat at his favorite table at the Giardino Blu restaurant in the Radisson Blu Hotel at the Zurich airport. During his meal he allowed his gaze to play over the airport scene in front of him. As he watched the takeoffs and landings of the airliners at this important European air hub, he wondered, as he always did, how many potential clients might be on board. As was his habit, he waited until he'd finished his dinner and Ramon brought him his favorite after-dinner cocktail, a rusty nail—Drambuie and scotch—before he allowed himself the pleasure of shifting his gaze toward the real reason he always chose this restaurant—his unobstructed view of the Freeport Naff-Zurich across the street.

The 362,000 square-foot, four-story rectangular edifice gleamed brightly as the setting sun exaggerated the gold color of the building's exterior, as if to say, "What's inside is pure gold." It wasn't all gold, of course, although it held a fair share of bullion to be sure, but it might as well have been. Inside its secured storage vaults, rented by some of the wealthiest art collectors on the planet, sat almost fifty-billion-dollars worth of rare exquisite art.

Naff, a pioneer in the freeport-for-art business, enjoyed recalling how he'd started. He'd grown up in Zurich, and after taking a degree in art history at the University of Geneva, worked as a buyer for a small auction house in Zurich. During his years there he came to meet men whose wealth was beyond anything he'd ever imagined. One thing they all had in common, he discovered, besides their wealth, was an almost religious fervor for avoiding paying any tax they could possibly get out of. These included capital gains taxes when they sold expensive pieces of art and made a substantial profit, as well as value-added taxes when they brought pieces they'd purchased abroad back to their luxury homes. These taxes, while different in each country, nevertheless amounted to hundreds of thousands of dollars on their expensive purchases and sales of important art.

But it wasn't until he discovered another problem common to these wealthy collectors that Naff began to get the germ of an idea. He sipped his drink as he reminisced. Most of these collectors were truly appreciative of their art. They loved it for its own sake, so of course they wanted to see it. The problem was that after years of collecting, they'd purchased so many pieces they'd run out of wall space to display it, even though they generally owned numerous enormous stately homes. Thus, they were forced to either put it in storage or sell it, both of which involved more cost and tax.

So, Quentin came up with the perfect solution. He'd build a storage facility near the Zurich airport where art could be temporarily stored in secure and impregnable vaults and where the owners could take advantage of a unique set of tax law exemptions for goods in transit. His facility would offer a solution to almost all of the problems these major collectors faced. If he could get several of them to use his facility, they could store their treasures free of the value-added tax they would have to pay when they took

them to their homes. Since there was no limit on how long
"in-transit" was, the art could stay there for long periods of
time, perhaps forever, tax-free.

An even bigger advantage might be that if one owner
decided to sell to another owner under the discreet cover of
his facility, the deal could be transacted entirely beyond the
gaze of state officials, and thus no capital gains to report.
And finally, if he could give the owners an attractive
alternative display space, available only to them, they could
have their cake and eat it too: safety, a tax-free
environment, and a museum-like setting in which to enjoy
their masterpieces. It was the perfect plan and he knew it
could work. There was only one problem: money. He
needed capital to start.

His chance had come one day about ten years earlier.
A man, an American, came into the auction house and
asked about the possibility of auctioning a painting he
owned—a seventeenth-century Italian landscape by Claude
Lorrain. Quentin Naff had examined a photo of the painting
and commented on its beauty and the high price he was
sure they could get for it. When he asked him why he
wanted to sell it, the man said he didn't feel it was secure
enough in his home.

Over coffee and casual conversation, Quentin told him
of his concept for a freeport for art. He said that owners of
art would be able to keep their paintings in the facility he
wanted to build and be able to visit them whenever they
chose. Further, the paintings would be safe and free from
tax liabilities if and when the owners ever chose to sell
them. Their only cost would be the rent they'd pay for the
service. The facility he envisioned would have climate-
controlled vaults equal or superior to any bank's.

To Quentin's surprise, the American seemed unusually
interested in his idea and told him he needed time to speak
with some other people and he'd be back in touch with him
soon. Two weeks later the man returned saying he

represented a group of five owners of rare and valuable fine paintings. They called themselves the Legacy. Between them they had twenty-five paintings by the Dutch Masters, van Dyck, Rembrandt, Hendrick Averkamp, and Jacob van Ruisdael as well as masterpieces by Italian, German, and Belgian artists. Naff did the math; the estimated combined value of the paintings was impressive. But even more exciting than the possibility of beginning his endeavor by providing the group with all the features he'd described to the American, was their surprising offer to supply him with the capital funding needed to launch his freeport.

He'd never understood why they were so willing to fund an untried, speculative endeavor. He was grateful, of course, but he couldn't figure out why they'd take the risk. Nevertheless, true to their word, they put up the money, and with it he purchased the land he was staring at now, the land that now housed the hugely successful Freeport Naff-Zurich.

It started out considerably less grandly, of course. While the Legacy comprised the initial renters to store pieces at the freeport, business grew exponentially over the next few years. Before long he was planning the beautiful large facility he regarded now as he sipped his drink. By the time he cut the ribbon for its grand reopening a year ago last September; he had a long waiting list.

He'd decided that the freeport idea was working so well that it was time to expand. So he opened an Asian freeport in Singapore and recently the first one in the United States. The 250,000 square-foot facility at the Tampa International Airport was already eighty-five percent rented.

Just a month ago he'd been leafing through an art magazine when he saw a story about one of the twenty-five paintings the Legacy had been storing in the Freeport Naff, a Caravaggio portrait of a young man selling fish. The article said the painting was once owned by the Duke of

Modena in Italy but had been looted by Napoleon's army and may have ended up in the hands of Jean-Baptiste Wicar, Napoleon's chief art thief.

This painting, along with an estimated twenty-nine more, was missing. No one knew where they were, but there had always been speculation that they might be in the hands of Wicar's heirs, and if so, they should be returned to the City of Modena. Naff read on and found a reference to two more paintings thought to be in the group stolen from the Duke. Some professor at Cambridge was doing the work.

So that's why they'd been so willing to fund him ten years ago, Quentin Naff realized. The five members of the Legacy must be Wicar's heirs. Now he understood why they didn't want the paintings on display and would have been willing to capitalize him to build his freeport.

Then, six years ago one of the Legacy cousins, not the American, approached him with a plan to sell the group's paintings under the cover of the freeport. He said he was representing the Legacy in this transaction. The man wanted Quentin to find a buyer for the twenty-five paintings currently being stored at Naff's facility.

Quentin Naff remembered being surprised when one of his new renters—a man he didn't know very well—an enormously wealthy industrialist from Germany—offered to buy the whole lot for four hundred thirty-two million dollars.

Naff sat back, sipped his cocktail, and closed his eyes in thought.

20

MARIE ARSENEAU SAT AT HER DESK when she heard her husband shouting her name.

"Marie. Where's my paperweight?"

She heard him but refused to answer his screaming. He was now obviously storming down the stairs of the 12,000-square-foot mansion and getting more irritated the longer he looked. "Marie. Where the hell are you?" he yelled with even more vehemence. Still she didn't reply.

He finally found her in her study.

"Can't you hear, woman? Are you deaf? I've been calling for you."

Marie Arseneau lifted her eyes slowly from the paperwork on her desk to regard her husband, who'd just barreled into the room. "And what can I do for you?"

He didn't miss the sarcasm in her voice, not for a minute.

"You can tell me where my goddam paperweight is."

"Your paperweight?"

"You know damn well what I'm talking about. That stupid maid must have moved it or put it somewhere. I'm telling you for the last time, if you don't fire her I will."

"I'm not firing another maid because you can't keep track of your things. She's working out well and doing a good job. Go upstairs and do a little searching. It's there somewhere." With that she returned to the paperwork on her desk. "I can't help you; I'm busy with Ringling business."

He pounded her desk with his fist. "That damned museum. It's taken over your life. Ever since you got yourself elected to the board, you've had no time to run this house. Your responsibility is here, not with those artsy-fartsy friends of yours."

Marie took off her reading glasses and stared up at her Pierre, who loomed over her desk like a vulture ready to strike. She wasn't sure when the change began exactly, but she knew it had started just before she made the decision to take the painting and the paperweight. She was pretty sure it was right after the last time he'd hit her. He'd been drinking, and they were sitting on the lanai by the pool looking at the setting sun. The outdoor speakers were playing soft classical music. For any other couple it would have been a tranquil and pleasant setting, filled with wonder. But they weren't any other couple, not by a long shot.

She'd gotten up to refill her wine glass but accidentally tripped on a corner of outdoor carpeting and spilled a little on his shirt. He'd screamed at her and called her a stupid useless old cow, and then hauled off and slapped her so hard in the face she'd fallen backward into the pool. Instead of getting up to help her out, he'd pounded off into the house, swearing at her as he went.

Yes, that was it. She was sure of it. That was most definitely the moment. After she'd climbed out she had told herself, no more. From now on he was the enemy. Just like that, after so many years of abuse, it was over. She would do what she could to protect herself and Monica, but no more would she try to make this sham of a marriage work. She knew he was responsible for its failure, not her. There was something wrong in his head, something evil. She didn't know where it came from, but she knew he was always worse when he talked to his cousins in Europe, the group he called the Legacy. He wouldn't tell her what they did or what they talked about at their meetings, but she suspected it was illegal.

She did know about the connection to Jean-Baptiste Wicar, her husband's ancestor. Early in their marriage, when there was still some love between them, he'd explained about the looted paintings, and that the other members of the Legacy also had some of the paintings. When she'd asked him a few years ago why he only had one left, the van Ruisdael, he'd told her to mind her own fucking business, that they were his paintings, not hers. After that he'd gotten even worse. The insults and physical abuse increased, and whatever love had once warmed the marriage was on the road to evaporating completely.

He stared down at her now, waiting for an answer. "Well?"

"Well what?"

Breathing deeply several times, he glared. Finally he turned and stomped out.

Marie smiled slightly at her small victory and returned to her deskwork.

DR. JOYCE ATTENDED THE FUNERAL FOR CHLOE SLINDE but had no words to console her mother. The poor little girl hadn't responded to the massive antibiotic treatment they'd administered. Her colleague, Dr. Scanlon in the emergency room, who helped treat her when Carrie Slinde brought her in, was equally devastated. In the end, her organ system shutdown was too aggressive and widespread to allow her to survive.

21

THE SIXTEEN-FOOT STATUE OF DAVID THREW a long shadow across the courtyard lawn as Hunter and Genevieve walked toward the conservation lab in the Education Center.

"Is it my imagination," asked Hunter, or does that thing look taller than the original in Florence?"

"It's the same height—probably just looks taller because it's high up on a parapet. The Ringling version was cast in bronze in 1874 from a mold of Michelangelo's original marble. They made two others at the same time. One is in the Vatican in Rome and the other outside the Uffizi Gallery in Florence. Lots of tourist mistake that one for the real thing—pigeon poop and all."

Hunter laughed. "So what did Gretchen want? Did she sound excited?"

"Not so much excited as—I don't know—sly."

"Sly?"

"Yes. Like she had a secret and was going to tell us slowly—let us twist in the wind a little first."

Twist in the wind? She's really getting good at this.

Gretchen saw them coming down the hall through the large glass windows that allowed people to look in and see the conservator at work. She met them at the door and led them in to the lab. They took stools around her workbench where the van Ruisdael painting sat on a small easel, next to the paperweight.

"I'll start with the paperweight," Gretchen said. "I wanted to find out if it was old, but unfortunately the two techniques we most often use for dating old art don't do well with glass. The most suitable types of sample for radiocarbon dating are charcoal and well-preserved wood, although we can also use leather, cloth, paper, peat, shell, and bone. The other technique is thermoluminescence dating. That measures the effect of the high-energy radiation emitted as a result of decay or radioactive impurities. Unfortunately it doesn't read glass either."

"This doesn't sound good so far," said Genevieve.

"Ah yes, but don't forget 'Gretchen, the Incredible' is on the case. Fear not, ye weak of heart. Through an amazing third technique I was able to ascertain its age—to the day."

"To the day? You mean the day it was made?" Genevieve asked. "How on earth . . .?"

"Genevieve, I can tell you not only the day it was made but precisely *where* as well."

"How can you do that?"

"Simple. But before I tell you how I did it, let me tell you what I found out. This paperweight was made along with eleven others in a glass smelter in Paris on December second, 1804."

"The day Napoleon was crowned Emperor," Hunter said, somewhat proud of his newfound realization of this fact.

"Precisely," said Gretchen. "I'm impressed, Hunter. Twelve of these were made to commemorate that event. Five of them are in museums, including one in the Louvre. The others have gone missing—that is, until this one showed up at the Ca' d'Zan. Now we know where six of them are."

"So how did you learn this?" Genevieve asked. "What amazing bit of science did you use?"

"Ah, yes. Well, first let me say it took a skilled technician with incredible talent and fortitude."

"Oh boy," Genevieve said, rolling her eyes. "All right, let's hear it."

Gretchen laughed. "Okay. All it took was a trip next door to our very own library. A little clever examination of our holdings, and bingo—up came this." She reached into her drawer and removed a book entitled *Napoleonic Symbols*, and opened to page 234. There it was, the paperweight and its story.

"Great work Gretchen," said Hunter. "Now, what did you learn from the painting?"

She closed the book with the paperweight information. "Not so much, I'm afraid. I found no hidden messages. The canvas under the painting is blank, meaning the artist didn't paint over an earlier work. There are no items concealed in the frame, no little compartments where something might be stored. It's a genuine Jacob van Ruisdael. It's just what it appears to be."

"So we're back to square one," said Genevieve, obviously disappointed.

Hunter thought about that for a moment. "Maybe not. The painting is genuine, and according to your father it was one of the fifty pieces from the Wicar heist at Modena. The paperweight is a genuine antique also linked to Napoleon. Let's consider the note."

The van Ruisdael is just the first step in the dance
Have Genevieve Swift trace its history
Her father's life hangs in the balance
If she's unable to solve its mystery

"If the writer of this note is so concerned for your father's safety," Hunter went on, "why not warn him directly? Why tell you? If there's nothing hidden in the painting itself, then the mystery referred to must be somewhere else. Maybe the mystery is just what we dismissed earlier—that the painting is part of the Wicar heist at Modena. Maybe the paperweight was simply meant as a clue to suggest the Napoleonic era. The note writer is telling you where to look. In this case, the Napoleonic theft, carried out by Wicar, at Modena. And then there's the whole question of why this person doesn't contact you directly, Genevieve. Why the enigmatic note? It must be just what we speculated earlier. Someone wants to help you but is afraid or unwilling, for whatever reason, to identify himself—or herself."

"That would make sense," said Gretchen.

"It would seem that it's someone in Sarasota or at least in this area," Hunter added. "When I talked with James Knox's neighbor, he said that the woman who visited him on the morning of his death—the day he left the painting in the museum—appeared to be well-to-do and drove off in a late model black Lexus sedan. The car and the woman were completely out of place in that neighborhood. It was rundown in every way. It's likely, I think, that she gave Mr. Knox the painting to place in the museum, and she may also be responsible for leaving the paperweight clue in the Ca' d'Zan. If we can identify her, we just might get the answers."

Genevieve pointed to the first line of the note that Hunter had placed on the table.

The van Ruisdael is just the first step in the dance

"Maybe that means the rest of the paintings are also somewhere in the Sarasota area. Maybe Wicar's heirs—the ones my father is looking for—are right here."

"Maybe somebody in the family is leaving the clues, the painting and the paperweight, so we'll find them and they're afraid to be openly identified because they'd be a traitor of sorts." Gretchen offered. "Their life might even be in danger."

Genevieve's cellphone rang. She took it out of her purse, and then put it on speakerphone so they all could hear. "Hello, Father. I've got you on speakerphone. Hunter is here, as well as Gretchen Ceisel, the conservator here at the museum. I want us all to hear whatever you've got."

"All right. It's about the man who was killed after breaking into our study at home. The police have identified him as Tony Carsten, a dangerous man suspected of being a killer for hire. His fingerprints were on file. DCI McCormick examined the man's phone records, and guess what? He received a call from the United States the day before breaking into our home. The number had a 941 area code."

"That's right here in Sarasota," Genevieve shouted.

"Yes. DCI McCormick said the call was made on a throwaway one-use cellphone—the kind the police call a burner. They couldn't trace it other than the area code."

Genevieve told him about the paperweight, that they were beginning to believe that things were being orchestrated in Sarasota, and that the other paintings as well as the Wicar heirs might be here as well.

Hunter told him about the mystery woman in the black Lexus.

"We're going to do all we can on this end to try to identify her. Hopefully, she'll have some answers. She might be afraid for her own life if she's betraying the family by leading us to them through her clues."

"You two be very careful," said Addison Swift. "Obviously these people aren't afraid to kill to protect themselves. Oh, there is one other thing, something else the police learned. The man wrote down two words on a notepad near his phone: 'Legacy' and 'Freeport.'"

Hunter added the words to the paper with the note on it.

They ended the call with father and daughter each telling the other again to be careful.

Back at the house Hunter tried to make a connection between the Cambridge felon and the call from the 941 area code. The dead man, Tony Carsten, had talked with someone in the Sarasota area who had used a "burner' phone." He knew that anyone who wanted to remain anonymous could go into a store, pay cash, and leave no credit card trace with personal information attached. A person looking for additional security might even wear a disguise while buying it; perhaps use a fake accent. That way, if the phone was ever traced to that store, there would be no connection digitally or even a reliable recollection of a clerk. Then, if the person wanted maximum security, he wouldn't make the call from his area because the cell towers will identify the calling area code. Apparently the caller hadn't taken this extra level of care.

Using Genevieve's computer, Hunter discovered that the 941 area code included the southwest Florida counties of Manatee, Sarasota, and Charlotte. Tracking who bought the phone and made the call was next to impossible. Still, the 941 area code meant the source was surely in this area.

He thought of the recent information made public about the NSA's surveillance of phone calls on US citizens. He'd learned that Verizon had been turning over cellphone records to the NSA on a regular basis. In 2012 a federal appeals court ruled that people using prepaid cellphones had no "reasonable expectation" of privacy and the government was free to track them. In short, the prudent bad guy who wanted to conduct his nefarious business using a burner had better not use it from his house or business, or any other location with which he had an identifiable connection.

22

GENEVIEVE WAS AT HER DESK in the Education Center when her phone rang. It was Monica Arseneau, her friend from the Sorbonne who lived in Sarasota.

"Hi, Genevieve. I was wondering if we could meet for lunch again, like, maybe today?"

Genevieve picked up a note of melancholy in her voice. "Sure. Today would be great. Do you have a place in mind?"

"How about the Muse at the Ringling? That's close for you, and I've always liked the place."

Two hours later Genevieve walked through the Ringling gardens to the restaurant, five minutes from her office. Genevieve spotted Monica at a table next to the window and joined her immediately.

The waitress took their orders and while they waited for their iced teas to arrive, Genevieve said, "So what's up? Anything new in the past couple of weeks?"

Monica didn't answer right away, but her eyes began to water and she bit her lower lip.

"Monica, what's wrong?"

She sniffed and wiped away the tear that was beginning to form. "Oh, I wasn't going to do this," she got out in a trembling voice. "I just wanted to see you, a friend. I didn't want to do this."

Genevieve took her hand. "What is it, Monica? Can I help?"

Monica looked away out through the glass across the water-lilied pond to the Circus Museum on the Ringling grounds. Genevieve waited. After a long moment, Monica turned back to Genevieve and in a voice that now carried a hard edge said, "It's my father."

Genevieve continued to wait.

"I told myself I wasn't going to do this, and here I am ready to tell you."

"Tell me what, Monica?"

The waitress returned with their drinks and left.

"Oh, where to start."

Genevieve could see her trying to organize her thoughts. She continued to wait, giving her friend all the time she needed.

"My dad's always been a brute. He's abused my mother for as long as I can remember. He's done the same to me."

"You mean . . ."

"No. Not sexually, he's not like that. He just demands complete obedience. He's a control freak. He's always been physically and mentally abusive to both of us. For me, it ended when I left home and got a place of my own. He has no control over me anymore. But Mom's not so lucky. At first, when I was little, I noticed bruises on her and I'd ask about them. She always said she'd fallen or accidentally hit herself, or something like that. Later, when I was a teenager and the same thing started happening to me, I knew."

Genevieve took her hand again. "How awful."

"Yesterday afternoon I went to visit her, and her jaw was swollen and starting to bruise. She didn't have to tell me what happened. She told me he's been worse lately. Something, she doesn't know what, has him more upset than usual. She's never seen him like this. He won't tell her what it is, but screamed that two of his art pieces have gone missing in the last week after a break-in at the house, and by God, he'll find out who took them."

Genevieve was immediately on alert. "Two art pieces? What are they?"

"One's an original old oil painting, a Dutch seascape, a van Ruisdael, I think, and the other's a glass paperweight he's had forever."

Genevieve stiffened and sat stunned, unable to speak.

Monica straightened, her eyes wide. "What is it, Genevieve?"

Those are the pieces. So they were stolen from her father and put at the Ringling? Is he the one who tried to kill us?

Remembering their pledge to limit this information only to those who had a need to know, she hesitated in answering.

Is he the Wicar heir my father's been looking for? Is Monica?

"Genevieve?"

Genevieve continued to stare out the window, trying to think it through, saying nothing. She had to talk to Hunter first. They had to process this before she brought Monica in. Maybe Monica or her mother was in real danger. Or maybe they were part of it, whatever *it* was. No, she had to talk it over with Hunter first. No question.

"Genevieve, what's wrong?"

"Oh, I'm sorry. Your talking about your father suddenly made me think about my own. He hasn't been well lately. Sorry I drifted off there for a moment."

Monica frowned with concern. "Is he all right?"

"Yes, but he's had a lot on his mind lately. I think it's taking a toll on him and my mother. When you mentioned the problems your parents were having, I just naturally thought about them too. I didn't mean to be insensitive to your situation."

"Oh, okay. I see."

They were quiet for a moment, each with their own thoughts.

"Look, Genevieve, I didn't want to talk about this stuff with my parents. My mom and I will deal with it. I'm sorry it came out. Let's talk about anything else, something fun. How are you and your boyfriend getting along?"

Happy they'd turned the conversation away from the two art pieces, Genevieve laughed. "Great. He's a wonderful guy. What about you? Any boyfriends in your life?"

"Not at the moment. I'm sort of in-between, if you know what I mean. Last guy didn't work out and the next one hasn't stepped up to the plate yet."

They spent the rest of lunch with girl talk and a promise to get together soon.

The moment Monica left, Genevieve called Hunter. "Can you come and get me? I'll meet you in front of the Visitors Pavilion."

"Give me ten minutes."

"You won't believe what I've found out."

23

"WHAT IS IT?" HUNTER ASKED, as Genevieve jumped into the car.

"Let's get home first. This needs our undivided attention. I don't want to be worrying about driving or traffic."

An unnecessary precaution, he thought, since she lived in a very quiet neighborhood and the traffic between the museum and her house was practically nonexistent. He figured she just needed time to digest whatever she'd learned and think about how to present it to him. Okay, he could wait.

Back at the house they went out to the bayside and sat in chairs on the lanai.

"All right, let's have it. What have you got?"

"My friend from the Sorbonne, Monica Arseneau. I told you about her. We just had lunch together. We barely got started when she broke into tears. It turns out her father is a controlling brute and has always abused her and her mother for as long as she can remember."

He clenched his jaw. Of all the things that set him off, this was near the top of the list.

"Yesterday she went to visit her mother, who had been beaten and could see that her jaw was swollen and knew what that meant. Her mother told her the father was furious that one of his paintings had been stolen, a Jacob van Ruisdael."

"Our Jacob van Ruisdael?"

"I'm sure it is. And here's the thing that clinches it. He also went nuts when a glass paperweight went missing from his desk."

Hunter whistled. "No way is that a coincidence."

"Now here's the thing, Hunter. I didn't mention any of this to Monica. She doesn't know anything about *our* having the painting and the paperweight. I didn't tell her that they showed up at the Ringling. I didn't tell her about the note. I just steered the conversation away to other things. We finished lunch and agreed we'd do it again. I was so shocked at what she told me I knew that we had to talk first and figure out what to do."

"Good. That was good."

"Hunter, he could have the other Wicar paintings. He could be the Wicar heir my father's been looking for. He could be the guy who broke into my place looking for the painting. He could be the one who's been trying to kill us."

"But how would he know about either one of us? How would he know about you or link you to the painting? And as for me, I had just landed at the airport when the car nailed me. How did that happen?"

"Maybe Monica told him about the lunch she and I had the week before you arrived. She probably would have said we studied together in Paris and that I was a visiting curator at the Ringling."

"Even so, he apparently has no idea that his painting is at the museum. He thinks it was stolen in a break-in. Even if he did find out it was at the Ringling, how would he associate you with it?"

"He couldn't," she had to agree.

"Something's missing, something we don't know." He paced the lanai. "Who did it?"

"Who did what?"

"Who wrote the note, and who paid Knox to place the painting at the museum? Was it his wife, Monica's mother? Did she take his painting and paperweight out of spite, some sort of payback for his abusive behavior? Does she drive a black Lexus?"

"Also," Genevieve said, continuing his train of thought, "if she wrote the note, she knows about my father's interest in the Wicar paintings. That would mean her husband somehow learned that my father was researching the Wicar looting. Maybe he was worried that my father might try to get the paintings repatriated. Of course, that *is* part of his plan."

"What's her father's name?"

"Pierre, I think. Pierre Arseneau."

"What about Monica? Do you think she's somehow involved?" he asked.

"No, I'm sure she's not."

"We need more information. We need to meet with her, see what she can tell us."

While Genevieve searched for Monica's address, Hunter strolled down to the water's edge and watched a black bird he'd learned was an anhinga successfully land a fish that looked too big for it to swallow. With a flip of its head, it repositioned the doomed fish and began to swallow it whole. In four gulps the fish disappeared down its gullet.

He heard Genevieve calling for him and reached the house just as she came out onto the lanai. "She'll meet us at her place in an hour. Her mother will be there too. I got the address."

MONICA'S PLACE WAS A QUAINT HOME in the Hillview district south of downtown Sarasota. The homes were mostly built in the same era, he guessed the nineteen fifties. They were very well kept up, and he imagined they were expensive when they changed hands. It represented a nice change from the mega-mansions along the shore.

Monica met them at the door and introductions followed.

Hunter smiled pleasantly at Monica, an attractive blonde, and then turned to study Mrs. Arseneau. An elegant, sixty-something woman, she certainly could fit the description James Knox's neighbor had given him.

"Hello Mrs. Arseneau, it's a pleasure to meet you," Hunter said, shaking the woman's hand.

"Shall we make it first names?" she asked.

"Sure," he said.

"And Genevieve," Marie said, "We've never met but I know about you and your position at the Ringling, since I'm on the board there. We're so happy to have you with us for the year."

"Thank you," Genevieve responded. "I'm happy to be here."

They assembled in the living room. The furnishings were new and expensive, yet they fit the style of the home perfectly. They weren't contemporary, and Hunter could only imagine how much searching she'd have had to do to find new furniture that looked like it belonged in the home forever. It surprised him that he'd even noticed.

Thank you, Annie, he thought.

Monica brought them each a glass of wine and set out a tray of nuts and fruit.

"So, Genevieve, what's this all about?" asked Monica. "You sounded so mysterious on the phone."

Genevieve told the two women about the painting that was left at the Ringling Museum, the note, and the paperweight with the Napoleonic bee. She told them about the man who'd dropped off the painting and who later died on the tram. She told them about how her house had been burglarized and she'd been attacked, then about Hunter's hit-and-run, and how they both had woken up in the hospital. She told them about the man who had tried to kill them by igniting the gas he set loose in her house, and about the man in the boat with the rifle who'd fired at them. Finally, she explained about her father's research into the

Wicar looting and how a man had broken into her parents' house in Cambridge and stolen his file on the Wicar heirs before being shot and killed by the police.

Monica listened open-mouthed with distress. "Oh my God. Oh—my God. How horrible," she kept repeating.

"We're trying to keep it quiet while we sort it out," Genevieve said when she finished.

"It has to be my father's van Ruisdael and his paperweight, but how did it happen?" Monica asked. "Who would do that? And the note, oh my God, the note. Who did that?"

Hunter observed her throughout the story Genevieve was telling. If Monica was faking her shock and dismay at what she was hearing, she was the best actress he'd ever seen. No, she had no idea what was happening, he was sure.

"So this old man, the one who died, must have stolen the items from my father's house. Do you know who he is?"

"Yes," Genevieve said. "His name is James Knox. He was seventy-five years old and a retired construction worker. He'd lived in the area all his life. But here's the thing; we don't think he did this on his own. We think he was most likely doing this for someone else."

Monica frowned. "Someone else?"

Genevieve looked to Hunter who took up the story from there. "Monica, a few hours before Knox planted the painting and the note in the Ringling Gallery, he had a visitor at his home, a woman in her sixties. She drove a black Lexus sedan. A neighbor saw her."

Monica's eyes widened as she gazed at her mother.

Marie Arseneau had listened without saying a word while Hunter gave his recitation. When he'd finished she sat quietly for a moment, and then said, "Monica, maybe you'd better pour each of us a little more wine. I've got a story to tell all of you."

Marie Arseneau made a steeple of her hands and brought them too her lips. Hunter, Genevieve, and Monica waited silently for her to speak while Monica poured more wine. Finally, making eye contact with Hunter, she began.

"My husband, Pierre Arseneau, Monica's father, is a difficult man."

Monica rolled her eyes at the obvious understatement, but kept quiet.

"I suppose the signs of his abusive nature were there even before we were married, but of course, I didn't see them then, and I'm not going to catalog the extent of his abuse now. Monica and I know it, and that's enough. It's also not germane to what I'm going to tell you."

Hunter nodded grimly.

"I don't deliberately snoop on my husband's phone conversations. I don't have to. He shouts loudly enough to be heard three rooms over. It seems that shouting has become his normal voice. Also, when he's on the line to his cousins in the Legacy, he's usually on speakerphone as well. He likes to pace while he's talking and that allows him to do it without carrying a phone around with him. So needless to say, I hear a lot."

Legacy? Hunter thought. That was one of the words on Tony Carsten's notepad.

"One day about a month ago, I heard the first reference to Genevieve's father. My husband was on the speakerphone, and I was able to make out that he was talking with someone from Cambridge University in England. He asked if Professor Addison Swift was in good standing with the University. I don't know whom he was talking with, but he must have been an official with Cambridge because he said, 'Of course, sir we're very proud of him. Who are you again, why do you ask?'"

"My husband's single colorful response to that statement was 'bullshit' and he hung up on the man. Later I heard him talking to someone at BIOMOD, his biochemical manufacturing company. He told the man he wanted copies of the two articles Professor Swift had written and published in *The Historical Journal*. He told the man to fax them to him within the hour or look for another job.

"Apparently the man succeeded, because I heard the fax printing about fifteen minutes later. I had no idea what this was about, but I decided to stay nearby to learn what I could. What I learned was that my husband's foul language repertoire was even broader than I imagined. Clearly he was reading whatever Genevieve's father had written and spared no pejorative adjective in describing how much it upset him.

"It wasn't until I heard him call Benoit Surette, one of the cousins in the Legacy, who lives in Prague that I got a sense of what it was about." Then, looking directly at Genevieve, she continued. "Genevieve, it was your father's research on my husband's family's looted art dating back to his ancestor, Jean-Baptiste Wicar. He told Benoit your father's research clearly showed that his intent was to find the paintings by finding the descendants and work for their repatriation."

Hunter kept waiting for something new, something he didn't already know.

"He told Benoit that this threat—Genevieve's father—had to be stopped before his digging into the family brought unwanted attention to their plans for the freeports. I don't know what that means, but apparently Benoit did. My husband listened for a while and then said, 'Good. Leave it to me. I'll take care of him.'"

Freeport, the other word on the memo. "You say this was about a month ago?" Hunter asked.

"Yes."

"Did your husband know that Genevieve was his daughter and that she'd be here for a year?"

"I don't know."

Hunter was starting to get an idea. "Go ahead with your story."

"I don't know if my husband knew Genevieve was here or not, but of course, I did. That's when I got the idea to place the painting and the note. I didn't want to come right out and contact you, Genevieve, but I felt I had to warn you, and through you, your father, about the threat my husband and his Legacy group posed. I'm not particularly proud of it, but my husband had recently gone too far in berating and beating me, and I told myself it was finally, indisputably over. I no longer owed him anything. The van Ruisdael painting was very important to him, being the only piece he had left of the Wicar collection. Taking it—I don't know, I just wanted to hurt him. I made it look like a robbery and arranged with a man to drop it, along with the warning note, in Gallery 17 of the museum."

"Mom!" said Monica

"That would be James Knox," Hunter said.

"Yes, the poor man."

"When you met him at his house the day he brought it to the museum, did you have someone with you, someone with a black Lexus?"

Marie looked up sharply. "Why do you ask that?" she asked in a suddenly anxious voice.

"I only ask, Marie, because if you did, that other person might also be in danger at some point. The more we know the better we can help."

Marie looked down at the floor and sighed, her shoulders slumping forward. "My friend, Gayle Morrison. She helped me. She rode with me to his house and kept the motor running and stayed low in the passenger seat while I went in to see him."

"All right, Thank you. Go on, Marie."

She turned to Genevieve. "I thought the note to you would alert you to the threat to your dad, and I wanted to make sure you realized it was directly tied to the research he was doing on the family. The follow-up delivery of the Napoleonic paperweight was to reinforce the link. I know what I did might not be enough, but I was frightened. Pierre's wrath is nothing to be trifled with."

"If your husband knew that Genevieve was Addison Swift's daughter and that she was here in Sarasota," said Hunter, "there's a good chance that he might be behind the break-in at her house. He might have been looking for his painting, figuring that she'd stolen it for her father. He might have been responsible for her being in the hospital. Do you think he's capable of that?"

"Oh my God. What have I done?" Marie dropped her face into her hands, and then looked up. "Yes, he's certainly capable of that, at least hiring someone to do it."

Hunter continued. "He might also have somehow found out I was coming to help her and maybe he arranged for the hit-and-run that put me in the hospital at the same time."

Marie let out a stricken cry. "And the other attempts on your lives as well. Oh, my dears, I'm so sorry. What have I gotten you all into?"

24

PIERRE ARSENEAU SAT IN HIS STUDY and quietly swore. He'd just listened to the entire conversation between his wife, his daughter, Hunter McCoy, and Genevieve Swift thanks to the FlexiSpy System he'd installed on his wife's phone. Even though she didn't have her phone turned on and it was in her purse, it had become a microphone, picking up all conversation in the immediate area and broadcasting it in real time to Arseneau's receiver.

So it wasn't the Swift woman who'd stolen his painting, he realized, it was his own goddamn wife. After all he'd done for her and his ungrateful daughter, she'd decided to turn on him. She knew the significance of the painting to him and still she took it. The only thought in his head was how to avenge this treachery, how to settle this score.

When they were first married, he didn't have a dime. She was the one with the money. Her parents had been killed six months earlier in an automobile crash and left everything to her. The inheritance included the oil leases in the Gulf of Mexico, twelve million dollars in securities, and the Lido Key property. They'd both graduated from college, but in his egotistical mind it was his drive and determination that generated all the financial success they'd had since then. In the beginning she'd been satisfied to help him in any way possible, including staying home and raising Monica.

Sure, he'd hit her once in a while when she got out of line, but so what? His dad had done the same with his mother and that had turned out okay. Then Monica needed a good slap every now and again too. That was the way it's supposed to be. But then, when their daughter moved out, Marie said she needed something else to give her life meaning. Apparently taking care of him was no longer sufficient.

She started working at the Ringling as a volunteer. More and more of her time and interest shifted to that place—away from him. Soon she was spending more time at the museum than at home. No man should have to put up with that, and he hadn't. He found the need to hit her more frequently than before. Still she wouldn't toe the line. Then, when she became a member of the board, thanks solely he reasoned to *his* financial success and status in the community, she began to ignore him completely. And now look what she'd done. Well, he thought, this is the last straw.

He knew exactly how he was going to deal with this. Sitting back in his chair, he recalled his excitement a month ago when his chief biochemical engineer called him to the lab.

"Mr. Arseneau, I've got something to show you. Come with me please."

Pierre had followed the little man in the white lab coat down the hallway in Building Six of the BIOMOD research facility to a small lab at the end. The scientist, Dr. Algarve, unlocked the door and they'd entered.

"What have you got, Algarve? I'm a busy man."

"You're going to like this, sir. I think it's what you've been looking for."

"You mean—?"

"Yes. I believe I've done it. Come over here."

He showed him to a lab bench where a small oil painting lay flat on the surface.

"This painting is thirty-five years old. The paint is thoroughly dried."

Algarve plucked a small amber-colored bottle, not much bigger than a woman's tube of lipstick, off the shelf.

"You can see this bottle has a small spray cap. Inside is a solution of my latest manipulation—Lot 83. Please watch."

With that, the scientist depressed the spray cap once, and sprayed the solution directly onto the surface of the painting. Arseneau watched. The surface appeared slightly wet.

"So now what?" he demanded. "What happens?"

"In twenty-four hours the change will be dramatic."

"You mean I have to wait twenty-four hours for—?"

The scientist held up a palm. He opened a drawer in the desk, took out another old painting, and laid it alongside the one he'd just sprayed. The surface was significantly damaged in three areas. "Exactly twenty-four hours ago, I sprayed the surface of this painting with Lot 83 in the three places you see deterioration. Now, I want you to look at this." He took out a lab notebook and opened it to the first page. Arseneau saw what must have been a photograph of the painting before the man had sprayed it with Lot 83.

"This is the painting twenty-four hours ago." He turned the page to another photo. "This is the same painting one hour later."

Arseneau squinted. He couldn't see any difference.

The man turned the page again. "Six hours later."

Arseneau looked again. In the three areas where the man must have sprayed he could begin to detect a dulling of the surface.

Algarve turned the page again. "Twelve hours later."

Now it was becoming obvious. "That's bacterial growth," Arseneau said.

"Yes sir. It is. Now take a look at eighteen hours later."

Arseneau watched as the growth spread and the underlying oil paint was consumed.

"As you see, sir, there's no doubt the microbes are breaking down the oil paint."

"But what about the pigments, the heavy metals?"

"Solved. I've solved it, sir." The little man looked quite pleased with himself.

He should be, Arseneau thought. If he truly found a way to keep the mercury and lead normally found in paint pigments from killing the microbes when they ingested it, the man deserved a raise.

"It took months of natural selection and thousands of generations working with *Alcanivorax borkumensis,* but by watching for strains that survived the heavy metals and concentrating them, I was able to identify a strain that not only survived, but actually seemed to thrive on them."

"But what about the enzymes? *Alcanivorax* doesn't have enzymes to digest oil paint."

"Right. So once I had a strain that survived the heavy metals, I switched out its genes with some that would produce enzymes to digest triglycerides and fatty acids like those found in linseed oil and walnut oil, the unique oils in artists' oil paints. But there was still a problem."

"What was that?" Arseneau asked.

"It was just too slow. I needed more digestive enzyme, and I needed a bacterium able to digest the oils both internally and externally. That way, I figured, it could double its digestive speed. So I took genes from *Vibrio vulnificus,* a bacterium that is able to release enzymes to the outside, and spliced them into *Alcanivorax.* Bingo. That was it. They started digesting oil paint like mad. The result is Lot 83."

"Excellent work, Dr. Algarve." Arseneau patted the man on the back for this amazing piece of work. "And are you telling me all it took was a single spray of Lot whatever to do this kind of damage?"

"Yes sir, Lot 83, one application."

Arseneau smiled. *This could be it,* he thought. *Now there is just one more test to run.* "Dr. Algarve, you said this painting is thirty-five years old."

"Yes sir."

"What if the painting were, say, several hundred years old? Say the oil paint had hundreds of years to dry. What do you suppose your Lot 83 could do with that?"

The man thought for a moment and shrugged. "I don't know. I don't know where to get a painting that old to try it on."

Arseneau wrapped his arm around the little man and grinned. "I believe I do. Let me have your sprayer."

As Arseneau recalled this incident he also recalled with satisfaction the success he had achieved when he'd subsequently sprayed the lion's face on an almost five-hundred-year-old oil painting by Lucas Cranach the Elder in Gallery 3 of the Ringling Museum of Art—one of his wife's favorites.

25

CHRISTOPHER WHITFIELD, EXHIBITIONS SPECIALIST with the Ringling Museum of Art, was supervising the unpacking of three old masterpiece paintings that had just been returned from storage in the Freeport Naff in Tampa. Two of them were going to other museums for temporary loan. The third painting was going to be on display right at the Ringling in an exhibit curated by Sharon Grandholm and Genevieve Swift, the pretty exchange curator from the Louvre.

Christopher, twenty-six years old, was new at his job, having been hired in March. Even though he was an art major and had a degree in preservation, making him a good fit with the needs of the museum, he knew he'd been lucky to get the position. Jobs like this one were few and far between. Only after he'd been hired did he learn that there were over one hundred applicants.

Christopher's assistant moved the first crate to a large tabletop, where he helped to carefully remove the packing material. It contained a beautiful Giorgione. Christopher carefully examined it to be sure it hadn't been damaged in any way. The frame and the painting itself appeared to be in perfect condition.

They repeated this procedure for the next painting Again they found no damage.

As each of the masterpieces was carefully uncrated, he marveled at seeing them for the first time. He'd never seen them before because they'd been in storage at the freeport for the past four years. Seeing them now gave him a sense of how lucky he was. He was truly living the dream.

When they uncrated the third and last masterwork, however, a beautiful Thomas Gainsborough landscape, Christopher immediately saw that something was wrong. On close examination, he noticed that the surface was wet in spots.

What's going on here?

He put his fingers to the liquid. No question, it was definitely wet with something. He sniffed his fingers. The liquid didn't smell. Was it just water? Probably, he thought, as he reluctantly tasted it, determining it was a little soapy.

He reached for a clean towel and very carefully dabbed the wet surface. It didn't appear that the liquid had caused any damage. Still, he was going to make a note of this in the records he was required to keep on the uncrating process. It was the freeport's job to see to it that the paintings were never subjected to moisture of any kind.

Later, when his workday was over, Christopher was headed for his Volkswagen Jetta parked in the museum's staff parking area, when a cramp in his stomach almost doubled him over. He reached his car and sat there for a moment. *What is that all about?*

The cramp subsided but he was beginning to feel sick to his stomach. Maybe he'd just go home and rest for a bit before he and Lea went out for dinner like they'd planned earlier. The air conditioning helped as he drove home. He was actually beginning to feel a little better.

He lived on the second floor of a four-story apartment building just on the edge of downtown Sarasota. The elevator wasn't working again, so he walked up the single flight of stairs and down the hall to the apartment he shared with his girlfriend, Lea Greber.

"Lea? Are you home?" he called, knowing she probably wasn't. Her job at the hospital, where she was a nurse, meant she usually got home after he did. True to form, she wasn't here yet so he decided he'd lie down for a while and wait for her.

"CHRISTOPHER, ARE YOU ALL RIGHT?" Lea had found him in bed under the covers and shivering. She put her hand to his forehead. "You're feverish. When did this start?" she asked, concerned.

In a voice so weak it scared her, he answered, "At work, I guess, about the time I left to come home."

"He cried out as another cramp curled him up under the covers.

Lea took his temperature and was alarmed to find it was one hundred and two. She brought him a glass of water and two Tylenol and helped him get them down,

"Just try to rest. The fever should break pretty soon, and you'll feel better." She brought him another blanket and tucked it around him. "I'll look after you, love. Just try to rest now."

Christopher's fever didn't break, and by the next morning it was at 104.5. On his way to the toilet he threw up on himself. Lea cleaned him up and helped him to the toilet. Afterward, she helped him back to bed. He told her he had a headache and his neck hurt.

She took his face in her hands and could feel the heat. "Christopher, listen to me. I'm going to take you to the emergency room at the hospital. We have to get this fever down, and nothing I'm doing is helping."

She assisted him getting dressed and helped him down the stairs and out to her car. On the way to the hospital Christopher kept his eyes closed against the morning sun and occasionally moaned. When they got to the entrance to the emergency room, she left the car with a parking attendant and walked him up to the admitting desk.

"I'm Lea Greber, a nurse. I work here and this is my boyfriend, Christopher Whitfield. He has a soaring fever that won't come down. He needs to be seen."

Within five minutes an emergency room nurse came to get them and brought them to a room where she left them alone so Lea could help Christopher out of his clothes and into a hospital gown. Within minutes the nurse was back, and helped him into bed, and brought a warm blanket to cover him. She said the doctor would be in to examine him shortly. Lea held his hand and comforted him while the nurse returned and took Christopher's temperature and drew a blood sample. The doctor came in a few minutes later.

"Hello, I'm Doctor Scanlon. You're Christopher Whitfield?" he asked, stepping up to the bedside. Christopher nodded, without speaking. "And you are?" he said, indicting Lea.

"Lea Greber. He's my boyfriend. I'm a nurse here, and I've been trying to get his temperature down since I came home from work yesterday. It was 101 at that point and hasn't responded to Tylenol. It was 104.5 so I brought him in."

"I see." Doctor Scanlon turned to Christopher. "I'm going to examine you now. Is that all right with you?" Again, Christopher nodded faintly. Lea had never seen him look so pale. While the doctor examined him, the nurse returned and showed the doctor the reading she'd just taken of his temperature—105. His blood pressure was 78 over 52.

"Let's give him IV Fluids, antibiotics, and if his blood pressure doesn't come up we'll try vasopressors."

Christopher, his eyes shut to avoid the overhead lights, seemed barely aware of his surroundings. Terrified, Lea stayed by his side as they moved him to the ICU.

CHRISTOPHER WHITFIELD SURVIVED the night in Sarasota Memorial Hospital. His fever had broken and was down to 100.5. His blood pressure was back up to 130 over 85. When he woke up from a fitful night's sleep he felt like he might actually live. Lea was by his bedside and wiped the perspiration off his brow.

"Hey, you," she said. "Welcome back."

Feeling better but still weak, Christopher smiled at her. "Thank you. Really, thank you. I don't know what I would have done if you hadn't been there. What happened, anyway?"

"The doctor said you had some kind of bacterial infection. It must have been bacterial because you responded to the antibiotics so well."

"Where did I get it from?"

"Who knows? Anywhere, I guess. The point is it's gone now and you're going to be fine."

Christopher lay back on the pillow, closed his eyes and thought, *I'm going to be okay.*

26

CHRISTOPHER WHITFIELD HAD RECOVERED sufficiently to return to work and help Sharon Grandholm and Genevieve Swift prepare for the landscape exhibit they were curating.

He got to help because one of the paintings they wanted for the exhibit had to come out of storage at the freeport, and that was his job. Then it turned out that the one they wanted, the Gainsborough, had been damaged. That wetness on the surface had somehow messed up the image. He'd brought it to Gretchen Ceisel as soon as it became apparent that the wet spots were damaging the painting.

Gretchen recognized immediately that the damage to the Gainsborough was identical to the damage to the face of the lion in the Lucas Cranach painting from two weeks before. But unlike Chris Whitfield, who was convinced the damage to the Gainsborough happened at the Freeport Naff-Tampa, she wasn't so sure. After all, the Lucas Cranach had been displayed where it had been for several years, on the easel in Gallery 3. It had never been in the freeport.

Most of the preparation work for the Exhibit, *Landscapes Through The Ages,* had already been done before Genevieve was attacked. She and Sharon Grandholm had arranged for all the art that had to come in from loans by other galleries, museums, or private collections. All of it, except for the Gainsborough, had already arrived and was on the walls. The signage had been completed and installed the day before in anticipation of tonight's opening reception.

LANDSCAPES THROUGH THE AGES. The large, beautifully crafted sign greeted visitors to the Searing Wing of the museum as soon as they entered the hall. The opening reception for Friends of the Ringling and other financial backers opened at 5:30 PM. with wine and cocktails on the veranda overlooking the beautiful courtyard and its tropical foliage and statuary. Wait staff moved effortlessly through the crowd bearing constantly replenished trays of hors d'oeuvre.

Sharon and Genevieve mingled with the group; answering questions about the show they were about to see once the doors to the gallery itself were opened at 7 PM. The two women had put the final touches on the exhibit the previous night finishing around nine.

Dressed in slacks, an open collar shirt, and a light jacket, Hunter carried his perfect Canadian Club Manhattan on the rocks to a concrete railing and watched the crowd. As much as he wanted to stay in the background, the pretty young waitresses kept offering him trays of goodies. No stranger to this kind of flattery from women, he thanked them politely and kept his eyes on the guests. He recognized Kyle Klinger, and they nodded across the veranda but didn't approach each other. Hunter assumed the security man was doing the same thing, looking for anything unusual.

Ever since the meeting with Marie Arseneau and her daughter, Monica, Hunter couldn't help thinking Marie was in danger beyond living with a brute of a husband. He spotted the two women at the wine bar just as they turned, each with a glass of white wine, to mingle with acquaintances. They waved in recognition, and then began talking with a middle-aged couple nearby. Marie's description of how she had faked the burglary of the painting and then later took the paperweight left him wondering how Arseneau would react to that. Of course he'd never met the man, so he didn't have any basis to judge, but he imagined he would be suspicious of his wife and anything she did. It was standard behavior for men who beat their wives. He'd attended a seminar at the medical school the previous fall featuring an expert on domestic abuse. Paranoia and suspicion were common on the part of the abusers.

"Hello, Dr. McCoy, enjoying the view?"

Startled, he turned and saw Director Bertram, with an attractive woman at his side. "I'd like you to meet my wife, Grace. Grace, this is Genevieve's friend from Virginia, Hunter McCoy."

"Dr. McCoy? Are you a physician?"

"No, I'm an academic." He wondered how much the man had told his wife. He quickly found out.

"So, what are you doing to keep yourself busy while Genevieve is hard at work curating the show?"

"Oh, I'm just taking in the sights and enjoying the great weather. She and I actually get plenty of time together even though she's working."

"What about you?" she asked. "How do you get the time off?"

"I don't have a class to teach until the fall, and my research lab is being run by my postdocs while I'm here. It's good experience for them."

"Well, enjoy your stay in Florida. It was nice to meet you, Hunter," she said as she pulled Bertram away to talk to a well-dressed couple she spotted across the way.

Director Bertram nodded and raised an eyebrow as if to confirm he hadn't even told his wife about the painting, or at least Hunter's part in searching for answers.

Hunter continued to scan the crowd for another ten minutes. Finally he spotted Genevieve and Sharon at the door to the Searing Wing and the Exhibition. He figured the show was about to start. The doors opened, and the well-disciplined crowd slowly began to move into the exhibit hall. He hung back, letting most of them move in and mingle before he followed them into the exhibit area.

Almost immediately it was apparent that something was wrong. Off to his left several people were exclaiming and pointing to one of the paintings. He walked over to see what the commotion was and spotted it at once. The large landscape painting showed a naked man standing in a boat on a pond. But the water under the boat was off, somehow. On closer examination he saw what the other guests saw: the paint had disappeared and left the boat floating. It was as if someone had taken an eraser and wiped out the area immediately beneath the boat in this part of the canvas. The rest of the painting appeared to be all right.

Hearing a commotion in the next gallery he quickly walked over to witness a similar scene. The crowd was pointing and talking at a loud level not usually found in a museum. Again, one of the paintings was disfigured. This time a village at the base of a mountain had been erased.

What's going on here?

"Hunter!"

He turned and saw a frantic Genevieve waving him to the other side of the room, where she and Sharon were gesturing at a canvas. He quickly joined them, pretty much knowing what to expect.

"Hunter, mon dieu, someone has ruined this painting. Look."

Again, he saw a huge erased area. This time what appeared to be hay in a field was missing, erased like the others. The canvas underneath was intact but the paint was gone.

"This is awful," she whispered.

They heard a commotion near one of the two other defaced paintings. It was Marie Arseneau. Seeing Genevieve, Marie ran over to her, obviously distressed. She took Genevieve's hand. "It's the Patinir and the Eckenbrecher. Both of them are ruined. It's my fault."

"Your fault? What do you mean?" Hunter asked, while Genevieve tried to calm the poor woman as she led her to a bench in the center of the gallery.

"Both of them. I arranged with both of their owners to lend them to us for the exhibit."

Genevieve gasped. "Sharon and I did almost all of the negotiating for the loan of the paintings in the exhibit," she whispered to Hunter. "But Marie, through her personal art connections, arranged for three of them, the Joachim Patinir, the von Eckenbrecher, and the Pieter Brueghel. She twisted to look back the way they'd come. "Oh my God," she cried, "the Brueghel, it's damaged too, like the one we just came from, Hunter."

Monica joined her mother as Marie slumped against Hunter.

"All three? It's my fault. I can't believe this," the woman cried. "What have I done?"

Sharon Grandholm approached the trio on the bench. "You've seen?" she asked Genevieve.

"Yes. How many all together, Sharon?"

"It looks like just the three."

Leaving Marie with Monica, Genevieve, Sharon, and Hunter approached the Brueghel.

"Look," Sharon said, pointing at the place on the painting where men were cutting hay to stack, "The canvas is intact but the paint is gone."

Peering closely at the area, they couldn't see any scrape marks or any indication that the pigment had been scratched away. Also, it didn't look as if a solvent had been used, as the edges between the missing paint and the rest of the painting were clearly marked.

"Is Gretchen here?" Hunter asked.

"I don't think so," Sharon said.

Monica with Marie joined them just as Kyle Klinger and the director appeared.

"What happened here?" Bertram demanded, looking directly at Genevieve for some reason.

"We don't know, but three paintings have been damaged."

"When did it happen?" he barked, as if they'd know somehow.

"We don't know," Sharon said, "but I can tell you this. All three were intact when we closed up last night."

"How can you know that?" he asked.

"We know it because Genevieve and I personally walked the entire exhibit just before leaving as a final check to be sure that we hadn't left something out and that every piece was where it should be. Believe me, we would have seen this damage."

"Then it must have happened between closing last night and the opening of the exhibit a little while ago," Hunter said, looking at Kyle Klinger.

"We'll check the CCTV," said the security chief. "If someone was in here, we'll see him. Sharon, I suggest you and Genevieve check all of the paintings to see if there are any others. McCoy, let's you and I go over the video feed."

While the director and his wife tried to assure the crowd that everything was under control, and Monica tried to comfort Marie, Klinger got the tape and he and Hunter went back to the security office to view it.

They could see that Sharon and Genevieve were the last two people in the exhibit gallery before Klinger locked the doors at 9:30 the night before. They started viewing at that point. Klinger fast-forwarded, and they continued watching until the doors were opened that night at 7 PM. They saw nothing. No one had entered or approached the paintings during the almost twenty-four hours.

"We have to get Gretchen to examine those paintings, see if she can figure out what happened to the paint," Klinger said. "I'll call her now." He put his cell on speaker so Hunter could hear.

"Listen, Gretchen, we've got a problem at the exhibit opening and we need your help. Three of the paintings have been damaged and there may be more; we're still checking. It looks like paint has been removed in portions of them."

"Whoa, that's not good."

"Can you get down here now and look at them?"

"Now?"

"Yeah, afraid so. Here's what we'll do. McCoy and I'll meet you in your lab with the paintings. Grab a sandwich. You might have a long night."

27

"SO WHAT DO YOU THINK, GRETCHEN?" Klinger asked after the conservator took her first look at the three damaged paintings.

"It looks very much like the damage I saw to the Lucas Cranach painting from Gallery Three and then again when Chris Whitfield brought in the Gainsborough that had been in storage at the Freeport Naff in Tampa."

"Tell me about the Cranach again," Hunter asked, remembering that she'd mentioned it the day he met her in Genevieve's office.

"Almost two weeks ago, a valuable sixteenth-century painting from our permanent collection showed damage similar to this. I couldn't find out what caused it and I've started work on restoring it to its original condition. It was only partially damaged—the face of a lion, actually—but I hope to get it fully restored."

"And you say this looks like the same thing?"

"Take a look at this." She indicated one of the three damaged paintings. "If you examine it through this magnifying glass, you'll see that the paint appears to be—I don't know—in the process of being destroyed."

"Destroyed?" Klinger exclaimed. "You mean like acid, or something like that?"

"It doesn't look like that. It's more as if the paint is being erased, except there are no smudge lines like you might get with an eraser. I just don't know. But it is wet, with something. Look here." She dabbed the wet surface with her fingers and wiped them on her lab coat. "Notice that the surface is wet only in the areas where we see damage, almost as though someone either wiped them or sprayed them with something that's erasing the paint."

"Who would spray priceless oil paintings to damage them? What would they get out of that?" Klinger asked to no one in particular.

Something was bothering Hunter about all this. He couldn't put his finger on it, but suspected the answer was right in front of them. He walked over to the window and stared out at the courtyard where a few guests still mingled, continuing to think about the damaged oil paintings. If it wasn't a natural accident of some kind that affected the painting, it had to be deliberate.

Returning to the group he said, "Gretchen do you have a micropipette and a small vial of some kind? I want to take a sample of the moisture on the paintings. I think I know how to get it analyzed. That will at least tell us what it is."

THE NEXT MORNING AFTER THE DISASTROUS exhibition opening, Hunter left Gretchen with the task of figuring out how to possibly restore the damage to the paintings. Klinger was focused on going over CCTV footage with his staff to find out how the vandalism had been done during the hours the exhibit was closed. Sharon and Genevieve were dealing with the lenders of the damaged paintings, and Monica Arseneau was trying to console her mother, Marie.

Hunter needed to take the samples somewhere and get them analyzed. He was beginning to get an idea, a hunch really, but had to get an answer. The task would require more science than Gretchen could supply. Still, he agreed with the director, they couldn't involve too many outside people.

He called his own lab in Charlottesville. After two rings he got an answer.

"Hi, Kurt," he greeted his post-doc. "Do you remember when we went to the medical conference last year in Boston, and we had dinner with the microbiologist who was doing the research on blood vessel receptors that sniffed chemicals made by gut bacteria? It was a blood pressure regulating mechanism."

"Yeah, sure, Gil Glick. It was fascinating stuff."

"That's the one. I recall he was from Florida somewhere. Do you remember where it was?"

"Give me a minute."

Three minutes later he was back. "He's at the University of South Florida in Tampa. He's head of the Department of Cell Biology, Microbiology, and Molecular Biology, Dr. Gilbert Glick."

Two hours later, after a drive from Sarasota, Hunter was sitting in the office of Dr. Gil Glick, on the USF campus in Tampa.

"I remember you, McCoy, you're the vascular guy at Virginia. We had dinner in Boston."

"Right you are."

"So what can I do for you?"

"Can you prepare a slide from the little liquid sample I have here and tell me if there's anything there?"

"Oh, I love a mystery." Gil Glick, a jovial man who appeared to enjoy his work, took a microscope off his shelf and a clean slide and coverslip from a box next to it. Then, using a micro-suction bulb, extracted a tiny sample from Hunter's tube, placed it on the slide, and covered it with a slip. Then the microbiologist examined the slide under high power.

"*Alcanivorax borkumensis*," Glick said, "One of at least seven species of bacteria that can eat compounds of petroleum as part of their diet. They're nature's way of removing oil that ends up in the ocean, whether the oil is there because of oil spills or natural oil seeps. The oil spill response community calls the process bioremediation."

"Bacteria?" Hunter said.

"Yup. That's what you have here."

"Where are they found?" he asked, thinking about the recent BP oil spill in the Gulf of Mexico.

"Species of oil-eating bacteria are found in all the world's oceans, from the warm waters of the Gulf of Mexico and the Persian Gulf to the arctic conditions of the Chukchi Sea north of Alaska. Each species is most adept at oil eating in its native environment. So, for example, if you took bacteria from the Persian Gulf and transferred them to arctic conditions, they wouldn't eat oil as fast as the native cold-water bacteria. The same would be true in reverse."

"How do they digest the oil? What are the byproducts? I mean do they pollute the water?"

"Ah, now that's really interesting," said Glick, slipping into full professorial mode. "As they feed they multiply, so the local population expands considerably if the food source is abundant. And the little rascals are ecofriendly. Their main byproducts are carbon dioxide and lipids like fatty acids that become fish food and nourish biovegetation."

He beamed, reexamining the slide as he talked. "Other factors that influence their activity are the types of oil they're eating. They eat gasoline and diesel faster than they eat heavy petroleum products like fuel oil or heavy crude oil. In fact because asphalt, the heaviest oil product of all, is eaten so slowly—if at all—we can use asphalt for roads without worrying about it being consumed by our little friends."

Dr. Glick looked up from his microscope. "So what's your mystery here, McCoy? Where did your sample come from?"

"This sample was taken last night from the surface of a four-hundred-year-old oil painting. It was taken from an area of the painting's surface where the oil paint had disappeared, leaving bare canvas. It looks like our little friends here have developed a taste for oil paint."

"Impossible," Glick said, waving a hand. "The surface of an oil painting is dry. They couldn't possibly thrive in that environment. Also, they have no digestive enzymes that can eat oil paint. They couldn't consume it."

Glick returned to the microscope and spoke as he scrutinized the slide. "They're clearly eating something though. Maybe it's something that was on the surface of the oil paint." Then he continued, answering his own question. "But you said the oil paint was gone, right?"

"Right. The paint was gone but the canvas underneath was intact."

"Do you have more samples?" Glick asked, clearly intrigued.

"Yeah." Hunter removed a second small vial from his pocket and handed it to Glick. It contained samples from all of the damaged paintings.

"Good, I can analyze this in our lab here and should be able to tell you if they're actually eating old oil paint. But I still don't believe it. The lead and mercury in the paint alone would kill them. They couldn't survive that."

"Maybe they could with sufficient genetic engineering?" Hunter offered.

Glick ran his hands through his thick head of bushy brown hair. "That'd be quite an amazing bit of engineering." Then he looked up as a thought occurred to him. "You know, you might try BIOMOD."

"What's that?" asked Hunter, although something about the name rang a bell.

"They're a bioengineering company down in Sarasota. They've developed strains of oil-eating bacteria that are commercially available for use in oil spills and other industrial applications. Essentially, they select microbes for their particular affinity for consuming hydrocarbon-based pollutants, and then further train them to enhance this hydrocarbon affinity."

"That sounds promising," Hunter said. "Do you know anyone over at BIOMOD I might talk to?"

"No, though I'm sure someone over there would be intrigued by what you'd have to show them. But why don't you wait until I get these fellows analyzed? Give me about two hours and we should have an answer."

28

HUNTER FOUND A NEARBY RESTAURANT and went in for lunch. While he waited for his order to arrive, he thought about the damage to the paintings. The first was the Cranach, followed by the Gainsborough and then the three paintings at the exhibit Marie Arseneau felt responsible for.

Christopher Whitfield had felt that the Freeport Naff in Tampa was somehow responsible for damage to the Gainsborough, but the other damaged paintings were never there. Was the Tampa freeport the one referred to on the Cambridge killer's notepad?

While Hunter waited for a call from Dr. Glick, he decided it was time for a little help from his old friend at Interpol headquarters in Lyon, France, Eduard Gautier. The two men had never met in person. It was the strangest thing. Over the years they'd spoken many times, and Eduard had supplied him with critical information on many cases he'd worked when he was with the Defense Intelligence Agency, tracking down international criminals. Hunter's boss at the DOD, Deacon Wogen, knew Gautier very well and had introduced Hunter to him during a case he was working that involved tracking a Mideast gun-smuggling ring based in Southern France. Eduard's intel had been critical in their capture and arrest. Hunter had written to Eduard's boss at Interpol and pointed out how his exceptional diligence had led to the arrest and elimination of the operation. Somehow, Eduard had found out about this letter of commendation and they'd been friends ever since. Hunter smiled thinking of it. He shouldn't have been surprised. Eduard had a way of finding out almost anything.

Hunter dialed a series of numbers known only to a few individuals. He knew what was happening on the other end. His ID number and name, along with the full dossier Interpol had on him, was coming up on Eduard Gautier's computer screen. He waited for the inevitable wisecrack.

"Ah. I guess the academic world must be as boring as they say. Why else would the august Hunter McCoy be seeking the help of Interpol?"

"Hi, Eduard. Nice to hear from you too."

"So what is it this time that requires the unique skills of yours truly?"

"Humble as ever I see."

"Sometimes it's hard, but I try."

"I can see that," he said with a chuckle. "Listen, Eduard, I may be on to an international operation dealing in fine art. All I've got is two words on a notepad, Freeport and Legacy. I'm fishing here, so whatever you can come up with might be useful."

"Do you mean Freeports like the Freeport Naff in Zurich?"

"What's that?" *Is it like the freeport in Tampa?*

"You've been shut away far too long in the dreary halls of academe, my friend. The Freeport Naff is an operation at the Zurich Airport that is said to house billions of dollars in fine art. People who own expensive art and don't have room at home to show it, or think it's too expensive to keep at home, or who simply own it as investment pay rent to store the stuff there—tax free. That is its real selling point."

"And you know all this how?" Hunter asked.

"Surely by now, mon ami, you know that I know everything." He laughed. "Actually the Swiss police have been looking into Mr. Quentin Naff, the owner of Freeport

Naff for a shady deal he might have been doing under the umbrella of the freeport. We've been helping them."

"I see. Can you see if there is any connection between the two words, Legacy and Freeport—perhaps the Freeport Naff?"

"I can. And because it's a case we're actively working on this end, it shouldn't take too long. I'll call you when I have something."

Hunter spent the next half hour searching the web on his cellphone for information on Quentin Naff and the Freeport Naff in Zurich. He found several references to the case that Interpol was making against Naff. He was being accused of swindling one of his clients, a German industrialist named Horst Mueller, who had just opened a vault in the freeport. Apparently Mueller had agreed to buy several paintings from another renter. Naff operated as the broker. The industrialist claimed Naff took his money but never delivered on the paintings and the industrialist was suing.

His phone rang. It was Gil Glick. "McCoy, You'd better get over here—you won't believe this."

As he walked back to Glick's lab his phone rang again. It was Eduard Gautier.

"I have some info."

"What took you so long?" Hunter asked in jest. It hadn't been thirty-five minutes.

"Well I wanted to make sure you had time to eat your lunch. Besides, I do want to get home today. You do realize it's seven PM here?"

"So you put the hammer down?"

"Pardon?"

"It's an American idiom. Means you did it as fast as possible."

"Right. I put the hammer down. The Legacy is a group of five men who supplied the funding for the original freeport set up by Quentin Naff at the Zurich airport. It seems Naff had the idea, and when he told it to this group—the Legacy—they decided to invest. They made a lot of money and then took the profits and sold their shares back to Naff. Not too smart a business move on their part. If they'd have stayed in they could have made a lot more. But then again, now that we're investigating Naff, maybe they weren't so dumb after all. We'll see."

"So these five men all had a lot of money."

"Right. Each one is independently wealthy. Together, they could easily have funded Naff in his early days. Jacques Koehl is a banker from Zurich who owns one international bank and has shares in three others. Henri Seneschal lives in Paris and owns a shipping line that carries freight throughout the Mediterranean. Francois Paternoster from Lille, France, owns and operates granite mines in Italy. His products are shipped all over the world. Benoit Surette from Prague owns automobile manufacturing plants in the Czech Republic. Pierre Arseneau is the only American in the group. His money comes from selling oil leases in the Gulf of Mexico. He also owns a biochemical manufacturing company called BIOMOD."

"What did you say?"

"He owns a company called BIOMOD."

That's the company Glick just mentioned—and Marie too: her husband's company.

"Is this BIOMOD located in Sarasota?"

"Yes. Do you know it?"

He was getting his juices flowing now. "Not yet, but I will. And you say Pierre Arseneau owns it?" *Marie told us that at Monica's house.*

"Yes. His company is the world's largest supplier of products to treat oil spills. Nice business to be in if you also sell oil leases, right?"

It certainly is. "That's great, Eduard. What would I do without you?"

"You'd be lost, of course."

He laughed.

"Seriously, Hunter," Eduard continued. "if you find anything that relates to the case against Naff, be sure to let me know."

"You got it. I'll call if I do. Oh, one other thing. Does this Naff own the freeport in Tampa, Florida?"

"Yes, and one in Singapore, too."

As he walked to Glick's lab he thought about Pierre Arseneau. He was Monica's father and Marie's husband. He and four other men belonged to a group called The Legacy that funded the freeports. What was the group's purpose? Did they just meet to invest in startup companies like the freeport? And now he had a Freeport Naff in Tampa, where the damaged Gainsborough came from? Arseneau was a Wicar heir according to Marie, and he owned one of the stolen paintings—the van Ruisdael—that Knox left in the museum. Were the Legacy cousins also heirs?

Maybe the Legacy was up to something illegal, something serious enough to kill for. Maybe that was the real reason for the attempt on all their lives. Was Pierre Arseneau behind it? Was it just a coincidence that he owned a company that produced oil eating bacteria for profit and that the oil paintings at the Ringling had clear evidence of bacterial damage? Had he found a way to genetically modify the bacteria to eat old oil paint in spite of the heavy metals? Why would he do that? What would he gain? But surely it was more than a coincidence that three of the five paintings that had been damaged involved his wife's efforts.

QUENTIN NAFF KNEW SOMETHING WAS GOING ON. Even though he still had waiting lists in Zurich and Singapore, some clients were pulling out their holdings. He knew about the rumors, and even though he suspected where they might be originating, there seemed little he could do to stop them. But even worse than the rumors was the report of actual damage to a painting previously stored in the Freeport Naff-Tampa. The owner, the Ringling Museum of Art in Sarasota, was blaming his company, saying somehow the painting had become contaminated with something while at the freeport. It was nonsense, he knew, but if the word spread, other clients might pull out as well. He decided to fly to Tampa and get to the bottom of it.

29

DR. GLICK LED HUNTER OUT OF HIS OFFICE BUILDING, through a connecting skywalk, to a laboratory building adjacent to it. When they entered Glick's lab, Hunter could see that someone else was already there.

"Dr. McCoy, this is Sally Bennet, one of our post-docs."

Hunter greeted the young woman in her late twenties, whose short black hair might have looked Goth were it not for her crisp white lab coat.

"Sally is our top chemical analyst. I intend to try to keep her when her post-doc is up, but unfortunately I'll have to contend with the big money boys to do that."

Sally blushed.

"Hunter, I want you to know that I told Sally nothing about these samples or where you found them. I didn't want to influence her analysis or interpretation."

"Okay," said Hunter. "Good idea. So what did you find, Sally?"

"What I found makes no sense. Morphologically these are petroleum-ingesting bacteria of the genus and species *Alcanivorax borkumensis*. Their diet is exclusively petroleum-based. Things like gasoline, crude oil, or diesel fuel. These little puppies of yours—true to form—are eating oil, but it's not petroleum. I found samples of linseed oil and walnut oil, as well as the breakdown products of both. As you know, neither linseed oil nor walnut oil is petroleum-based; they're triglycerides, they're fats. So the question is, what are they doing there and where did they come from?

"The particulate matter in their cytoplasm appears to be undigested pigment, like you might find in oil paint. There were also trace amounts of lead and mercury, and that's really strange. If I had to guess, I'd say these little buggers have been eating artists' oil paint. Like I said, it makes no sense. Those heavy metals should have killed them. Oh, and one last thing. Your solution contained a small amount of detergent. You're going to have to start rinsing your glassware better, I'm afraid."

Hunter eyed Dr. Glick, who shrugged. "There you have it, an independent opinion."

"Where did you get these," Sally asked.

He knew that he had to keep this close to the vest. "From the surface of an oil painting four hundred and fifty years old."

"I knew it!" she yelled, almost jumping up and down with excitement.

"You knew what?" Glick asked, confused by her outburst.

"I compared the concentrations within the samples to current oil paints. They were all wrong. My research said the paint had to be very old, before the modern era."

"Very nice work, Sally," said Hunter, impressed. "Maybe I'll compete with Dr. Glick here and hire you for my lab instead."

She blushed again.

"Now, lady and gentleman, if you'll both follow me," Glick said, "I have a demonstration for you to see."

He led them through a door to an adjacent laboratory, then over to a side bench. Hunter instantly recognized the setup. On the bench was a high-power microscope that was video-linked to a screen somewhere. Hunter saw where, when Glick clicked open his laptop on another bench. This setup allowed whatever was happening on the microscope slide to be simultaneously shown on his computer screen.

They didn't need to look through the eyepiece; they could see it all on the screen in color and in motion.

"Let me tell you what I have here," Dr. Glick said. "I wanted to give our little friends a potential feast, so I chipped off a tiny piece of oil paint from a painting in my office. The painting has been in my family for a while— at least one hundred years. All I needed was to take a pin and flick out a small piece of paint. It doesn't even show on the painting, so I didn't damage it at all. But as far as your little devils are concerned, McCoy, it should be a veritable feast. I put it on the slide and added the live sample of bacteria you gave me. Let's take a look, shall we?"

Glick punched a few keys, and his screen came alive. What they saw was astonishing. The bacteria were clearly consuming the paint. They appeared to be concentrating on a crevice in the paint chip. They must have found this easier going than the broad, flat areas. Some of the bacteria, instead of consuming, were holding back, away from the main site of feeding activity. It appeared they were up to something else. Then Hunter saw it. They were reproducing.

"This is amazing," Sally said. "They're thriving on a meal that should be unpalatable for this species and lethal for them as well."

"Right," Glick said. "But look at them, they couldn't look healthier."

Leaving the bacteria to feast on the paint chip, the three of them took seats on lab stools.

"All right," said Hunter, "I'm no microbiologist, but I have to think that this strain of microbe didn't just happen to develop on its own. If it's manmade, how was it done, Gil?"

Glick handed Sally and Hunter cups of coffee then poured one for himself.

"I'm sure you know that bacteria are great evolvers. They can do it fast and on a large scale. Part of this can be explained by their short generation times and large population sizes. So if a random gene mutation occurs that happens to be beneficial and therefore increases the chances of that individual surviving and reproducing, it's favored by natural selection. Mutant gene variants are passed from parents to offspring, and the traits are carried on that way. This is called evolution with vertical transmission—down the family line, so to speak. And again, because bacteria have short life cycles and produce large populations, beneficial mutations spread rapidly."

"Yes, but do you think this is natural evolution?" Sally asked.

"I'll get to that in a minute," Glick said. "So bacteria acquire genetic variation through random mutation. But unlike humans, they also regularly get new gene variants through the process of horizontal transfer — that is, they can pass DNA back and forth directly from one individual to another."

"How does that work?" asked Hunter.

"For example, bacterial genes can be incorporated into small self-replicating circles of DNA called plasmids, which can be injected into other bacteria. The receiving bacterium can even incorporate some of the new DNA from the plasmid into its own genome and pass those genetic sequences on to its descendants. In terms of evolution, this means that bacteria do not have to rely on random mutation to produce a beneficial gene variant.

"In fact, this type of transfer can even occur between two different bacterial species. That means that a beneficial trait in one species can be horizontally transferred to another species that had no part in the original mutation. One species might pick up an advantageous gene from another species, and then the normal process of natural selection could begin to act right away, spreading the new variant through future generations."

"That's how antibiotic-resistant bacteria develop, right?" Hunter asked.

"Exactly, and the antibiotic resistance spreads both vertically and horizontally even from one species to another."

"So we have vertical transfer—parent to offspring— and horizontal transfer, between individuals," Hunter mused. "But how would it be beneficial for a petroleum-eating bacterium to start eating old oil paint? How would natural selection favor that?"

"It wouldn't," Glick said. "If a random mutation that would favor eating oil paint occurred in an individual in a petroleum-rich environment, it would not reproduce and would die out. It wouldn't be favored by natural selection."

Hunter nodded. "What if it were deliberate? What if you took petroleum-eating bacteria and put them exclusively on a diet of oil paint? Presumably one or two might randomly have a mutation that would let them eat it. The others would die out, but if you took the few that survived and let them multiply, could you get a population that would favor oil paint?"

"Bingo, Dr. McCoy. That is the kind of research they do down in Sarasota over at BIOMOD. I told you about them earlier. They've used techniques like that to develop strains of microbes that specialize in consuming light crude oil, heavy crude oil, gasoline, diesel, and probably a lot more as well."

Did they also produce strains that specialized in artist's oil paint? Hunter wondered. *Pierre Arseneau is the owner of BIOMOD. Is he behind all of this? What would he have to gain from destroying oil paintings?*

He thanked Sally Bennet and Gil Glick for their help and asked that they keep this business quiet for the time being.

Driving back to Genevieve's house he wondered about BIOMOD. How was he going to find out if they had developed the paint-eating bacteria? He couldn't just ask them directly. If Arseneau's company did develop it, would it have been deliberate and with the clear intent to damage paintings? Why would he do that? Surely it wasn't just to hurt his wife's reputation by damaging paintings she felt responsible for. There had to be more to it than that.

He and his cousins had been partners in a business to preserve paintings, not destroy them—at least until they sold out. Maybe that was it. Maybe they didn't part ways with Quentin Naff in a congenial way. But if that were true, it still didn't explain why he'd develop such a strain of bacteria.

It's time I pay a visit to BIOMOD.

30

THE DAY AFTER HIS TRIP TO TAMPA, Hunter found the BIOMOD campus on Google and set the Beemer's GPS to take him there. Driving east on Fruitville Road, he thought about the previous night, when he and Genevieve had a chance to catch up on events since the disaster at the exhibition. Actually it was a disaster only from the point of view of the Ringling staff and Marie Arseneau. Genevieve and Sharon had continued to work the crowd and discovered that most people weren't even aware there'd been a problem. The damaged paintings had been immediately taken to the lab for Gretchen to examine. The rest of the show had been a resounding success. Now came the painful tasks of coping with the collectors whose art work had been damaged and with insurance adjusters demanding answers they didn't yet have.

Before setting his course for Pierre Arseneau's biochemical engineering facility, Hunter had stopped at the museum and informed Klinger, Gretchen, and Director Bertram what he'd learned about the bacteria from Gil Glick and Sally Bennet. The question of who was at fault still loomed.

Now Hunter passed orchards and landscaping farms dedicated to supplying the Florida lifestyle to an ever-increasing number of gated communities. Turning left onto Sarasota Blvd. he drove for another three miles before coming to the BIOMOD facility. It had a small parking lot in front of a white building that looked to be the office. Hunter parked in one of the slots that was designated VISITOR. He noticed that he appeared to be the only visitor among seven or eight other cars he assumed belonged to employees.

Dressed in what he hoped was Florida business casual—a jacket, open shirt, and slacks—he entered the building and was immediately greeted by a receptionist oddly positioned with her desk against the front wall. He would have walked past her without seeing her except for her greeting.

"Welcome to BIOMOD. May I help you, sir?"

"Yes. I'd like to talk with someone about how I might clean up a rather large spill on my property."

"Of course, I'll see if Mr. Miller is available. Would you like a cup of coffee in the meantime?"

"Thank you. Black, please."

The young attractive woman brought him the coffee, and a few minutes later an eager young man in a nicely pressed dress shirt, not much older than the secretary, extended his hand. "Please step into my office, Mr.—?"

"McDill, Harry McDill."

Well, the initials are the same anyway.

"Please have a seat and tell me what we can do for you, Mr. McDill."

Hunter had only partially thought this through and hoped it would be enough.

"It's the pond behind my house, you see. I live up near Ocala, and my property backs onto a county road. At least once a week some nut decides to use it for a dumpsite because it's so rural and they have little chance of getting caught. You wouldn't believe the stuff I've had to cart out of there. Anyway, someone recently dumped three fifty-gallon barrels of linseed oil into the pond. I know it was linseed oil because I still have the barrels. Anyway, I understand you have microbe products that can safely clean up problems like this. Have I got that right, Mr. Miller?"

"Yup, bioremediation for spills is certainly one of the things we do here, but it's with petroleum spills—things like oil, gasoline, stuff like that. Linseed oil is a fat, if I remember correctly, a triglyceride. I'm pretty sure we don't have anything for that. What does it look like on your pond?"

"Awful. It just sits there on the surface as a kind of scum, and it's getting worse as it picks up dust and dirt from the air. My wife is so upset she says we'll have to sell the place if I can't get it fixed. Isn't there some way you can help me?"

Young Mr. Miller stood up and beckoned. "I'll tell you what. Come with me and I'll take you back to the lab. You can talk to our head molecular biologist and see what he has to say about it."

When they exited the back of the building Hunter saw for the first time that the BIOMOD complex was much bigger than it appeared from the parking lot, where he could only see the one building he'd just been in. Now he saw what appeared to be two rows of flat corrugated-steel buildings extending straight back from the front office building. He counted twelve identical buildings in all, six in each row, separated by a paved walkway through a grassy area and well-kept palm trees on either side of the walkway. Miller led him to the second building on the left, and they entered through the single metal door.

"Dr. Algarve, this is Mr. McDill," Miller said as he introduced him to a sixtyish balding scientist wearing a while lab coat who sat at an enormous table with papers spread all over it. The man looked up and greeted him, while barely acknowledging young Mr. Miller.

"Give me just a minute here while I finish this series of equations," the scientist said.

Hunter took the opportunity to look around. They were in a very large room with lab benches around the perimeter. He could see that this room was a research laboratory and not a production facility. He assumed production occurred in some of the other buildings. Here he saw file cabinets, chemical storage closets, refrigerators, a few sub-zero freezers, and analytical equipment common to research laboratories.

Finally, Algarve pushed back from the table. "There we go. Now what can I do for you?"

"Mr. McDill has a spill problem involving linseed oil and wonders if we can help him,"

"Linseed oil? How did that happen?"

Hunter explained about the bogus pond and the bogus dumping and watched as Algarve thought this over. Then, seemingly coming to a conclusion, Algarve said, "Our bioremediation products are all geared toward petroleum accidents. We don't have anything for fats. You could use a detergent, I suppose, but that could end up being an even bigger problem than you already have."

"Nothing?" Hunter said, feigning despair. "You have nothing?" A series of emotions spread across the man's face. Hunter left him alone. Algarve went over to a file cabinet, pulled out the bottom drawer, and shuffled through some files. Then he closed the drawer, walked over to a bench on the other side of the large room, and examined some more papers in a locked file. Finally he returned.

"How big is your pond?" he asked.

"I'd say it was maybe a half an acre."

"Hmmm," the man said, obviously thinking something over. "There's an outside chance we might have something you could use, but we'd have to grow it up to a concentration that would work for you."

Jim Miller, surprised, said, "I didn't know we had anything for linseed oil."

Algarve whipped his head around and fixed the young man with a cold stare. "We don't, but I still might have something that could work." Turning his attention back to Hunter, he said, "Give me a few days and then check back. I should know by then."

"Oh damn," Hunter said, "I was hoping to return to Ocala today. I guess I can find a place to stay and hang on for a bit. A few days, you say?"

The man paused, then said, "How about tomorrow? Check back with us after lunch tomorrow. I'll know by then whether I can help you."

He thanked the scientist and walked back to the office building with Miller.

"So," Hunter said, "is this the corporate office for BIOMOD?"

"No, this is the research and production facility for the company. The corporate offices are downtown in the One Sarasota Tower building."

"Who owns BIOMOD?" Hunter asked even though he knew the answer.

"That would be Mr. Arseneau."

"And his office is downtown?"

"Oh yeah. I've never seen it, of course," the young man said with a shrug. "I'm not important enough."

On the way back to the Ringling, Hunter thought about the possibility of Pierre Arseneau being behind all the trouble. He'd never met the man, but what he'd learned implied he'd be capable of it. His wife even admitted as much. Was it possible his company had developed a strain of bacteria that could destroy oil paintings? If it had, and Arseneau wasn't a scientist himself, then maybe his chief chemist, Dr. Algarve had developed it for him. But again, why? Did he just dislike his wife so much he'd try to destroy her credibility with the art community by destroying the paintings she helped bring in? Did it have anything to do with the freeports?

Passing the orchards again, he wondered what Algarve might have that could help his fictitious problem with the linseed oil spill. Maybe he had developed the bacterial strain that was destroying the oil paintings for whatever reason, and was thinking that the same critters might actually be used for a legitimate purpose as well. Maybe that's what he meant when he said, "We might have something but we'd have to grow it up to a concentration that would work for you." Presumably the amount needed to apply to a small part of a painting wouldn't be much, but to treat a half-acre pond would require the population to grow quite a bit.

Could he do that by tomorrow? Hunter wondered.

DR. ALGARVE THOUGHT ABOUT THE MICROBES. He hadn't wanted to comply with Arseneau's request to develop the strain. Still, the excitement he'd experienced as a molecular biologist in actually being able to do it was thrilling. Of course the boss wouldn't tell him what it was for, but he was no fool. It could only have one use, to damage art, to destroy oil paintings, and probably old and rare ones at that. Well, if that were true then maybe, just maybe, finding a legitimate use for the same strain would salve his conscience a little.

31

HUNTER WASN'T SURE EXACTLY WHEN IT HAPPENED, but somewhere on the drive back to town from BIOMOD he decided it was time to meet Pierre Arseneau. He wanted to get a feel for the man in his public life before he began to dig into the grimy underbelly he was increasingly beginning to believe was really there. There was no reason anyone at BIOMOD should suspect "Harry McDill" of meddling in company business. As far as they were concerned, he had time to kill until tomorrow afternoon anyway, so what could be more natural than paying a visit to the corporate offices of the company that might be able to help him out with his environmental problem?

He was slowly beginning to find his way around the city. If he just kept driving west on Fruitville, it would take him right downtown and very near One Sarasota Tower. Inside he studied the directory on the wall near the elevators. BIOMOD was on the seventh floor along with two other firms.

"May I help you?" asked the woman at the BIOMOD reception desk.

"I hope so," he said. "My name's Harry McDill, and I was just out at the research facility and spoke with Dr. Algarve. He was quite helpful. Your company is looking into helping me with a problem I have with a spill. Anyway, if he has a moment, I'd like to speak to Mr. Arseneau. I apologize for not having an appointment."

"I see. Can I tell him what it's about?"

"The products the company produces sound like they are a great environmental asset. So I'm wondering about investing in the company, and when I do that I like to meet the top man. I promise, it won't take long."

"Just wait here, and I'll see what his schedule is like today."

The receptionist's desk was in an open part of the hallway with two large logos of BIOMOD on either side of a double glass door between them and behind her desk. She got up and went back through the doors, which closed behind her.

She was back in a few minutes. "Mr. McDill, Mr. Arseneau has a few minutes free right now, but I have to tell you he has an important meeting in fifteen minutes, So, please keep that in mind."

She led him back to an office, gently knocked on the door, and opened it slightly. "Mr. Arseneau? Mr. McDill is here."

Hunter walked into a large office with glass on two walls from floor to ceiling. The west-facing view was spectacular, showing the vast expanse of Sarasota Bay and the Ringling Bridge crossing it to Lido Key. As it was 2:30 in the afternoon, the sun was shining directly into the office. But surprisingly, the tinting was such that looking directly at it was no problem.

The man came around his desk and extended his hand to Hunter. "Mr. McDill, won't you come in." They shook hands and Arseneau indicated a chair, and they both sat. Arseneau was a large man, as tall as Hunter, dressed in a business suit. His head was also large, almost inordinately so, with a full head of dark hair turning gray at the temples. He smiled and said, "I'm delighted to hear you're thinking of investing in BIOMOD. What's the nature of the problem that brought you to us?"

Hunter knew he had to be careful here. "I live on a rural property near Ocala, and have a half-acre pond on the property. It backs up to a rural road with a treeline and heavy scrub separating the road from the pond. People dump stuff back there. Well, somebody dumped three fifty-gallon drums of raw linseed oil directly into my pond. I have no idea why; I mean, that stuff is worth almost a thousand dollars a barrel. Anyway, it's polluted my pond. I heard about your company and thought, why not? Maybe they can help me."

"What did you learn?" Arseneau asked.

"Well, your man Jim Miller said you did bioremediation for petroleum spills but he didn't believe you had anything for my problem. Still, he took me back to meet your top science guy, Dr. Algarve. I explained my problem to him and he agreed you had nothing. Then, he must have thought about it some more, because he said maybe he could help. He asked me to come back tomorrow and he'd let me know, something about growing up the stock."

No longer smiling, Pierre Arseneau said, "I see."

Hunter could tell that he was thinking something through. Finally Arseneau stood up and extended his hand again. "Very nice to meet you, Mr. McDill. I hope you invest with us. The receptionist can give you materials about the company. I'm afraid I need to get to that meeting now."

Hunter shook hands, thanked him for his time, and turned to leave. That's when the painting caught his eye. Over a credenza on the wall near the door was an oil painting that he thought he recognized. On his way out he tried to memorize the scene depicted.

Once in the elevator on his way down he tried to recall what he'd seen. At the bottom he got out of the elevator and typed what he could remember as a note on his cellphone. Genevieve's father had emailed him a list of the Wicar paintings whose whereabouts were still unknown. Each was accompanied by a color image of the original. He thought the painting in Arseneau's office might be one of them. They were on Genevieve's computer. He knew he had to check on it right away while the image was still fresh in his mind, so he drove directly to the Ringling and went up to Genevieve's office.

"Hi," she said when she saw him coming. "I hope your day's been better than mine."

He took a seat and said, "We'll see. Can you bring up the paintings your father sent, the ones he called the Wicar paintings? I need to see them right away."

"Did something happen?" she asked while locating them in her files.

"Let me take a look at them and I'll tell you."

Hunter began to scan them one by one. Finally he said, "That one. Bring that one up."

She clicked on the one he'd pointed to, and it filled the screen. He could see immediately that the paintings were different. He consulted the notes on his cellphone. The two paintings had similar themes of angels surrounding naked maidens in the woods, but they were definitely not the same.

"What is it?" she asked.

"Pierre Arseneau had a similar painting in his office downtown. I just saw it."

"You were in his office? What were you doing there?"

He explained about his trip to the BIOMOD facility that morning and his phony story about a linseed oil spill on his fictitious property in Ocala.

"I'm hoping that tomorrow when I go out there they'll have a product for me. If so we can compare it to the bacteria Gretchen found on the paintings."

"But you said you went to Arseneau's office."

"I did. I just wanted to meet the man. I told them I might want to invest in the company. When I told him I'd been out to the research facility, I could see that he was thinking something over. If I'm right, he may get on the phone to Algarve and chew him out for agreeing to create this special product for me. I may have stirred the pot a little bit."

Genevieve pushed her hair back from her face and sat back in her chair. "I'll say. You'd better be careful with him. If he's really the guy behind the attempts on our lives, he's no one to mess with."

"If that's true, he'll learn that I'm no one to mess with either." He paused as if something had just occurred to him. "Didn't Marie Arseneau say that her husband only had one painting from the Wicar group, the painting that she stole and dropped at the Ringling?"

"Did she say that?"

"Yes. She said it was the only piece he had left of the Wicar collection."

"I wonder what happened to the others?" they both said together.

AFTER HUNTER LEFT HIS OFFICE, Pierre Arseneau sat and pondered what had just happened. That man wasn't Harry McDill. That was Hunter McCoy. He recognized him from the photo he'd given his hit man—the man who failed with his hit-and-run attempt. He also recognized the voice from the conversation he'd overhead on Marie's phone when he'd met with her, Monica, and the Swift woman at Monica's home.

32

GRETCHEN CEISEL WOKE UP WITH A HEADACHE. She assumed it was all the activity of two nights before, the call from Klinger, the damaged paintings at the exhibit, the all-nighter in the lab, and the discovery of the bacteria by McCoy. Dreaming about bacteria eating the paintings in her care, she hadn't slept well. She assumed that's why she was also a little nauseous. *Oh well,* she thought, *I'll be okay once I get to work.*

She ate her usual breakfast of Cheerios and blueberries with skim milk. It wasn't until she had her coffee that the abdominal pain began. *It must be the caffeine,* she thought. Unfortunately the idea of decaf for breakfast just didn't cut it. "Coffee is supposed to perk you up, for crying out loud," she said to herself through her discomfort.

She finished her breakfast, got dressed, and drove to work.

HUNTER ARRIVED AT THE BIOMOD RESEARCH FACILITY at two PM. He figured that shouldn't be pushing it too much, since Algarve did say in the afternoon. He parked in front as he'd done the day before and entered the admin building, where Jim Miller found him immediately.

"Mr. McDill, how are you?" the young man asked, offering his hand.

He shook it and said, "I'm doing fine."

Looking nervous, the young man said, "I'm afraid there's been a problem in fulfilling your request."

Feigning surprise, Hunter said, "Really, what's that?"

"Dr. Algarve, actually. He's sick."

Now this was a surprise. Hunter hadn't expected that.

"His wife called and said she'd had to get an ambulance in the night, when he developed a fever and a rapid heart rate. I called her a little while ago, and she said the doctors told her he had septicemia and was very ill."

"I see," said Hunter. "I'm sure he didn't have time to do anything about my problem with the linseed oil, then. I hope he's going to be all right."

"I know he'd started on it," said Miller, "and then he didn't feel well and went home early. He said he'd gotten a call from Mr. Arseneau. I have to tell you, he didn't look good. He was pale and kind of hunched over."

"Poor man. I hope he comes through okay."

"If you want to give me a phone number, Mr. McDill, I can call you when he gets back if he can come up with a product for you."

"That's all right. I'll just stop in again sometime."

He left and drove away out of sight of the building, then pulled over and parked.

What's going on here?

He wasn't surprised that Arseneau had called Algarve. He suspected Algarve had created the oil-paint-eating-bacteria for Arseneau. Why, he didn't know. But if he had and he was going to juice up a batch for "McDill" to use on his linseed oil spill, he figured that Arseneau would call him and demand to know what was going on.

What he didn't understand was the chemist's illness. It didn't seem likely he was faking it, not if his wife had to call an ambulance. On top of that, his diagnosis was septicemia—blood poisoning. Were the bacteria he created pathogenic? He hoped not, since he and Klinger and Gretchen had all been in contact with it.

He made a decision. He had to get back into Dr. Algarve's laboratory.

No one else had been in the lab when he was in it the day before. He wondered if it was always that empty. If so, he might have a chance to get in there and look around without being seen. If Miller or someone came in and found him, he could say he'd left something there yesterday and didn't want to bother them in finding it.

The parking lot was on the side of the main building, out of sight if you were in there. He returned and parked at the farthest part of the lot that was actually closest to the back buildings. The second building on the left, where Algarve's lab was, was unlocked. Much to his relief it was as unpopulated as the day before. He quickly went to the bench where he'd seen Algarve look at files before deciding that he might be able to help "McDill." It seemed as good a place as any to begin.

The single four-drawer file cabinet was locked. *Rats.* Taking a chance, he reached behind the cabinet to see if a spare key was taped there, you never know. Nothing. He tried the desk. The center and side drawers were also locked. He spotted a Bonsai tree in a pot on Algarve's desk. He picked it up and checked under it. Again he found nothing. *Damn,* he thought, *Okay, Larry, it's up to you.* Hunter took out "Larry" his lock-picking tool, and went to work on the file cabinet. In twenty seconds he was in.

He started with the top drawer. The files were alphabetical. Not knowing what he was looking for, he had to hope something would jump out at him. It did, midway through the second drawer, the same drawer that Algarve had looked in the day before. The file was titled "Masterpiece Oil Paint." He pulled the file just as he heard voices and the door to the lab open. He quickly closed the drawer and ducked down between it and the desk.

Two men carried in a large cardboard box and set it down next to the door. He would be in plain sight if they looked this way.

"The guy said the doc wasn't in today. Just set it anywhere."

The second one said, "That looks like anywhere to me." They laughed and left.

Hunter opened the file and quickly scanned it. It held a half a dozen sheets. Handwritten inside the file cover was a label. "Notes for Mr. Arseneau's project for bacterial action on oil paintings." This was it. He quickly looked around and spotted a copy machine.

Do I have time to do this?

Stop thinking and just do it.

He took the file to the copier and quickly made copies of all six sheets, as well as the note on the inside of the file folder. Then he replaced the file and locked the cabinet, folded the sheets in his pocket, and was about to leave the same way he entered when Jim Miller walked in.

"Mr. McDill? What are you doing here? I told you Dr. Algarve was sick today."

"Right. I know. It's not that. It's this."

Hunter produced his pocket notebook and handed it to Miller. "I left this here yesterday when we were in here. I was going to take notes, but as you know, I didn't. Anyway, I didn't want to bother you and I was out here anyway, so I just came in and there it was, right where I left it."

Not looking completely convinced but not having any reason to doubt the story, Jim Miller leafed through the notebook and handed it back to him. "You'd better leave now. No one is supposed to be back here unsupervised."

"Sure thing," Hunter said. "The last thing I want is to get you in trouble. You and Dr. Algarve have been great to me. I'll get in touch with him again, when he's better and back to work."

All the way on the drive back he wanted to stop and examine the papers, but knew he wouldn't be able to do it properly until he got home and had access to the computer. Then he'd get some answers.

On the way his phone rang. It was Klinger. He pulled over and answered. "What's up?"

"Another note. This one warns that we only have thirteen days left until the museum is ruined."

33

HUNTER PULLED INTO THE CARPORT at Genevieve's house about 2:30, thinking about Klinger's call. Given this new threat to ruin the Ringling Museum, he'd better get into the folder as soon as possible. He had a few hours to examine it before Genevieve got home. He made a cup of coffee and spread the papers out on her kitchen table, and began to read. It was molecular biology—not a field he was particularly skilled at—and heavy on mechanism. Still, with the help of a little research on the computer whenever he came to terms and procedures he wasn't familiar with, he was able to figure out what Algarve had done.

BIOMOD, or at least Dr. Algarve, had engineered a type of bacteria that if sprayed on the surface of an oil painting would begin to feast on the dried oil in the paint and destroy it.

Hunter wondered, what is the point? BIOMOD was a legitimate company that among other things biologically engineered bacteria to consume environmental oil spills. But why produce a bacteria designed to ruin oil paintings, valuable oil paintings at that, like those damaged at the exhibit?

Then a thought hit him. He looked at the date on the papers when the development of the bacterial species had been completed. He checked it against the date of the damage to the Lucas Cranach painting, with the ruined lion's face. The painting was damaged exactly one week after Algarve finished the project.

It must have been a test. They wanted to see if it worked and needed an old oil painting to try it on. The

Lucas Cranach was just sitting there on an easel in Gallery 3. It would have been an easy target.

He poured more coffee and walked out onto the lanai overlooking the water. He thought of the Gainsborough and the three paintings that were damaged in a similar way at the exhibit. He'd seen the bacteria in Glick's lab and knew they'd caused the damage. The note in the file clearly showed that Pierre Arseneau was responsible. He owned the company that produced the paint-eating bacteria. He abused his wife. Of the ninety-seven paintings in the exhibit, only three were damaged, the three that Marie Arseneau had arranged for. Was all of this—the development of the paint-eating bacterial strain—just another way to abuse his wife, or was it something else?

Was *Arseneau* going to "ruin" the museum? Was *he* behind the threatening notes? If so, what did May third and the number twenty-one mean? Maybe he should ask Marie or Monica if the date and the number meant anything to them.

Then he thought of something else. Jim Miller, the office manager at BIOMOD, said that yesterday afternoon Dr. Algarve told him that after he got a call from Mr. Arseneau, he hadn't felt well. He was going home. Then he ended up in the emergency room at the hospital. Did Arseneau think that Algarve was going to give "McDill" a sample of the paint-eating bacteria to use on his phony oil spill? Did he call to threaten him? Is that why the man went home? Of course, that didn't explain why he was now in the hospital.

Or did it? He examined the papers again and thought he might have an answer.

He knew he couldn't wait for Genevieve to get home. He called Klinger and told him he needed to get everyone together, including the director, Gretchen, Sharon, and Genevieve. He had something to show them, and he'd need a room with a dry erase board. Then he gathered up the papers and drove to Genevieve's building at the Ringling.

An hour later the five of them were sitting in a classroom looking expectantly at Hunter. He went to the front and began.

"Five hundred years ago, and even today, artists would make their paint by mixing linseed oil into pigment and stirring it into a paste. There were no bacteria available to eat linseed oil, much less oil that had dried for hundreds of years."

"So what's your point, McCoy?" asked Director Bertram.

"I believe that BIOMOD, a biochemical engineering company right here in Sarasota, has developed a bacteria that *can* eat five-hundred-year-old oil paint. And further, I believe a solution of these bacteria was sprayed on the three paintings at the exhibit, as well as the Gainsborough, and was tested earlier on the Lucas Cranach painting in Gallery 3."

The others waited for Hunter to continue.

"BIOMOD started with a well-known oil eating bacteria called *Alcanivorax borkumensis*. This species is always present in low numbers in seawater until an oil spill occurs. Then they rapidly flourish in the oil-rich environment and begin consuming the oil. It's their principal food source so they eat and multiply. They normally produce enzymes that are specialized for digesting petroleum oil.

"Now by its very nature, oil is not soluble in water. Remember the phrase 'oil and water don't mix'? This is potentially a problem for bacteria trying to consume oil in an oil spill because they have to internalize it—take it inside themselves—in order to break it down, using their specialized enzymes. To do this the oil has to somehow become water-soluble. It turns out that these bacteria have evolved a neat trick to do just that. They produce what's called a biosurfactant on their surfaces that break up the oil into tiny microdroplets that are much more water-soluble and can be readily absorbed. It works like a detergent does when you're washing dishes. The detergent dissolves the grease by breaking it up into smaller particles, making it water-soluble.

"Of course oil spills and oil paint are not the same thing. Oil spills are petroleum products and *Alcanivorax borkumensis* has the enzymes to digest it. But oil paint is an entirely different matter. It's usually made with linseed oil or walnut oil combined with pigments. They're not petroleum products. They're triglycerides—fats—that also don't combine with water. So if *Alcanivorax borkumensis* wanted to ingest it, the fats would have to be made temporarily water-soluble, and as I just told you, it produces a biosurfactant to do this."

"But wait a minute, McCoy," the director said. "An oil spill in the water is one thing—it's all liquid. But the linseed oil in a five-hundred-year-old painting is solid. It's dried. How could the bacteria do anything with that?"

"That, director, is an excellent question. How shall I put this—I managed to pilfer a copy of the file from BIOMOD on how they did it. The spray that was used to spread the bacteria on the surface of the paintings is a mixture of water and several other ingredients, including a solubilizing detergent—a biosurfactant. We also found traces of this detergent when I had the samples from the paintings at the exhibit analyzed."

"Still," Gretchen said, speaking for the first time, "even if the detergent did that and the bacteria managed to take up the linseed oil from the painting, I don't imagine they'd have the enzymes to digest it, would they?"

"You're right. So here's what they did. The genome for *Alcanivorax borkumensis* had already been completely sequenced. This means BIOMOD knew exactly which genes produce the enzymes for digesting petroleum. So using a technique that is pretty common these days, they snipped out those genes and replaced them with genes for the synthesis of lipase and esterase, the enzymes that would easily digest the fats in oil paint."

"So they custom-made bacteria to eat oil paintings?" Klinger asked.

"Yes, but they didn't stop there."

Gretchen frowned. "What do you mean?"

"This whole process is pretty slow. If the bacteria had to solubilize the oil, ingest it, and then digest it with its new enzymes, it could take days. So BIOMOD developed a mechanism to speed up the process so it would only take a few hours."

"How did they do that?" asked Bertram.

"This is where it gets tricky," said Hunter. "Some bacteria—not our petroleum-eating friend, *Alcanivorax borkumensis* here, but some—digest their food outside of themselves first, and then ingest the digested products for internal use. Of course in order to do this, they have to move their digestive enzymes to the outside. They do this by packaging the enzymes in tiny vesicles and transporting them through the cell wall to the outside environment. Once they're out there they do their thing and digest the oil.

"So what the engineers at BIOMOD did was to attempt to add this capability to the linseed-oil-eating bacteria they'd already produced. The idea was that if they could get the bacteria to not only digest linseed oil that they'd taken in from the outside, but also to package some of these enzymes in vesicles and ship them to the outside, they could speed up the paint-eating process by a considerable amount."

"Yeah," said Gretchen, "but how do you get a bacteria that doesn't ship vesicles full of enzymes to the outside to start doing that?"

"Here's what they did. It's ingenious, really. They looked for a type of bacteria that was already a big-time secretor of enzymes to the outside, and they found one. It's called *Vibrio vulnificus*. Then they attempted to transfer *Vibrio's* secreting capabilities to the linseed-oil-eating bacteria they'd engineered from *Alcanivorax borkumensis,* and apparently they succeeded."

"So in theory," Genevieve said, "these guys should be able to digest oil paint internally and externally."

"Right, and in a speedy way."

"So you're saying the bacteria we saw digesting the oil paint on the paintings were doing it by secreting enzymes outside and onto the surface of the painting, as well as chewing up the paint and absorbing it inside to digest?" Gretchen asked.

"Exactly."

"That's ingenious," she said.

"But there was a problem with *Vibrio's* protein digesting enzymes," said Hunter. "Algarve tried to remove the machinery by which they produce them. I think he may have failed with this part of it and accidentally transferred them to *Alcanivorax*."

"So what?" asked Klinger. "There's no protein in paint, is there? And even if there was, and the purpose was to destroy the paint, wouldn't that just be a bonus?"

"It would if the bacteria stay on the painting and don't come into contact with humans."

"Oh dear," said Bertram. "I don't like the sound of that."

"You are right to be concerned, Director," Hunter replied. "This bacterium, *Vibrio vulnificus,* the one Algarve used because of its unique ability to secrete enzymes to the outside, is involved in several nasty disease conditions."

"Like what?" asked Sharon Grandholm.

"Have you ever heard of flesh-eating bacteria?"

34

"FLESH EATING BACTERIA?" Gretchen squealed. "What's that?"

Hunter saw the anxiety and fear on her face but didn't understand why right away, so he continued.

"I wasn't sure either, so I read up on it. It seems that *Vibrio vulnificus* is a highly lethal human pathogen responsible for the overwhelming majority of reported seafood-related deaths in the United States. It's common in coastal marine environments worldwide and is found in water, sediments, and a variety of seafood, including shrimp, fish, oysters, and clams. Symptoms include fever, chills, abdominal pain and nausea, diarrhea, septic shock, and the formation of secondary lesions on patients' extremities. That's where the flesh-eating term comes from. Blood poisoning is the most lethal consequence, with an average mortality rate exceeding fifty percent."

Gretchen leaped up and stared at Hunter, shaking. "Oh my God," she said. "I've got it."

"Got what, Gretchen?" Genevieve asked in alarm.

"That—bacteria thing. I've got it. I woke up this morning with abdominal cramps and I've been nauseous all day. I handled all of those paintings. I must have got it from them. Oh my God."

Director Bertram came to life and took over. "All right, we have to get you to the hospital right now to get checked out. McCoy, you'll go with her, as you seem to have the most knowledge of what's going on here. Have any of the rest of you actually touched the wet surface of the paintings?"

All of them shook their heads, saying no, they hadn't actually touched the surface. Even Hunter, when he'd taken the samples to bring to Glick, hadn't actually touched it, not because he thought it would harm him, but because he didn't want to contaminate the sample before Glick got to examine it.

Hunter drove Gretchen to the emergency room at Sarasota Memorial Hospital and used the time on the way to call Glick and warn him of the potential danger from the samples. Then he turned to Gretchen, who looked pale and scared.

"From what I've read, the bacteria should respond well to antibiotic treatment."

Gretchen nodded, remaining quiet and looking worried, not seemingly comforted by that.

The emergency room staff immediately put her in a bed while he went to the lab and talked to the head tech, Carole Brindly. After introducing himself and stating his own connection to medicine, he asked the woman if she'd ever identified a *Vibrio vulnificus* infection before.

"Only once," she said. "As I recall the patient died from fulminating septicemia. Why do you ask?"

"Because I expect you're shortly going to get your second case, but you're not going to believe it."

"What do you mean?"

"Before I tell you that, let me ask you another question. Have you ever seen a case of *Alcanivorax borkumensis* infection?"

"I don't even know what that is," she said, her face a question mark.

"It's a common bacterium in seawater, including out there in the Gulf, that thrives by digesting oil. It feeds on oil spills and natural oil seepage from the seafloor. It's never been known to be a human pathogen."

"Well, that explains why I've never seen it in here then," she said, appearing relieved that her lack of knowledge of it was understandable. "So what does it have to do with *Vibrio*?"

"I've just brought in a friend to the emergency room with abdominal cramps and nausea who's been exposed to a bacterium I believe is basically *Alcanivorax borkumensis* but with the capability to secrete the *Vibrio* digestive proteins. The patient's name is Gretchen Ceisel; you'll be getting a blood sample to examine soon. I wanted you to know what to look for ahead of time. I've got to talk to the attending doctor about this now."

"Wait," she said. "How did this happen?"

"I'll explain later. I have to see her doc now," Hunter called as he walked away, leaving the lab tech no doubt staring at his back in confusion.

He made his way back to the emergency room, where the doctor attending Gretchen, Dr. Scanlon, had just stepped out of the curtained examining room.

Hunter explained about the two bacteria and the fact that Gretchen might be infected with a hybrid that retained the worst components of the pathogen *Vibrio vulnificus.*

Dr. Scanlon asked Hunter to accompany him back to his desk. The doc's desk wasn't his own, of course. They all shared them. Still, he did have a drawer all to himself.

"How do you know this stuff about *Vibrio*?"

Hunter explained that he was a physiologist at the University of Virginia Med School and he told Dr. Scanlon what he had learned about the development of the bacteria at BIOMOD and its potential danger to anyone who came in contact with it.

"Jesus, McCoy, you've got to go to the authorities with this. Wait, a minute," Scanlon stood up. "Miss Ceisel out there works for the Ringling Museum, doesn't she?"

"Yes. She's their art conservator."

"I had a patient in here a few days ago, also from the art museum. He'd been pretty sick. Said he'd come in contact with a painting that was wet with something. He didn't know what, just that it was the only thing he could think of that was unusual."

"Was that Chris Whitfield?" Hunter asked.

"Yes. Do you know him?"

Hunter nodded. "Say doc, if he was infected with this pseudo-*Vibrio* bacteria, how did he get better? I mean, if it's a cousin to the flesh eating bacteria we hear about, shouldn't he have gotten worse?"

"Not necessarily," Dr. Scanlon replied. "While *Vibrio* is an extremely virulent bacteria, it causes three types of infection. One is acute gastroenteritis, usually from eating raw or undercooked shellfish, usually oysters. The patient gets severe abdominal pain and explosive diarrhea, but responds to normal treatment and antibiotics. That was Mr. Whitfield. He told me he tasted the wet stuff on the painting."

"So, no flesh-eating effect if that's all that happens?"

"Right. For that, you'd need the second type of infection from *vibrio*, a necrotizing infection. In this case, the patient comes in contact with infected seawater and the bacteria enter the body through an open wound of some kind. These patients usually develop a blistering dermatitis. That's where the flesh-eating story comes from. It can be very nasty. But the worst case is the third type of infection, where the bacteria enter the bloodstream and cause systemic septicemia. These patients get all the effects of the infection, and if they already have a compromised immune system or any kind of liver disease, it can be lethal."

Hunter nodded. "So, in Whitfield's case, he's probably out of the woods. We need to see if Gretchen Ceisel tasted the wet surface or had any open cuts on her fingers."

"Very good, McCoy. We'll do that. We've already started her on fluids and antibiotics. I'll double check to see if she has any liver or immune system disorders that might make her more susceptible. Now that we know what to look for, I'll have the lab do a thorough bacterial evaluation."

"Dr. Scanlon, have you had any other patients with these symptoms?"

Hunter watched as the man did a mental recall. "Yes, two. One was a little girl who had full-blown symptoms and died a little over a week ago. Her mother said she'd never eaten shellfish, and she hadn't been to the beach. She had the full set of symptoms, including septicemia and blisters."

Scanlon slapped his forehead. "Oh My God."

"What?" Hunter said.

"The little girl. She also had childhood autoimmune hepatitis. Her family doctor had it under control but she would still have been a prime candidate to get the full-blown infection."

Hunter patted the man's shoulder. He was clearly distraught at having missed it.

"There's no way you could have known. None of us knew."

Scanlon looked at Hunter in anguish. "I had one more too. A man, what was his name?" They walked to the nurse's station and he checked the records. "Yes, here it is—Algarve. He came in with intestinal problems similar to Whitfield's."

Algarve?

"Is he still in the Hospital?"

"No. He improved and he's gone home."

Doc, I think you should try to get tissue samples from all of them, including the little girl's body, and see if they carried the modified *Alcanivorax,*" Hunter said. "Meanwhile, I'm going to see to it that this stops here."

35

THE YOUNG WOMAN WHO ANSWERED THE DOOR had dark circles under her eyes, her posture sagging with grief.

"Mrs. Slinde, my name's Hunter McCoy," he began when she answered the doorbell. "Thank you for agreeing to see me. As I said on the phone, I'm working with the hospital, trying to determine what happened to your daughter. I am very sorry for your loss. I can't begin to imagine what you're going through."

The young woman wiped away a tear. "Thank you." She invited him into her small living room and asked him to sit. "Chloe was my only child."

Hunter nodded in sympathy.

"I don't know why this happened to her," the woman said in anguish. "Are you going to find out?"

"Well, that's why I'm here today. If we can find the answer to that, maybe we can prevent it from happening again."

"It's too late for my poor little Chloe." her voice so weak and plaintive that Hunter almost wished he'd left the poor woman alone. She choked back a sob and held a palm up toward Hunter when he began to stand. "I'll be all right. Please sit down. How can I help?"

"I know you told the people at the hospital that Chloe didn't eat shellfish and that you hadn't been to the beach in several months. This might sound strange, it even does to me, but was Chloe around any old oil paintings recently?"

Carrie Slinde looked up sharply. "Why yes. We had gone to the Ringling Museum the day she first felt sick. Why do you ask that? Do you know something?"

Hunter sensed they might be on the threshold of something.

"I'm not sure. We're just following a lead at this time. Do you remember if Chloe touched any of the paintings?"

"She did, yes. I remember telling her you don't touch paintings in a museum."

"Now this is important, Mrs. Slinde. Do you perhaps remember which painting it was that Chloe touched?"

"Of course. I remember because she said it was wet."

Getting excited now, Hunter asked. "Where was this painting?"

"It was right after we'd gone through the big Rubens gallery at the beginning of the museum. We turned left and it was in that next gallery. The painting was sitting on an easel. It had a lot of red in it. I remember that Chloe was interested because there was a funny-looking lion in the painting. She said his face was wet."

HUNTER FOUND DR. ALGARVE IN HIS LAB at BIOMOD.

"Mr. McDill, is it? You were going to come back to the lab, and I'm afraid I got sick and couldn't meet you."

"That's right," Hunter said. "How are you feeling now?"

"Better, much better. I actually had to go to the hospital emergency room. Worst stomach problems I've ever had. I wouldn't wish it on anybody."

If you only knew, Hunter thought.

"Funny thing, too. That doctor, the one who treated me in the emergency room, had me come back yesterday to give a blood sample and to take some tissue swabs. Said he was still trying to figure out what I had."

He doesn't know. He doesn't know it's dangerous.

Hunter knew he had to take a chance. "Dr. Algarve, I'm going to level with you, and I hope you do the same with me."

Algarve stiffened a little at this. "What do you mean?"

"I want you to hear me out before you say anything. I'm not accusing you of anything and I'm not threatening you. I'm just trying to gather information. You strike me as an honest man. Hear me out and show me that my evaluation of you is justified."

"What the hell are you talking about, McDill?"

"First, my name isn't McDill. It's McCoy, Hunter McCoy. I don't live in Ocala and I don't have a pond contaminated by a linseed oil spill. I'm a professor of physiology at the University of Virginia School of Medicine."

Algarve frowned. "I don't understand. What's this about?"

"It's about a solution of bioengineered *Alcanivorax borkumensis* that digests oil paint. Bacteria that you developed right here for Pierre Arseneau."

"How do you know about that?" Algarve asked, a line of sweat beginning to bead his forehed.

"Because I read your notes."

"What?"

"I was impressed," Hunter said, deliberately choosing a calm, warm tone. "Very ingenious the way you genetically engineered *Alcanivorax* so it would produce fat-digesting enzymes rather than its normal petroleum-digesting set. But even more ingenious was the way you transferred the vesicle-secreting genes from *Vibrio vulnificus* to *Alcanivorax*. You only made one mistake, unfortunately a fatal one."

He watched Algarve's face. The scientist looked genuinely confused. "What do you mean? What mistake?"

"When you spliced out *Vibrio's* genes for vesicle secreting, you also took its genes for secreting its own native proteolytic enzymes."

Algarve's eyes widened at the implications. "Oh shit. No, I couldn't have. I was very careful not to."

"Well you did, nevertheless."

"But that would mean . . ."

"Exactly. Your little oil paint eaters became human pathogens. Little killers."

"Oh, my God. If anybody came in contact with it they could . . . Wait. That's why I got sick!"

"Not just you, Dr. Algarve."

"What? Who?"

"Before I tell you that," Hunter continued, "answer me this. Why did you do it? What was the purpose?"

Algarve sighed, and his shoulders slumped. "I'm sure this will cost me my job. But I never liked the feel of this project. Mr. Arseneau, the owner of the company, he asked me to develop it. He would never tell me why. There certainly is no economic need for such a solution. In fact, when you came in with your phony linseed oil spill, it was the first time I'd ever heard of a potential commercial use for it. I have no idea what he was going to use it for—although he did want to make sure it would digest old, dried oil paint, like you find in the old masters. I'll admit I was suspicious."

"Did you test it on any?"

"Old paintings? No. I didn't have one. The best I could do was a painting about thirty years old."

"Tell me about the solution," Hunter said.

"Well, it contained a concentration of the bacteria, of course, and a surfactant detergent to help break up the old oil. That was necessary to give the bacteria a soluble mixture to work on. I set it up in a spray canister so it could be sprayed on. Mr. Arseneau was quite impressed by the results of my demonstration with the thirty-year-old painting, but he wanted to test it on one much older. I told him I didn't have one. He just smiled, took my sprayer, and said 'I do.' "

Then Algarve gasped. "Wait. You said someone else got sick. How did that happen?"

Hunter explained about Chloe and that he believed Arseneau had tested the molecular biologist's sprayer on the face of the lion that the little girl touched in the painting at the Ringling Museum.

Algarve dropped onto a nearby stool and broke down in tears. Hunter almost felt sorry for him, but not quite. He told him that two others had gotten sick as well.

Then, in as firm a voice as he could generate, Hunter said, "Think very carefully before you answer this next question. Did you personally spray your solution on any other paintings besides the thirty-year-old one you used to demonstrate for Arseneau?"

"No, of course not."

"You didn't spray the Cranach, or a Gainsborough recently removed from the Freeport Naff in Tampa, or three paintings at the recent exhibit on landscape painting at the Ringling?"

"God, no. I would never do that."

Hunter believed him. It was time to meet Mr. Arseneau, this time as Hunter McCoy.

36

PIERRE ARSENEAU SAT BACK IN HIS FIRST CLASS seat on Air France as it carried him high over the Atlantic Ocean to Prague, where he was on his way to meet with his cousin, Benoit Surette. The two men shared a certain resolve, he reflected. Neither of them could tolerate losing in anything. Benoit was the one cousin in the Legacy Pierre could go to now for help.

The fifteen-hour flight touched down at Vaclav Havel International Airport at 9:05 AM. Benoit's chauffeur met him at the baggage claim. Pierre didn't know the man, but he'd held up a card with Arseneau's name on it. Pierre wasn't surprised that Benoit didn't meet him in person. As owner of the country's largest automobile manufacturing facility he was, after all, one of the most easily recognized people in the Czech Republic.

After a forty-five-minute drive in the back seat of the huge Mercedes sedan, Pierre arrived at Benoit's home in the hills above the city.

"Welcome to Prague, cousin," Benoit Surette said as Pierre entered the man's home. It was more a castle, really, built of stone, and huge—larger even than Arseneau's mansion on Lido Key.

"Thanks for making time for me, Benoit. I know you're a busy man."

"You know that I'm always willing to talk family business. At least I assume it's family business, since you didn't give me much information on the phone," said Benoit, formally without a smile.

Pierre Arseneau hadn't said much on the phone since he'd learned that his wife was checking up on him. He knew he'd have to be careful. He and Benoit had a history that, no doubt, still simmered just below the surface in the Czech.

"It's too early to offer you a drink, Pierre, but if you haven't had breakfast, you can join me for mine."

"I had coffee on the plane but wasn't hungry enough for breakfast. Still, I wouldn't turn it down now."

"Let's go to the back porch; we'll eat out there."

Pierre had never been here before and had to admit his cousin lived large. The house and furnishings were reminiscent of a Gothic cathedral without the religious trappings. Beamed ceilings, stained glass windows with historic and woodland scenes, antique pieces that looked as old as the home strived to be. Pierre knew it had been built only twenty years before. While there was plenty of art on the walls, he didn't see the Botticelli that he knew Benoit kept as his part of the Legacy. He figured he'd see it somewhere later.

After walking through the house they emerged onto a sunny covered porch that ran the entire length of the back of the house. It must have been twenty feet deep by maybe two hundred feet in length. Evenly spaced Corinthian-topped columns held up the roof. The floor was marble. But most spectacular was the view overlooking manicured gardens of hedges, flowers, trees, and stone walkways, with more hills behind. The effect in the morning sun was an explosion of color the likes of which Pierre had never seen in a private home until now.

Benoit caught him staring. "Quite spectacular, isn't it."

"Breathtaking," exclaimed Pierre as they sat down to eat.

Benoit's manservant brought them coffee and quiche with cups of chopped fruit and then left them alone.

"So, Pierre, what's this all about? What circumstance required you to fly all the way here that couldn't be resolved on the telephone?"

"I have a problem with my wife," Pierre began.

"Ha," Benoit laughed, "don't we all."

"No, really. It turns out she's the one who stole my painting and paperweight."

"Paperweight? She took that too? Why?"

"She eavesdropped on some of our phone calls. I made the mistake of having us on speakerphone; she overheard me talking about Addison Swift and his research into the family history. She got the idea that I was a threat to his life, and felt she should warn him. It turns out that his daughter being at the Ringling was just a coincidence after all. But my wife is on the Ringling Board and had been working with Swift's daughter on an exhibition at the art museum, so in an effort to warn her she left my van Ruisdael at the museum with a note apparently warning the daughter to find out what she could about the painting to protect her father."

Pierre stopped at this point. Benoit waited. Finally, he said, " "So what aren't you telling me, Pierre. There's more to it than this, isn't there?"

Pierre sighed. "Yes. I was sure the Swift woman had my painting, so I hired a local thug to search her house for it. The imbecile didn't find it, of course, but when she came home and surprised him, he hit her on the head with something and sent her to the local hospital. But a bigger problem is her boyfriend, a guy named Hunter McCoy. She was on the phone with him when my man hit her. The man had enough presence of mind to check the phone and see whom she'd been talking with. That's how I got his name."

Now completely scowling, Benoit Surette said, "And?"

"It gets worse. I did a quick check and found that the nosy bastard, this McCoy, is a skilled criminal investigator of some kind. I figured he'd fly to Sarasota immediately to help her. So I had the thug meet him and try to take him out."

"Take him out? Take him out?" Surette stood up, his fist on the table. "Are you out of your mind? What the hell's the matter with you?"

"I know, I know. It was stupid. I wasn't thinking."

Pierre Arseneau saw, in his cousin's eyes, the steely dark menace that Benoit's industrial adversaries must have faced whenever they crossed this man. Even Pierre was a little intimidated.

"What happened?" Benoit demanded.

"My guy tried to run him down with a car at the airport in Sarasota. McCoy ended up in the hospital but survived— intact from what I've been able to learn."

"I'm almost afraid to ask. Is there more or is that it?" Benoit hissed.

"Two more. My man, in a final effort to get rid of him, rigged the Swift woman's house, where McCoy is staying, for a natural gas accident. That didn't work either. Then later he shot at them from a boat near her home. Again, he missed. McCoy is getting way too close. Using an alias, he came to my company with a phony story about an oil spill. He might know about my spray."

Benoit stared at Pierre. If looks could kill, Arseneau would be dead. Benoit Surette stood up and walked to the edge of his porch and gazed out at his beautiful grounds. Pierre left him alone while he processed everything he'd just heard. Pierre knew the man was a tactical genius. He also knew he could be a lethal adversary. The other three European members of the Legacy didn't come close to his level of ruthlessness. The only member who even approached it was Arseneau himself, and truth be told, he was a little afraid of Surette. Of course, he'd never let the man know this.

Finally, Surette returned to the table, sat down, and took a sip of his coffee. "All right, here's what we'll do," he told Pierre. "You'll leave this to me. Your stupid employee with the poor driving skills is going to suffer a fatal accident. A different kind, but equally lethal accident will end the threat from Hunter McCoy. Unlike you, I know how to do this efficiently. Your skill only appears to be getting innocent people killed."

A long silence followed during which both men recalled what that meant, the suicide of Benoit's son, while he lived with the Arseneau's a few years before.

Finally Benoit spoke. "We'll leave the daughter alone and we'll leave her father alone. We'll deal with them only if we see them becoming a real threat."

"All right. I agree," Arseneau said. Then after a pause, "Benoit?"

"What?"

"There is one last thing I didn't tell you, and I promise this is it."

"Good God, man, what?"

He took a deep breath to calm himself, and then told him about the failed break-in at Addison Swift's house in Cambridge.

37

PIERRE ARSENEAU WAS ALONE IN HIS ROOM at Benoit Surette's mansion. Earlier that evening they'd had dinner, drunk cognac, and examined his painting collection. He finally saw Surette's namesake painting, a whimsical oil of Mars and Venus painted by the Italian master Sandro Botticelli in the late fifteenth century. Along with eight other old masters Surette had collected legitimately over the years, the Botticelli was on display in a climate-controlled room off his massive library. The lighting was perfect and each painting was beautifully illuminated. Pierre was impressed. At the end of the room was another door—quite formidable—and Pierre asked him where it led. He couldn't get Surette's odd response out of his mind.

"Nowhere, it's just a storage area," his host responded a little too sharply.

That was odd. Why the attitude? Pierre wondered. So he pressed a little. "What? You keep your *very* old masters in there?"

"I told you, it's storage, forget it. It's off limits," Surette snapped, not amused.

Pierre couldn't help wondering what was behind the door. *But well,* he thought, *the man is entitled to his secrets.* Over the next three days he planned to visit Rembrandt, Correggio, and van Dyck for an overnight in each of their homes. As the three Legacy members most committed to opening up the freeports so the art could be more open to the public, they were also the three most committed to spreading rumors about the compromised safety of the freeports, leading to clients pulling out. At their recent five-year meeting at his home on Lido Key they'd explained in general how this worked, but he wanted to sit down individually with each of them to get the details.

It occurred to Pierre—not for the first time—that while his motive for bringing down Quentin Naff was revenge, and the three cousins he was going to visit over the next three days were primarily motivated by concern for the public, he never did know what Benoit Surette's primary motivation was. In many ways the man was an enigma. When he'd suggested using his newly developed oil-paint-eating bacterial spray to help bring down Naff at their recent meeting, the three had been absolutely against it. They were horrified at the thought of damaging paintings, even Quentin Naff's paintings. They insisted that the rumor campaign was working and was all they needed for operation *Payback*. So with three votes against him he told them he'd put the bacterial spray project on hold.

Benoit Surette had voted with Pierre however, although he hadn't expressed an opinion one way or the other. In fact, he hardly ever spoke evil of Naff the same way the others did. While he was as involved as the rest of them in *Payback*, it was as if his heart wasn't in it to the same extent as the others.

Then there was the issue of the suicide of Benoit's son, Paul Ballard. The young man, who'd been living with Surette's ex-wife in France, took a job as a security guard at the Ringling Museum a few years before. Benoit wanted Paul to follow him into the family business in Prague, but the boy said he needed a year or two abroad before he'd be ready to settle into it. Benoit arranged for him to live with the Arseneau's during this time. When Paul hung himself on the grounds of the museum, Surette held Pierre and the Ringling personally responsible. It made no sense, but there it was.

HUNTER DROVE DIRECTLY TO One Sarasota Tower, and took the elevator to the seventh floor and headed for Pierre Arseneau's office. It was way past time to confront the man. At the very least he was indirectly responsible for Chloe Slinde's death. He was certainly morally responsible. There could be no good reason for developing the oil-paint-eating bacteria. It was either just a juvenile attempt to punish his wife or he had an even more sinister motive. And beyond that, the man might very well be behind the attacks on him and Genevieve, maybe even Addison's break-in in Cambridge. Determined to get some answers today, Hunter told the receptionist that he needed to see Mr. Arseneau immediately because he had critical information that Arseneau would want.

"I'm sorry, sir, Mr. Arseneau is currently out of the office. In fact he's out of the country."

"Where is he?" asked Hunter.

"I'm really not at liberty to say, sir."

"And when will he be back?"

"I'm sorry, sir, I was instructed not to give that information."

"Really. Who gave you those instructions?" Hunter snorted, more sure than ever of the man's guilt.

She shrugged, implying that information too was not to be forthcoming.

Disgruntled, Hunter left, and on the way out of the building a uniformed chauffeur with the BIOMOD logo on his shoulder walked past him into the building. Taking a chance, he called to him. "Hey. Wait up a minute."

"What?" the man said, stopping and turning to Hunter.

"I've got some papers I was supposed to give to Mr. Arseneau before he left, but I missed him. Did you take him to the airport?"

"Yeah, why?"

"Oh boy, I've really messed up," Hunter said. "Do you know what time his flight gets in? Maybe I can email it to him once he gets off the plane."

"You did mess up. He left yesterday afternoon. His flight would have gotten into Prague this morning about nine."

Prague?

"Oh crap," Hunter muttered. "He'll need these papers."

"Too bad. He's staying with his cousin, Benoit Surette. Just give him a call at the house and make arrangements. If you can't reach him there, you're out of luck. I don't pick him up for the return until Friday. I gotta go."

"Hey, thanks, pal," Hunter said.

Benoit Surette. That's one of the Legacy members Eduard told me about. Marie said her husband called him. What are they up to?

He called Marie and explained Pierre had left the country. "I was told he's in Prague with his cousin, Benoit Surette."

"I didn't even know he was gone," said Marie. "He never tells me his plans and frankly, I don't care. I can run the house and get along without him quite nicely."

"Apparently he left yesterday. Did he give any hint as to why he might go to Prague? Anything at all?"

"Well, he was upset again, but that's not unusual. He's always upset at something or someone. I did hear him screaming at his attorney, something about a fouled-up oil lease in the Gulf. Something about he'd been damn well assured the feds wouldn't notice. I don't know what it was about."

Hunter filed that bit of information away. "Has he been to Prague before—to visit Surette?"

"I don't think so. Of course, Benoit Surette and the other three cousins—The Legacy, he calls them—were here just a few weeks ago for their five-year meeting. My husband had also met him at other meetings of the group in Europe, but I don't believe he's ever been to Prague."

Damn, he thought. *Just when I had enough evidence to confront the man he leaves the country.*

"Hunter?" Marie said. "Hold on, I'm on my cell and I just walked into his study. I'm going through his desk calendar. I see he's written something on the date two days ago. It's a name. Bergen, and the words 'incompetent overrated asin.' I don't know anyone named Bergen."

"Asin, did you say?"

"Yes, A S I N."

"Marie, I've got something else to tell you. I'll pick up Genevieve and come out to your house. I want to tell you in person."

There was a pause before Marie answered hesitantly, "Okay."

"We'll be there in half an hour."

Hunter drove back to the museum, picked up Genevieve, and her Beemer's GPS took them directly to the Arseneau house on Lido Key. But to call it a house would be to say a Rolls Royce Corniche is just a car. The term house didn't even begin to describe it.

First, it was huge. Hunter knew that Pierre Arseneau and Marie lived there alone. Of course he knew that the question wasn't how much house do two people need, but rather how much could they afford? In this case the answer was apparently a lot. A black wrought-iron fence punctuated by concrete pillars surrounded the entire compound. This left the house visible to anyone standing outside. As they approached the gate, it opened automatically. Marie must have seen them coming through a camera setup of some kind. They drove into the sprawling courtyard with a cascading waterfall in the center, pulled around it, and parked in what appeared to be the vicinity of the front door. Again, as they approached the door, it opened, and Marie welcomed them in and took them to a lovely living room area.

"I'm not going to like this am I?" she asked with no ceremony.

"I'm afraid not. But you've been honest with me so I'm going to be honest with you. Maybe we'd better sit down."

"Oh, God. It's that bad?"

"Yes, I'm afraid so." Hunter got right to it. "Your husband had his head scientist at BIOMOD, a man named Algarve, engineer a bacteria specifically to eat old oil paintings. The man confessed it all to me."

"Pierre's responsible for damaging the paintings?"

"Yes, and there's more. Dr. Algarve, who developed the bacteria for your husband, thought the engineered bacteria were safe, but they're not. They're pathogenic and can cause severe sickness and even death. The bacteria are delivered by a spray canister to the surface of a painting and within twenty-four hours can completely digest the oil paint. It was first tested on the Lucas Cranach painting in Gallery 3. A little girl touched the wet surface and put it to her mouth. She died a week ago. The second use that we know of was to spray the Gainsborough that was coming from the Freeport Naff in Tampa for your Landscape exhibit. We don't know how the spray got there but Christopher Whitfield touched the wet surface on it and ended up in the emergency room at the hospital. Luckily he recovered. The other three sprayed paintings you already know about."

Marie began to cry.

"I don't yet know if he's involved in the violence against Genevieve and me, or for that matter her father in England, but I'll tell you this. He's going to be stopped, Marie, and I'm going to do it."

The elegant woman sobbed quietly for a few moments, then composed herself. "I knew the man was deranged, but

I had no idea how bad he'd gotten. It's as if I've never really known him. He must hate me more than I realized. Are Monica and I going to be safe while you do whatever you're going to do?"

"Your safety, along with Monica's and Genevieve's is my highest priority. You can be sure of that."

When they left Hunter called Captain Rand Conrad of the Sarasota Police Department, the division commander Ringling Security Chief Kyle Klinger had introduced him to. "Captain, it's Hunter McCoy."

"What do you want, McCoy?"

"Do you know a local bad guy with the name Bergen?"

"McCoy, jump in your car and get your butt down here right now."

"Whoa, so it rang a bell, huh?"

"Just get down here now. We need to talk."

Hunter dropped Genevieve off at the house and a half hour later was sitting in the hot seat at Conrad's desk. An unsmiling Conrad asked, "All right, what do you know about Benny Bergen?"

"Benny? That's his first name?"

Conrad drummed his fingers on his desk. "All right," Hunter went on, "The name was written on a scrap of paper on Pierre Arseneau's desk. He's the owner of BIOMOD, a biochemical engineering facility east of the city. The name Bergen was accompanied by 'incompetent overrated asin.' I'm investigating some irregularities at BIOMOD and have evidence pointing to the complicity of the owner. I have no proof, but suspect Bergen might also be behind the violence directed against Genevieve Swift and the hit-and-run against me. What do you know about Bergen?"

"I know he's dead."

"What? When?"

"A few hours ago. Apparently he was taking a bath and his electric hairdryer fell in the tub. Shorted out lights in his building and a neighbor found him almost right away. The body was still warm when the ME got there."

"The medical examiner? Why was he there? You think this was a crime?"

"She, the ME's a she. And maybe. We know Benny Bergen. He's been a career troublemaker, in and out of jail on minor stuff mostly. Never been to prison. But he had a violent streak. Liked to think of himself as trouble for hire. If he's the Bergen your man Arseneau referred to, he could have hired him to go after your girl and you."

"Makes sense," Hunter agreed. "Asin could be assassin."

"Tell you what, McCoy, I'm going to have a talk with Mr. Arseneau."

"Good luck with that. He just left the country yesterday."

"Where is he?"

"Prague, I believe."

"Prague? Do you know when he's coming back?"

"According to his chauffeur he'll be back Friday."

38

QUENTIN NAFF'S FLIGHT WAS STILL TWO HOURS away from landing at Tampa International Airport. Arrival was scheduled for 9:05 AM after a grueling eight-hour flight from Zurich. He didn't enjoy flying all that much but knew he had to get to the bottom of this newest threat to his system of freeports. He'd suspected for a long time that the Legacy group was behind the rumors that the freeports weren't safe. They just wouldn't believe that he wasn't responsible for the theft of their paintings, and he'd done everything he could to convince them otherwise.

In retrospect, he had to admit that he hadn't done sufficient due diligence. Horst Mueller had only recently taken out a unit at the Freeport Naff-Zurich and hadn't yet moved any of his holdings into the vault assigned to him. He'd examined the paintings in the Legacy's vault and made the offer to buy them all in a single sale. The funds, four hundred thirty-two million dollars, were to be transferred from Mueller's account at Deutsche Bank to a brokerage account maintained by Freeport Naff, Inc. Quentin maintained this account to process sales under cover of the freeport. The agreement was that the art would be transferred first, and when that was completed and verified, the funds transfer would follow instantly. He'd done this before with other sales for other clients and never had a problem.

Quentin verified with Deutsche Bank that the German industrialist's bank account held sufficient funds to complete the sale. Later, Horst Mueller claimed he never received the paintings but that he *had* transferred the money—which the Legacy never received.

The Legacy believed that Quentin Naff was behind it all and had swindled them out of their money. So he was convinced *they* were behind the smear campaign about the safety of his freeports. And it was having a devastating effect. Clients were pulling out. It wasn't enough to be a serious problem yet, but it could be if it kept up. But now, with this mysterious charge that a painting had been damaged while at the Tampa Freeport, things could get out of hand fast. If there was one thing owners won't put up with it was the possibility of their treasures being damaged, thus his presence on this miserable airplane. He had to find out for himself if there was any truth to the charge being made by the John and Mable Ringling Museum of Art, and if so, to correct it immediately before the fallout ruined his empire.

PIERRE ARSENEAU REGARDED the CEO of the Credit Suisse Group, one of the largest and most successful financial conglomerates in the world. The CEO was Jacques Koehl, and in the Legacy group he went by the name Rembrandt. When meeting individually, like today, Legacy members typically used their real names.

"It's been quite easy, Pierre, really no trouble at all. Many wealthy men owe their financial success to me. They generally cooperate with me on anything I ask if it isn't illegal or doesn't hurt them personally. Three such men had been holding valuable art at the Freeport Naff-Zurich. I merely gave them an alternative possibility. I asked them to make arrangements to have their art on display with the Kunstmuseum here in Zurich as a permanent loan to the museum. That way they still own their pieces and have all of its monetary value, while turning the responsibility for its safety over to the museum. Also, it would save them the considerable cost of storage at Naff's Freeport."

"I understand," Pierre said. "But how do you spread the rumor that it's not safe at the Freeport Naff? That's what we're trying to do, right?"

"Don't forget, we're trying to do two things, cousin. One, we want the art on display, not merely out of the freeports. This technique accomplishes that. Where better to display art than in public museums? Two, we want to shut down freeports in general and Naff in particular. In order to accomplish the latter, I simply drop hints among the rich and famous, whenever I see them, that I've heard people are leaving because the facilities aren't as safe as the art owners thought, or that local governments might be preparing to shut them down for tax fraud. I also hint that Naff has been taking illegal commissions on transactions between art owners under the freeports. Believe me, Pierre, in this position, I spend almost as much time at cocktail parties as I do in the boardroom, so I have plenty of opportunity to spread the word."

"Very good. That's ingenious," Pierre said.

"Yes, it is. And as a bonus, nothing about it is illegal."

"Excellent."

39

IT HAD BEEN TWO DAYS SINCE HUNTER had brought Gretchen in to the hospital, and he knew she was planning to leave today. Fortunately, the progress of her illness had been like Christopher Whitfield's, relatively mild. Still, Dr. Scanlon wanted to keep her for observation, given the level of the threat. Once Gretchen knew she wasn't going to die or be horribly disfigured, she became a real pain-in-the-ass to the staff. Hunter had to laugh thinking about it.

"Look, I'm ready to go home—now," Gretchen's exasperated voice echoed down the hall as Hunter approached her room. "The doctor said I could leave this afternoon. It's almost five o'clock. What's the holdup? I have a real job, you know."

As Hunter entered, Gretchen's nurse left, rolling her eyes at him.

"Hey, Gretchen, what if I told you that you had to stay here another two days?" he said jokingly.

"I 'd claw your eyes out, for starters," she said. "I'm going home tonight, no matter what. This is the first time I've ever been overnight in a hospital. It's driving me nuts."

"I never would have guessed."

The nurse returned. "Gretchen, your discharge papers are on the way over right now. As soon as they're here, which should be just a few minutes, you'll be able to leave."

Gretchen threw her arms in the air. "Hallelujah."

Twenty minutes later, Hunter drove her home. After dropping her off, saying he'd see her tomorrow at work, he picked up a thin-crust brick oven pizza and drove home to wait for Genevieve's call. Earlier she'd told him that she and Sharon would be working late, trying to tie up the remaining loose ends from the disaster at the exhibition. She'd asked him to pick up a pizza from her favorite Italian place, take it home, and she'd call him to pick her up at the office when she was finished.

On the way he couldn't stop thinking about the two notes the director had gotten, threatening to 'ruin' the Ringling Museum of Art. *What the heck was that all about?* What did it say? *Thirteen more days until your precious museum is ruined. Have a nice day.* Somebody had a serious grudge against the museum and now there were only ten days to go.

He made a mental note to check with Klinger and the director to see if they'd found anything more on the May third date and the number twenty-one. Thinking Pierre Arseneau might be behind the threats, he'd asked Marie and Monica if the date and numbers meant anything to them, but they'd both drawn a blank. What he couldn't get out of his mind was the wording. The threatening notes sounded personal as if someone had been wronged or hurt by the museum or believed he was. Had anyone been fired on that date? Was someone injured on May third of some year?

Once he got to the house he called his dad on Face Time, using his iPhone. He liked being able to see his dad while they talked, and he knew it made his dad feel closer to him as well. He propped the phone up against the counter so his dad would be able to see him as he set the table for dinner with Genevieve. Just as the Face Time connection was completed, but before either of them had a chance to say anything, a man appeared in the doorway to the kitchen wearing a business suit and tie. He held a very lethal-looking weapon, rock steady and aimed squarely at Hunter's chest. Slim with neatly trimmed black hair going gray he had the easy confidence of a professional.

"Sit down, McCoy."

Eastern European accent, Hunter thought. Seeing no option and sensing the man posed no threat in the next ten seconds or he wouldn't have him sit down, Hunter pulled out a kitchen chair and did just that.

"I have several questions for you. If you answer them satisfactorily you can walk away from this and you won't see me again. If you don't answer them, or your answers are not satisfactory. . ."

"Who are you?" Hunter asked. He hoped his dad was watching on the cellphone and smart enough to keep quiet. He also hoped the man didn't see the phone.

"No, no. I have the questions, remember?"

"What do you want to know?"

"First, let me tell you what I *do* know. I know that Miss Swift did not steal the van Ruisdael painting from Pierre Arseneau."

Hunter tensed and leaned forward, frowning.

The man stared hard at him. "Do not move again, please."

He sat back. He also noticed for the first time that the man looked pale and was sweating.

"The man who attacked her in this house, rigged her gas lines, and shot at you from a boat is now dead. I know this because I killed him myself—a little accident with a hairdryer in his bathtub."

He killed Benny Bergen? Who was this guy?

"I also know that her father, Professor Addison Swift, is trying to identify the heirs to the Wicar paintings. And I know about you. I know you're a dangerous man; almost as dangerous as I am."

"What do you want to know?" Hunter asked, sensing the time was right for a question.

"Are you familiar with the Legacy?"

"A group of five cousins, presumably Wicar's heirs, who own thirty looted paintings."

"Do you know their names?"

"Yes." Hunter could see the man process this. He didn't look happy.

"Do you know who Quentin Naff is?"

"Yes, he owns art freeports and is currently under investigation by the Swiss Police for some kind of art fraud."

"You're well informed, but not so much as you think. Did you know, for instance, that Quentin Naff swindled the Legacy out of twenty-five of the paintings you referred to?"

This was news to Hunter. "How and when did he do that?"

"Six years ago. The Legacy decided to sell them, and Naff brokered the deal. Only it was a sham. The Legacy lost their paintings and got no money in return."

"Why are you telling me this?"

"I would have thought that was obvious. Let me explain. I'm talking to you, and not Miss Swift or her father, because you're the driving force here. Tell Addison Swift that he can stop looking for the heirs because they no longer have the paintings; Quentin Naff does. My employer has no interest in you, Miss Swift, or her father—*if* he quits this line of inquiry. If you can't convince him to stop, I'll kill all four of you including the professor's wife."

The two men glared at each other for a moment. "You said Naff swindled them out of twenty-five paintings. There are thirty Wicar paintings. What about the other five?"

"Each of the Legacy members kept one."

That explains why Marie said he had only one left, the one left at the Ringling.

Suddenly Hunter got a hunch. "What if the Swifts stop looking, but the Ringling Museum of Art keeps investigating? We can't control them."

"Ah yes, the Ringling Museum of Art. I'm afraid its fate is already sealed. It is going to be ruined on schedule."

There it is, the voice behind the threat to ruin the museum.

"Why would your employer do that?"

"He has his reason."

"Who is your employer?"

"Someone you don't want to meet, McCoy. You also don't want to meet me again." Then the man disappeared, just like that, as quietly as he appeared, Hunter could have sworn he was looking at him one moment and not the next. He was gone before Hunter could ask him about May third and the twenty-one day countdown. He checked the house to make sure he was alone, then returned to the kitchen.

"Dad, are you there?"

"Hunter," he heard his dad whisper, "is he gone?"

"Yeah, he is."

"Jesus, Hunter, what the hell was that?"

"There was a man with a gun and—"

"I know. I think I got a picture of him."

"A picture? How did you do that?"

Hunter knew his dad was using Face Time on his MacBook Pro computer. Hunter had bought it for him the previous summer and his dad had been getting better at using it ever since. He'd gone from "I don't need that silly thing" to "wow, this is pretty neat." He'd also gotten his dad an iPhone and told him to keep it with him so they could stay in touch no matter where either of them was.

"Here it is. Look."

Hunter checked his phone's screen and saw a great closeup of the face of the man with the gun. "How did you—?"

"I used the camera feature on the iPhone to take a picture of the computer screen that had him on it. I set it for a closeup and snapped away. Would you like me to email it to you, or should I text it?"

"Dad, you are—amazing. There's no other word for it. That was great work. By all means email it. Wait, did you say text it? I can't believe you know how to text. When did you learn that?"

"I think it was right after Ben Franklin and I did that thing with the kite. You remember that? It was in all the papers."

40

AFTER ASSURING HIS DAD HE WAS ALL RIGHT, and while waiting for Genevieve's call, Hunter thought about the man with the gun. He had to be working for someone. Was it Pierre Arseneau? Had Arseneau hired Benny Bergen to look for his stolen painting because he thought Genevieve had it? But if Arseneau hired Benny Bergen, why would he have this guy kill him? Unless Bergen just screwed up by attacking Genevieve physically and Arseneau had him killed in turn for his bad judgment.

No, Hunter thought, that didn't wash. This guy worked for someone else, but who? It had to be the Legacy or someone in it, since his employer wanted Addison to stop his research into the Wicar heirs. The Legacy was the only group that would care. So if it wasn't Arseneau, it had to be one or more of the other four members. But then, what goal would they have that would be different from Arseneau's? Did one or more of them have an agenda of their own? Was one of the others behind the threat to ruin the museum? But then, why?

His thoughts turned to Quentin Naff. Could he have sent the gunman? If the guy had told the truth and Naff stole their paintings, Naff was no friend of the Legacy. But then why would he care about Addison's research on the Wicar heirs? Of course, it would bring unwanted attention to the freeports if it became common knowledge that the looted Wicar paintings had been stored there. And, Hunter thought, for a man already under investigation for fraud, he certainly wouldn't want an investigation into the missing Wicar paintings that might point at him. But if the gunman worked for Naff, why would he tell him that Naff stole the paintings?

Fully aware that the gunman had been a professional hired killer, Hunter knew he had to be careful not to put Genevieve or her father or the Arseneau women in any danger. He had to keep them safe while he investigated.

Genevieve called and asked him to pick her up. In thirty minutes they were back in the house. They poured wine and decided to eat out on the lanai instead of in the kitchen. Over pizza he told her what had happened.

"What's going on here, Hunter?"

"I don't know, but there are only nine days left. I'll call Klinger and the director in the morning."

In the morning, before calling them, he called Eduard Gautier from Interpol.

"What have you learned, Hunter?"

"I was just visited last night by a very nasty man with a gun. He told me he was responsible for the murder of a smalltime local thug who was probably responsible for the attack on Genevieve. It's possible he's working for the Legacy or even Quentin Naff."

"Naff?" the Interpol man said, surprised. "Naff's hired a hit man?"

"I don't know, but the man is here in Sarasota. I've got a photo of him. I'll send it to you in a minute. What I want to know is, can you check him out and see who he is?"

"How did you get a picture of him if he had a gun on you?"

"That's a great story in itself. I'll tell you later. Oh, he also had an Eastern European accent of some kind. See what you can do with it."

"Okay. Send it over."

QUENTIN NAFF INTERVIEWED EVERYONE who had anything to do with the Ringling's Gainsborough. His security chief ultimately found out how it had been damaged. Initially, the only oddity the chief found was that the employee who crated the Gainsborough, a fifty-two-year-old man who'd been with them for eleven years, died of an apparent heart attack two days after crating it for delivery to the Ringling Museum. CCTV footage in the relevant areas showed no unauthorized person at the freeport in proximity to the painting after it was crated. Further, the head of the department swore the painting was unblemished when he examined it and had the man crate it.

It was his security chief at the freeport who found the answer. After the museum director complained about the damage and the man who did the crating died unexpectedly while presumably in good health, the chief got suspicious. He learned from other employees that the man was apparently having financial problems. The solution to what had happened came when the chief examined the man's locker at work and found an envelope with a large amount of cash—almost ten thousand dollars. No one, including his wife, could offer any explanation for the source of the cash. The obvious conclusion was that someone paid him to damage the painting, and he either died naturally from the heart attack or was killed.

QUENTIN NAFF RETURNED TO THE OFFICE of the director of the Tampa Freeport and told him to call the director at the Ringling Museum of Art and set up an appointment with the man. "Tell him I've come from Zurich to meet with him personally in his office at his convenience."

41

PIERRE ARSENEAU, BENOIT SURETTE, and Quentin Naff. Hunter knew one or more of these people was somehow involved in everything that had happened. Arseneau had likely hired Benny Bergen and was definitely behind the development of the paint-eating bacteria. He could also be behind the threat to the Ringling. But what was his motive? Did the man's abuse of his wife extend so far he'd threaten the institution she supported? They were definitely going to find that out when the man got back from Prague.

He knew much less about Surette and Naff. Surette was clearly working with Arseneau on some project dealing with the freeport, but what was it? And then there was Naff. Had the man really swindled the Legacy out of their paintings? What was his game?

Just as he was thinking he needed to know more about Surette and Naff, he got a call from Kyle Klinger.

"McCoy, I just learned that the owner of the Freeport Naff in Tampa, Mr. Quentin Naff himself, arrived in Tampa two days ago. He called Director Bertram and told him he was very concerned about the damage to the Gainsborough that Whitfield found and consequently had come to Tampa to investigate. He has an appointment with the director at two o'clock this afternoon. Do you want to be there?"

"Yes, of course." *Great*, Hunter thought, *now maybe I can at least get some answers about Mr. Naff.* "Will you be there too?"

"Sure. It will be you, me, and Whitfield, along with the director and Naff."

Hunter wasn't sure how to approach Naff about his suspicions or even if he should. He figured he'd just play it by ear and see how the meeting went. He wondered if there was any truth to the gunman's claim that Naff had stolen the Legacy's paintings. He thought Whitfield might not know that bacteria on the Gainsborough had caused him to be sick, and he figured this was probably for the best at this point. He didn't want the young man accusing Naff.

At two o'clock, Hunter showed up at the director's office and Hilda ushered him in. Already present were the director, Kyle, Chris Whitfield, and a slim elderly man Hunter assumed was Quentin Naff. The director introduced him to Naff.

"Now that we're all here," Director Bertram continued, "I'd like to say that from the perspective of the Ringling Museum of Art and its administration and staff, we are pleased that you've taken this seriously enough to have come all the way from Zurich to address the issue."

Quentin Naff put up his hand at this and interrupted the director. "Sir, the charge you've leveled at our facility in Tampa is more than enough cause for me to take this seriously. I assure you, if the Freeport Naff Tampa is responsible in any way, however small, for the damage to your painting, it is in my company's best interest to correct whatever might have caused it as quickly as possible and to pay you for any damage you've had. In fact, I can report to you now that we are almost certain we've found the cause."

"What? You know what's caused it?" Director Bertram blurted out.

Hunter and the others perked up at this admission. "What caused it?" Chris Whitfield asked.

"We believe one of our employees, the man who crated your Gainsborough for transport to the Ringling, was paid a large sum of money to damage it during the crating. He died two days later so we can't interrogate him. We're continuing to investigate and we're coordinating with the local police."

"Mr. Naff," the director said, "in light of this information, I'd like a moment to confer with my people."

"Of course." Naff stepped into the outer office and pulled the door shut.

After he closed the door, the director said. "If this is true, Naff has been a victim of sabotage as much as we have. I'm wondering if we should tell him of the damaged painting problems we've been having here. What do you think?"

"I agree," Hunter said, "but I'd like to ask him several questions, if that's all right with you, Director?"

"Okay."

Hunter invited Quentin Naff back into the office. When everyone was seated comfortably, he began.

"Mr. Naff, you've been honest with us, and your investigation has paid off in that you know the damage to the Gainsborough was deliberate. The question is who paid your man? Who's behind this? We might be in possession of some information that can help in that regard."

Naff sat up straighter in his chair.

"In addition to the Gainsborough that was damaged deliberately in your facility, four other paintings have been defaced in a similar way here at the Ringling. None of them were ever in your freeport. He described the damage to the Cranach and the three landscapes while on exhibit at the museum.

"My God," Naff said, clearly agitated by this news, "What's going on here? Do you know who's behind this?"

"I believe so," Hunter said, "and I'm afraid it's someone that you know as well."

"Someone I know?"

"Yes. But before I tell you, let me explain how the paintings were damaged. The perpetrator used a spray containing a carefully engineered population of bacteria specifically designed to consume oil paint in old paintings."

"You mean someone deliberately designed bacteria to do that?"

"Yes."

"Who would do that? And why?"

"The bacteria were engineered right here in Sarasota by a company called BIOMOD. Does that ring a bell with you?"

"BIOMOD? No I—wait a minute. Wait a minute!" Naff shouted, standing up. "Pierre Arseneau. He owns that company."

Hunter smiled grimly and waited now that the fuse had been lit.

"That son of a bitch. I *knew* he was somehow behind all of this. That bastard has been spreading rumors that the freeports aren't safe and I've lost several big customers in Europe and Asia as a result. He and his Legacy group are doing this. This is the proof we need. They think I swindled them out of their paintings. That's what's behind the lawsuit against my company by Horst Mueller. That's why Interpol is on my ass. Goddamn him to hell. I haven't swindled anyone."

Then, composing himself again, he asked Hunter, "How do you know this? Do you have proof?"

"Yes, we have irrefutable proof that he specifically asked his chief molecular biologist to create bacteria designed to eat oil paintings. We don't have him spraying these paintings personally, but we have very good evidence that it was done at his direction."

Naff paced around the director's office for a moment thinking, taking it all in.

"Would you mind describing your issues with the Legacy?" Hunter asked. "It may help us put a stop to all this."

"Certainly," said Naff. "Arseneau and his four cousins in the Legacy initially funded my first freeport. When it succeeded beyond all expectations they sold their shares back to me and took a huge profit in the process. That was fine with me. I was happy to finally be the sole owner of my own idea. When I expanded with even more success, they wanted to buy back in. I didn't need them at that point and said 'Thanks, but no thanks.'

"Then, with Benoit Surette speaking for the group, they asked me if I could find a buyer for the twenty-five paintings the Legacy was storing as a group at the freeport. I said I'd see what I could do. About that time an art collector named Horst Mueller opened a storage area at the Freeport Naff-Zurich. He told me he was looking to buy, and I suggested the holdings of the Legacy might be of interest to him. With Benoit Surette, I arranged a meeting during which the three of us examined the Legacy's twenty-five paintings, still in their storage vault. Mueller said he was interested in buying the entire lot and came up with a very generous offer of four hundred thirty-two million dollars.

"Surette conferred with his cousins, and the deal was agreed upon. I did my due diligence and checked to see if the man was good for the money. He was. It was set up so that the funds would be transferred from Horst Mueller's account to a holding account that I use to broker transactions like these. Once the funds were in my account I would take my commission and transfer the balance to the Legacy's account at Credit Suisse. The plan was that the twenty-five paintings would be placed aboard an electric motorized delivery vehicle we use within the freeport. Once the vehicle with the paintings reached Mueller's storage area, his doors would be opened and the paintings placed inside. Two Freeport Naff guards accompanied the delivery vehicle throughout its entire trip, and they unloaded the paintings into Mueller's storage area. We have it all on CCTV. Mueller saw it and signed off on the completion. The plan then called for him to transfer the funds to my brokerage account.

"It was a perfect plan, except that it wasn't. The funds were never transferred, and the paintings went missing. Mueller claims he never got the paintings and that he did transfer the funds to my account as directed. He is suing me for taking his money and his paintings. The Legacy claims *I* stole their paintings. Both sides believe I swindled them. Gentlemen believe me, I'm the one who's been swindled. That money and those twenty-five paintings are somewhere, that's for sure. But I don't have any of them."

42

QUENTIN NAFF OFFERED TO PAY THE Ringling Museum of Art for the complete restoration of the Gainsborough and a year of free storage at the freeport for their troubles, and he assured the director that the security breach at the Tampa facility had been significantly tightened and the Ringling's remaining holdings there were perfectly safe. At the conclusion of the meeting, Hunter volunteered to drive Naff back to Tampa and much to his surprise, the man accepted. Hunter knew the drive over the Sunshine Skyway Bridge would take about an hour.

During the drive, Naff was reflective.

"The integrity of the freeports is of incredible importance to me, Dr. McCoy. This whole business—the sabotage of the paintings and the malicious rumors—has to be stopped. The Ringling Museum had every right to be incensed at the damage to their painting. Believe me, it won't happen again."

Impressed with the man's sincerity, Hunter believed he meant every word. "Do you mind if I ask you some questions about the deal to sell the Legacy's paintings?"

"Not if you answer a question of mine first," Naff said.

"Sure, go ahead."

"What's your connection here? You don't work for the Ringling, the director told me you're a medical school professor—and you have no background in art. Do I have that right?"

"Spot on, and guilty on all charges. I'm here because my friend, Genevieve Swift, who is currently at the Ringling as a visiting curator from the Louvre, was attacked in her home. What the director didn't tell you was that her father, a professor of history at Cambridge in England, has been trying to trace the heirs of Jean-Baptiste Wicar who may still be in possession of paintings looted by Wicar during the Napoleonic wars in Italy. One of those paintings, currently owned by Pierre Arseneau, was recently left at the museum by his wife, along with a note warning Genevieve about the risk the Legacy posed to her father if he continues looking into the family history."

"I see," said Naff. "I can tell you for certain that the Wicar paintings the professor is looking for are the twenty-five that went missing, and the members of the Legacy are probably the heirs as well. Arseneau and his damned group are convinced I swindled them, and they're trying to put me out of business by spreading malicious rumors, and now they're even using this bacteria thing. It's possible they still have all the paintings somewhere, although I believe Horst Mueller, who's suing me actually has them and all of his money as well."

"The thing that bothers me about that," Hunter said, "is if Mueller has the paintings and the money, why sue you? Why bring all that publicity and the ensuing police investigation on himself, as well as you? Why not simply enjoy the paintings and the money and keep quiet?"

"I've wondered that myself," Naff answered. "McCoy, I have another question for you. You think like a cop; where does that come from?"

Hunter told him.

"I knew there was more to you. Give me a few minutes to think about something."

They drove in silence for another fifteen minutes, while Hunter had to admit to himself that he was beginning to take the elderly gentleman's side. Finally Naff spoke again.

"My security people have been all over the case of the missing paintings and the supposed money transfer.

They've found nothing out of the ordinary. Still, I know something went wrong with the transfer, something we've missed. You say your mission is to protect your friend whose father is investigating the looted Wicar paintings. I believe the twenty-five paintings missing from my facility are those twenty-five. Could I persuade you to accompany me back to Zurich to look at the facility there, and do your own investigation into the transfer process, and see what you can learn? Of course I'll pay all your expenses along with a hefty fee for services. I believe that anything you find out that helps me will also help you in your task. What do you say?"

Hunter considered the idea. There wasn't anything else for him to do in Sarasota at the moment. The police would meet Arseneau as soon as his plane landed back at the airport on Friday and probably take him into custody. But there was the question of the gunman and his threat if Genevieve and her father continued looking into the Wicar heirs.

Hunter's phone rang. It was Eduard Gautier. "Eduard, I'm driving right now. I'll pull over at the next exit, hold on."

He pulled into a rest area just at the foot of the Skyway Bridge. Turning to Naff, Hunter said, "Excuse me, but I need to take this call." Then he stepped away from the car, far enough that Naff couldn't hear. "Okay, Eduard, what is it?"

"Your gunman. His name is Petr Havel. He works for Benoit Surette, one of the Legacy members from Prague. He's a nasty piece of work. It's said he moves like a ghost. He does the more unsavory work a powerful man like Surette needs from time to time. Watch out, Hunter, he's bad news."

"Do you know where he is right now?" Hunter asked.

"Yes. Yesterday he took a Delta Airlines flight out of Tampa to Prague. He's still there."

"Anything else?"

"Nope, that's it for *now*," Gautier said.

"Thanks, Eduard. Oh, and Eduard. I didn't mention it earlier, but when Havel had the gun on me he didn't look well—as if he was sick or something. It may not mean anything. Just thought you should know."

He resumed the drive. With Havel back in Prague and Benny Bergen dead, Hunter felt that Genevieve would be safe if he took Naff up on his offer and went to Zurich. But he had a few questions first.

"Let's consider the transfer of the paintings and the cash. The way I see it, these are the possibilities: One. Horst Mueller has the paintings and still has his money, and he's lying about having transferred it to your brokerage account. Am I correct that this is your position?"

"Yes."

"Two. You have the paintings and the money that Mueller transferred to your brokerage account. This, of course, is *not* your position."

"Absolutely not. In fact I don't personally own any paintings. I get enough enjoyment out of seeing everyone else's. That's one of the perks of operating the freeports."

"And yet you believe the Legacy is convinced you have both, as is Horst Mueller."

"Yes."

"Let me ask you something. Do you believe the Legacy is acting as a unified entity? Are they all in agreement on this? Is it possible that one or more of them believe differently and may be acting independently?"

"I don't understand. What do you mean?"

"Two nights ago a gunman accosted me at home and said Genevieve and her father were of no interest to his employer and they should stop looking for the Wicar heirs because they no longer had the paintings, you did. He said you stole the paintings from the Legacy and the money from Horst Mueller. He also told me he had killed the man who attacked Genevieve Swift. I have reason to believe that man was working for Pierre Arseneau. Arseneau thought she'd taken his painting, and the man was in her house looking for it when he startled him.

"Now, I just learned from Interpol a few minutes ago, that the gunman works for Benoit Surette. If the Legacy is working together, why would one member, Surette, have another member's thug—Arseneau's—killed?"

Naff wrinkled his brow. "Where are you going with this, McCoy?"

"Who approached you with the request to find a buyer for the Legacy's paintings?"

"It was Benoit Surette. He showed up one day and told me that the group had met and decided it was time to find a buyer. They knew I brokered such deals."

"And how did you find Horst Mueller?"

"Well, he sort of found me. Two days after I met with Surette, Mueller approached and said he needed space in the freeport for his art and mentioned he was looking to buy additional art as well. I told him I had space for him and I told him about the Legacy's intent to sell some pieces. We secured a space for him, and when Surette and I showed him the Legacy's paintings, he offered to buy the lot."

"It didn't strike you as an almost too good to be true coincidence that such a buyer would show up so soon after meeting with Surette?"

"I certainly thought it was good fortune. Do you suppose that Benoit Surette struck a deal with Horst Mueller to steal the paintings from the other members of the Legacy? Maybe Mueller gets to keep his money, and perhaps some of the paintings, as payment for his part in the scam."

"Or," Hunter offered, "maybe Surette somehow got it all, the paintings and the money, and made it look as if you got it all. That would explain why Mueller and the others in the Legacy are so convinced that you swindled them and why Mueller is suing you."

"My God, you may be on to something. I always thought there was something off about Surette."

"I'll tell you what, Mr. Naff. I'll take you up on your offer to check out things at the freeport in Zurich."

43

"LADIES AND GENTLEMEN, THIS IS HUNTER MCCOY." Quentin Naff was addressing his security staff. "I've brought him in to take a fresh look at the transfer of paintings and funds supposedly carried out here between the Legacy group and Horst Mueller. You're all aware of the lawsuit brought against us by Herr Mueller. Dr. McCoy is just going to go over all we've already uncovered regarding this sale. I'm asking that you give him your complete cooperation. We're all on the same side here."

Quentin Naff turned the floor over to Hunter. "Dr. McCoy."

Hunter surveyed the group who were the brains of the operation. The four men included the head of the security department and his three divisional leaders. The two women made up the cyber department. Previously, one guy had run it, but after he won the lottery or something he left, and the two women replaced him.

"I'd like to start with a tour of the facilities and storage areas," Hunter said in a genial tone. After that I'd like to look at the relevant CCTV, and finally, ladies, I'd like to have you show me how the money transfer was supposed to work. Let's get started."

Hans Farner, the head of security, led the tour. Hunter was somewhat surprised to find that in spite of the vast wealth of art hidden behind locked doors, the hallways were quite ordinary-looking, with nothing on the walls and rows of discretely numbered doors. The quiet hum of air conditioning was the only noise, as the walkways were exquisitely carpeted. Farner pointed out that the facility was completely climate-controlled. This included temperature, humidity, air quality control, and light. The doors to the individual vaults were bright cherry wood over solid steel and featured a maximum-security retinal-scan locking system.

As they walked Farner pointed out that in addition to Mr. Naff's vault, there were a total of two hundred fourteen vaults and that the list of items stored at the freeport included not only fine art and gold bullion, but also jewelry, watches, gemstones, precious metals, antiques, vintage cars, wine, cigars, carpets, and confidential documents.

Farner pointed out the video monitoring equipment, located throughout. An art collector from Geneva was now renting the unit previously rented by the Legacy; they could only see it with the man's permission. Hunter told Farner to skip it for now. If he felt it was necessary later, he'd contact the man. Finally they reached Horst Mueller's vault, which was still empty as long as the lawsuit was going on. Using the freeport's bypass system, Farner was able to open this unit for Hunter's inspection.

Hunter scanned the interior, impressed. He might have been in a gallery somewhere without any paintings on the walls. Farner told him that Mueller hadn't yet moved any of his paintings to the vault. After the lawsuit was filed, the authorities examined his art—held by a competing freeport facility in Geneva—and Mueller had papers for all of it. None of the Legacy paintings were part of that collection.

The room was about twenty by fifty feet with comfortable chairs and sofas evenly spaced throughout. The floor was inlaid hardwood, and the beautifully furnished room featured a bar and wine cabinet in one corner. Hunter thought the superrich certainly knew how to live. He noticed a steel door on the back wall. "Where does that go?" he asked.

"It leads outside. It can only be opened from this side. There are no handles or locks on the outside for security. If an owner wants to take something out he can, but he can't get back in that way."

"So when the transfer occurred, when the Legacy paintings were presumably brought into this room, there were no paintings on the wall at all?" Hunter asked.

"That's correct."

Hunter moved over to the bar, an L-shaped counter with two stools. Behind it was a small sink, and a wine cabinet, which was empty. There were no bottles of any kind on the back counter. He checked the cabinets and found them empty as well. The bar was clearly ready for the next client.

Farner pointed out the security cameras throughout the room and asked Hunter if he'd like to see anything else.

"Are these cameras on at all times, twenty-four-seven?"

"Yes," Farner answered, "unless the owner turns them off temporarily for privacy reasons. Sometimes they don't want us snooping while they have guests in here."

"I see. Can they accidentally leave them off when they leave?"

"No. As soon as the room is empty—determined by sensors— the cameras come back on. It's automatic and the owner can't change it."

"Are all the units exactly like this one?" Hunter asked, beginning to get an idea.

"No, some are smaller, and two are larger and even more luxurious."

"What about those on either side of this one?"

"Oh, those are exactly like this one. In fact this entire wing is made up of identical units."

"When you say identical, do you mean everything—the flooring, the walls, the bar, the lights?"

"Yes. They're exactly alike."

"I'd like to see the units on either side of this one."

"I can show you one but not the other, which is occupied. That owner has been using that unit since the freeport opened. You'd have to get his permission to get in there."

"Okay, show me the empty one."

Next door, Hunter saw the exact same room. The floors, walls, furniture, and bar were identical. The cabinets behind the bar were empty as before. There was an unopened bottle of wine in the wine cabinet, but otherwise the bar was empty.

"Looks like someone forgot that," Hunter said, pointing at the bottle.

Farner opened the glass door and removed the bottle of wine. "Wow, this is a vintage Chateau Lafite-Rothschild. It must be worth a few grand. I'll take it to Mr. Naff."

Satisfied with this part of the tour, Hunter said, "I'd like to see the CCTV footage now."

"Of course, follow me."

Back in the security center Farner had his TV monitor chief run the footage. He started with the removal of the paintings from the Legacy storage facility. As they watched Hunter could see each piece being carefully loaded onto the driverless transport by the two men from loading. Farner gave Hunter their names. They'd each been with the freeport for over ten years and were highly trustworthy. The paintings weren't crated for this short trip, and were clearly visible. As Hunter watched the monitor he could see the date and the time moving forward by the second. When the transport was loaded, the two men guided it down the hallway to Mueller's storage area. Mueller had previously given permission to open it in order to receive the art. He wasn't there personally, as he had business in Berlin at the time.

Hunter watched the men unload the twenty-five paintings, stack them against the walls, relock the door and leave. The entire operation had taken about forty-five minutes.

Farner looked at Hunter. "There you have it. That's what we've got."

Hunter had to admit. The footage was pretty conclusive. The paintings had clearly left the Legacy's storage area and were transferred to Mueller's.

So where are they now?

"All right," he said, "we may come back to this later. Now I'd like to look into the money transfer."

Farner brought Hunter to a room adjacent to the main security area, where they found two very excited women at their computer keyboards.

"That's it. My God, Ina, that's how he did it. We've got him."

Hunter wondered what all the excitement was about. The two women had been quiet and subdued when he'd been introduced to them earlier, but now the two were agitated and high-fiving each other.

"What have you got?" Farner asked, bewildered by their jubilation.

"Okay, okay," said the woman called Ina. "When Dr. McCoy, sorry—Hunter—said he wanted to look at the case with fresh eyes, Millie and I decided to do that ourselves. It's been a while since we dug through all this, so in a way we were also looking at it with fresh eyes. They just happened to be our own."

"So what did your fresh eyes find?" Hunter asked.

"Plenty," Ina said. "We have a copy of the complete transfer setup from Horst Mueller's computer. He'd shared this with us earlier as proof that he made the transfer to Mr. Naff's brokerage account. We also have a copy from the police. Millie and I have been over it many times, and on the surface it appears that Mueller did just what he said he did. His computer sent the funds to the brokerage account number that we supplied him. That way, when he pressed send on his computer, the money should have automatically shown up in the brokerage account. Deal done, money transferred.

"Only it didn't happen. The transferred funds never got here. So what happened? If Mueller sent them, and we didn't get them, where did they go? The only possibility is the account number was changed for a surreptitious side transfer to some unknown account and then immediately changed back to the Brokerage account."

"Is there any record of that? Can you check that out?" asked Hunter.

"Can and did." The two women high-fived again.

"Normally there would be a digital record of a change in the account number," said Ina. "You can't make a change like that and not have it recorded. If it happened, it will be there somewhere. Of course we looked earlier and found nothing. All indications were that the only number on the account was the brokerage account. Still, when you said we should look at it with fresh eyes, we decided to take another look. Millie found it. Tell them, Millie."

Millie beamed. "You have to understand that the goal here was to change the routing number for the transfer, then change it back to the brokerage account, while leaving no record of the change. How do you do that? So I thought, how would I do it? I'd write a small program to change the number to another account on the 'send' command that would automatically revert to the original number when the transfer was complete. A second part of the program would erase any digital footprint of the event. The program is not on the sender's computer, so there is no record of it there. All it takes is a clever hacker with access to the sender's computer.

"How do we know it would work, you ask? We just did it. Ina just tried to send one dollar to the brokerage account, using the account's proper number. It never got there but showed up in my bank account instead. I hacked into her computer ahead of time, activated the program on my computer, and when she pressed send, the numbers changed, and I got the dollar. The program erased the record of the change on her computer, and I backed out of the hack. Easy peasy. Done deal."

Hunter nodded his approval. "Fantastic work, Millie. You too, Ina."

"A hacker?" said Farner. "So you're saying that Mueller is a victim instead of the perpetrator? Then where did his money go?"

"Where indeed?" asked Hunter. "That, Mr. Farner, is the next question."

44

BACK IN THE COFFEE ROOM WITH FARNER, Hunter considered the implications of Mueller being a victim.

"If Mueller was hacked and he's been telling the truth about transferring the money, where did it go? Since it clearly left his account and clearly never showed up here, it had to go somewhere. And wherever it went, it was at the direction of the person or persons responsible for a huge swindle involving the money and the paintings. We've got a lot of victims here. Mueller was swindled because he claims he lost his money and didn't get the paintings. The Legacy presumably was swindled because they claim they lost their paintings and didn't receive the money. And Naff has been charged with fraud and faces a lawsuit because he is being accused of taking Mueller's money but not delivering the paintings, plus he says he's suffering from unfounded rumors perpetrated by the Legacy designed to ruin his business."

"So we have two issues here," Farner said. "One, who got the money, and two, where are the paintings."

Hunter finished his coffee and stood up. "Let's go back over that CCTV footage again. Maybe there's something there." Then, chuckling, he added, "We'll do what Ina and Millie did. We'll look with fresh eyes."

Forty minutes later they concluded there was nothing new to be learned from watching the paintings being loaded onto the transporter at the Legacy's storage area. They looked at it four times and nothing new showed up.

"All right," Hunter said, "let's try the transport from the Legacy area to Mueller's area."

Again, nothing new showed up after four reviews. The two guards and the transporter slowly worked their way from one area to the other with no incident.

Next they went on to opening the door lock and entering Mueller's vault. Hunter saw the room was exactly as he'd seen it earlier. They watched as the two men carefully removed each painting from the transporter and placed it upright on the floor against the wall. Farner told him earlier that Mueller had specifically requested this so that he could see they were all there. One of the men had been instructed to call Mueller when the paintings were in place. Then he was to use Face Time on his iPhone to slowly scan the room to assure him that all twenty-five of the paintings were safely in his facility before the transfer. When he was satisfied that everything was in order, Mueller transferred the money.

They watched the CCTV footage showing them entering the room and placing the paintings three more times; again, nothing new. About to give up, Hunter said, "One more time."

The CCTV camera inside the room was stationary and didn't scan. It just recorded everything that happened in front of it. The entire room was visible. Hunter had been focusing on the men unloading and placing the paintings. He hadn't spent much time looking at the rest of the room. This time he did and saw nothing unusual, just the familiar chairs and sofas, and, in the corner, the bar. The bar was clean and empty. He could see part of the glass door in the wine cabinet around the side of the bar, but not all of it. That's when he saw it: the single bottle of wine. There had been no wine in Mueller's wine cabinet, but there was a single bottle of wine in the vault next door.

"Farner," Hunter said, "look at that. What do you see?"

"Where?"

"In the wine cabinet. What do you see?"

"Shit. That's the room next to Mueller's. That's where the paintings went. You've found it, McCoy."

"Not exactly," he said. "The paintings aren't there now, are they? Can you get those two men up here? Let's talk to them."

"I already have, but in light of their going to the wrong room, we'll do it again."

Ten minutes later both men were sitting in the security office shifting nervously.

"We already told you everything, Mr. Farner. We got the orders to move the art and we did it. Just like it said."

"Not exactly like it said. You two took the art to the wrong storage vault."

"No we didn't, we checked it twice. Transfer the twenty-five paintings from A67 to A32 and place them standing up against the wall."

"Not A32, you imbecile, A33."

"No sir, A32. Here, look. This is the copy of the order sent to us."

Farner grabbed it from the man, read it, and frowned. Then he read it again.

"McCoy, look at this."

Sensing what he was going to see, Hunter took it and his fears were confirmed. The order said to deliver to A32, just as the man had said. "Who sent this order?"

Farner winced uncomfortably and licked his lips. "I did."

"It has to be another hack. You'd best get Ina and Millie on this right away."

Farner excused the two men with a gruff apology, and then slumped down in his chair. We've been played, McCoy. We've been played by an expert."

"Back to the paintings, Farner. We know when they went into A32. Can we look at CCTV footage of them leaving?"

"Sure."

They ran it from the time the two men left after delivering the paintings to see what happened. Approximately an hour after the two men left, the camera showed a single man entering A32. He wasn't recognizable as he had his back to the camera, which went blank almost immediately and stayed that way for forty-five minutes. When it came back on the paintings were gone.

"Shit, shit, and shit," Farner said slamming his fists on his desk. "He shut off the camera and it didn't come back on until he closed the door. By then he'd removed the paintings. He must have used the back outside door. We didn't live-monitor this vault because it wasn't occupied."

Farner called the security desk at the entrance. "Check the log for—he looked at the time and date on the camera—Thursday, July 16 six years ago at 13:23."

"Six years? Boss. What are you looking for?"

"Who had A32 at that time? And who checked in to access it on July 16 at 13:23?"

"Let me check; I'll call you back."

Ten minutes later he got the call back. "A32 was owned by Baptiste Sublette of Orleans. He checked in at 13:20 on July 16 and checked out at fourteen hundred."

"So," Hunter said. "He checks in, goes to A32, shuts off the CCTV, props open the back door, loads the paintings presumably into a vehicle waiting outside, closes that door, exits through the main door in the hallway, the cameras come back on, and he proceeds to leave building through the front entrance."

"Must be," grumbled Farner.

They called up the CCTV for the entrance and the hallways the man would have walked through and didn't get much, as he had a hat pulled low over his face.

"What about outside coverage of his getaway vehicle? Do you have cameras outside?"

"Of course. Let me check."

They watched it together. The man with the hat pulled low over his face loaded a van with the paintings and then reentered the vault through the propped-open back door that he then closed. A few minutes later, after exiting through the front door he can be seen walking around the building to the van and driving off. Of course the van had no plates.

Not surprisingly, when they tried to trace Baptiste Sublette of Orleans, they found that he *had died* three years before the transfer.

"We've got to tell Mr. Naff what we've learned," Farner said. "He's not going to be happy."

Hunter and Farner went to Naff's office and found the man staring out the window watching the planes taking off and landing at the airport. Fifteen minutes later, after being told what had happened to the paintings, Naff returned to the window and watched the planes again. Then, still staring out the window, he muttered. "So, we've all been swindled—by a dead man, at that. Baptiste Sublette. Nice name. Does it remind you of anything, McCoy?"

"Yes—Benoit Surette."

"Exactly."

"Farner, when did Baptiste Sublette take A32, when did he let it go, and did he ever have art in it, other than the twenty-five missing paintings?" Hunter asked.

Farner examined the printout on his lap. "He opened it on June 15 and closed it on July 17. He never moved any art into it."

"So," Hunter continued, "if Sublette is Surette, he's got the paintings and maybe the money as well. Also, he stole the paintings from his cousins in the Legacy. He's quite happy to have them think you swindled them, Mr. Naff, since it keeps them from looking at anyone else—like him."

"A clever plan," Naff said. "You've done very well, Hunter. Your 'fresh eyes' were just what we needed. Now it's time to bring in the police, and get this damn lawsuit and fraud charge off my ass."

45

QUENTIN NAFF DROVE HUNTER to the departure terminal at the airport for his return trip to Tampa. Naff told him to check his bank account when he got back. "Believe me, this time the transfer will go through."

"Thank you. I'm sure it will," Hunter said.

"Today, I'll have my attorney call Mueller's attorney. He's been ripped off, and I've been falsely sued and maligned. I'll also call in the police with the new information that you uncovered. You know, in retrospect, I don't know how we missed it all."

"Fresh eyes, sir. Fresh eyes."

"I'm going to give the police the circumstantial evidence we've uncovered that Benoit Surette may be the person behind all of this. Maybe they can dig up evidence that shows it. Anyway, thank you, Hunter. I'll keep in touch and let you know if we find anything."

"I'll do the same and let you know if I uncover anything of value."

WITH THE TIME ZONE CHANGES flying west, Genevieve met him that same night at 8:45 at the Tampa Airport and threw her arms around him when he exited the secure area. The kiss was sweet indeed.

"Whoa, I need to be gone a few days more often. That was nice."

"You think that was nice? Just wait, Yooperboy."

"Yooperboy?"

"That's another one, right?"

"Right you are, but where did you learn it?"

"I called your father yesterday to see how he was. We had a great talk, and he let on that people from the Upper Peninsula of Michigan—the UP—are often called yoopers."

"Can you imagine yourself a year from now? People will think you were born here. Of course, that French accent just might give you away."

"You don't mind, do you?"

"I'll show you how much I mind." In the middle of the terminal, with people everywhere, he wrapped her up and kissed her again like there was no tomorrow.

During the one-hour drive south to Sarasota, he told her everything they'd uncovered at the Freeport Naff in Zurich. He explained how the money was stolen, even though they didn't know where it went, and how the paintings had been stolen as well. The police would try to track the van that took them away from the back door of vault A32 at the freeport, though that would probably be a dead end after six years and no plates. They'd also try to track the man posing as Baptiste Sublette, who may have been Benoit Surette, or perhaps someone he hired.

She reported that Rand Conrad from the Sarasota PD called. "His men are planning to meet Pierre Arseneau's flight into the airport from Europe and bring him in for questioning. If Pierre Arseneau is guilty of engineering a bacterial spray to ruin oil paintings," Genevieve said, "and it can be proven that he was responsible for damage to the five paintings we know about, the police should be able to arrest him, right?"

"Right. And don't forget, he's also likely responsible for hiring Benny Bergen who tried to kill us. That's attempted murder. He's in big trouble."

"Is he also responsible for the threat to 'ruin' the museum?"

Hunter shrugged. "I guess he has a motive. He resents the fact that his wife spends so much time there, with her duties on the board and all. But what's the significance of May third or the number twenty-one? Maybe Klinger or Bertram came up with something in their searches. They were both going to check to see if the date and the number have any significance."

They stopped for a light dinner on the deck at Marina Jack, overlooking the downtown harbor and Sarasota Bay. It was a moonlit night, and Hunter diverted from his normal Manhattan and had a glass of cabernet sauvignon. Genevieve chose an excellent Argentinian Malbec that she described as "chewy."

"Chewy?"

"Sure. Compare it to your cabernet. You'll find your wine is a little 'thinner,' not quite so 'chewy' as this."

"Hmmm." He took a sip of both. "You know, I believe you're right."

They finished the excellent dinner and drove back to the house, where Genevieve showed Hunter that he wasn't as tired as he thought he was. There was no need to turn on any lights, as the full moon beyond the large windows illuminated the interior in a pale blue glow.

THE NEXT MORNING, SATURDAY, Genevieve found an email from Director Bertram wanting to meet with both of them in Klinger's office after lunch.

"What did you learn at the freeport in Zurich?" the director asked by way of getting the meeting started.

"Quite a bit, actually," Hunter replied. He summarized the elaborate double theft and swindle that had set both the Legacy and Mueller against Quentin Naff, while the perpetrator waltzed off with the paintings and the money.

"So the police don't know who the mastermind is, and they don't know where the paintings are," Bertram said, shaking his head in disbelief.

"That's pretty much it," Hunter agreed, "except for one thing."

"What's that?" asked Klinger.

"Look at the name, Baptiste Sublette. Does it remind you of anything?"

It didn't click right away with Klinger or Bertram, but it did with Genevieve. "Benoit Surette," she said.

"Right. According to Naff, it was Benoit Surette who first approached him and asked if he could find a buyer for the Legacy's paintings. And quite apart from the similarity of the two names, there is the fact that Baptiste is the middle name of Jean-Baptiste Wicar, the family's thieving ancestor. On top of that, Naff believes that Surette approached him to sell the paintings before he'd even discussed it with the other four members of Legacy. Eventually they agreed, but it was Surette's idea from the beginning.

"When Pierre Arseneau arrives tomorrow at the Tampa airport, the police will meet him and bring him in for questioning concerning the bacterial spray, your damaged paintings, and the physical attacks on Genevieve and me. I talked to them this morning, to give them several other questions to ask him as well, questions about the Legacy's role in the sale of the paintings and Arseneau's relationship with Surette. And there is one other thing. Naff believes that Arseneau and the Legacy are behind the rumors that have caused him to lose valuable clients over the past few years. I believe the police will have lots of questions for Mr. Arseneau."

"McCoy?" the director asked.

"Yes?"

"We have one more very large question that we don't have an answer for yet. Who is planning to ruin the Ringling Museum of Art in six more days, and why? And what are they planning to do?"

46

HUNTER LOOKED FROM BERTRAM to Klinger and back. "Have you two found anything?"

Klinger went first. "I searched our records for the past ten years for the date, May third. I got seventeen hits. Most were normal, things like delivery dates, appointments, and stuff like that. Two showed a little promise until I got into them, and then they disappeared as possibilities. The first involved a collision between a visitor walking on the grounds and one of our volunteer people driving a tram. The visitor was slightly injured, but I have to assume she was not irritated enough to be the cause of our threat."

"How can you assume that?" Bertram asked.

"Because after the accident she and the tram driver started dating and today are happily married and expecting their first baby. He still volunteers for us."

"Oh, okay. What was the other one?" asked the director.

"On May third three years ago, we had an incident in the Searing wing, where a nine-year-old child climbed up on an exhibit and knocked it over. The mother apologized profusely and helped set it up again. There was no follow-up to that, but it seemed to end well. I couldn't find any significance to the number twenty one, nothing at all."

"What about you, Director?" Hunter asked.

"The only thing I could find," Bertram said, "was not on May third, but on May first. It was also a security issue. You probably didn't find it, Kyle, because you searched only for May third. Seems that four years ago on May first we had some major vandalism in the courtyard. That was before my time. One of our new security people, a young guy from Europe, decided, for some reason known only to himself, to spray yellow paint on an outdoor sculpture in the courtyard. He claimed the culprit left the can there and ran off, but the only fingerprints on it were the guard's. Of course he had to be let go."

"I remember that," Klinger said, "He was just a young kid. I liked him. I don't know what made him do it. What was his name . . .?"

"Ballard," Bertram said. "Paul Ballard, from somewhere in France, I think the report said."

"Right, Paul Ballard," Klinger said. "It was a real shame. He killed himself a few days later."

Hunter's head snapped up. "A few days later? Maybe on May third?"

Bertram went to his computer. "Yeah, that's it. He killed himself on May third."

"I'm afraid to even ask this next question," Hunter said. "How old was he?"

Bertram went back to the computer. "Let's see, he was born on—May third. How about that? My God, he killed himself on his birthday. He would have been . . ."

"Twenty-one," Hunter said, guessing the answer.

"Yes. That's it. He killed himself on this twenty-first birthday on May third. That's got to be it," Bertram exclaimed.

Kyle and Hunter agreed. "Okay," Kyle said, "we need to check this out. Maybe someone is blaming us for his death, and this is their way of getting revenge."

"It is rather far-fetched but it fits," Hunter said. "It also explains why there were no conditions attached to the threat. What could the museum do to make it right? Nothing. Somebody thinks this is a righteous response to what happened to the young man."

"So," Klinger said, "our letter writer is either someone here in the Sarasota area, given the postmarks on the envelopes or the writer comes here to post them. We've got to find a way to look into Paul Ballard's past relationships to find this person. How do we do that?"

"What do your employee records have on him? They must at least have his address in Europe before he came here. It must be on an application," Hunter offered.

"I've got the employment records of those hired by my department back in my office," Kyle answered. "Come with me McCoy, we'll go through them. Director, maybe you can see if you have any more in the files you can access."

Klinger and Hunter retreated to the security office, where the security chief found Paul Ballard's folder.

"Ballard's birthday was on May third, and he'd have been twenty-one," he read aloud. "That checks out. He's from Beaulieu-sur-Mer, France. I don't know where that is, do you?"

"I believe it's on the French Riviera," Hunter replied. "I'll check it out. Just a minute." He used the map feature on his cellphone and found the location on the Riviera just southwest of Monaco. "Yeah, that's where it is. What else do you have?"

"There's an address and a phone number. Let's see, we also have a short paragraph telling why he wanted the job. Here, take a look."

He handed it to Hunter, who read it out loud.

> *My name is Paul Ballard. Above all else, I am honest and I never lie. I owe this to the upbringing and nurturing of my mother, Elise Ballard. I am an only child. I am a student studying painting at the Marched School in Aix-en-Provence. I am taking two years off from my studies to live and*

*work in the United States to
expand my English language
skills as French is my native
language. I believe this position
will give me the opportunity to do
that in a beautiful setting of art.*

"Doesn't make sense that an art major would spray paint on that sculpture, does it?" Hunter asked.

"No, it sure doesn't. And he was a nice kid as I remember, polite, always on time. Never missed work. He must have had some dark secrets, though, to have killed himself like that."

"How did he do it?"

"That was weird too," Klinger replied. "He hung himself from one of our banyan trees. Maybe you've seen those aerial stringers that reach down from the trees? He made a noose out of one of them and did it that way."

"How do you know it was a suicide and not a murder?"

"The police investigated and concluded it was a suicide. He even left a note. It was definitely in his handwriting. I remember seeing it. But that was also weird. Something about never meeting expectations and he saw no other option. Oh, and something about his mother. Said it wasn't her fault."

"Tell you what, Kyle, I'm going to go downtown and see if they'll let me read the police report on this thing. There might be something in there."

A HALF HOUR LATER HUNTER WALKED IN to Rand Conrad's office for the second time that day.

"McCoy, again? I hope you don't think we're going to put you on the payroll."

"Not likely. I already have a job, remember?"

Also, Quentin Naff just deposited twenty-five thousand dollars in my bank account for find-and-correct work at his Freeport Zurich.

"So what is it this time? I told you this morning that we don't need you tomorrow night at the Tampa Airport. I'll have a detective and two officers meeting Pierre Arseneau when he steps off his flight at nine thirty-six. Thanks for the extra questions. We may arrest him when they're done. We'll see."

Hunter nodded. "Good, you take care of Arseneau. You know what you're doing. I have a question about something else, though. You remember I told you that Elias Bertram, the Ringling Museum of Art's director, received a threatening message that said the museum would be ruined in twenty-one days from May third? It wasn't a demand for anything. It simply said it would happen. He's had two follow-up notes since then, and we've come up with a possible explanation of the May third day and the number twenty-one. Here's where you can help.

"On May third exactly four years ago, on his twenty-first birthday, a security guard at the museum committed suicide by hanging himself from a banyan tree on the grounds of the Ringling. He'd been fired after the museum administration accused him of vandalizing an outdoor sculpture. He left a note. Were you involved in that case?"

"No, I remember it though. That was Wally Osborn's case. He's in homicide. You want to talk to him?"

"Yeah, and it would help if you told him I know what I'm doing and have a legitimate right to know."

"I'll see what I can do."

47

WALLY OSBORN WAS A BIG MAN, EVEN BIGGER than Hunter, whose handshake enveloped Hunter's grip. He was pushing sixty and getting a little wide in the beam in the process. Still he had a ready smile and highly intelligent eyes.

"Conrad told me you're interested in the Ringling suicide four years back. Paul Ballard. That right?"

"Yes. Anything you could give me would be helpful. We think someone close to him may be planning to cause some damage to the museum in six days." He explained how they arrived at that conclusion.

"What we're after is someone who might have taken such offense at his being fired and killing himself for what he said he didn't do—damaging the sculpture—that they'd make such a threat. Did you come across anyone like that in your investigation?"

Osborn took a long pull on his coffee and set the mug down. Then he just regarded Hunter with steady eyes. "I heard about you, McCoy, at DOD. I was thinking about retiring when you came on the scene. I heard how you were recruited after you captured Mahmud e Rac in Pakistan. I also heard you lost your brother in that raid. Sorry about that. Anyway, I followed your career for a while just to see how you'd do. You did good, and then you quit. What happened?"

So Osborn apparently quit the DOD and became a homicide detective in Sarasota. Hunter was a little amazed that someone he hadn't personally told knew about his background with the department. If he remembered correctly, this was the first time it ever happened.

"I went back to school," he answered. "I'm a med school professor at the University of Virginia."

"From cop to professor. Don't imagine that happens much. But now you're being a cop again."

"Sort of."

"Hmmm." Osborn opened the folder on his desk and began to read aloud.

"Ballard, Paul. Age twenty-one. Death ruled a suicide. No evidence of homicide. He left a note. Mother: Elise Ballard. Father: unknown, no siblings. Mother's address: 16 Boulevard Edouard VII, Beaulieu-sur-Mer, France. Telephone number: +33 4 93 01 01 04."

Osborn looked up from his notes. "I called her, McCoy, Broke the news to her. Oddly, I had the feeling she wasn't surprised. I mean, she was broken up, of course, but she didn't sound surprised. Anyway, that's pretty much it. No other names came up. We had to close it the way it looked—suicide."

Hunter stroked his chin. "Not much there, is there?"

"No, sorry."

"Would you mind if I give Madame Ballard a call and push her a little to see what I can find, given the impending threat to the museum?"

"Be my guest. Just tell me anything you learn."

"You got it."

Hunter got up and the two men shook hands. "I'll be in touch," Hunter said.

GENEVIEVE WAS AT WORK so Hunter drove home, where he used the computer to look up Beaulieu-sur-Mer. It turned out to be a lovely seaside village on the French Riviera between Nice and Monaco. He examined the interactive city map that accompanied the website and determined that 16 Boulevard Edouard VII was on the periphery of the city in what looked to be the hills behind it. He assumed it was a primo property region with a great view down onto the town, the harbor, and the sea.

He did a quick calculation of the time difference and figured it to be early evening if she was home. He assumed she spoke English if Osborn interviewed her. Then he thought, What if Osborn speaks French? Maybe he should have Genevieve do this. In fact, that might be a good idea for several reasons. She might be more open with a woman than with him.

He drove to the Education Center and found her at her desk, just getting off the phone.

"That was the last owner of the damaged paintings," she said. "When we explain it to them, it's amazing how understanding they've been. Gretchen is hard at work restoring them all. When the owners get them back, they shouldn't even notice the difference."

Hunter nodded. "That's good."

"So what's up? I can see something's on your mind."

He explained what he wanted her to do and why. "What we're looking for is someone who might have taken his suicide so seriously that they'd threaten the Ringling like this. You'll have to be careful, because it might even be her. She was his mother, after all."

"All right. Make the call and hand me the phone."

He did, then sat back and listened for twenty minutes to a conversation completely in French that he couldn't understand a word of. Obviously the woman was willing to talk. Genevieve took copious notes. Hunter glanced over and saw they were also in French. He supposed it was faster for her that way. Oh well, she'd translate for him later, he reasoned. He got up, poured himself a cup of coffee, and strolled around her office looking at the books. Finally she ended the call, and he took his seat again.

"Well?" he said.

"Nice lady."

He tapped his foot.

"Here's everything I learned." She pushed her notes across the desk to Hunter and looked at him with that superior smile again.

"Hmmm."

"So, is there anything else I can do for you?"

Hunter rolled his eyes.

"Perhaps you could translate this for me?"

"One of these days, my darling, you're going to have to learn French."

"Right. But for now?"

"All right." She picked up her notes and began.

"Paul lived at home with her when he wasn't away at school in Provence studying art. He was a good kid and rarely got into trouble. When he did it was minor. He had a girlfriend in high school, but that apparently ended when he went off to college. The girl still lives in town and is now married with a child. When I told Elise Ballard about the threat to the museum and why we were looking into Paul— the May third date and the number twenty-one—she seemed to think it was a stretch on our part, but understood why we were looking into it. When I asked her if Paul was a happy boy, she waffled a little."

"Waffled?"

"Another idiom, huh? How am I doing?"

"I'll tell you when you tell me how she waffled."

"It felt as if she was weighing how much to tell me— or that she didn't want to put things in my head that might not be true."

"Okay, waffled is good in this case. Nice job."

Smiling, she went on. "Anyway, she'd always been proud of him and his desire to be a painter. She told him he could be anything he wanted as long as it made him happy. She only wanted that, for him to be happy."

Hunter sensed a "but" coming.

"But not so for his father."

"Who's his father?"

"She wouldn't tell me."

"Didn't or wouldn't?"

"Wouldn't."

"Hmmm. Are they divorced?"

"Yes. And she wouldn't tell me anything about him, nothing at all. I'm not sure, but it might be that she's afraid of him. Anyway, she said that his father wanted the boy to follow his path in business. He had no use at all for a son who wasted his time painting pictures. The father told Paul that if he didn't give up this nonsense and follow him into the family business, he and his mother would be completely disinherited."

"She wouldn't tell you his name or what the business was, or where he lived?"

"The only thing I could get was that he was in Europe but didn't live in France. Anyway, the boy was chronically conflicted. He wanted his mother taken care of, but he wouldn't bend to the father's will. She said he'd been extremely depressed for the two years prior to his death. That was why he wanted to get away from home. He thought a different environment might help, and his mother agreed."

"That sure adds to the likelihood it was a suicide."

"I agree," Genevieve said.

"I think I know a way to find out who the father is," Hunter said as he picked up his phone. "I'll call Eduard."

He made the call and got through immediately.

"Eduard, I have some information for you and a question."

"Okay, let's have the information first. Tell me it's about the case against Naff."

"Yes and no. Yes, it's about the Naff case; no, it doesn't make for a case against him."

"All right. Let's have it."

Hunter told him about going to the Zurich Freeport with Naff, and finding pointing to both Mueller and Naff being swindled by someone else. Eduard listened to everything, and when Hunter was done asked him a question. "So who do you think did it?"

Hunter had been thinking about this a lot since Zurich and came to the conclusion that as much as he disliked Pierre Arseneau, he didn't think it was him. "I would say Interpol should be taking a very close look at Benoit Surette."

"Okay, I'll give all this information to the chief investigator. Don't be surprised if he contacts you for more information. So what's your question?"

"A woman named Elise Ballard lives at 16 Boulevard Edouard VII, Beaulieu-sur-Mer, France, Telephone number: +33 4 93 01 01 04. She's divorced and had a son named Paul Ballard who committed suicide in Sarasota, Florida four years ago. I need to know the name and location of the husband who divorced her. He may very well be the person who is threatening the Ringling Museum of Art with serious ruin in five days."

"That shouldn't take long. Stay by the phone."

Ten minutes later Eduard called back. "You're not going to believe this, Hunter. The man who divorced her is none other than Benoit Surette."

48

PIERRE ARSENEAU WAS LOOKING FORWARD to getting home. He could afford to stay in the finest facilities, but still preferred his own bed. As the KLM flight made its final approach to Tampa International Airport he felt the last-minute trip had been worth it. The rumor mill his three cousins had been churning out had been clever and was working well, and Benoit was going to take care of Benny Bergen and Hunter McCoy. He shuddered a little at the utter ruthlessness of the man. Benoit was not someone he'd want as an enemy.

He cleared customs and looked for his driver. The man was supposed to meet him and accompany him to baggage claim. Annoyed, he scanned the crowd. Where was the idiot?

"Pierre Arseneau?"

He turned at the mention of his name then frowned in confusion at the sight of three serious-looking men.

"Who are you?"

"I'm Detective Osborn with the Sarasota Police Department. Are you Pierre Arseneau?"

"Yeah. What do you want?"

"We'd like you to accompany us to police headquarters in Sarasota, where we have several questions for you."

"What the hell is this? I'm not going anywhere with you."

"You can either come with us and call your attorney on the way if you wish, or we'll just arrest you here and take you in. The choice is yours."

Arseneau looked nervously over the man's shoulder, searching the area.

"Oh, and don't bother looking for your driver. He's not here."

"Arrest me for what? What's this all about? Why are you doing this?"

NINETY MINUTES LATER, WITH HIS ATTORNEY at his side, Pierre Arseneau was staring daggers across a table at Wally Osborn. Rand Conrad had assigned him to the case given his earlier connection to the Paul Ballard suicide. Also watching Arseneau through the one-way mirror glass in the interview room was Hunter McCoy.

Osborn began his questions. "Are you the owner of BIOMOD?"

"You know damn well I am. What the hell is this?"

Arseneau's attorney put his hand gently on his arm, silently telling him to calm down and answer the questions.

"Did you have your chief molecular biologist develop a bacterium that could eat oil paint?"

Pierre whispered in his attorney's ear and didn't look happy with him at the response.

"So what?"

"I ask you again. Did you have your chief molecular biologist engineer a bacterium that could eat oil paint?"

Arseneau shifted in his seat and replied reluctantly. "Yes."

"And what was the purpose of this oil-paint-eating bug?"

Hunter watched amused while the man struggled for a plausible response and then was stunned by the brilliance of his answer.

"My company engineers bacteria to digest oil in oil spills. It's an effective and ecologically safe way to deal with these disasters. But these bacteria are only effective against petroleum-based spills. There is nothing on the market to deal with commercial-grade triglyceride spills, things like linseed or walnut oil. A bacterium that can do that would be a commercial success. I had him build a species for that purpose."

Hunter couldn't believe it. He'd fed the bastard a defense.

Osborn got up and walked out of the room, then in to Hunter on the other side of the glass.

Hunter spoke first. "That's a crock. I told him about that when I went to his office. He'd had Algarve engineer the oil-paint-eating bacteria before he ever heard of a linseed oil spill. I'm sure Algarve will back that up."

Osborn went back into the interrogation room. "Give me the statistics on triglyceride oil spills that would make developing such a bacterium economically feasible."

"I don't have those figures here."

"How about some round numbers? Generalizations, if you will."

"Dammit, what's this all about?"

"It's all about your oil-eating-bacteria being sprayed on, and intentionally damaging, five paintings at the Ringling Museum of Art. The first was a Lucas Cranach oil painting in Gallery 3 at the museum approximately three weeks ago. The next was a valuable Gainsborough that was being removed from the Freeport Naff in Tampa for an exhibit on landscape paintings a week ago. At that same exhibit three paintings, all arranged for by your wife, were also sprayed and damaged."

Pierre Arseneau looked genuinely confused. Hunter watched the play of emotions across his face, as did Wally Osborn. It seemed as if Arseneau might know about the Lucas Cranach, but he appeared to be genuinely surprised by the others.

Arseneau's attorney stood up. "Unless you're charging my client with something, this meeting is over." He took Arseneau's arm to help the man up.

"Sit down, counselor," said Osborn. "I have more questions for your client here."

Still looking as though he was trying to process something he didn't understand, Arseneau sat back down. "This is bullshit. Now what?"

"Do you know a man named Benny Bergen?"

Pierre Arseneau turned white, sighed noticeably, and closed his eyes.

"Mr. Arseneau?"

Pierre Arseneau looked away from Osborn and stared at the wall, saying nothing.

"Mr. Arseneau, do you know a man named Benny Bergen? Did you hire him to burglarize Genevieve Swift's home and assault her, sending her to the hospital? Did you hire him to drive a car into her friend Hunter McCoy with the intention of killing him? Answer the questions."

Finally recovering a little, he whispered to his attorney, who listened and then said, "I'm going to instruct my client to say nothing more. Unless you're arresting him, we're leaving now."

"I'm not done yet, counselor. Mr. Arseneau, do you know of a man named Tony Carsten, in Cambridge, England? Did you hire him to burgle Professor Addison Swift's home to find out what he'd learned about the Legacy?"

Arseneau again closed his eyes and sighed, saying nothing.

"Did you threaten to 'ruin' the Ringling Museum of Art exactly twenty-one days from May third?"

Arseneau popped open his eyes, looking totally confused. "What? What the hell are you talking about?"

"You deny sending a note to the director of the Ringling Museum on May third threatening to ruin the museum in twenty-one days?"

"Of course I deny it."

"Stand up, Mr. Arseneau. I'm arresting you on the charge of aiding in the burglary and assault of Miss Genevieve Swift, and the attempted murder of Hunter McCoy. I'm also charging you with aiding in the burglary of Addison Swift in Cambridge, England."

Osborn read him his Miranda rights, and Arseneau buried his face in his hands as he was led away by two police officers.

"He's definitely guilty of something, McCoy," Osborn said to Hunter later, "I'm just not sure what. We've pretty much got him on the more serious charges of hiring Benny Bergen and Tony Carsten. But did you see his response to the charges of damaging the paintings?"

"Yeah," Hunter said. "He'd seemed to know about the Lucas Cranach damage, but the other paintings caught him completely by surprise. Either he didn't expect we'd link them or they were news to him. His total surprise at your question about the note to ruin the museum also looked genuine. I'm putting my money on Benoit Surette." Earlier, Hunter had told Osborn that Interpol identified Elise Ballard's former husband and the father of Paul Ballard as none other than Surette.

"The judge will set a high bail, given the attempted murder charges, but he'll be able to post it and be out right away," Osborn said. "We'll keep gathering evidence."

THE MORNING AFTER ARSENEAU'S ARREST, Hunter and Genevieve enjoyed an omelet on the lanai and discussed the impending ruination date of the Ringling Museum of Art, now only four days away.

"I've got to think Benoit Surette is behind the threat to the museum in retaliation for his son's being fired and his subsequent suicide. I'm also pretty sure that he's the big swindler in the loss of the Legacy paintings and Mueller's money. I think we need to get a complete picture of this man. When we go in to work, can you pull up everything

you can on Benoit Surette from the internet while I bring
Klinger up to date on the arrest of Arseneau and Surette
being Paul Ballard's father?"

"Sure, I can do that," Genevieve said.

At work she went into the Education Center while
Hunter walked across the lot to Klinger's office in the
Security building. Director Bertram was already there, and
they were going over precautions for "ruination day."

"Come in, McCoy," Klinger said. "We've decided that
we should close the museum for the day. We'll leave the
rest of the buildings and grounds open as usual, but close
the art museum under the pretense that we have a gas leak
that is being fixed. We'll put on extra security people that
day throughout the building and monitoring the CCTV.
We'll have guards at all potentially vulnerable locations
throughout the buildings. We've got four days left, so
starting today we'll be doing continual visual inspections of
every cranny and crawl space in the facility, looking for
anything suspicious. I've told my men to report anything
they find that's unusual, whether they believe it's a threat or
not. The County Sheriff's bomb-sniffing dogs will be used
after hours when the visitors are gone. If anything
dangerous has already been placed here or is placed over
the next few days, we'll find it."

Hunter nodded. "That sounds very thorough, Kyle. I
can't think of anything else you can do."

Bertram spoke next. "In the event he's planning some
kind of financial attack, we'll be freezing the museum's
bank holdings for thirty-six hours, starting six hours before
midnight on the day before and ending six hours after
midnight the day after. Also, we've changed the passwords
on all museum accounts."

"Now, as it happens my contact at Interpol
headquarters in Lyon can find out almost anything. I asked
him if he could find out who the husband was in the Elise

Ballard divorce proceedings. In ten minutes he had the answer."

"That's great, McCoy. Who is it?" Bertram asked. "He might be the note writer."

"I agree. His name is Benoit Surette. He's a cousin of Pierre Arseneau, one of the Legacy members. And he's beginning to look like the person who swindled Horst Mueller out of millions and his own family out of the Legacy paintings. I believe he also swindled Quentin Naff. If he believes that the Ringling Museum is in any way responsible for his son's suicide, he won't hesitate to take revenge. I'm sure he'd see the Ringling firing Paul as the real reason for his son's depression and suicide, rather then his own treatment of the boy."

"So what do we do now?" Bertram asked.

"I suggest that you two continue what you're doing. I'm going after Mr. Surette."

49

"BEN, WHAT ARE YOU DOING IN THERE? Hurry up. The driver will be here in ten minutes, and I don't want to be late. The ambassador and the deputy prime minister will be there."

Benoit Surette's head jerked, startled by his wife's voice. He'd been thinking about his son rather than the gala charity event his wife had orchestrated for that night. "I'll be ready, I just need a few minutes more."

He stood in front of the full-length mirror and applied the studs to his tuxedo shirt. His body was going through the motions of getting ready, but his mind carried him back four years to the news delivered to him personally by the American ambassador, Charles Linden. He supposed that the Americans saw him as an important enough person that news of this magnitude should be personally delivered by their highest-ranking official. "Your son is dead," the ambassador told them. "He's taken his own life in America. I'm truly sorry."

It made no sense. Paul had taken a job at the Ringling Museum of Art in Sarasota, Florida as a security guard and by all accounts was doing well. Of course Ben and his second wife wanted more for the boy but Paul had said he needed to "find himself" first, whatever that meant.

Ben recalled how he'd told his son that if he continued with this nonsense of studying painting instead of joining him in his automobile empire, he'd disinherit both him and his mother. It must have had an effect, as Paul had called him and told him that he needed time away in America for two years and then he'd come home and take a position with his father. In spite of everything, he'd loved his son and had given his blessing to this temporary diversion in his career path.

Because the job with the Ringling Museum of Art was in Sarasota, he'd contacted his cousin, Pierre, to inquire if Paul could live with him during the two years. Pierre had agreed and Benoit thought everything was going well until he got a call from Arseneau's daughter, Monica. Apparently Arseneau's disdain for the museum his wife worked at boiled over into contempt for Paul as well. Monica told him that Arseneau belittled the boy at every opportunity. Apparently he didn't treat his wife and daughter any better. She'd told him that Paul was getting more and more depressed and she was becoming seriously worried about his mental state.

Paul had always been a troubled youth. With his artistic temperament he'd suffered bullying in school, but had always seemed to deal with it—at least Benoit thought he had. Paul had suffered bouts of depression, and counseling seemed to have little effect. Still, he was a relatively happy young man when the depression wasn't dominating. Benoit thought he'd been doing well at the museum, and in their occasional phone calls Paul had assured him things were fine. That's why the suicide was so unexpected.

It wasn't until later, with the help of a private detective, that Ben got the whole story. A disturbed young man apparently came into the museum and sprayed yellow paint on some outdoor sculpture and then, just before running out, had thrown the can away. Paul had picked it up. Since his were the only fingerprints on the can and no one else saw anything, he was accused of the vandalism. CCTV footage didn't show the actual vandal. Paul insisted on his innocence but was dismissed from his job anyway. A few nights later he hung himself from a banyan tree on the museum grounds. Ringling officials said they were sorry, but they had to act on the evidence they had. That was the extent of their culpability as they saw it.

But Ben didn't see it that way, not by a long shot. His seething hatred of the place that he deemed responsible for his son's death could never be placated by the pious statement of their administration: "We're sorry for your loss, but we don't see his suicide as having anything to do with the Ringling Museum."

Then there was Pierre Arseneau. His continual badgering of Paul was equally responsible for Paul's depressed state. The Museum and Arseneau: the two killers of his only son.

He'd killed himself on his twenty-first birthday. Ben considered the number. He'd started his company when he was twenty-one. Against all odds he succeeded enormously. Life had been full of promise and opportunities, and he'd had the energy and enthusiasm of youth to take the chances necessary to set himself up for success. Life was wonderful, full of energy, hope, and promise. He was now one of the most wealthy and powerful men in the Czech Republic.

He should have been passing on this success to his son. But he never would. His son was dead. Murdered by the Ringling Museum and by Pierre as surely as if they'd put the noose around his neck themselves. Well, they were about to pay the price. Beginning on May third, to commemorate the twenty-one years of his son's life, he had started the twenty-one-day countdown to his plan to make them pay—the Ringling Museum of Art, and his cousin, Pierre. *Twenty-one*, he thought, *a fitting number*. He checked his watch. They would learn that in four more days, and he planned to be there to watch the fun.

"Ben, are you ready? The car's here."

"Yes, dear, I'm more than ready."

HUNTER LEFT KLINGER AND BERTRAM and went back to Genevieve's office to see what she had learned about Benoit Surette.

"The man is a major success story, Hunter. At fifty-four, he is probably the most recognized man in the Czech Republic after Miloš Zeman, the third and current President of the country. He is the sole owner and CEO of Czech Motors, the foremost automobile factory in the country. In addition he is the principal builder of those gorgeous tour buses that you see all over the continent. He doesn't even get much competition from other car manufacturers, as he has the franchises for selling most other luxury cars in the country like Mercedes, BMW, and Lexus, not to mention Toyota and Honda and others. In the press he's often called 'Mr. Motor.' Forbes lists him among the top twenty-five wealthiest men in the world.

"He's apparently a self-made man. He started Czech Motors at twenty-one, when he bought a gas station and garage. He quickly expanded that to a network and eventually bought out a small automobile manufacturing plant and grew it into a regional competitor. From then on he just gobbled up everything automotive in sight until today he practically owns it all."

"And he wanted his son to take over, only he wasn't interested," Hunter said. "He wanted to be an artist, a painter."

"He must have wanted that badly, to have turned all that down," Genevieve said.

"What about his personality?" Hunter asked. "Did you find anything that might lead us to suspect he'd be capable of enough revenge to 'ruin' a museum?"

"Only one thing. Give me a minute, I bookmarked it. Ah. Here it is, a story on the darker side of Mr. Surette. Three times over the past ten years the police have questioned him concerning violence to competitors. In each case the company was one Surette wanted to buy but they wouldn't sell. In one case an owner was beaten up; in another, the man's wife was harassed continually; and in the third—the most damaging—when the man wouldn't sell his auto parts plant to Surette, he claimed that Surette had his business torched and burned to the ground. None of these cases even made it to court, but they taint the otherwise shining picture of the man. In any case, Hunter, he doesn't sound like a man who would take kindly to an institution he thought had treated his son poorly—poorly enough to drive him to suicide."

"No, he sure doesn't."

Hunter walked around the office, thinking. *If I were this guy, what would I be doing four days from now? Would I go about my business waiting for a news report that my plan, whatever it is, had worked or would I want to be there to see it happen?*

"Genevieve, I think he's coming here. He'll want to enjoy his revenge personally. I think he has to come. I'm no psychologist, of course, but I think he is going to have to be present to get the full satisfaction he needs out of it."

"Why don't you call your friend Eduard and see if he can tell you where Surette is right now? It seems like Eduard can do almost anything."

"He'd disagree with your use of the term 'almost.' He'd tell you he *could* do anything, no almost about it. I'll call him now."

50

"EDUARD, I NEED SOME MORE INFORMATION on Benoit Surette. The threat to ruin the Ringling Museum is scheduled for four days from now, according to the note writer. I have reason to believe that person is Surette. I think he's planning to cause major harm to the museum on that day in revenge for his son's suicide. He holds the Ringling responsible, and I believe he'll want to be here to watch whatever it is he has planned."

"Are you kidding me, Hunter? Do you know how big a fish Surette is? The man's almost untouchable. No one's ever been able to make anything stick against him. He's ultimate Teflon. What do you want from me?"

"I need to know where he is. If he's in Prague now, he'll have to fly to Sarasota in the next few days. Is there any way you can track him for me so I know where he is and when he moves?"

"I'll see what I can do."

Hunter turned to Genevieve. "He said he'd see what he can do. That means he'll do it."

"You're lucky to have him on your side, Hunter."

"I know. I never take him for granted. Now there's something I think you should do. Call your father and tell him to lay off any research on the Wicar heirs for the time being until we get this resolved. You can tell him that it's likely that the Legacy group are the heirs, and the missing twenty-five paintings are probably part of the thirty he's been looking for. You can give him the names and locations of the five Legacy members we got from Eduard. And finally, tell him about the threat from Surette's gunman, Petr Havel. Come to think of it, I'd better call Eduard back and have him keep an eye on Havel too."

While Genevieve made the call to England, Hunter walked over to the library in the Education Center and browsed through the current art journals. He had to admit that the glossy graphics of paintings, sculpture, and other works of art that adorned the pages made the rather drab graphs and charts that typically made up a science journal article look unimpressive by comparison. *When this is over,* he thought, *I'm going to have to take a class on art appreciation at the university.* One of the advantages of teaching at a university was the opportunity to interact with highly educated experts in so many different areas. Further, most academics were delighted to have a colleague in an unrelated area sit in on one of their courses.

Hunter was reading an article on Sandro Botticelli, a fifteenth-century Renaissance painter, when he remembered something Arseneau had said while being questioned at police headquarters. Osborn asked him whom he saw in Prague. He'd said Botticelli, and then quickly corrected that to say his cousin, Benoit Surette. What was that about?

Figuring that Genevieve had had enough time for her call to her father, he had started to head back to her office when his phone rang.

"What have you got, Eduard?"

"Surette has a private jet, a Gulfstream G550 easily capable of flying between Prague, where it is currently in a hanger at Vaclav Havel Airport, directly to Sarasota if he chooses to do so. If he uses this, his pilot will have to file a flight plan and I'll know it immediately. If he flies commercial or by some other means, he'll be harder to track but I should still be able to do it."

"Does a flight plan also list the names of anyone on board?"

"It will list the principal passenger and the total number on board but won't necessarily name all of them. Why?"

"I'd also like to keep track of Petr Havel, Surette's hit man."

"We're still following him. Right now he's with Surette at his house. I'll keep you informed of any move either of them make in your direction. I've been instructed to give you any help you need, since your case overlaps with the Quentin Naff investigation. The Swiss and the Czech police are very interested and demand that you keep them informed of any developments through me."

"You got it. Thanks."

He returned to Genevieve's office, where she was just putting down the phone.

"Okay, that call's made. Father was delighted with all the information we gave him and said he'd throttle back any public conversation on his research until this is over."

"Throttle back? You just said throttle back?"

Genevieve shot him that superior smile of hers.

THE NEXT MORNING—WITH "RUIN DAY" three days away— Hunter called Wally Osborn to see if he'd learned anything else from Pierre Arseneau. If Arseneau wasn't behind the threats to the museum he might know who was. Hunter thought they needed to grill him on it.

"Not surprisingly, he's been released on bond," Osborn said. "The judge had him turn over his passport and ordered him to stay in the county during the investigation. We can still go to his house and question him though. Do you want to come with me and do it?"

FORTY-FIVE MINUTES after Osborn picked him up, they drove into the Arseneau compound on Lido Key and knocked on the front door. Marie answered, and Osborn identified himself.

Marie nodded. "Okay, I'll get him. Hi, Hunter, nice to see you."

A few minutes later an unsmiling Arseneau came to the entrance.

"What do you want? I don't have to talk to you without my lawyer." Then he glared at Hunter. "McCoy? What are you doing here?"

So he knows who I am, thought McCoy.

Osborn took over. "We have a few questions and you can decide whether to answer them or not. May we come in?"

Arseneau continued to stare at Hunter, seemingly trying to make a decision. Finally he said, "All right, come in."

He led them to a large sitting area in the front of the house adorned with enormous paintings everywhere. Hunter didn't recognize any of them but assumed they were originals. Arseneau, no doubt in an attempt to appear unthreatened, asked if they would like coffee. They agreed, and a few minutes later a uniformed maid appeared with a pot and three cups. When they each had theirs, and were comfortably seated, Arseneau asked, "All right, what do you want to know?"

He and Osborn had agreed earlier that Hunter would begin the session. "Before I ask any questions, Mr. Arseneau, I'd like to tell you what we know. I'm sure some of this you already know, but I'm equally sure that some of it you don't. We know that six years ago, you and your cousins—the Legacy—arranged for Quentin Naff to sell twenty-five paintings that had originally been looted by your ancestor, Jean-Baptiste Wicar, from the Duke of Modena. We also know that the initiator of the idea to sell them was your cousin, Benoit Surette, but you all agreed. The buyer was to be Horst Mueller from Germany, who was to pay your group four hundred thirty-two million dollars for them. The deal went bad, and you lost the paintings and never received any money for them."

"Yes, that bastard Naff stole the paintings and the money." He narrowed his eyes at Hunter. "How do you know this?"

Hunter explained what he'd learned at the Freeport Naff in Zurich from the CCTV footage. "Quentin Naff didn't take your paintings, and he never received the money. Someone else did. Whoever that is swindled you and your group and put the blame on Naff. It was very cleverly done, and so far he's gotten away with it."

Arseneau got up and paced the large room. Wally and Hunter left him alone so he could take it all in. Finally he stood directly in front of them and asked Hunter the right question.

"Who owned the vault next to Mueller's?"

Hunter smiled inwardly. This was exactly the question he wanted Arseneau to ask, and he watched the man's expression closely as he answered.

"It was reserved one month before and closed one week after the sale by a man from Orleans, France named Baptiste Sublette. The only Baptiste Sublette from Orleans is on record as having died three years earlier."

Arseneau stiffened and closed his eyes as if in pain.

"Benoit Surette."

51

HUNTER AND OSBORN WATCHED AS ARSENEAU set his jaw and repeatedly clenched his fists. Obviously, the man was coming to the same conclusion as Hunter: Benoit Surette could be behind the whole swindle. What Hunter wanted to know was whether Arseneau thought his cousin was capable of it, and apparently he did.

"What did you want to ask me?" Arseneau asked, still clenching his teeth.

Hunter had thought through the questions he was going to ask so as not to have the man clam up and call for his lawyer.

"At the Police Station earlier we asked if you had anything to do with the five paintings either belonging to or on loan to the Ringling Museum of Art that were damaged recently when sprayed with your company's newly engineered bacteria, the one that is capable of digesting triglyceride spills like linseed or walnut oil. Four of these five were to be on display for a recent exhibit called Landscapes Through The Ages at the Ringling Museum. They included a Gainsborough recently removed from Freeport Naff in Tampa and three others on loan to the museum. You said you had nothing to do with their damage. Is that correct?"

"Yes. I told you that earlier. How could that even happen?"

"Now consider my next question very carefully before you answer. Did you have anything to do with similar damage to a fifteenth-century painting by Lucas Cranach in

Gallery three of the museum approximately three weeks ago?"

Arseneau turned away, and then replied with a scorching look. "I won't answer that question without my lawyer present."

"All right, let's go back to the other four paintings that were linked to the exhibit. Since they were damaged by your company's product, can you think of anyone who could have or would have done it? Who had access to the spray?"

Hunter and Osborn both watched, as the man truly appeared to be thinking exactly that. If he didn't do it, who did?

"I don't know," he finally said. "All the product is at the plant. I suppose someone could have broken in and taken some, but I can't think of who that would be."

"Did you write notes to Elias Bertram threatening to ruin the museum twenty-one days from May third?"

"Good God, no. I told you that already. What is that all about?"

"Can you think of anyone who would make such a threat, someone who might wish harm to the institution for some reason?"

He shrugged and said, "No. No one."

"I see. Well that's all the questions I have. How about you, detective?"

Hunter knew Osborn wouldn't ask him any questions about Benny Bergen and the attacks on himself and Genevieve, or Tony Carsten and the break-in at Addison Swift's house, since his arrest on those charges required the presence of his lawyer.

"Nope, that's it," said Osborn. "Thanks for your cooperation, Mr. Arseneau."

At the door, Arseneau said, "I didn't know any of that about the art sale, six years ago."

Hunter nodded, accepting that fact as they left.

Hunter asked Osborn to drive him to the Ringling, since Genevieve was already there with the car. "So what's your take on his answers to the sprayed paintings?" Hunter asked.

"Pretty much the same as we had on Friday when we questioned him. He's got something to hide about that first one, the Lucas whatever, but he seems genuinely adamant that he doesn't know anything about the other four."

"My thoughts exactly. In fact he's not only confused about who did it, but that they did it at all."

"Looks like he came to the same conclusion you did about Benoit Surette, though," Osborn said. "If he tries to contact him we'll know; we've got all his numbers covered. What about the threatening notes to ruin the museum? Do you believe what he said?"

Hunter felt in his gut that Arseneau was genuine here.

"I don't think he did it, even though he has no love for the place according to his wife. Still, he might have some idea who did, or at least would have a reason to do it. He has to know about Benoit's son's suicide"

Then changing the subject, Hunter asked, "How are you doing on linking him to Benny Bergen or the guy in Cambridge, Tony Carsten? Anything there?"

"It's slow going with Carsten. They've triangulated the towers that picked up the call to Carsten from the burner that was used. The general area was just south of downtown Sarasota. If we could find the phone we could learn where it was purchased and show photos to the sales staff to see if they recognize Arseneau, but without that it's a dead end. What we *do* have is Carsten's notepad with the words 'Legacy' and 'Freeport' next to his phone. It's a circumstantial link but still powerful.

"We've absolutely linked him to Benny Bergen, though. Apparently he hadn't yet decided to use a burner when he made the call to Benny. We have phone records that clearly show Arseneau calling Benny three days before the attack on your girlfriend. Oh, and Benny's fingerprints are all over her house. If that isn't enough, Benny actually used his own car to take a run at you. Fibers from your pants were found on his dented grill. You're lucky to be alive, McCoy."

"That's what the emergency room doc told me."

"So with the note on Arseneau's desk that his wife found with the words 'Bergen' and 'incompetent overrated asin,' coupled with all the rest we have, the DA is starting to think we might actually have a case."

"HOW DID THE INTERVIEW WITH ARSENEAU GO?" Genevieve asked when he entered her office. He told her all about it. "So I think he's taking a good hard look at his cousin, Benoit. He was really pissed."

"Pissed? What is pissed?"

"You know, Genevieve it isn't necessary to pick up every American idiom you hear. Let's just say he was upset, okay?"

"Do you think he'll call him like you hope?"

"I don't know. I've certainly given him enough to think about, with everything we've learned about the Naff swindle. He was stunned, and like us, he's now beginning to think that Benoit Surette was somehow behind it all. He could be upset enough to call him, and if he does, Osborn will pick it up. He's also put a tail on him, so we will know anywhere he goes."

Hunter's phone rang. It was Klinger.

"McCoy, we're holding a general strategy session at one o'clock. My entire staff will be there, along with the director. I want you and Genevieve there as well. The plan is, that we'll open the floor for ideas, try playing the bad guy. What could he or they *possibly* do to ruin the museum? The idea is that maybe we're missing something in our precautions. If someone comes up with a threat we haven't considered, we still have time to take steps to prepare."

"Sounds like a good idea. We'll be there."

After lunch everyone gathered in the assembly hall. Hunter was surprised by the size of the relatively large security staff. After Klinger introduced Hunter and Genevieve to those who hadn't met them, he proceeded to tell them the reason for the meeting.

"I want you to put on your bad guy hats. You all know what precautions we've already taken in advance of the threat coming up in three days. I want you to think outside the box. What could you do, if you had the resources, to bring this place down, that we haven't taken precautions against? I wish I could tell you there's an all-expenses-paid trip to the destination of your choice as a prize, but I'm afraid I can't do that."

"How about a raise, Kyle?" a man in the back of the room called out. Everybody laughed.

"Right, maybe next year, Johnson," Kyle answered with a chuckle. "Seriously guys and gals, we need your input, so let's have it."

The room erupted into conversations for a few minutes. Finally a hand went up.

Kyle acknowledged a woman leaning against a window. "What have you got, Cheryl?"

"Suppose some guy is running one of those drone things with a bomb attached and he flies it into the building? How do we stop that?"

"Hey, I just saw a You Tube video on that," a young man called out, "and it showed an eagle swooping in and bringing down the drone. Course, I don't know where you'd get a trained eagle to do that."

"Maybe we could station a few guys outside with shotguns or something, to shoot one down if it comes in the area," another offered. "Or maybe there's some kind of jamming device we could use."

"Okay, okay," Klinger said, putting his hands up. "Thanks, Cheryl. We'll look into drone defense. How about other threats? Anyone else?"

A hand went up in the front row. "Jim, what have you got?"

"Well, presumably no one will be able to get in the museum on the day in question. The place will be closed to the public. So nothing destructive could be brought in that day. But what if it's already here? Maybe it's been here for some time. I mean, whoever is doing this surely had plenty of time to prepare."

"That's true," Kyle said. "That's why we've been doing the daily searches of every space in the place. If he hid something, that's our only way to find it."

"But don't forget, he warned us twenty-one days in advance," said Jim. "He must know we'd be doing that kind of searching. I don't think it would be anything as relatively easy to find as a bomb of some kind. I don't know what, though."

"What about a gas?" someone said.

"Yeah, but you'd still need something physical to deliver it," another answered, "like a gas tank, presumably something we'd find."

It went on like this for another hour. Almost everything that came up was something that Klinger's existing precautions would discover. Finally he thanked everyone and told them to keep thinking and to call him immediately if anyone thought of anything useful. Afterward, Hunter and Genevieve joined Klinger in the director's office.

"It didn't sound to me like we got much useful information out of that Kyle. What did you think?" Bertram said.

"I agree. It seems as if we're doing everything we can. What did you think, Hunter?"

"The only thing I heard that made sense is that whatever is going to do the damage must already be in place and probably not visible. That was a good comment, about our having a twenty-one days warning, so surely the bad guy—and remember, I think it's Benoit Surette—knows we'd be looking. My contact at Interpol has a team watching Surette constantly. They're also watching his chief thug, Petr Havel. I believe that Surette, if he's our man, will come here to watch the fun in person. I don't think he'll be able to resist. If he flies here, we'll know for sure it's him."

Bertram shook his head and just looked at Hunter. "And to think I was going to throw you out as an amateur who'd only get in the way."

Hunter chuckled. "Thanks, but my plan now is to get in the way of Benoit Surette."

52

BENOIT SURETTE HAD JUST DISMISSED Petr Havel after giving him instructions for the next several days. As he often did, he strolled to his gallery to relax in the timeless pleasure of fine art. Passing though the gallery he'd shown to Pierre Arseneau, he stopped at the door the man had asked about, the door he'd told him was to a storage area. *How amusing,* he thought. It was a storage area, all right, but most certainly not for mops, pails, and brooms. No, this storage area was his sanctuary. No one came in here but him, not even his current wife. No, this was his and his alone.

He brought his eye to the retinal scanner disguised as a wall thermostat some fifteen feet from the door to his sanctuary so as not to link the two in the minds of any visitors to his more public gallery. He heard the familiar and satisfying *whoosh* as the door opened and then closed behind him after he entered.

Instead of walls of wood or plaster, he might have stepped into a rough-hewn cave of rock. The floor was a beautiful hardwood pattern, all the more startling in its modernity when it came up against the crude rock outcroppings that composed the walls and ceiling. The cave itself was twenty-by-twenty-five feet. There were no windows, and the only door was the one he'd just come through. The center of the room held a leather swivel lounge chair and side table with a beautiful lamp for reading or just sitting. Against one wall was an old oaken desk with several oak file cabinets.

The lighting was magnificent with no bulbs visible, having been cleverly hidden among the rock outcroppings. Benoit poured himself a small snifter of Cuvée Léonie cognac, and put his feet up, and thought of the coming retribution.

PIERRE ARSENEAU SAT IN HIS STUDY on the second floor of his magisterial home and stared out at the Gulf. He knew he was in trouble. He'd been stupid to get involved with either that idiot Bergen or Tony Carsten. The charge of attempted murder was serious, and even his lawyer might not be able to get him off if the police gathered enough evidence against him.

In spite of this, he couldn't get over the duplicity of his trusted cousin. Hunter McCoy had apparently discovered in a very short time what the other Legacy cousins, himself included, had missed all along. Here they'd been plotting against Quentin Naff when all along the real asshole was Benoit Surette. Arseneau thought back to all the times they'd been together at meetings, and then during his visit to Prague just a few days ago, when Benoit's behavior had seemed a little strange, not quite in tune with the others. He'd always put it down to Benoit just being a little different. Well, he was different all right, the lying bastard. He had their paintings and Mueller's money, Pierre was sure of it.

What he couldn't figure out was who had damaged the other four paintings McCoy and that cop had mentioned. He hadn't done it, and he was the only one with the bacteria. Yeah, he'd sprayed that first one, the Cranach as a test, but he hadn't done any others. It wouldn't have been Algarve; he'd have no reason to do it. It had to be someone who was trying to frame him, but who, and why? Did Benoit do this too, somehow? But how would he get access to the stuff, and even then, why would he do it?

Pierre sat back, musing. Had he done anything that would make Benoit do this to him personally? He figured it was one thing to steal the paintings and probably Mueller's money but why would he try to frame him for doing damage to Ringling's paintings? Then it hit him. McCoy had asked if he'd written notes threatening to ruin the Ringling Museum. Maybe Benoit was planning to do that for some reason, and is planning to frame him for it, and what better—and more convenient way to do it than to have their best paintings ruined by BIOMOD's bacterial solution? That had to be it. Benoit must have gotten the stuff from the lab somehow when he was here for the meeting. *What irony,* thought Pierre. He'd developed the solution to ruin Quentin Naff and how his own double-crossing cousin was using it to ruin him.

But wait, he thought. Why would Benoit want to damage the Ringling? Pierre closed his eyes and thought back, of course, his son. Paul had been staying with them while he worked at the museum. He and Marie lived for that place and they were thick as thieves. That's all the kid could talk about, the art and the museum. Pierre couldn't stand him and argued with him all the time. Then the boy had hung himself—at the Ringling, after he was fired for messing up a statue or something.

Pierre sat straight up. Is that it? Did Benoit write notes to threaten to ruin the Ringling Museum because his son chose their tree to hang himself? Not likely, he thought. Then he got an idea. He opened his computer and Googled 'suicide by hanging at the Ringling.' he found the newspaper story from four years ago in which Paul Ballard— a security guard at the Ringling Museum of Art—was accused of vandalism to some sculpture by the administration and fired. He claimed he was innocent and that someone else had done it. Apparently he became depressed and took his own life by making a rope out of hangings from one of the banyan trees on the grounds. He died on May third.

"That's it," he shouted out loud. Benoit was planning revenge by ruining the Ringling Museum of Art and setting up a frame to blame him for it. The shit. Damn him to hell. Arseneau stormed around the room pounding anything he came near, the walls, his desk, and his open palm. *The bastard,* he thought. *Well, Benoit, it's not over yet.*

Maybe if he cooperated with the police, told them what he'd realized, maybe worked some kind of deal with them. He sat down and closed his eyes again. He had to think this through. Finally he made a call.

"McCoy, it's Osborn. We have a development."

Hunter was on his way to the house when he got the call. "What's up?"

"It's Arseneau. He wants to talk. He and his lawyer are coming to the station—now."

Twenty minutes later Hunter and Wally Osborn sat across the table from Pierre Arseneau and his Attorney.

The attorney started. "My client has just figured out some of the answers to the questions you asked him earlier. He'd like to cooperate with you, but would hope that his cooperation will be reciprocated. He's not asking for anything specific, only that you consider his willingness to cooperate."

"Understood. So what do you have to tell us, Mr. Arseneau?" Osborn asked.

"I believe my cousin, Benoit Surette got hold of my company's bacterial solution and is responsible for damaging the paintings you mentioned in an effort to frame me for it. He would expect you to come after me since my company developed it. Further, I believe he is behind the threat to ruin the Ringling Museum. He's doing it in retaliation for the death of his son. I believe he blames the Ringling for the boy's suicide because they accused him of vandalizing some sculpture and fired him. The boy became depressed and hanged himself from a tree on the grounds. By damaging the paintings at the exhibit Benoit intended to implicate me, so that when he does whatever he has planned for Thursday, I'll be blamed."

Pierre sat back and waited.

Hunter and Osborn looked at him. Finally Hunter said, "Is that it? Is that all you have to tell us? You see, Mr. Arseneau, we already know all of this. It's great that you've confirmed it, but you haven't told us anything new."

Arseneau's expression quickly turned from surprise to dejection.

"Do you have any idea what your cousin might be planning? If you do, *that* would be useful information. You know the man. What *might* he do?"

Arseneau shook his head. "I thought I knew him. But after what you found out about his stealing our paintings and the money, I'm not sure anymore. I can tell you this. He is completely ruthless and capable of anything."

I'm sure Marie and Monica would say the same about you, Hunter thought.

"What about the bacteria?" he asked. "How much of the spray exists? Could he be planning to use it to damage a large number of paintings? That would surely count as ruining the museum."

Arseneau wrinkled his brow. "I don't know how much Algarve made. But if Benoit has it and uses it that way, you would surely see the wet surface. If you have people constantly checking you could easily wipe the painting clean and dry before the bacteria got to work."

"We need to check with Algarve and find out if any of the solution has been stolen," Hunter said.

"We'll go out there next," said Osborn.

"Do you have anything else to tells us, Mr. Arseneau?"

Arseneau looked at his attorney and shrugged. "No, that's it."

A half hour later, after calling Dr. Algarve to make sure he was there, Hunter and Osborn drove to the BIOMOD plant, hoping that Algarve would tell them nothing was missing.

53

DR. ALGARVE WAS AT HIS DESK in his lab when they arrived.

"Hi," he said when he saw Hunter. Then he looked curiously at the man with him. Hunter introduced him.

"Dr. Algarve, this is Detective Wally Osborn with the Sarasota Police Department," said Hunter.

He then went on to bring the man up to date on everything he needed to know, including that his boss, Pierre Arseneau, was under arrest for attempted murder. He told him about the Thursday deadline, now just days away, for ruining the Ringling Museum of Art, and that they suspected the perpetrator was likely a man from Prague, Benoit Surette, though they didn't know what he was planning. The man had been a guest of Pierre Arseneau a few weeks ago.

"Dr. Algarve," Hunter said, "we need to know two things. First, have you ever seen this man before?" With that, Osborn took out a picture of Benoit Surette and showed it to him. Algarve examined at it and said no. He'd never seen him. "Secondly," Hunter continued, "can you account for all of the bacteria that you produced for Arseneau? Can you show us where it is and how you keep in under control?"

"Sure, come with me."

He led them out the building and down the path that Hunter had taken on his earlier visits, to the last building on the left. Inside, Algarve took them to a series of incubation chambers that lined the room. Each was numbered, and

Hunter counted ten in all. Each was about the size of a refrigerator freezer with a lift top.

"These incubators are where we keep the stock," Algarve explained. "Of course they're completely climate-controlled, allowing us to maintain them for long periods of time. We don't need to keep much, because when we get an order we can take a sample of the variety we need from these incubators and quickly grow them in the building opposite this one to the large volumes demanded by the particular job. It's actually quite efficient. We don't have to hold a large inventory; we just have to maintain the stock in these incubators."

"Can you show us the stock you made for Arseneau?" Hunter asked. "The oil-paint-eating bacteria?"

"It's over here in number three."

Algarve lifted the lid, revealing Petri dishes in a row numbered one through twelve.

Algarve frowned in puzzlement.

"What is it?" asked Hunter

Algarve picked up the dish numbered twelve and examined it. "Something's wrong here. This dish has no bacteria in it. See how it is different from the others? And look at the number twelve. I didn't write that. That's not my handwriting. Look at the rest—you can see for yourself, that it's different."

"Someone's been in here and made off with a dish of bacteria, and you're just finding this out now?" said Osborn. "When might this have happened?"

Algarve shrugged haplessly. "You've got to understand, there's no demand for this product and so no need to check it regularly. This could have been switched out anytime in the past four weeks."

"How could someone take a sample and keep them alive if you need a fancy incubator like this to do it?" Osborn asked.

"I don't know, but bacteria are tough, Captain. They might go dormant, rather than die."

"Do you have any way of telling who's been in here during that time?" asked Hunter.

"No, we don't keep a log. We haven't seen any need to check people in and out—until now, I guess."

"Given your boss's arrest, I say you no longer have any need for these little devils. You could probably trash the lot— safely."

"I'll do that, right away. Aside from enjoying the technical challenge of engineering them, I'll be happy to see them go. They've been nothing but trouble."

———————————

THE NEXT MORNING, TUESDAY, Hunter's first thought was: *we have less than forty-eight hours.* He called Eduard.

"Nothing's happened, Hunter. The plane hasn't moved from the hangar and Surette hasn't left his house."

"What about Havel?"

"He left yesterday morning. They followed him downtown to Surette's office building, where he maintains a residence. He's still there."

"Damn. I was sure he'd come here."

"He could still do it, but he'll have to leave soon—I'd say in the next few hours, given the time change if he plans to be in Sarasota like you think he will. Don't worry. If any of them move, Surette, the plane, or Havel, I'll call you right away."

"Thanks, Eduard."

Hunter drove Genevieve to the Ringling. Genevieve went to her office, and Hunter sought out Klinger. He found him in the North Wing checking the storage space behind the baseboards in Gallery Eight.

"Still haven't found anything, McCoy. What about you?" Klinger said as he slid out of a crawl space behind the wainscoting.

"Maybe." They each took a seat on the viewing bench. "We went out to BIOMOD and talked to the molecular biologist who built the bacteria. One of the Petri dishes with a colony on it was missing. It could have been taken any time in the past few weeks."

"So you think he's planning an attack on the paintings like we saw earlier?"

"It could be."

"If he is he'll have to get close enough to spray them," Klinger said, "and I'll have so many people in here he'd never be able to do it. No one but my people will even be in the building."

"I know, and that's what bothers me," Hunter said. "How could someone spray them if they're not right in front of them?"

Tapping his feet on the floor, Hunter considered the problem. "How about this. You have a sprinkler system in case of fire, right? Could he get the stuff into that somehow and then set it off and spray everything at once?"

"I don't see how, but I'll check it out just the same."

"How does it work, anyway?"

"We have what's called a wet-pipe system with a pre-action activation system. A wet-pipe system means the overhead pipes throughout the museum are filled with water, right up to the sprinkler heads in the ceilings and walls throughout the galleries. The sprinkler heads have heat sensors. At a predetermined temperature, usually 135 to 225 degrees Fahrenheit, they activate, releasing a plug and allowing water to escape. The flow of water in the system triggers an audiovisual alarm that can be heard throughout the building. The water is directed onto a diffuser designed to not only break up the water into droplets of a specific size, it also directs the spray to cover a specific floor and wall area. Each sprinkler head is individually activated by heat. According to the authorities, in the majority of fires just one sprinkler head is triggered, and that is sufficient to deal with the fire.

"To avoid the system releasing water accidentally—if say someone bangs the sprinkler head with a ladder or something—most museums, including us, have what's called a pre-action activation system. That means the water won't be released unless the sprinkler head is activated normally by exceeding the temperature setting."

"Doesn't the release of water damage the art on the wall?" Hunter asked.

"Not as much as you'd think. A fire department pouring in water with high pressure hoses would cause much more damage."

"Is there a control panel for the system?"

"Sure. It contains valves to shut off the water and houses the alarm systems that are activated when water starts to flow anywhere in the system."

"Doesn't sound like he can do much damage there."

"No, but I'll have a man on duty at the control panel just in case."

"You know what I'm afraid of, Kyle?"

"What?"

"That there's something right in front of us that we haven't considered."

54

HUNTER AND GENEVIEVE WOKE UP WITH ONE DAY left before the deadline. While Genevieve went to her office, Hunter joined Klinger reviewing the security measures. The call from Eduard came through as Hunter and Klinger were on their way to the South Wing.

"Hunter, the Czech police who followed Havel out of Surette's house to his apartment in the downtown office two days ago screwed up. When they went in to check on him, he wasn't there. They found the clothes he was wearing in the apartment. They also went back to the house, and neither Havel nor Surette were there. They lost both of them. The only good news is the plane is still in the hangar at the airport."

"So if I have this right, they've both had almost two days on their own without surveillance. They could be anywhere."

"Correct. The only thing the cops know for sure is they haven't gone anywhere on that plane. Oh, and we also know they haven't used their passports to either leave the Czech Republic or to enter the United States. We'll keep monitoring this. Of course the man is incredibly wealthy. He could have some other way of traveling that bypasses the normal security routes. We'll keep looking on this end, but you'd better be prepared. They might show up there any time."

"Thanks, Eduard."

Hunter told Kyle what he'd learned, and the two men knew that the threat level had just been increased. Interpol had supplied Hunter with photos of both Benoit Surette and

Petr Havel, and Klinger said he'd have them reproduced and in the hands of all security people within the next few hours, instructing them all to be on the lookout for either of them. He'd also supply copies to the main entrance at the Visitors Pavilion with instructions to call him immediately if either of them were spotted.

While Kyle continued his rounds, checking on all his enhanced security procedures, Hunter thought about the missing Petri dish. He called Algarve.

"Dr. Algarve, is there any possibility that the missing Petri dish with your engineered *Alcanivorax* could have just been misplaced?"

"No, absolutely not. Those dishes and any of the others are never even removed from the incubators. When an order comes in—of course it wouldn't for that one—we just use an auto-pipette to remove what is needed and place it on growth medium in a new dish for transfer to the culture building across the way. The original dishes, the ones you saw, never leave the incubator. And of course the modified *Alcanivorax* that I made for Arseneau has never been used for a job."

"Well, that's not quite correct, is it? You must have made some up for Arseneau's test because it was used on at least five paintings that we know of."

"Yes, of course. I did grow up a small amount for him for use with an atomizer. I gave that to him."

"Did he ever give it back?"

"Yes, as a matter of fact he did. He also said his test was a success."

"Really. When did he give it back?"

"Oh, just a few days later. He didn't have it for more than two days at the most."

"Where is the atomizer now?"

"It's in my office in an incubator."

"Can you check to see if it's there?"

"Sure, just a minute. I'll go over there. I'm working in the receiving room now."

Hunter waited for a few minutes until Algarve came back on the line.

"McCoy, it's not there. It's gone."

That's not good.

Hunter said, "Arseneau must have brought it back over three weeks ago. How long has it been missing? When did you see it last?"

"I don't know. I had no use for it, so I didn't pay attention. It could have gone missing anytime during that period."

"So we have a missing atomizer and a missing stock Petri dish containing your little monsters. This just keeps getting better and better. If you still have a job and a company when this is all over, you're going to have to do something about your security. It stinks."

Disgusted, Hunter called Osborn and told him what he had just learned from Algarve. "If Arseneau brought the atomizer back when Algarve said he did, five weeks ago, and the other four paintings were damaged two weeks ago, then he didn't do it. Someone else stole it out of Algarve's desktop incubator and sprayed those last four paintings. I've got an idea. I'll call you back."

Hunter hung up and called Eduard Gautier. "Eduard, you said that you tracked Petr Havel flying back to Prague from Sarasota on a commercial flight the day after he showed up and stuck a gun in my face."

"Right."

"When did he fly to Florida in the first place? Can you check that?"

"Sure, give me a minute."

Hunter paced until Eduard came back on the line. "Okay, here it is. Immigration has Havel entering the country with Benoit Surette after going through customs in Tampa almost one month ago. They came in together on

Benoit's jet. It must have been for the Legacy meeting at Pierre Arseneau's house that you told me about. Surette left and returned to Prague three days later. Havel stayed until the return commercial flight four days ago."

"Thanks, Eduard." Hunter sighed. Given BIOMOD's lack of security and Havel's ability for ghost-like moves, the man could easily have stolen the aerosol from Algarve's desktop incubator and sprayed the Gainsborough and the three paintings at the exhibit. He also could have stolen the Petri dish with the stock solution from incubator 3 at BIOMOD. But he didn't spray the Lucas Cranach. That happened before he was in the country. That had to be Pierre Arseneau testing the solution. No wonder he didn't want to answer that question.

Arseneau's theory must be correct. Surette probably had Havel spray the last four paintings to make it look as if Arseneau had done it, and then, when he did whatever damage he had planned for the museum, the obvious culprit would be Arseneau. Hunter had to admit, it was a pretty clever frame.

Still, he had too many questions and not enough answers. Was the misdirection in Prague designed to allow Surette and Havel to reenter the US without alerting customs, by some means that a man with enough money and power, like Benoit Surette, could easily arrange? Were they planning to somehow spray the paintings in the museum and ruin them? How did they imagine they could do that, knowing that with a twenty-one day warning the museum would take every precaution? They surely weren't planning to just walk through and spray. Taking the Petri dish with the stock solution suggested they might be planning to grow a large volume of the stuff. But even so, how could they apply it with all the security they surely knew would be in place?

How would they be able to grow the stock solution? Neither of them was a biologist, as far as Hunter knew. He felt sure Algarve wasn't helping them, so where could they have it done? He called Algarve back and asked him.

"It's not that hard. Anyone with an incubator, a few basic supplies, and a little knowledge of basic bacteriology could do it."

Hunter called Wally Osborn next to tell him what he'd learned from Eduard and Algarve. "If I give you Petr Havel's cellphone number, can you get a subpoena for his phone records to see who he's called in the past few weeks?"

"Sure. Since he's a subject in an international criminal investigation, it shouldn't be a problem."

"You know we're up against a deadline and running out of time."

"I know you need it yesterday. I'm on it."

IT WAS NOW 4:30 PM, seven and a half hours until Thursday; the day the note promised the museum would be ruined. Hunter had been chasing leads all day and felt he was getting closer. He was now almost certain the ruin would involve bacteria and the museum's valuable paintings. He just couldn't figure out how Surette was planning to pull it off. He decided to pick up Genevieve and go get something to eat. He hadn't had anything since breakfast.

He drove to Cafe L'Europe on St. Armand's Circle, an elegant shopping district, where they were surprised to find that the chef was offering a unique special for that night only. Apparently during the month of June, some sixty-five restaurants in the Sarasota area normally offered fixed-menu multi-course meals for only $29.95 to try to attract new customers during the off-season. The program was called Savor Sarasota, and even though this was only May 2nd, the chef wanted to try out his planned menu ahead of time and get some feedback. They looked at each other and shrugged. Why not?

So they had lobster bisque, followed by scallopini of salmon sautéed with capers, wild mushroom, and beurre blanc, and for dessert, Crepes Suzette for two. Hunter enjoyed a perfect Manhattan on the rocks while Genevieve had a glass of fine white wine. The dining was wonderful, but they were both wracked with worry about what tomorrow might bring for the museum.

Hunter's phone rang. It was Osborn. "I think I have what you're looking for."

55

"WE GOT PETR HAVEL'S CELLPHONE RECORDS," Wally Osborn told Hunter. "Two days after Arseneau returned the aerosol to Algarve who put it in his desktop incubator, Havel made a call to ACELMICROBES, a bioengineering firm in Tampa. He made one other call there a day later. One day after that he received a call from them. We have the number and a name, a Dr. Winkler. Since I'm the one here with official law enforcement status, I should contact him. I assume you agree we should call rather than drive up there since time is running short."

"I agree," Hunter said, "but let me tell you the technical questions to ask him first."

"Okay, shoot."

Hunter gave him a list and then he and Genevieve drove home. They'd just gotten into the house when Osborn called back.

"The man's dead. Four days ago he was found shot in his home. The cops up there are calling it a burglary gone bad. Some cash, a watch, and wallet were taken. He was single and lived alone. I don't buy it."

"Neither do I," agreed Hunter. "Four days ago. That's just before Havel flew back to Prague. This Dr. Winkler must have done something for Havel with the bacteria— maybe both the aerosol and the missing Petri dish—and then Havel killed him to silence him. I believe the threat to the museum tomorrow somehow involves these bacteria. I'll call Klinger to tell him. Can you have some police presence here tomorrow to back up the Museum security staff? Like I said earlier, I believe Surette and probably

Havel will have found a way to be here. They won't want to miss the spectacle."

"Already taken care of. We'll have twelve cops working the museum. They'll have reviewed photos of the two and know who to look for."

"Good. See you tomorrow."

He called Klinger next and told him what he'd learned from Osborn and that he was convinced the threat was going to be to the paintings, somehow using the bacteria.

It was now ten o'clock, just two hours until midnight. They had no idea when the threat might be realized. Would he be at 12:01 AM or sometime during the day? They were both exhausted and knew they had to be fully awake for "Ruin Day," so they decided to get some sleep but set the alarm for 6 AM.

Hunter was up first at 5. He showered and shaved. By then Genevieve was getting ready herself.

Over coffee they reviewed their plans for the day. Hunter knew Klinger and Bertram were concerned for the safety of their people. In the event that Surette had something truly catastrophic planned, such as somehow blowing up the museum, he didn't want more people exposed than was absolutely necessary. On the other hand they needed all the eyes they could get, looking for someone or something that could do harm. It was a delicate balance, and Hunter imagined Klinger hadn't gotten much sleep. Still he believed the attack would be against the paintings, using sprayed bacteria like they'd seen before. But how could they do that if they couldn't physically get near them?

Genevieve took a sip of her coffee. "Maybe it will be someone dressed in a security guard uniform who goes unnoticed."

"But even if he could get in and not be recognized by the others, how could he do much damage? As soon as he starts spraying, someone will spot him," Hunter said. Then he hopped to his feet. "But if he somehow got the bacteria into the fire sprinkler system? Klinger explained that the museum has what's called a wet-pipe system. The water pipes to each of the sprinkler heads throughout the museum are charged with pressurized water right up to the head. All it takes is to exceed the temperature threshold on a head and it goes off spraying water, including on the paintings."

Hunter grabbed his phone. "That could be it. I'm calling Klinger. He needs to shut off the mains to the system while we check to see if the water in the lines is contaminated."

Invigorated by the chance to finally take some action, Hunter finished his coffee in a gulp and phoned Klinger. Not surprisingly, Klinger was already in the building and said he'd head to the control room right then and close the valves to the system. Next Hunter called Algarve and told him to get his ass over to the Ringling Museum immediately with something that would let him test the water for the presence of his lethal bacteria.

Klinger wouldn't allow anyone into the museum other than his staff and the plainclothes police that Wally Osborn arranged for. The only exception was Hunter. He'd told Algarve to meet Genevieve in the Education Center and told him how to get there. Genevieve would stay with him until hopefully Hunter could bring a sample of the water in the preloaded pipes. He felt the immediate threat would be contained as soon as Klinger got to the control room and shut off the main water pipes to the sprinkler system.

Driving them to the museum, Hunter wondered how he'd get the water sample. If they'd charged the system with bacteria some time back, they'd have diffused to an equal concentration everywhere in the system. If that were true he could take the sample from anywhere—right behind a sprinkler head, or even in the control room if there was an access point. He'd have to wait until he got there to find out. After driving faster than he should, but knowing they were in the end game, he pulled into the lot and parked.

"Wait in your office, Genevieve. I told Algarve how to get here. He'll identify himself to the security guy at the entrance, who'll call you down to take him up to your office. As soon as I have a sample, I'll bring it over and he can do his thing."

She nodded and headed into her building while Hunter sprinted to the art museum building next door. Klinger was already there when Hunter made his way to the fire control room.

"Okay, I've shut off the main valves," Klinger told him. "There are three of them. These guys right here." He pointed to three black steering-wheel-sized circular valves.

"The system is now closed between this point and the hundreds of sprinkler heads throughout the place. No new water can flow into the system with these valves closed, but the water already in there must have some pressure on it."

Hunter studied the piping. "I'm figuring I can either get a sample in here somehow or pop one of the heads and collect some water that way."

They both examined the piping in the control room. It quickly became obvious to both men that without taking one of the three valves apart, there was no way to get to the water in there.

"It'll have to be a head," Hunter said. "Can you identify a head where the spray can't reach a painting?"

"Yeah, I know one. Grab one of those buckets and follow me."

Klinger headed for a hallway in a gallery where the paintings had been temporarily removed to resurface the walls. On the way he called someone and told them to bring a ladder to 14 on the double. Once they got there the ladder arrived almost simultaneously, and the workman set it up under the head Klinger identified.

"What will you do?" Hunter asked.

"Remember I told you we installed a pre-action system? Most museums have it. It's designed to prevent accidents. Suppose a workman happens to bump a sprinkler head while they're handling an exhibit or moving things. You don't want the system going off and spraying water needlessly. A pre-action system requires that the sprinkler head will only open if activated by the proper method, namely high heat. Like I'm going to do right now."

Klinger climbed the ladder with a bucket in one hand, and then took a lighter out of his pocket. When he reached the head, he placed the bucket over it to catch any water released and lit the lighter and brought it close. The plug popped, and water immediately sprayed a ten-foot circumference—then almost as quickly slowed to a trickle and stopped.

"Great, with the mains shut off the pressure is almost minimal," he said.

By the time he got down the sprinkler head released only a few drips.

Klinger instructed the workman to mop up the little that got on the floor and wash his hands completely when he was done. They went back to the control room. Klinger gave Hunter the bucket with about three inches of water in it.

"All right, here's what I'm going to do," he said. "These three valves each control different zones in the museum. In case our bad guys managed to get into only one of them, I'm going to get you a bucket from the other two as well. You can take this one over to your guy in Genevieve's office so he can test it now. I'll bring the other two as soon as I have them."

Hunter nodded. "Good, see you in a bit. Be sure you wash your hands too."

When Hunter got to the entrance to the Education Center, Algarve was just getting out of his car. Hunter waved him over. The man raised a palm up as if to say, "wait a minute." Then he opened his trunk and pulled out a large black case that Hunter assumed contained his equipment. He imagined it was some kind of microscope. It must have been heavy, as the little man struggled with it. Hunter came over and exchanged loads, giving Algarve the bucket of water while he took the case. Algarve was happy to switch, and they headed up to Genevieve's office.

Hunter introduced Genevieve. "Maybe you can set up on that table over there."

Genevieve cleared the surface while Algarve unpacked what Hunter recognized as a very expensive light microscope. He also removed a slide box with cover slips. He set out a box of Chemwipes and a rack with an auto pipet for drawing up samples, and then looked questioningly at Hunter.

Hunter put the bucket on the table.

Algarve removed a fresh slide from the box, put a new tip on the auto pipet, and withdrew a small sample of water from the bucket. Then he carefully pipetted a drop onto the center of the slide, covered it with a new coverslip, and placed it on the stage of the microscope. He examined it for a moment as he moved the slide under the high-power lens of the scope. Then he sat back in his chair and said, "Nothing here but water."

"Are you sure?" Hunter felt disappointed, then worried that he might be wrong and Surette was planning something else they hadn't considered.

"Look for yourself."

Hunter did. No bacteria or anything else.

"Where did this water come from?" Algarve asked.

"We took it from the fire sprinkler system in the museum. I thought that someone might have put some of your sample in the water system and planned to set it off somehow, spraying the paintings and causing serious damage. We suspect the person who stole your samples had the bacteria grown at a lab in Tampa."

"Oh jeez."

"I have two more samples coming. The museum's fire sprinkler system has three zones, each with its own water system. You just looked at one of the three."

Hunter's phone rang. He thought it would be Klinger, but it was Eduard.

"Hunter. Just so you know. The Czech police have been unable to locate Surette or Havel. It's as though they've disappeared off the face of the earth. Apparently that's not unusual for Petr Havel, but it's almost unheard of for Surette. We have no information on them crossing any borders that require passports, but like I said earlier, for a man with Surette's wealth, that's not a real problem. Keep your eyes open over there. I have a feeling he's going to show up on your patch any minute now."

Hunter hung up just as Klinger came in with two new buckets.

The little man nodded and indicated Klinger should put the buckets on the floor next to him. Then Algarve repeated the process he'd just completed, now with the new samples. He took a little longer this time, but in the end the results were the same.

"No bacteria. Nothing but water."

56

THE STOOPED OLD MAN SLOWLY PUSHED HIS WALKER down the path from the Visitors Pavilion, where he'd paid cash for a ticket to enter the grounds. When he pushed past the tram stop, the driver asked if he'd like a ride. The old man waved him away with a smile, implying he'd like to walk. He continued on the path heading toward the bridge over the pond that separated the Visitors Pavilion and gift shop from the Ringling Museum of Art. The old man didn't cross the bridge, though; he just went as far as the bench in front of a tropical garden, where he took a seat, removed a sandwich from a bag, and waited.

He thought of the long journey he'd just completed to be here. He assumed the police would be watching the house in Prague and he knew the only access view they'd have would be of the front. The first thing he'd had to do was to get out of the house without being seen. He'd managed that by strolling back through his lush garden and up and over the hill behind. He'd always kept a car back there for occasions like this, when he had to travel unseen. He'd driven southeast to Brno, where he boarded a flight to Barcelona using one of many passports he had in several nationalities under many names, each with his photo on it. In Barcelona he boarded an American Airlines flight to Atlanta using yet another passport. Finally in Atlanta, using a third passport, he flew to Sarasota, where he rented a car and took a hotel room at the Ritz downtown. That was two days ago. Now, looking entirely unlike his passport photo, he'd emerged from his room as an old man with a walker and driven to the Ringling, where he'd parked and entered the grounds.

Havel had also flown back to the states using a phony passport under an assumed name. Havel had done well, he thought. It was too bad such a useful man was going to be sacrificed. He'd served Benoit Surette well over the years, always doing his bidding and never complaining. Still, what he had planned for today was too big to allow anyone to know about, even Petr. He patted the bag on his lap and smiled. Then he thought of his son, Paul.

Like his cousin, Pierre Arseneau, he didn't really care for the women in his life. Oh, he knew all about Pierre's treatment of his wife and daughter. The man had told him often enough. But he didn't have a son like Benoit had had. Even worse, he'd badgered Paul into an even deeper state of depression, no doubt contributing to his decision to kill himself. In spite of Paul's refusal to join him in his empire and desire to become a painter, he'd still loved the boy and always held out hope he'd come around. Then, just as he'd finally seen the light and told Benoit he only needed this short time in America before joining him in the business, he was gone.

The previous director of the Ringling Museum of Art had written him an email—an email, not a letter or a phone call, an email—and said Paul must have been a troubled young man to have vandalized the sculpture the way he did. Of course they didn't know he'd commit suicide when they fired him, and in any case it wasn't their fault. Still, they felt his pain and asked if there was any way they could help with his grief. He'd never responded to this. He had nothing to say to them at the time. Now he did. And oddly enough, it was his cousin Pierre who had given him the answer. And how fitting the solution was, truly poetic justice. He recalled how excited Pierre had been a month ago, when he'd told the group about his bacterial spray solution and how fast it could begin to eat the oil paint. He'd told them all about his test on the sixteenth-century painting at the museum. The idiot actually believed his three other cousins in the Legacy would agree to destroy priceless artworks, just to get back at Naff. Pierre was actually shocked when he lost the vote three to two.

But it was that idiot Pierre who provided Benoit the solution he'd been looking for—the truly appropriate way to answer that email's cynical offer to *"help in any way with your grief."* He'd had Havel stay behind while he flew back to Prague after the meeting. His mission was to get the bacteria and develop a supply sufficient to destroy every painting on every wall in the Ringling Museum. He'd told Petr that it had to be done in such a way that even with the twenty-one-day early warning he was going to give them, they couldn't stop it. In this respect, Havel had exceeded expectations. Again he smiled and patted the bag on his lap. It was now 5:30, and at exactly 7:00 PM this evening the inevitable would begin.

HUNTER RUBBED HIS TEMPLES. He'd been convinced that the water in the pipes was the delivery system to spray the paintings. He was back to square one, with no idea how it was going to happen. Klinger had insisted that the fire sprinkler system be activated again, in case the threat was somehow setting fire to the place. At least they'd have that protection. Hunter couldn't argue with that. Still, given what they'd learned about the stolen aerosol, Petri dish, and Havel's contact with a Tampa lab capable of helping multiply the stock—a biologist who later turned up murdered—he was still convinced the target was the paintings.

He turned to Dr. Algarve, who had just put away his equipment. "Any ideas, doc? How can it be done if we're watching? How can anybody get near enough to those paintings to spray them?"

"They can't."

Suddenly Genevieve shot out of her chair. "Wait a minute. Wait a minute. I just thought of something. We may have this all wrong, Hunter. The target might not be the museum at all."

"I don't understand."

"What about the freeport in Tampa?"

"What do you mean?"

"I don't know how much art *we* have there but I imagine it's a lot. If it's anywhere near the industry standard of 80% of the museum's art, then destroying that would surely constitute ruining the museum, even if he doesn't touch the art that's here on the walls."

"You might be right." Hunter immediately called Klinger and told him what Genevieve had come up with.

Klinger said, "I like it. Good idea. I'll call Tampa now. I'll have them get all the people they can over to our holdings. We have three vaults there. We can't send any of our staffers up there—it would take too long. Maybe you can talk to Osborn, and he could get some police presence up there."

"Right, I'm on it."

In two minutes he was talking to Osborn, who was walking the museum. "Wally, the museum has more art stored at the Freeport Naff in Tampa than it has here in the museum. I don't know why we didn't think of it before, but it's an even bigger target than the museum here. Klinger is calling them and telling them to get as many people over to their three vaults as soon as possible. Maybe you can get some police presence there as well. It's a ninety-minute drive to the freeport from here, but I don't think I should leave. It might be another dead end."

" I agree. I have contacts at Tampa PD. I'll make a call."

57

PIERRE ARSENEAU STARED OUT THE WINDOW of his second floor home office on Lido Key, clenching and un-clenching his fists. He couldn't remember ever feeling this betrayed in his entire life. First his own wife set him up by stealing his family heirloom, the van Ruisdael, and his antique paperweight. She collaborated with the Swift woman and McCoy to help that damn professor in England. And, his only child, his daughter Monica, was in it with them. So much for family loyalty. Marie was even convinced that he damaged her damned paintings for the exhibit when he'd had nothing to do with it. The only painting he ever did anything to was that Lucas Cranach in the museum. It was just a test. Even there, he only sprayed the face of the lion. He never touched her paintings.

But who the hell did? He wanted to believe it was that asshole cousin, Benoit, but he would have been in Prague at the time. And how would he have gotten the spray solution, anyway? He called Algarve.

"Do you still have that aerosol I gave back to you?" he demanded.

Algarve hesitated, then replied, "Sir, the aerosol was stolen, along with one of the stock Petri dishes from the incubators.

"Dammit, man. How could you let that happen?"

"There was no reason to check on it. You didn't ask for it and no one else would want it. It had no commercial use."

"Well, somebody wanted it, and I know who." With that he hung up.

Benoit Surette, his cousin, a member of the Legacy. Traitor. What McCoy and that detective had told him made sense. Benoit was planning to bring down the Ringling Museum as revenge for his son's death. That was fine with Pierre; he didn't care about the place either. But Benoit was planning to frame him for the destruction.

He checked his watch. Today was the twenty-first day. The place would be crawling with police and security people. How did Benoit think he was going to pull it off?

He'll want to be there, the bastard, Pierre thought. *He'll either do it himself or be having it done. In either case he'll be there.*

Pierre walked to his desk and opened the second drawer down on the left. He lifted out the small handgun and slipped it into his pocket. He knew it was loaded. He always kept it that way. He sat in his chair and stared out at the Gulf waters. He thought of the attempted murder charges against him. He knew if the police found enough evidence to link him to Bergen or Tony Carsten, he'd be convicted. Could he survive life in prison? Would he want to?

He took out the gun and stared at it. He thought of how Benoit would emerge the winner in the end. He'd have the twenty-five paintings, Mueller's money, and now he'd even get his revenge on the Ringling while Pierre went to prison for it. He stood up, resolved that the bastard wouldn't get away with it. He put the gun back in his pocket and went downstairs and out to his car.

KYLE KLINGER WAS EXHAUSTED. He hadn't slept much the night before and the phone call from the director a few minutes ago wanting to know if he'd found anything didn't help. He hadn't. In fact he was no closer now to knowing what Surette—if he was even the guy planning the trouble—was going to do than they did earlier. Almost as frustrating as not knowing what the madman planned was not being able to figure out when he'd do it. Sure, he'd given us the day, but what time during the day? Tired and out of ideas, he called Hunter.

"McCoy, where are you and what are you doing?"

HUNTER IMMEDIATELY RECOGNIZED the exhaustion and anxiety in Klinger's voice. He could only imagine the man's feeling of impotence. He was the top security official responsible for all security at the entire facility. It included not only the Ringling Museum of Art, but also everything else in the entire complex as well. He'd taken every precaution imaginable over the past week or so and still they had no idea what was planned. On top of that, if it all went south, Klinger would be the man in the hot seat. He'd be the man whose job would be on the line.

"Hey, Kyle. I'm here with Genevieve in her office."

"Okay, I've got a job for both of you."

"What's that?"

"Figure out what time today this is supposed to happen."

"That's all?"

"Get on it." He hung up.

Hunter turned to Genevieve who was beginning to look as exhausted as the rest of them. Her clothes were disheveled, her hair a mess, circles under her eyes, and her face uncharacteristically drawn. He'd never seen her this unkempt. "That was Klinger. He wants us to figure out exactly when it's supposed to happen."

"How do we do that?"

"Let's try. Okay, we think Benoit Surette is going to use Algarve's bacteria somehow, to do it, either here or at the Freeport. We believe it will be done in retaliation for the Ringling accusing his son of vandalism and firing him, resulting in his suicide."

"Okay," Genevieve said.

Hunter sat up straight. "What time did he die? What was the time of death? Twenty-one days from his son's suicide on May third at exactly the same time of day."

Hunter found his phone and called Osborn.

"Osborn, you worked the Paul Ballard suicide. What was the coroner's estimated time of death?"

"I don't remember. I'm over here in the south wing, why?"

"It might tell us what time today Surette is planning to do it. It would complete his plan. You've got to find it."

"I'll call headquarters and get it. Stay tuned, I'll call you back."

While they waited for Osborn to get the information, Genevieve went to her computer and Googled "Paul Ballard suicide at the Ringling." She found the story in the *Sarasota Herald Tribune* and scanned the article. "Here's something," she said, and then read it aloud.

> *The young man's body was found hanging from an aerial root of one of the many banyan trees on the grounds. It had been made into a crude noose, and he'd apparently stepped off a folding chair that was lying on its side under him. A night watchman discovered the body at nine-thirty PM. The police reported that there was a note but wouldn't disclose the contents. The police have not identified the man pending notification of the next of kin."*

"That's it. Just that he was found at nine-thirty at night."

Hunter nodded. "We'll have to wait for Osborn. I would think that he must have just done it, though, or someone would have found him earlier, when the grounds were still open. If so that's good news." Hunter checked his watch: 5:30. "We don't have much time if this idea is correct."

His phone rang. It was Osborn.

"The coroner estimated the official time of death at seven PM. "We've only got an hour and a half."

"Thanks, Osborn. This could be important. I'll call Klinger and tell him."

"No need, McCoy, I see him just ahead of me in the next gallery. I'll tell him."

After hanging up, Hunter strode nervously around the room. He stopped, clasped his hands behind his head, and stared up at the ceiling. "All right. That worked well. Let's try some more thinking. There's something about this whole bacteria thing that we're missing. Let's try to think it through, together."

"Okay, I'll start," said Genevieve. "He can't just walk up and spray the paintings. There's too much security out there."

Hunter was next. "Even if he could, he couldn't spray enough paintings to qualify as ruining the museum before being brought down."

"He can't spray it through the fire sprinkler system because it's clear. You and Klinger just checked it."

"All right, if you can't spray them, how else do you get the bacteria on the paintings? You can't put them in the air-conditioning system and distribute them that way. Klinger's men have already checked that several times. Besides, they'd need to be wet in order to be active."

"What if they weren't wet?" Genevieve asked. "What happens to them then?"

"They'd go dormant, I guess. I think that's what Algarve said," Hunter offered.

"So what does that mean?" she said.

"It means they sort of wall themselves off from the unfriendly environment and stop functioning until a favorable climate returns."

"So they're not dead?"

"Apparently not."

They both saw the light at the same time. "What if the bacteria are dormant and already on the paintings?"

58

PETR HAVEL WASN'T FEELING WELL. He'd been getting sicker every day for a week now. He had terrible stomach cramps and knew the reason why—the bacteria. He'd also developed blisters on his arms and neck. Mr. Surette had asked him to stay behind in Florida when he flew back to Prague after his meeting with his group a month ago. Before he left he'd taken Petr to dinner at the Ritz Carlton on Lido Key and told him a story he hadn't known before. He told him how his son had been driven to suicide by the Ringling Museum of Art. Then he told him how he was going to take his revenge. And Petr, who had done enough wet work for his boss over the years, knew it wasn't going to be pretty.

It had been pathetically easy to break in to the BIOMOD facility and take the spray aerosol and the Petri dish of the engineered bacteria. The biologist at ACELMICROBES was more than happy for the money he paid him to expand the samples from the Petri dish to a colony large enough to do the job on the Ringling's paintings. While he was doing that, Havel had to start the ball rolling framing Pierre Arseneau.

Surette had told him that Arseneau abused his wife and hated her work at the museum and was also responsible for his son's death. When he learned about the upcoming exhibit, he knew this was his opportunity. Surette had always valued Havel's ingenuity, and when Havel came up with the plan, Surette was pleased. He'd threatened the Freeport Naff employee at the Tampa facility that he'd kill his wife and child if he didn't cooperate in spraying the Gainsborough as he'd crated it. He paid the man and he did the work. Later Havel killed him with a potassium solution that made it look as if he'd suffered a heart attack.

Havel should have suspected the bacteria when he learned later the museum guy who uncrated the painting got very sick and had to be hospitalized, but he hadn't made the connection. So a few days later he took his second opportunity to spray the three paintings at the exhibit. That was a different spray though. That one was still delivered through an aerosol, but the biologist from ACELMICROBES had put them into a dormant state.

The three paintings that Arseneau's wife arranged for had arrived three days before the exhibit, and had been uncrated, and were lined up against the wall in the Searing wing of the museum, waiting to be hung. While the room was technically off limits to visitors during that time, he found it astonishingly easy to walk through and casually spray the three paintings without being noticed. After he did it and inspected them, he immediately saw the difference between this aerosol and the one he'd given the workman to use on the Gainsborough at the Freeport. The surface was dry, with no sign of moisture, no sign of his spraying them, no sign of anything.

The bigger task, the one that took two weeks, was to visit every gallery of the museum during that time, wearing a different disguise every day. On each visit he would walk up to a painting, holding the aerosol with the new dry spray in such a way that it looked like he was contemplating the painting with his hands folded in front of him. When he was sure that no one was looking directly at him he'd spray. The good thing about the aerosol was that it made no noise. It didn't have that escaping gas sound characteristic of an ordinary spray can. He supposed it was because this one had less pressure. He'd only had two close calls, one with a visitor and one with a security guard. The guard asked him if he'd been in there the day before. He'd told the man no, he'd not been in the museum.

A few paintings were hung too high on the wall to spray. There wasn't anything he could do about that, but he figured he'd covered close to 90% of the paintings in the north and south wings, even the lower parts of the huge Rubens in the first two Galleries. Surette would be satisfied. He'd completed the task two weeks ago and was glad he'd done it then. They hadn't yet begun to beef up security as Surette's threatened day of ruination approached. He couldn't risk being seen over there now, but he'd gotten close two days ago to observe the increased activity.

He could relax now. Everything was in place, and he'd given Surette the activator yesterday in his room at the Ritz.

Up until then he had been a loyal soldier in Benoit Surette's army. He'd been with the man for twelve years and had never failed to deliver on an assignment, and Surette had treated him well, even giving him an apartment in the office building. All that had ended two hours ago in Algarve's office at BIOMOD. He'd been getting sicker every day now for a week. Suspecting it might be the bacteria he'd gone to BIOMOD and held a gun to the temple of the terrified little man who'd created it.

"Does your bacteria make people sick?"

Algarve had swallowed hard. "Who are you?" he managed to croak out in a weak, frightened voice.

"I'm the man who's going to kill you if you don't answer."

"Yes. It can make you very sick. It wasn't supposed to, but it can, especially if you have a compromised immune system or a liver problem."

Havel never drank but he had been diagnosed with nonalcoholic cirrhosis of the liver. He definitely had a liver problem. "What are the symptoms?"

"They can include fever, vomiting, diarrhea, and abdominal pain. If your immune system is weak because you have any kind of liver or kidney disease or diabetes, the infection can cause more severe symptoms."

"Like what?"

"High fever and chills; low blood pressure; redness, swelling, and blisters on the skin."

"Like these?" Havel rolled up his sleeves to reveal open sores.

Algarve looked and closed his eyes, finally seeing where this was going. "Yes, exactly like those. If the bacteria come in contact with an open cut, you may get a severe skin infection like that. If not treated, it can spread to your bloodstream and it's lethal."

"Why did you do this?"

"I was ordered to by my boss, Pierre Arseneau."

"Did he know it was deadly?"

"No one knew at the beginning."

"What about later?"

"We all knew."

"I want you to think very carefully about your answer to my next questions. Do you know who Benoit Surette is?"

"I learned who he is from the police. I didn't know him before."

"Did he know the bacteria was deadly?"

"I don't know. Probably. He might have learned it from Arseneau."

Havel was silent for a moment, and Algarve said, "You don't look well. Are you all right?"

Havel took the gun away from Algarve's temple and stepped back several feet still keeping the gun trained on him. "No, I'm not. I have a liver disease and all the symptoms you just described. I've been in contact with your bacteria since I took it out of your incubators several weeks ago. No one told me it was toxic to humans. I was only told it would eat paintings. I've sprayed it, touched it, and breathed it for weeks. Now what would you think of a boss who would order you to do that, knowing it would kill you?"

Algarve had no answer. He knew who was really responsible for the man's condition. He was. He'd created the little killers. It was his carelessness that turned them into lethal timebombs. He was responsible for the little girl's death. He was responsible for this man's illness.

"I'll tell you this, Algarve, Pierre Arseneau and Benoit Surette are dead men walking, but not for much longer."

Havel kept the gun steady and focused on Algarve for a long moment as if considering what to do. Then he slowly lowered it and left.

59

HUNTER CALLED GRETCHEN CEISEL and told her to meet them in Gallery 3 of the south wing right away, and to bring some cotton swabs, slides, and cover slips. If their thinking was correct, they should find some evidence to support it. Over time someone could have sprayed a dormant form of the bacteria on the paintings with the idea of somehow activating it when they wanted to begin the destructive process of digesting the paint. They'd try to figure out how that could happen if the bacteria were there.

They arrived at the gallery at the same time as Gretchen.

"What do you want to do with this stuff?" she asked.

"We think the paintings may already have a dormant form of the bacteria on them, just waiting for a signal to re-activate. We've got to see if they're there."

Hunter supervised as Gretchen dipped a cotton swab in water and wiped a part of the first painting they came to. Then she wiped the slide with the swab and placed a cover slip on it. She repeated the process with a fresh swab, slide, and cover slip on eight more paintings.

"All right, Gretchen, let's go back to your lab and look at these under the microscope."

A few minutes later, in her lab in the Education Center, they were doing just that. Hunter peered through her scope, transfixed by what he was seeing. Since this whole thing with the bacteria had started he'd being doing a lot of reading on the Internet. The samples on the slides confirmed their worst fears. Before his eyes he could see inactive bacteria shedding their shells and becoming active again. Clearly the water had been the trigger that brought them out of dormancy and prepped them for their destiny, digesting oil paint. The key was water. Hunter grabbed his phone and called Klinger.

"Kyle, the bacteria are already on the paintings," he nearly shouted into the phone. "They're dormant. Surette plans to spray water on them to activate them. It's got to be the fire sprinkler system after all. Get down there. I'll meet you right away."

———————————————

BENOIT SURETTE, STILL SITTING on the garden bench opened his eyes. To a casual observer he would have looked like an old man napping for the past hour. He hadn't been. He'd spent the time recalling the days when he and his young son, then just a boy, had played in the garden behind his mansion in Prague. It was a happy time, before the divorce. In spite of the rift in his marriage, he had great things in mind for the boy. As Paul grew into a young man Benoit made plans for him to become a partner in the business. And when the two years at the Ringling were over, the boy had agreed to do just that. Then he killed himself, and all hope ended. Benoit considered it a murder. Paul may have taken his own life, but they were responsible, and now, on the anniversary of his death, they were going to pay.

How ironic, he thought, that his cousin Pierre had supplied him with the very means to do it, his cousin whom he loathed; the cousin who contributed to Paul's suicidal depression. And now, because Pierre's own bacterial invention would place the blame squarely on him, Benoit's revenge would be that much sweeter.

He checked his watch. Just a few minutes now.

———————————————

"SOMEHOW HE'S PLANNING TO SET OFF the sprinkler system, Kyle. I know it."

"We've got to shut off the main valves again." The two men were running toward the fire sprinkler control room as fast as they could. Arriving out of breath, they each started turning one of the three valves. When they'd been shut off, Klinger worked on the third until it too was closed.

"There," Klinger said, "Seven PM on the dot. Now if he has some way to set them off all together, the paintings won't get wet and the bacteria will stay dormant."

Both men relaxed and fell back against the wall, breathing heavily. Hunter heard it first, a sizzling, crackling sound overhead. It seemed to be coming from the preloaded pipes they had examined earlier. Hunter grabbed a chair, stood on it, and touched one of the pipes. It was hot.

"He's heating the pipes somehow. If they get hot enough the heads will pop. Remember, when we did this the other day there was still enough pressure in the pipes even with the valve's shut off to get the paintings slightly wet. That's all it takes to activate the bacteria. Humidity might even do it."

Hunter saw that the pipes passed through a wooden panel into the wall. He pushed the panel. It was loose.

"Hold the chair steady, Kyle. I'm going to knock this out."

He hammered on the panel with his fist until it loosened enough for him to pull it out. Then he saw it, the source of the sound and the heat. A metal belt was wrapped tightly around each iron pipe, and they were attached to what looked like some kind of power source, a metal box about two feet square.

"Kyle, over there, on the workbench. Give me some wire cutters or pliers, something, anything. Fast."

Klinger pulled out drawers in the bench. Finally he found a pair of large pliers. He tossed them up to Hunter, who quickly yanked out the wires from the box to the belts, and the crackling noise stopped.

Kyle got on his radio to his people. "Has anyone seen a sprinkler go off anywhere? Tell me now. Come on people, I'm waiting."

"Negative."

"No sir."

"Nothing."

Everyone reported in. No sprinkler discharge. They'd stopped it. They'd stopped him.

"Now let's find that bastard," Kyle said.

"Let's go," Hunter said, simultaneously calling their head of security at the Tampa freeport, a man Hunter had brought into the search earlier. He told him what to look for in their system and asked him to report back as soon as possible.

SURETTE HAD THROWN THE SWITCH on the device Havel had rigged for him a few minutes earlier. The signal would turn on the power source attached to the pipes. The pipes would be heating now, and the sprinkler heads going off any minute. He could only imagine the panic inside when that happened. He smiled as he thought of the destruction Pierre's little creations were about to produce.

Now that the system was activated he got up and pushed his walker back toward the Visitors Pavilion, where Havel was going to pick him up for the drive back to the Ritz. Then he'd wait for the television news reports or the morning paper, whichever was first with the story. He smiled as he thought of that.

Passing through the lobby of the Visitors Pavilion, he exited through the front gate where Havel, as instructed, was waiting with the car. He got into the back seat and removed his old man disguise, his gray-haired wig and glasses, and as he asked for the bottle of scotch he'd told Havel to have available, he noticed the man hadn't spoken. Then he noticed something else. They weren't driving downtown toward the Ritz but were heading north instead, past the airport. Confused, he opened his mouth to demand that Havel explain this when suddenly he felt a blinding pain, accompanied by stars and bright lights, followed by oblivion.

Pierre Arseneau, already tied and gagged in the trunk, heard the commotion and knew that things were only going to get worse.

60

HAVEL DROVE FOR TWO HOURS, not concerned in the least for the comfort of the two men now tied up and gagged in the trunk. He rather enjoyed what he could only imagine to be their confusion. They'd easily recognize who the other was, he was sure of that. They'd be absolutely confounded as to why they were in this predicament. He was sure they hated each other and would be all the more outraged to find themselves equally in trouble. And they were in big trouble.

He eventually drove back to the Ringling, where he knew the compound would be closed for the day. He parked in the lot by the Education Center. It was dark, with only a sliver of a moon to supply a ghostly light. He marched both men at gunpoint, with their wrists duct-taped in front of them, to a large banyan tree near the secret garden where John and Mable Ringling and his sister were buried and had them sit on the ground under the enormous arms of the spreading tree. Then he removed his silenced pistol and carefully shot each man in the leg. Still gagged, they could do little more that scream silently and thrash on the ground. He waited for them to realize they were still alive and gave them time to deal with the pain. Then he began to talk.

"Let me begin with you, Pierre Arseneau. I'll tell you why you're here. You're here because you've killed me. Yes, that's right. I'm a dead man, and you killed me."

Arseneau vigorously shook his head. If he weren't gagged he'd probably scream, "What the hell are you talking about? I don't even know you. I've never seen you before in my life." Of course he couldn't say these things, so he just continued to shake his head and stare wild-eyed at the man with the gun.

"Let me tell you how you killed me," Havel went on. "Those little bacterial monsters of yours cause serious human infection to anyone who handles them. In addition to eating oil paint, they also eat human flesh. But then you know that, don't you?"

Again Arseneau wildly shook his head.

Then, directing himself to his former boss, Havel said, "And you did too."

Surette just stared at Havel with malevolent hate obvious in his eyes.

"For a full month you had me deal with this stuff. I stole those bacteria from his lab for you. I had it grown into large volumes for you. I sprayed paintings for you. All the time you knew I'd be killing myself."

Havel watched as Arseneau looked in confusion at his cousin, who continued staring at Petr with undisguised rage. Then Havel shot each of them in the other leg. Arseneau passed out while Surette silently screamed again and lunged at Havel, who slapped him in the face with the gun.

"I've served you faithfully for many years, and this is your response? In the end I'm nothing more than trash to you. And what do you do with trash? You throw it away. Well, you've succeeded. I've been thrown away. But I'm not going before I have my revenge. You and Arseneau are about to leave my final message to the world."

IT WAS A BEAUTIFUL MORNING IN SOUTHWEST FLORIDA, and even though the tourist season was pretty much over, there were still plenty of them wanting to see the sights. Bill and Judy Collins, from Denver, Colorado wanted to see the famous John and Mable Ringling Museum of Art. They bought their tickets and boarded the tram at the Visitors

Pavilion for the ride to the Ca' d'Zan, where they were told they'd see the Circus King's palatial mansion on lovely Sarasota Bay. The tram driver, a veteran volunteer, pointed out the sights and answered the frequent questions of the six passengers along the way.

After leaving the Pavilion they drove around a lovely pond with tropical water birds and colorful fish and turtles, to the front entrance of the art museum building, where the driver pointed out a remarkable bronze statue of a naked woman, Lygia, strapped to the horns of a bull from the Quo Vadis story of first-century Rome. She was an early Christian in love with a Roman soldier persecuted by Nero.

The driver stopped while three visitors disembarked and two others got on. Next the driver took them past Mable's Rose Garden, the oldest continual rose garden in the state of Florida and the personal delight of Mable Ringling. As they approached the Ca' d'Zan mansion, which they could now see emerging before them, the driver gestured to the huge, twisting Banyan trees, explaining there were fourteen such trees on the grounds, some of which were almost one hundred years old, having been there during the time of the Ringlings themselves.

"Now just up ahead, ladies and gentlemen," the driver announced as the tram approached a large banyan tree in front of the mansion, "if you look closely you'll see what can happen if you stand too long next to one of these beauties." The driver waited for the laughter that always accompanied their seeing the concrete statue that had long been enveloped by the tree itself. Instead he heard a woman scream, "Oh my God. Look!" Others shouted as well. Confused, the driver turned toward the enveloped statue and saw what his passengers had seen.

Hanging by their necks from aerial roots behind the statue were the bodies of two men. Seated below them on the ground, propped up against the tree, was a third man, dead apparently from a gunshot to the head.

KLINGER CALLED HUNTER, WHO CALLED OSBORN. It didn't take long to identify the three bodies as Pierre Arseneau, Benoit Surette, and Petr Havel. The park was immediately closed and all visitors were asked to leave. The crime scene people did their work while Hunter, Klinger, and the detective speculated on what had happened. The body of Dr. Algarve had been discovered earlier. After the coroner did her work the bodies were removed, and she told Osborn she'd have a report for him later in the day.

"We may find that Algarve was killed by the same gun that was found lying next to Havel, although why he did this, I can't imagine," Detective Osborn said. "It looks like two murders and a suicide. Why would he kill them and then kill himself?"

Hunter was stumped too.

"It's got to have something to do with Surette's attempt to damage the paintings," said Klinger. "Thank God we stopped that. Gretchen and her people are going to be busy for quite a while cleaning the bacteria off every painting in the place; we'll need to keep the museum closed for several more days. By the way," he added, "we've found no trace of bacteria on the paintings in the freeport. It looks like the only target was right here."

"That's good, at least," Hunter said. "Still, something just doesn't add up here. We may have stopped the immediate threat to the paintings, but something else is going on. Something we know nothing about. I'm sure of it."

HUNTER AND WALLY OSBORN WERE DEVOURING enormous Reuben sandwiches with fries at a downtown deli when Osborn got the call from the coroner's office. She told him she had time and cause of death and something else as well.

He'd better get over there on the double and bring McCoy with him.

"What's up doc?" Osborn asked, twenty minutes later, imitating Bugs Bunny.

Ignoring him, she began. "Cause of death for both Arseneau and Surette was asphyxiation. The hanging did it. However, they'd both lost a lot of blood before that from a single gunshot wound to each leg. It's impossible to tell how long he waited after he shot them before he strung them up. He didn't hit any major arteries so he could have had as much as an hour or so with them before the hanging.

"Now as for Havel. Gunshot residue shows that he pulled the trigger on himself. But what's really weird—and that's why you're here, McCoy—It appears that he was very sick with the bacteria you told me about earlier, the oil-eating-bacteria that acts like the pathogenic bacteria, *vibrio vulnificus*. I'm quarantining these bodies until they can be properly disposed of."

Back at the station Hunter and Osborn considered what they'd learned.

"So Havel was sick, probably dying," Osborn began. "Probably explains his suicide. But first he kills those two. Why? Does he blame them for his condition? He no doubt learned—either from Algarve or more likely Surette—that Arseneau was responsible for developing the bacteria in the first place and killed him for that. If the bullet that killed Algarve turns out to be from Havel's gun, then he most likely figured out that Algarve made the bacteria deadly, blamed him for it, and killed him too."

"Right," Hunter said. "And he killed his boss, Surette, because he'd had him stay here in Sarasota, steal the sample, and spray the paintings. He had to blame him for his getting infected. Surette might not have known the stuff was dangerous, but Havel wouldn't have known that. So he took his revenge and then put himself out of his misery."

"Sounds reasonable," Osborn said.

Hunter called to update Genevieve who said she was in the director's office and asked him to join them. Hilda ushered him in as soon as he arrived.

Director Bertram got right to it. "Hunter, I can't thank you and Genevieve enough. You both really saved the place from destruction. I don't know what we would have done without you. All the paintings are safe. Gretchen's found a way to vacuum the painting surfaces without getting them wet, and then she destroys the bags with the bacteria. She's being very careful in the process, not wanting another stay in the hospital."

Hunter laughed. "I can imagine. She wasn't too happy the last time."

"So thanks to you two, and Kyle and his people, we're going to get back to normal around here," the director said. "Thank you again for all your help. Oh, there's one other thing. I know how your find-and-correct remuneration system works. Kyle told me. You can expect an appreciation gift in the mail from the Ringling within the week."

Hunter took Genevieve to dinner at a place he'd heard about south of downtown on Phillippi Creek, called The Table, or as Genevieve called it, La Table. They toasted each other with a fine Italian Tuscany red and ordered dinner.

"Well, Hunter, it looks like everything's been taken care of. The bad guys are dead, the mysteries have been solved, my boss is now happy with me, Mother and Father are safe, and I've got you."

"Almost right. They're just two things left we don't have answers to."

"What do you mean? I thought we had everything wrapped up."

"Not quite. If you'll remember, we still don't know where the twenty-five missing Wicar paintings are. And there's the little matter of the elusive four hundred thirty-two million dollars?"

61

Two Weeks Later

HUNTER RUBBED MORE SUNBLOCK on Genevieve's back, even though they were sitting on low beach chairs under a wide umbrella on Venice Beach, just off downtown. Rather than being populated by touristy tee shirt shops and other junk, West Venice Avenue was a high-quality destination shopping area only a half-hour from downtown Sarasota, Hunter and Genevieve preferred it to the more populous Siesta Key beach. They'd been kicking back and relaxing, finally getting the time together they'd planned all along before Benny Bergen had attacked her in her house almost six weeks before.

Hunter knew he had to get back to Charlottesville soon, but couldn't get the feeling out of his head that the whole affair they'd just been through wasn't over yet. He'd been disturbed by the call he'd gotten yesterday from Eduard Gautier. As he'd informed Genevieve, Eduard had told him that the Czech police had done a thorough search of Benoit Surette's home and found no trace of the twenty-five missing Wicar paintings that they all expected to be there. It had taken considerable effort for the authorities to open a locked vault off a small gallery he kept in the house, where they were sure they would find the paintings. But it seemed he kept this vault only to store records of the illegal business he used Petr Havel for. It turned out that all of those cases where they suspected he'd used force to run competitors out of business were true. The evidence was in the vault.

What really had Hunter confounded was the lack of any evidence for the painting swindle. They found none, none at all. If Benoit kept incriminating documents of a lifetime of business corruption and even murder in a locked large vault in his house, why not evidence of the freeport swindle? Gautier told him that the authorities had raided and examined all other properties that Surette owned and found nothing. Examination of his personal computers by experts found no evidence that would suggest he had the paintings or had received the four hundred thirty-two million dollars, nothing.

"What are you thinking about?" Genevieve asked. "I can hear the gears grinding."

"The gears grinding? There you go again. By the end of your tour here you'll sound more like an American than I do."

"Is that a bad thing?" she asked, bending to kiss him on the lips.

"Nothing about you is bad."

They gazed happily into each other's eyes for a moment, and then sat back to admire the beautiful blue-green Gulf waters.

"So who has the paintings and who has the money?" she asked, fully aware of what the gear grinding was about.

"Eduard said that Interpol talked with each of the other three European cousins in the Legacy. They all said that each of the five members kept only one of the original paintings and the others were kept in the Zurich Freeport until they were stolen. For a while there I thought that Arseneau had two when I saw that one in his office but, of course, that one wasn't a Wicar painting. I wonder, though. Did *he* somehow carry out the swindle? Did *he* get the paintings and the money? Were we all wrong? If that's the case he put on quite a show with Osborn and me when we told him that Surette was the swindler. I'd swear he didn't fake his surprise."

"What about Arseneau's house on Lido Key? I'm sure Marie would give permission to search it."

"I'm sure she would too. I'm going to call Osborn and see what we can do."

It had been two weeks since the banyan tree murders, and Hunter and Genevieve had met several times with Marie and Monica since then. While they were horrified by the manner of the deaths, neither of them missed Pierre very much. Hunter knew that they'd both cooperated with the police in their investigation, and while they no doubt wanted to put the affair behind them, he suspected Marie wouldn't object to another official visit.

Today was Sunday, so the next morning he took Genevieve to work and drove downtown to see Osborn, where he laid out what he'd learned from Gautier and what he wanted to do next.

"No kidding. The Czech guy didn't have it? He didn't have the art or the money?"

"Not according to Interpol, and they did a thorough search of everything the man owned."

"So where is it?"

"Maybe we need to revisit Marie Arseneau. It might be that Pierre Arseneau was the swindler, although I can't imagine how. You were there when we laid out the case that his cousin Surette did it. His response looked pretty genuine to me."

"Yeah, it did. It looked like he'd have strangled his cousin if he'd been there."

"That's what I thought. Maybe we were wrong, and he was just a great actor. I'd like to have us go out and see Marie again, and this time let's ask her about the possibility that Pierre might have done it."

Osborn called Marie, and an hour later they were invited into the living room. As a bonus Monica was present as well. Now that Pierre was gone, she had moved back in to keep her mother company in the enormous mansion.

"Marie, I'm sorry to bother you again," Hunter said, taking the lead. "You know the police have been trying to find the missing paintings and the money that Horst Mueller paid for them. The theory was that Benoit Surette worked the swindle and had it all. But the Czech police, working with the full cooperation of Interpol, have turned up absolutely nothing to suggest that Surette ever took the paintings or the four hundred thirty-two million dollars from Mueller. Nevertheless, somebody did. Is there any chance that your husband did it without your knowledge?"

Monica shook her head. "I truly don't know. He never told me about any of his business with the Legacy. Somehow he felt that was completely his business and none of mine. I think he always resented that fact that it was my money that got us started in the first place, so the paintings were his and his alone. I didn't care. Let him have them was the way I looked at it."

"Have you been through his office upstairs? Did you find anything that might suggest he had them somewhere?" Osborn asked.

"No. To tell you the truth, I haven't even been in the room for two weeks. I guess I've avoided it."

Osborn nodded. "Would you mind if we examined it?"

"No, go ahead. Monica, would you show them where it is? I'm going to stay here."

Monica led them up an enormous winding stairway to the second level, then to the side of the house facing the Gulf where Arseneau had his office. Immediately Hunter noticed that the van Ruisdael painting and the paperweight were back lying on his desk—returned to Marie by Director Bertram. Monica left, and Hunter and Osborn spent the next ninety minutes going through files and desk drawers.

Behind a tapestry of a hunting scene they found a large wall safe with a door like one would see in a bank.

Neither man found anything related to paintings of any kind. There were also no records of the Legacy, their meetings, or even a mention of their names. They also found nothing relating to Quentin Naff and the freeport or their having funded it.

"It looks like we've gotta get in that safe, McCoy," Osborn said.

Two hours later, with Marie's permission, a firm the local bank recommended sent a man out with a van full of tools. After forty-five minutes of work, he was in. Marie paid him, thanked him, and he left.

"I guess I'd better stay for this," said the elegant widow.

The vault was large enough to step into, about six feet high, four feet deep, and four feet wide. It was completely lined with shelves and files. When they saw a cellphone, Hunter said, "Maybe that's the burner he called Tony Carsten in Cambridge with."

Osborn, wearing gloves, dropped it in an evidence bag and said he'd check it out. They hit the jackpot with the files. They were the complete records of the Legacy. They included detailed minutes of all their meetings, plans for something called *Payback*, information on all of the current members, and paperwork concerning funding the initial freeport in Zurich and the eventual sale of their interest for a huge profit. While Marie and Monica looked on, periodically bringing iced tea, Hunter and Osborn went through everything, emerging bleary-eyed two hours later with the full picture.

The Legacy's initial investment to fund Quentin Naff had paid off big time. They cleared almost a five hundred percent earning on their money when they sold their shares back to him. At the urging of Benoit Surette, the group had asked Naff to find a buyer for the twenty-five paintings they were storing in the freeport. Naff found Horst Mueller, and after showing him the Legacy's paintings, Mueller offered four hundred and thirty-two million dollars for them. The deal was carried out—only the Legacy lost their paintings, never got the money, and since Mueller never got the paintings, everyone accused Naff of the swindle, figuring he got it all, the money and the paintings. So they set out to ruin his business through rumor. The minutes also included the fact that if Arseneau had gotten the votes in their last meeting, they would have begun sabotaging paintings in Naff's freeports using his oil-paint-eating microbes. None of that would necessarily have gotten their paintings back, but the revenge would have been satisfying.

"There's nothing here to suggest that Arseneau—sorry, your late husband—had the twenty-five paintings or somehow got the money," Osborn said.

Hunter wasn't listening. He was staring out the window at the Gulf. He'd been looking only at bits and pieces of the puzzle, hoping somehow they'd mean something. But they hadn't. Alone they were only facts, only unusual events. Somehow they had to mean something collectively. He continued to watch the turquoise water, ignoring the others, until he finally saw it.

How had he missed it? The clues were right in front of him all the time. All he'd had to do was to put them together. He turned to the others in the room, Marie, Monica, and Osborn.

"I know who did it and I know how."

62

HUNTER SPENT THE NEXT THREE HOURS on and off the phone with Eduard Gautier at Interpol Headquarters in Lyon, France. During that time he told Gautier what he'd concluded. Eduard agreed it was possible and immediately contacted the Swiss police investigator looking into the case against the Freeport Naff at the Zurich Airport. The man had been working on the case with Interpol from the beginning. Right after the German businessman, Horst Mueller filed his lawsuit against Naff for swindling him out of four hundred thirty-two million dollars in exchange for twenty-five masterpieces he never received.

He then took an overnight Swiss Air flight from Tampa to Zurich. According to Eduard, Detective Jonas Hirtzel, the officer in charge, would meet him at the airport on his arrival. Hunter had to admit he'd been completely fooled. He'd been led all the way. He'd followed all the bread crumbs laid out in front of him without question. All of it was designed to mislead him into thinking that the ultimate thief of the twenty-five paintings and the four hundred thirty-two million dollars was Benoit Surette.

The more he thought about it, the more he was impressed by the finesse of the frame. All the evidence pointed to Surette. It was Surette who'd initially suggested the Legacy sell the paintings. When Pierre Arseneau found out that they'd completely cleared Quentin Naff of any involvement in the theft of their twenty-five paintings and they were looking for another suspect in the swindle, it didn't take long for him to arrive at the same conclusion they had. Especially after they told him they believed that

Benoit Surette was going to take his revenge against the Ringling Museum by damaging its paintings using Arseneau's own specially engineered bacteria to do it. That way Surette could get his revenge against the Ringling and place the blame squarely on his cousin. That would have been a double win as far as Surette was concerned.

So of course Arseneau immediately pointed the finger at Surette. And who could blame him? The clincher was the name of the man who'd actually rented the freeport vault next door to Horst Mueller's and been caught on tape stealing the paintings, Baptiste Sublette from Orleans. The framer certainly knew they would discover that the only Baptiste Sublette from Orleans had been dead for several years by that time.

Baptiste Sublette—Benoit Surette.

It was beautiful, and Hunter and the others had followed every clue to every planned conclusion. They'd been played by a master—suckered all the way.

After landing and clearing customs, Hunter spotted a dour-faced man in his fifties wearing a tie and jacket holding a sign that said "McCoy."

"Detective Jonas Hirtzel?" Hunter asked.

"I'm Hirtzel. You Hunter McCoy?" the man asked in flawless English with only a hint of accent.

Hunter extended his hand. "I'm McCoy. Thanks for meeting me, detective."

"Where are you staying? I'll drive you there and we can talk on the way."

"The Radisson Blu, near the airport. Shouldn't take long."

Fifteen minutes later Hunter had checked in and the two men went down to the hotel's restaurant, where they both ordered breakfast. Over the next hour and a half Hunter filled him in on everything he'd learned and outlined what he thought they should do. Detective Hirtzel listened quietly, only asking questions now and then to clarify a point or two. When Hunter was done Hirtzel just sat quietly for a moment. Then slowly, almost imperceptibly, a smile crept onto his face, and he nodded. "I like it."

QUENTIN NAFF LITERALLY LIVED IN A CASTLE. It had been built in 1790, and when it came on the market five years ago, he couldn't resist. It had sixty-two rooms, turrets, balustrades, a great hall and a spectacular view down onto Lake Zurich. It had already been upgraded with modern conveniences and was ready to move in. Few but the superrich could have afforded it, and now Quentin Naff was one of them. His freeports were so successful, he now needed an entire staff of people who did nothing but manage his investments.

Earlier, when he had gotten the call from Detective Hirtzel saying he needed to meet with him and was bringing Hunter McCoy, Naff was delighted, thinking they were going to tell him they were going after Benoit Surette and would stop harassing him for the theft of the Legacy's paintings and Mueller's money. So he met them at the door himself.

"GENTLEMEN, PLEASE COME IN. Dr. McCoy, it's nice to see you again, although I'm a little surprised you're back in Europe."

Hunter noticed that Naff appeared positively gleeful. "I'm frequently here on business," he replied, "and of course Genevieve lives in Paris, so it's not too unusual."

"That's great." Naff led them into a library off the entryway, where they took seats. He straightened his brocade smoking jacket and settled opposite them. "So what can I do for the police, Detective Hirtzel? I'm assuming you're setting your sights on Benoit Surette as the real swindler, after what Dr. McCoy uncovered at the freeport. And I must say it will be delightful to finally be out of your crosshairs."

Hirtzel took the lead. "Well, I'm afraid a few problems have recently come up concerning that."

"Problems?" Naff asked, puzzled. "What problems?"

"Did you know that Benoit Surette had a son?"

"No, I know nothing about the man's personal life. I know he is a wealthy industrialist in the Czech Republic—automobiles, I believe. He and his cousins in the Legacy were wealthy enough to fund the initial Freeport. What does his son have to do with anything?"

"Benoit Surette is dead. He was recently murdered in Sarasota, Florida."

"What? Dead?" Naff's eyes widened.

"Yes, it seems he was in the process of trying to carry out a plan to damage paintings in the Ringling Museum of Art in Sarasota. It was some sort of revenge plot in response to his son's suicide four years ago. He blamed the museum for the boy's death. His son had been an employee there at the time."

"That's terrible. But Benoit Surette was murdered, you say?"

"Yes, and not only him. His cousin, Pierre Arseneau, was killed along with him."

"My God. Who did it?"

"They were killed by Petr Havel, Surette's hired thug, who then killed himself."

"That's horrible. Arseneau too? But I don't understand. What's this all about? What does it have to do with me?"

"The police in Florida believe that Havel was fatally ill from coming into repeated contact with a lethal bacteria that was bioengineered at Arseneau's company to destroy old oil paintings. Surette had Havel spray paintings in the museum with the bacteria as his means of revenge for his son's death, and he was planning to frame Pierre Arseneau for it. We believe that Havel blamed both of them for his illness and killed them in retaliation. Then, already dying from the disease, he turned his gun on himself."

"That's just incredible. I'm speechless. But how does that affect me?"

"Well, now it gets interesting. You see, we agreed with you. All the evidence would suggest that Surette had stolen the paintings and somehow gotten the money that Mueller transferred electronically. So the Czech police did a thorough search of Surette's home in Prague, but found no evidence of the paintings. They searched his office building. They searched everywhere. No paintings. They combed through his computer files, his bank accounts, and there was no evidence of the four hundred thirty-two million dollars he supposedly took from Mueller. There was nothing to link him to the crime at all. He looked guilty, but he wasn't."

"I don't understand. I was sure it was him." Naff stood up and paced the room for a moment while Hunter and Hirtzel remained quiet and watched him. Finally he said, "What about Arseneau? Maybe he did it?"

Hunter had been expecting this. "It's funny you should say that. After Surette appeared to be innocent of the swindle, we searched Arseneau's home for evidence of the paintings or the money. Again, we found nothing. He did have a safe in his office, and when we got into that we found all the records of the Legacy. Everything they had, going back years. We even found records of their funding your early efforts with the Freeport. All of that was above board; everyone benefitted from it."

"Yes, that's true," said the old man. "Their early investment made it all possible, and they earned a lot of money later."

"Yes, they did," Hunter agreed. "And you'll be interested to know that they were so convinced that you had swindled them out of the paintings that they launched a program they called *Payback* to get even with you. Its main feature was to spread rumors that your freeports weren't safe anymore. Their plan was to put you out of business."

"Dammit. I knew it. I knew they were behind it. You have evidence, you say? Actual evidence that they've been doing this?"

"Yes. You were correct all along. In fact, there's more. Pierre Arseneau had his company, BIOMOD, engineer the oil-paint-eating bacteria precisely to spray some of the art in your freeports to show your clients that they weren't safe. Luckily for you, the majority of Legacy members voted against doing this. The only two in favor by the way were Arseneau and Surette."

"Damn them to hell," Naff yelled. "Then they got what they deserved."

"They did," Hunter agreed. "They were evil men, both guilty of many crimes including murder. But the thing is, they weren't actually guilty of one thing; neither of them was guilty of stealing the twenty-five Wicar paintings or of stealing Horst Mueller's four hundred thirty-two million dollars. You did that all by yourself."

"What? You're out of your mind. You've already seen it wasn't me. You came to the freeport and proved how it was done. You've shown it wasn't me."

"Yes. That was brilliant on your part, and it almost worked. In fact, to be honest, if the searches of the Surette and Arseneau properties hadn't turned up empty, I probably wouldn't have given it a second thought. But since they didn't do it, I took a new look at you, and here's what I came up with:

"When I asked you if you owned any art, you said, 'Absolutely not. In fact I don't personally own any paintings. I get enough enjoyment out of seeing everyone else's. That's one of the perks of owning the whole thing.'"

"Yes, I did, and it's true. So what?"

"Well imagine my surprise when your man Farner told me that you maintained a personal vault at the Zurich

Freeport. Why would you need a vault if you don't own any art? What could you be storing in there?"

Naff remained silent and gaped at Hunter, his white-bristled jaw quivering.

"But what really got my curiosity up was learning that your previous cyber department head was a man who everyone said had suddenly won a lottery or something and had decided to quit and lead a life of luxury."

Naff began to chew on his lower lip.

"When Ina and Millie showed me how the money transfer *could* have been diverted without leaving a digital record, I decided to take a close look at this mysterious lottery winner, your former cyber head. Guess what we found when I got the authorities to look at his bank records?

"Last night Detective Hirtzel, here, arrested the man. He confessed that he wrote a program—at your request—to divert funds to a numbered account at Credit Suisse. The next day, thirty-two million was transferred to the programmer's personal bank account. The other four hundred million was withdrawn and disappeared. The numbered account was immediately closed. The numbers involved here are just so interesting, don't you think? Thirty-two million, four hundred million, four hundred thirty-two million."

"I want to call my attorney."

"You do that, Mr. Naff," Detective Hirtzel said. "Tell him you're being arrested now for grand theft. Oh, and you should also know that my men are currently entering your vault at the freeport. I wonder what they're going to find? Any ideas, Mr. Naff?"

Epilogue

ED McCOY, HUNTER'S DAD, and Ed's best friend Henry Niemi were both in Genevieve's kitchen preparing dinner according to Curly Winston's instructions. Ed told Hunter and Genevieve to go sit on the lanai and relax. They'd prepare the fish. Earlier in the day Ed and Henry had been out in the Gulf fishing with Genevieve's neighbor, Curly. They'd had a great time catching grouper and red snapper. Ed and Paul, living exclusively in Michigan's upper peninsula were stream fishermen only and knew nothing about fishing on the open water of the Gulf. Curly, it turned out, was an excellent cook as well as a knowledgeable fisherman, and he gave them some suggestions on how to prepare the day's catch for dinner before taking a portion home to his wife.

A week ago, Hunter had found them a one-month rental cottage on Sarasota Bay, just two miles away from Genevieve's house, and both men were delighted when Hunter said he'd pay all their expenses. All they had to do was get down here, catch the occasional fish, and prepare dinner once in a while. They jumped at the idea.

The four of them devoured the fish, after which Genevieve complimented Ed and Henry on their fishing skill and culinary talent. Both men actually blushed. Hunter wasn't sure he'd ever seen his dad blush before. Now, with dinner out of the way, the kitchen cleaned up, and the sun setting in the west, they made their way to the lanai and each prepared the after-dinner libation of their choice. Henry had a beer, Ed fixed a Jack Daniels neat, Genevieve had a white wine, and Hunter made a small shaker of perfect Canadian Club Manhattans on the rocks with a twist of lemon.

With Hunter and Genevieve alternatively picking up the story over the next two hours, they told Ed and Henry the whole tale of the Wicar Legacy.

"So let me see if I have this right," said Ed. "This Naff character paid you twenty-five thousand dollars to find the bad guy who—wait for it now—turns out to be Naff himself? In other words, he paid you twenty-five grand to find himself?"

"That's right, Dad. Of course he figured we'd tap someone else instead. He'd done a masterful job of setting up Benoit Surette to take the fall for the swindle and it almost worked."

"So can I assume that Henry and I are enjoying all this," he spread his hands wide, "at least partly at the expense of Mr. Naff? Please tell me that's true."

"It's true Dad. Ironic, but true," and they all laughed.

"So what's the latest on Naff?" asked Henry.

"My friend at Interpol, Eduard Gautier, called yesterday. When Detective Hirtzel's men entered Quentin Naff's vault at the freeport they found the twenty-five Wicar paintings and the four hundred million dollars that was Naff's share of Mueller's money. Faced with this evidence Naff had to confess, and Hirtzel says he'll be convicted for sure."

"But here's the best part, Dad, and you'll love this; you too, Genevieve. It seems that Horst Mueller, the German industrialist who lost the four hundred thirty-two million dollars to Naff's swindle, had put up a five hundred thousand dollar reward for getting it back. It seems he believes that I deserve that reward, so I'll be getting that in the near future."

"What?" Genevieve yelped. "A half million dollars and you didn't tell me until now?" She punched him in the arm.

"Ouch. That's my bad shoulder."

"Hmmm."

Ed got up. "Henry, it's time we got back to our place. These two need to count their money."

At the door Genevieve hugged Ed and Henry and thanked them for the wonderful dinner. Then she hugged Ed again and whispered something in his ear. He smiled and kissed her cheek and they all said goodnight.

When they were gone, Hunter swept her into his arms. "What was that? What did you whisper to my dad?"

She smiled and kissed him deeply. Then heading for the bedroom unfastening her skirt along the way, she turned and said, "You're the detective; follow the clues."

Hunter grinned, unbuttoned his shirt, and did just that.

Author's notes to readers

This story is a work of fiction, and all characters and events are products of my own imagination with the exception of Jean Baptiste Wicar. Wicar, born in 1762 in Lille, France, was a skilled and successful artist who, at the direction of Napoleon, headed up a commission to loot art to enrich the museums of France. The stolen artwork also helped pay for the costs of the massive armies under Napoleon's direction.

The story of the Duke of Modena is also true. the Duke—having just been defeated by Napoleon's army—did sign an armistice that stated he was to grant twenty paintings to the Emperor's representative at the scene—Jean Baptiste Wicar. My story that Wicar actually took fifty, gave twenty to Napoleon, and kept the thirty that are the basis for this story, is entirely fictional. The story of Wicar's heirs—the Legacy—is also entirely fictitious. It is true, however, that as Napoleon's armies marched across the continent, Wicar kept many looted pieces for himself. The historical evidence for this is that he left over a thousand artworks to the city of Lille upon his death.

The concept of the art freeports is also true. The first one did open in Switzerland and its favorable tax environment was a huge part of its success. None has ever opened in Tampa and the storage of art in such a facility by the Ringling Museum of Art is entirely fictitious. Also, no one has ever hung himself or been hung from a tree on the Ringling grounds.

I got the idea for this book after reading about the art freeports in Europe and Asia. Then, when stories about 'flesh-eating-bacteria' recently made the news, I started to think of ways to blend them. As an emeritus professor of physiology, I'm always on the lookout for ways to bring science into the stories I write. The descriptions of the biology of *Vibrio vulnificus,* and its non lethal oil consuming cousin, *Alcanivorax borkumensis* are accurate. The story of BIOMOD, and the bioengineering of the hybrid bacteria used to spray the paintings in this story are completely fictitious.

Don Stratton

Acknowledgements

Writing a novel may seem like a solitary business but it's only possible because of the considerable help of many people. I'd especially like to thank my long time friend Rick Morrow for starting us both on the writing road, and I'm happy to say we're both still at it. I'm also indebted to my editor, Carol Gaskin, of *Editorial Alchemy* Her invaluable critiques improved the work immensely and I'm forever grateful. I'd also like to thank the many writers in Florida's Chapter of the Mystery Writers of America that I interact with at SleuthFest. Their encouragement is always greatly appreciated and their suggestions have born fruit throughout this work. Finally, a special thank you to those who painstakingly read proof versions of the book and offered their invaluable input including, Monica Hoover, Rick Morrow, Billie King, Pat Polazzo, Claire and Fred Norton, and of course my chief supporter and daily editor, my wife, Pauline.

Also By Don Stratton

A famous historian is brutally murdered with a samurai sword on Florida's Casey Key and Hunter McCoy's dad is arrested for the crime. Searching for the truth, Hunter is drawn deeper into an increasingly elaborate web of deceit.

During WWII, Dr. Li Qiang Chen, a Chinese country doctor is believed to have discovered an extraordinary medicine capable of preventing the development of diabetes.

When Hunter becomes convinced that finding the long dead doctor's missing research notebook is the key to clearing his dad of the murder charge, he teams up with Billie Chen, Dr. Chen's great-granddaughter.

Almost immediately, Hunter finds himself enmeshed in a continuing series of lies and misdirection that only deepens his dad's apparent guilt in the eyes of the law and potentially threatens everything Hunter holds dear.

Available in paperback and Kindle from Amazon.com

Also By Don Stratton

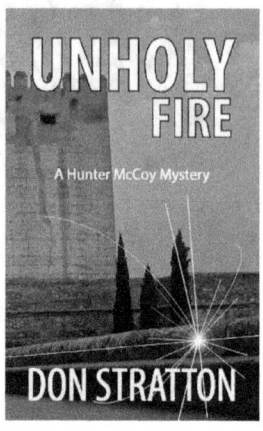

Young scientists scheduled to begin work at the Large Hadron Collider near Geneva are being systematically murdered . . .

Hunter McCoy discovers that their deaths are somehow linked to his search for a lost book—a book written by a Spanish physician who was burned at the stake by the Inquisition in the sixteenth century . . .

A shadowy group with ties to high-energy particle physics has its own compelling and deadly reasons to find the book first . . .

McCoy, trying to stay one step ahead of ruthless unknown adversaries is running out of time as his partner, a beautiful French archivist, is set to become the next victim—unwittingly unleashing a cataclysmic international disaster.

Available in paperback and Kindle from Amazon.com and most major ebook distributors

Also By Don Stratton

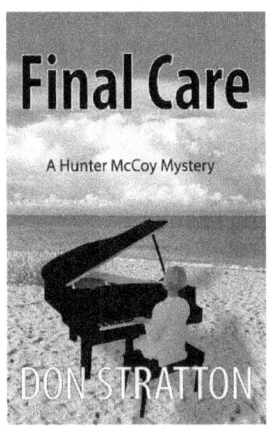

*A Widow In Florida Discovers The Body In The Coffin
At Her Husband's Funeral Isn't His*

Following emergency surgery for a head injury, a woman develops
virtuoso-like piano skills . . .

While on holiday in Italy a man suffers a stroke and inexplicably
becomes an accomplished juggler . . .

An embalmer with a secret past and his daughter face an
unimaginable choice in Brussels . . .

In a secret laboratory in Sorrento, marketable skills become a
valuable commodity . . .

Hunter McCoy is asked to locate the missing body and anticipates a
simple find-and-correct job. However his search quickly turns
deadly when he uncovers a sinister plot linking an international
funeral business and a world-renowned neurological institute—a
plot set in motion by a powerful and mysterious man, fueled by
decades of hate and revenge.

Available in paperback and Kindle from Amazon.com

About The Author

Don Stratton is a biomedical scientist born and raised in Michigan's Upper Peninsula. He was a professor of physiology for many years at Drake University. His research on blood vessel physiology was reported in over thirty-five scientific publications and his textbook Neurophysiology was published by McGraw Hill. Don was granted an endowed chair and named Ellis and Nelle Levitt Distinguished Professor of Physiology and Biology. He now lives as professor emeritus in Venice, Florida with his wife Pauline and dog Gracie where he's writing his next mystery novel.

www.ingramcontent.com/pod-product-compliance
Lightning Source LLC
Chambersburg PA
CBHW070152260626
47160CB00002B/321